With *A Winter Scandal*, *New York Times* bestselling author Candace Camp begins a sparkling new series sure to captivate readers who adored the unforgettable Bascombe sisters in her Willowmere novels. Read what critics have said about this breathtaking Regency trilogy!

## An Affair Without End

"Camp concludes the Willowmere trilogy with this delightful romantic mystery. . . . Cunning intrigue. With clever and witty banter, sharp attention to detail, and utterly likable characters, Camp is at the top of her game."

—*Publishers Weekly* (starred review)

"Sprightly dialogue . . . [and] a simmering sensuality that adds just enough spice to this fast-paced, well-rendered love story."

—*Romantic Times Book Reviews* (4½ stars)

## A Gentleman Always Remembers

"An intensely passionate and sexually charged romance. . . . A well-crafted, delightful read."

—*Romantic Times* (4 stars)

"A delightful romp set in the Regency period. Ms. Camp has a way with truly likeable characters who become like friends. The action pops . . . and the relationships are strong."

—*Romance Junkies*

W9-BDH-199

# CANDACE CAMP

## A WINTER SCANDAL

POCKET STAR BOOKS

New York   London   Toronto   Sydney   New Delhi

Pocket Star Books
A Division of Simon & Schuster, Inc.
1230 Avenue of the Americas
New York, NY 10020

This book is a work of fiction. Names, characters, places, and incidents either are products of the author's imagination or are used fictitiously. Any resemblance to actual events or locales or persons, living or dead, is entirely coincidental.

First Pocket Star Books paperback edition November 2011

POCKET STAR BOOKS and colophon are registered trademarks of Simon & Schuster, Inc.

For information about special discounts for bulk purchases, please contact Simon & Schuster Special Sales at 1-866-506-1949 or business@simonandschuster.com.

The Simon & Schuster Speakers Bureau can bring authors to your live event. For more information or to book an event, contact the Simon & Schuster Speakers Bureau at 1-866-248-3049 or visit our website at www.simonspeakers.com.

Designed by Jacquelynne Hudson
Cover design by Lisa Litwack, photo by Michael Frost, hand lettering by Ron Zinn

Manufactured in the United States of America

10   9   8   7   6   5   4   3   2   1

ISBN 978-1-4516-3950-6
ISBN 978-1-4516-3953-7 (ebook)

*For Grady*

# Acknowledgments

No book makes it to the shelf without a lot of work by a lot of people. As always, I am grateful for the amazing job done by my editor, Abby Zidle, and the whole team at Pocket. You guys really outdid yourselves this time!

Also, thanks to my agent, Maria Carvainis, and her staff. I couldn't do it without you.

And, as ever, many thanks to my husband, Pete. Sometimes I think the only thing harder than writing a book must be living with someone who is writing a book.

# A WINTER SCANDAL

# One

*The Squire's house was ablaze* with lights in the crisp December evening, and the boughs of evergreen branches festooned across the lintel added to the festive air. A groom hurried forward as the vicar's pony trap pulled to a stop in front of the house, and Daniel handed him the reins before going around to help his sister out of the open-air vehicle. It had been a cold ride over to Cliffe Manor, and despite the lap robe across their legs and the hood Thea had drawn up around her head, she was chilled, her cheeks pink. As soon as Thea stepped into the warm house, of course, her spectacles fogged up, and she had to take them off and wipe them before replacing them on her nose.

"Vicar! And Althea! How delightful to see you," Mrs. Cliffe, the Squire's wife, greeted them effusively, squeezing Thea's hands in both of hers. The Squire's wife, like her husband, was built along generous lines, and her rather square form was encased in a gown of green velvet with a wide, low neckline that revealed an alarming amount of white bosom. A pearl necklace, elbow-length white gloves, and a green turban with a long, curling peacock feather completed her ensemble.

Next to her, the Squire was far more soberly dressed, but his hearty greeting equaled his wife's. He shook Daniel's hand vigorously and bowed to Thea with more enthusiasm than grace. "Well met, Vicar, well met. Miss Bainbridge. It's a pleasure to see you. I am sure your dear sainted father would be proud of you both."

Daniel responded with only a bow, so Thea hurried to add her thanks. "It is kind of you to say so, sir. I know it is very important to my brother to strive for the excellence that our father achieved for St. Margaret's."

What Thea actually knew was that it was a small source of irritation to Daniel to be always compared to their father, Latimer Bainbridge, who was a most learned as well as spiritual man. She and Daniel were aware that Latimer had felt some disappointment that not all his children had measured up to his expectations. Their sister, Veronica, had been exactly as a girl should be, pretty and pleasant in nature, and she had made a good marriage, so Latimer had not been bothered by her lack of interest in intellectual pursuits. But while Daniel and Thea both had a scholarly bent of mind, the truth was that Daniel was more interested in exploring Roman ruins than in examining the human soul, and Thea, unfortunately, was a female. Thea could not follow in their father's footsteps, and while Daniel did take over the living at St. Margaret's, he did not invest the same time and interest in it that Latimer would have liked.

"If I know you, Vicar, you have been hard at work on your Christmas sermon," Mrs. Cliffe offered with a waggish smile. "I do so love to hear your thoughts on the Holy Word."

Thea wondered how the Squire's wife would view her brother's sermons if she knew that they were mostly written by Thea herself. Of course, Thea was not about to tell her that, but she could not think of another comment to make to Mrs. Cliffe, so she merely smiled. She was finding it more difficult to concentrate tonight than usual.

"Here, here, have a cup of Christmas cheer," Mrs. Cliffe went on, guiding Thea over to a narrow table, which held several cups of steaming broth. "'Twill warm you right up."

A footman came up to take Thea's cloak, and she picked up one of the small ceramic cups, gratefully curling her hands around the warm drink. While her hostess continued to chatter, Thea sipped at the spiced soup, to which a generous amount of negus had been added. The mulled Madeira in the negus was potent enough to make Thea's eyes water, but the heat of it sliding down her throat and filling her insides was delightful. She hoped it would serve to unknot the tangle of nerves in her stomach, as well. It was foolish to be on such pins and needles, but she could not seem to bring her rebellious nerves into order.

"Don't you look nice, my dear," Mrs. Cliffe went on. "So neat and orderly. I always say to my girls, take notice of Althea Bainbridge, that is just how a lady ought to conduct herself. She doesn't put on airs to make herself interesting or flirt with young men or spend her time fussing with her hair. She knows that there are more important things than looking pretty."

"Indeed," Thea murmured, with long practice turning aside the implied slight. She was well accustomed to being plain, after all, and could hardly fault others for realizing it.

"Of course my girls are still so young—all they think about is how they look. Sometimes I think there aren't enough mirrors in the house." The middle-aged woman let out a hearty laugh and looked down the great hall to where her daughters stood in a cluster, giggling and talking animatedly. There were four of them, all dressed in white, with enough ribbons and ruffles and frills to decorate a whole host of young ladies.

If the girls were being taught to emulate her, Thea thought, looking down at her own unadorned gray gown, they certainly seemed to have missed the mark. "Your daughters are all quite lovely tonight."

"Thank you, my dear." The Squire's wife gave Thea a self-satisfied smile. "They are a pretty sight, aren't they? They are absolutely humming with excitement about our 'very special guest.' No doubt you are above all that sort of silliness after all these years. But my little misses are like to faint from the anticipation. Even I, I vow, am awaiting Lord Morecombe's arrival most eagerly. No doubt it is different for you, since you are related to the Earl of Fenstone, but I have never played hostess to one of the peerage before."

"We are only distantly related," Thea demurred. Her father had been the youngest son of the youngest son of an earl, making him a cousin to Lord Fenstone, which meant that while their bloodline was unquestionably good, her family had never had an adequate fortune to take part in the life of the *ton*—not, of course, that Latimer, or she herself, for that matter, would have wanted to be a part of that society. "There is every reason for you to be excited," she told her hostess. "You scored a veritable *coup* in landing Lord Morecombe for your Christmas ball. I am sure everyone here is all agog to meet him."

Lord Morecombe, a bachelor of some note, had a few weeks ago purchased the house known hereabouts as the Priory, which had belonged to the Earl of Fenstone. Lord Fenstone had rarely made a visit to the Priory in all the years he had owned it, but Lord Morecombe had arrived for a stay two weeks earlier, bringing with him a number of his friends. Since that time, his lordship, his friends, and the goings-on at the Priory had been the central theme of all gossip in the village of Chesley. No matter how high or low, how old or young, how distant or near, everyone seemed to have a story concerning the newcomers, and everyone was always eager to hear more about him.

"Well, I must confess—" Mrs. Cliffe leaned a little closer and lowered her voice a trifle. "I did wonder if I should have done so. I mean, inviting these young men to be around young, impressionable girls? One has heard such unsavory tales.... Still—" She brightened. "I thought, after all, he is friends with Lord Fenstone's son. Indeed, the Earl's son is one of the young men staying at the Priory with him. An excellent family, of course, and doubtless Lord Morecombe is from a good family, as well. And one must expect young gentlemen to sow a few wild oats, now, mustn't one?" Her eyes twinkled merrily. "Of course, I should not be discussing such things with an unmarried girl like you. Though you're not really a girl anymore, are you? But still ..."

Thea clung a little grimly to her pleasant expression. She was well aware that she was considered completely "on the shelf." It was little wonder, given that she had reached the ripe old age of twenty-seven without the slightest hint of a proposal from an eligible man ... or, indeed, even from an ineligible one. Still, she had not yet become immune to such dismissals. She wondered when a woman *did* become accustomed to them. Her voice was a trifle brittle as she responded, "No, indeed, ma'am, you need not watch your tongue with me. I am well past the age of being an impressionable young girl."

"You have always been such a sensible young lady." Mrs. Cliffe beamed her approval at Thea. "Now, you should run along, dear; you have spent enough time talking with an old woman like me. Go join the younger set. Your friend Mrs. Howard is already here, though I'm not sure where she's got to." Mrs. Cliffe glanced around vaguely.

"Is she?" Thea brightened. "Indeed, I will go find her. Thank you."

Thea strolled through the great hall, nodding and smiling and stopping now and then to talk to someone. Her progress was slow, for she had lived in the village of Chesley all her life and was well known by its residents. She found Damaris Howard near the rear of the large room, standing with Mrs. Dinmont and a woman she recognized as the wife of the Squire's younger brother.

"Thea!" Damaris turned toward her, smiling.

Damaris's thick, lustrous black hair was pulled up and pinned in intricate arrangements of curls. Her almond-shaped eyes were an unusual shade of blue-gray that seemed almost lavender, an effect heightened today by the deep purple of her stylish silk gown. Her creamy white skin was in sharp contrast to the vivid color of her hair and eyes. Jet earrings and a simple jet-and-ivory cameo around her slender neck were the only adornments she wore other than a spray of diamonds in her hair. She looked, as always, far too beautiful and sophisticated for a remote village such as Chesley.

She had lived here for less than a year, and no one knew where she had come from. She had a faint aura of mystery about her that was both intriguing and difficult to pinpoint. Her rich contralto voice held no hint of accent. Mrs. Howard was obviously genteel, but she never spoke of her family connections, and though she said she was widowed, no one knew anything about her deceased husband. She was clearly familiar with London and Bath, as well as several foreign cities, yet she never really spoke of any place as her home. And though no one knew much about her, she never seemed secretive, so that one was left with a vague sense that one knew Damaris without really knowing many details of her life.

For one brief moment, Thea felt a pang of envy for Damaris's rich gown of royal purple and her artfully upswept hair. Both, she knew, were quite outside her reach. Thea could not have afforded such a glorious dress, and even if she could have, it would be foolish to waste so much money on a ball gown that would be worn only two or three times when she had a perfectly good one from last year. The vicar's family, after all, was always in the public eye, and it would not do for the vicar's sister to appear wasteful or vain.

And as for her hair—well, it was nonsense, Thea knew, to rail against the fate that had given Thea her wayward curls, which often managed to escape from mere hairpins and frizz wildly all over her head until she looked a fright. The best way to subdue her unruly mane was to braid it and wind the plaits tightly into a coil atop the crown of her head. The style did not enhance her looks, but at least it was practical.

Thea wore her spectacles for the same reason. When she was young, she had often abandoned her spectacles when she attended parties in an effort to show off her best feature, her large gray eyes. However, she had gotten over such vanity through the years. It was silly to sit through a dinner or go to a party and be unable to see clearly three feet from her face. And what good did it do, really, to pretend for a few hours that she did not look as she did?

As Damaris excused herself from the other two women and came over to Thea, smiling, Thea pushed aside her moment's longing for beauty. It was one's heart and soul that mattered, after all, as her father had always told her.

"Thea, I am so glad you have rescued me," Damaris murmured as she slipped her arm through Thea's and started to stroll away with her. "I vow I have been positively drowning in tales of Lord Morecombe."

Thea chuckled. "I have no doubt. Were they talking of the carriage full of women of doubtful character who drove over from Cheltenham? Or the wagonload of brandy and ale coming by night in a very suspicious manner?"

"Smuggling in liquor to his cellars? I doubt that would raise many eyebrows around Chesley," Damaris retorted. "Though the amount he brought in might. No, Mrs. Dinmont was regaling Mrs. Cliffe the younger with stories of shooting contests that involved picking out the candles of the chandelier. Mrs. Cliffe countered that the man has no maids in the house because no self-respecting female will work there. Of course, they both agreed that they are nevertheless waiting with bated breath to meet the legendary lord."

"Mm. Everyone seems to be." Thea refused to think about her own dancing nerves. "I am sure his fortune and the fact that he is a bachelor will overcome any objections anyone may have to his moral character."

"I believe his face plays a role, as well. Everyone agrees he is as handsome as Lucifer before the fall."

"Yes. I suppose." Thea could feel heat rising in her face, and she looked down at her glove, rebuttoning the little round button through its loop.

"Have you ever seen him?" Damaris went on. "I have not."

Thea shrugged as she turned her gaze out on the crowd. "His friend Lord Wofford is my second cousin, though I scarcely know Cousin Ian more than to say hello."

Damaris looked at Thea thoughtfully, but if she found it odd that her friend had not really answered her question, she did not say so. "Well, I shall be interested to see him, I admit, but I am growing rather weary of hearing about our local lord. Let us turn to a more interesting topic. You will be pleased to know that I received a shipment of books this week. You shall have to come round and look at them."

"Really? How delightful."

"They included Cantos I and II of Lord Byron's *Don Juan*." When Thea did not respond, her friend glanced at her, surprised. "Thea?"

"What? Oh, I am sorry." Thea blushed. "I am afraid my mind wandered."

"Are you all right?"

"Oh, yes, of course. I am just a bit distracted tonight. I am sorry. I fear you said something that I was not attending to—something about the books you received?"

"Yes. I got in Lord Byron's new poem."

"Did you?" Thea's eyes widened appreciatively. She understood now why Damaris had been so startled by her lack of response to the news. Thea was an avid reader, and until Damaris arrived, no one else in Chesley shared her love of books except her brother, Daniel—and his tastes ran more to the scholarly. Books of history or even the philosophical and religious texts her father had enjoyed were all very well, of course, and Thea read whatever her father or brother ordered from London. But she also had a love of poetry and novels and satire, which were all too scarce in the study at home. When Thea first met Damaris, and their conversation had turned to books, Thea knew she had found a friend. "Is *Don Juan* terribly shocking? It is supposed to be, but I confess, I cannot wait to read it."

Damaris laughed, and Thea joined in, though afterward she said, "I would not tell anyone but you that. I fear I am not a very good example to Daniel's flock."

"Well, they are his parishioners, after all, not yours."

"I know. But I do have a certain duty." Thea let out an unconscious sigh.

"I promise I shall not tell anyone that you are borrowing it."

"Have you read it yet?"

"My dear, the very evening I got it! Though I shall go back for a longer perusal, of course. But it is wonderful. You will not be disappointed, I assure you."

"I am sure that I will not. It is very kind of you to lend it to me."
Thea glanced toward the front of the hall, where the Squire and
his wife were still receiving guests. She noted that she was not the
only guest who kept turning to look at the entrance. Everyone, it
seemed, was awaiting Mrs. Cliffe's "very special guest."

"If Lord Morecombe does not attend, it will spell disaster for
Mrs. Cliffe's party," Damaris said, following Thea's gaze.

"It is foolish in the extreme, of course, to put so much interest
in the appearance of one person," Thea said, feeling a bit guilty at
being caught looking. Resolutely she turned so that her back was
toward the door.

"No doubt it is, but still, 'tis difficult not to be caught up in it."

Thea glanced around and let out a little sigh as her eyes fell
on the row of people seated against the wall. "I had better pay my
respects to the Squire's mother. Would you like to come?"

Damaris chuckled. "Thank you, but I have already done my
duty there this evening. I am afraid you must face the gorgon on
your own."

Thea had to smile at the comparison. The old woman, who
was wrapped in a shawl and grimly studying the occupants of the
room, often made one feel as if she could turn one to stone. "If you
think the experience is treacherous for you, think of those of us
whose every childhood misstep is known to her!"

Thea bade good-bye to her friend and made her way toward
the rear of the room to make her curtsy to the elder Mrs. Cliffe.

"It's good to see you, ma'am." The polite lie slid off Thea's tongue
with the ease of long practice. "I hope you are well this evening."

"Hmmph." The old woman cast a baleful glance at Thea.

"As well as I can be, I suppose, with one foot in the grave." She thumped her cane against the floor and nodded toward the chair beside her. "Sit down, sit down, girl, can't crane my neck looking up at you like that."

Thea sat down beside the old woman. She could not see the door from here, which would serve to keep her from glancing toward it all the time.

"Bunch of ninnies," Mrs. Cliffe declared, glaring at the rest of the room. "All agog over seeing some lord no better than they are, when all's said and done. Well, at least you aren't as big a fool as the rest."

Thea was not sure how to respond to this halfhearted compliment, so she merely nodded.

"Look at my granddaughters—putting on ribbons and lace and airs, just to meet some popinjay from London who won't take a second look at them. And their silly mother encourages them— as if some lord from London would have any interest in a bunch of young chits who've never been farther than Cheltenham. Isn't as if any of them are beauties, either. I always say, you only make yourself look foolish acting like you're a diamond of the first water when anyone can see you're merely paste." The old lady turned to Thea and gave her a sharp nod. "Now, you my girl, look just as you should. Neat and no-nonsense."

Thea felt a sharp, familiar burn in her chest, but she told herself not to be foolish. She could hardly fault the Squire's old mother for expressing the very sentiment Thea had used as her own watchword tonight: it was better to be thought a dowd than a fool.

"Course, no telling my son's wife that. Maribel's pumped the girls' heads so full of nonsense, they can hardly see straight. She's been in a tizzy all week, half the time up in the boughs over her catch and the other half worrying herself to a frazzle that he won't come. Hah! Serve her right if he didn't, for going around puffing it up to everyone that he'd accepted."

"Still, I am sure that you would not really wish to see her disappointed."

"I wouldn't be too sure of that." The old lady slid a dark, glittering glance at Thea, then let out a heavy sigh. "No, you're probably right. She'd spend the next week nattering on and on about it till I'd have to keep to my room just to avoid her."

Thea looked down at her hands to hide her smile.

"Well, tell me, girl," Mrs. Cliffe went on, "is that sister of yours coming home for Christmas?"

"Oh, yes." Thea smiled. "I am quite looking forward to it. We get to see her and her children so rarely. But it is always delightful to have all their noise and activity. It makes the house seem truly alive and filled with the spirit of Christmas."

"That is the life of a naval wife, I fear, stuck off in some seaport somewhere."

Thea did not point out that Portsmouth was hardly the ends of the earth, saying only, "Well, she will be here in just a few more days, so we are happy about that."

"Pretty girl, Veronica," the old woman mused. "Not surprised she made a good marriage. But I never did hold with her having a Season and you not. I told your father so, as well. 'Vicar,' I said, 'you're slighting your youngest, and she's got as much right as anyone to have a go at catching herself a husband.'"

"I was needed at home," Thea replied somewhat stiffly. "And, indeed, I had little interest in a London Season."

She hadn't wanted to have a Season; she really hadn't. Thea had known as well as anyone—better, really—that she hadn't the sort of looks necessary to make a splash in London. Veronica was the acknowledged beauty of the family. Whereas Thea's hair was a nondescript color, neither red nor brown, Veronica's hair was a lush, deep auburn, a beautiful contrast to her creamy white skin— which never, ever was touched with the freckles that decorated Thea's cheeks if she forgot to put on her bonnet when she went out into the garden. And no one would compare Thea's solemn gray eyes, hidden behind her spectacles, to the color of bluebells, as more than one young swain had said about Veronica's eyes. Veronica's form was sweetly curved and delicately feminine, and next to her, Thea's tall, thin frame looked distinctly storklike. Clearly, just as her father had decreed, it did not make sense to spend the money on Thea's Season, and anyway, her father had needed Thea to copy out his sermons and keep the house and the vicar's life running smoothly.

"Nonsense. Don't try to tell me you wouldn't have liked to go to London. I wasn't born yesterday, far from it." Mrs. Cliffe let out a cackle of laughter. "But you're a good daughter not to brook criticism of your father."

There was a rustle of movement near the door, and a swift susurration of noise swept around the room. Thea lifted her head, her pulse suddenly pounding in anticipation.

"Well?" Mrs. Cliffe demanded. "What's happened? Did he come? Don't just sit there, girl. Stand up and see what's going on."

Thea was happy to oblige. She popped to her feet, but too many people were between her and the door to see anything. All of the guests were shifting toward the front of the room, their faces turned toward the door.

"I think he must be here," Thea told her companion. "But I cannot see."

The elder Mrs. Cliffe grimaced and brought her cane down with an irritated thump. "Never mind. She'll bring him over to introduce him to me—Maribel won't be able to resist tweaking my nose with it. Sit down, and we'll pretend we didn't even notice. Always better to look like you don't care, I say."

"Yes, ma'am." Thea retook her seat. She wondered what it said about her that she found herself in sympathy with this crotchety old woman.

"Tell me about this silly live Nativity that Maribel says you're planning for Christmas Eve."

"I think it will be quite affecting, ma'am. St. Thomas Church in Holstead-on-Leach did it last year, and I believe it was very successful."

"Quite chilly, I'd say," Mrs. Cliffe snorted. "Hope you know what you're in for, letting my granddaughter play Mary. Course, you had no choice there. Maribel would have hounded you to your deathbed if her eldest weren't chosen."

Thea decided it was probably better not to comment on that. Instead, she launched into a description of their efforts to mount the production, knowing that the mishaps that occurred at each rehearsal would arouse Mrs. Cliffe's prickly sense of humor. As Thea talked, she kept an eye on the room in front of her. The guests, after the initial movement forward, began to part down the middle like water before the prow of a ship, and before long Thea could see the younger Mrs. Cliffe moving slowly through the room beside a tall, dark-haired man. Two other men were with him, but Thea noticed only the one to whom Mrs. Cliffe clung.

His hair was thick and black, swept back from a sculpted face. His brows were as black as his hair, sharp slashes over large, intense dark eyes. He was, as gossip had rumored him, sinfully handsome, and his black jacket and breeches were elegantly tailored to fit his muscular frame. His pristine white neckcloth was tied simply and held in place by a sapphire stickpin; he wore no other adornment save a gold signet ring on his right hand. Tall and broad-shouldered, he walked with the confident stride of one who was accustomed to being the center of attention.

Gabriel Morecombe. Thea's heart thudded so hard she feared it might leap right out of her chest. The blood seemed to rush from her extremities to her center, leaving her face pale. She tried frantically to pull her thoughts together, to have a smooth, polite greeting ready. The group moved slowly, Mrs. Cliffe stopping to introduce her prize to each guest. Beside Thea, Mrs. Cliffe's mother-in-law rumbled with a low laugh.

"Wants him to get a long look at all four of the girls—and Meg's just sixteen. Poor little sparrows; she's got their heads stuffed full of nonsense about catching a peacock."

Lord Morecombe looked, Thea thought, rather glassy-eyed. No doubt he was stunned by the succession of simpering Cliffe daughters—not to mention every other halfway marriageable female in the room. The thought made Thea chuckle, and it eased her nerves a bit. But then Mrs. Cliffe pivoted and led him toward where Thea sat, the other two men trailing along behind.

"Allow me to introduce you to Mrs. Robert Cliffe, my husband's mother. Mother Cliffe, this is my honored guest, Lord Morecombe. And his friends, Sir Myles Thorwood and Mr. Alan Carmichael." Thea noticed that her cousin Ian had apparently not joined the group.

Gabriel stepped forward and executed a formal bow to the old lady. "My pleasure, madam, though surely you must have married very young indeed to be the Squire's mother."

Mrs. Cliffe let out a short crack of laughter. "Ah, you're a smooth-talking devil as well as a handsome one."

"Mother!" The young Mrs. Cliffe's face flooded with color. She rushed on, "And this is another of our lovely young ladies, Miss Bainbridge."

Thea rose on somewhat shaky legs. "My lord."

Lord Morecombe turned to her, his eyes moving over her without interest. "Miss Dandridge." He sketched a polite bow before moving on with Mrs. Cliffe.

Morecombe's two companions bowed to her in turn, greeting her by the same name. Thea nodded to them instinctively, not really hearing them, aware of nothing but the hard, cold knot forming in her chest.

Gabriel Morecombe had not remembered her.

# Two

*Thea sat back down with* a thump as the men walked away.

"Well, I must say, he's a handsome one. They didn't lie about that," old Mrs. Cliffe said, turning toward Thea. "Are you feeling quite right? You look pale as a sheet."

"Yes, I mean, no—I—I'm not sure. If you will excuse me, ma'am, I do think I should leave the room. It's a trifle warm."

Scarcely waiting for Mrs. Cliffe's response, Thea slipped out the nearest door. A short distance down the corridor, she ducked into a small room, unlit except for the light spilling in from the hallway. She dropped into a chair and leaned back, closing her eyes.

Gabriel Morecombe had not remembered her. There had been not even the slightest glimmer of recognition in his eyes when he looked at her. She had tried to prepare herself for his reaction, whatever it might be. She had thought he might look at her, unsure, and she had little doubt that he would probably not remember her name. After all, it had been ten years since they had met at the wedding of Lord Fenstone's eldest daughter. She had even braced herself for the possibility that Lord Morecombe would remember everything, down to the last embarrassing detail, or that, even worse, he might blurt out something about that night. It had been her first ball of any consequence, and while Veronica shone as she always did, Thea had merely watched, hoping and yet dreading that the handsome young lord would take notice of *her*. In the years since, Thea had often thought of him as one would a fond dream—wistfully and without expectation of seeing it again.

But while she knew their encounter was for him nothing of consequence, she had not really considered that Lord Morecombe would not have even the smallest recollection of having met her. Danced with her. Kissed her.

Thea braced her elbows on her knees and buried her face in her hands, humiliation burning through her. The night that she had remembered so well had been such a small thing in his life that it had entirely slipped his mind. She had not expected him to recall it as vividly as she did. After all, he was a sophisticated London bachelor. No doubt since then he had kissed scores of girls—hundreds, even—whereas she . . . well, that had been the only kiss that the spinster Althea Bainbridge had ever received. But it scalded her that it had been so commonplace, so meaningless, so utterly forgettable that he registered not even the faintest recognition or, at least, some degree of discomfort.

She leaned back against the chair, and her mind went back to that long-ago evening at Fenstone Park when she had first met Gabriel, Lord Morecombe.

Thea's father, Latimer Bainbridge, was cousin to the Earl of Fenstone. Latimer's father had been the youngest brother of the family, and the Earl's father, the eldest. Latimer, in turn, was the youngest son of his family and had, in accordance with family tradition, gone into the clergy. He received his living from the Earl, as his son would receive it from the Earl after Latimer's death. While Thea's family moved in an entirely different world from the Earl's, on special occasions, when the entire Bainbridge family gathered for one reason or another at their family seat, Fenstone Park, Latimer and his wife and children were invited.

One of those occasions was the wedding of the Earl's oldest daughter ten years ago. Fenstone Park was packed with relatives and friends, so that not only did Thea and her sister, Veronica, share a chamber, but they shared it with their mother, as well. Latimer and Daniel were in another, equally small room. They were shunted off into the oldest wing of the house, and Veronica was acutely aware that their dresses were not of the first stare of fashion, as were those of most of the other girls. Thea frankly had not cared; she was simply glad that she was old enough to put her hair up and her hems down and participate in all the festivities as an adult instead of being thrust in with the nursery group as she had been three years before.

She saw the handsome Gabriel Morecombe the evening before the wedding when she came down for supper, but of course at the table she had been placed far away from the heir to the Morecombe title, and she wouldn't have dreamed of trying to catch his attention later in the evening when everyone mingled more freely in the music room and drawing room. No one in the village of Chesley, she knew, would have branded her shy, for she tended to take charge of matters, but the size and elegance of Fenstone Park, as well as the glittering sophistication of the people therein, intimidated her. Besides, Thea knew that when it came to social situations, she had little to offer. In the only area that counted among young women, beauty, she lagged behind the others. So she sat quietly beside Veronica, looking on as her pretty sister flirted with first one young man, then the other.

Once, when Veronica was for a moment free, Thea leaned in close to her sister, covering her mouth with her spread fan, and whispered, "Who is that young man? The one standing with Lord Wofford." She nodded her head toward where the handsome young man stood with their second cousin Ian.

Her sister looked in the direction Thea indicated, raising her own fan to hide the smile that curved her lips. "Ooooh, *him*. He's Gabriel Morecombe; he'll be a lord when his father dies. He and Wofford have been friends forever. He's a terribly good catch. Not only handsome as can be, but possessed of a nice inheritance, I hear." Veronica released a soft sigh. "Quite above our touch, I'm afraid."

"Oh." Thea felt her cheeks warm, and she looked down, twisting the fan in her hand. "I didn't mean—I never considered *that*. I just thought . . . I wondered who he was."

She raised her eyes again, unable to keep them from returning to Gabriel. He was flirting with two girls in satin evening gowns that Thea was sure cost more than her entire wardrobe at home. She watched, aware of an odd little clutch in her chest. She knew that her father would tell her she was being covetous, but right now Thea could not bring herself to care. For just a moment, she ached to be a fragile blonde with limpid blue eyes, dressed in satin and lace.

The next day Thea's eyes found Gabriel Morecombe wherever he was—sitting six rows in front of her in the chapel during the wedding, laughing as he walked down the hall with another young man, sitting on a bench in the garden south of the house, the sun glinting off his black hair. Once he glanced over at her, and she quickly looked away, her cheeks flaming with embarrassment. Had he seen her staring? Did he realize that she could not keep from looking for him wherever she went?

That evening she went down to the ball wearing her best evening gown—well, it wasn't hers, really, but the pale blue gown Veronica had worn to the County Assembly last month. Still, it was the nicest dress she had, and Veronica had given it up only because she was wearing one of the new dresses bought for her debut this year. Its blue color had been chosen with Veronica's dark auburn hair and blue eyes in mind, but it was a flattering enough shade for Thea, as well. And Veronica had insisted on doing Thea's hair herself, so that it hung in long curls from a knot at the crown of her head, and the soft, fine hairs that tended to pull out from their pins were twisted and tamed into feathery little wisps around her face. Thea had indulged in a final bit of vanity by removing her spectacles and leaving them on her dresser.

Without her glasses, she could see little more than a blur beyond a few feet in front of her, and at first, as she descended the stairs, she felt a little frightened by her lack of vision. However, when she followed Veronica into the ballroom and realized that the crowd spread out before her was nothing more than soft, fuzzy shapes and colors, she relaxed. It was quite pleasant, actually, not to see the people around her. She was, she thought with some amusement, rather like an ostrich sticking its head in the sand—unable to see anyone with clarity, she felt herself somehow invisible.

She took her usual place beside Veronica and her mother against the wall of the large ballroom. A small orchestra played at one end of the room, and couples danced in a haze of color and motion in front of her. Before long, Veronica was asked to dance, and Thea's mother, blessed with the same sort of easy social grace Veronica possessed, was deep in conversation with the wife of Sir Joseph Symonds. Thea plied her fan gently in the warmth and wondered what Gabriel Morecombe was doing. At least she could not embarrass herself this evening by looking for him since she could see only a few feet past the end of her nose.

After some time she was roused from her reverie by her mother's voice, saying, "Thea, dear, Lady Fenstone is here."

"Hmm?" Thea turned, somewhat reluctantly letting go of the daydream about a dark-eyed man that she had been spinning in her head, and looked over at her mother. The Earl's wife was standing in front of Mrs. Bainbridge, looking at Thea, and beside her stood Gabriel Morecombe.

It was all Thea could do to keep her mouth from dropping open in astonishment. "M . . . ma'am." Thea shot to her feet, sending the fan that had been resting in her lap tumbling to the floor with a clatter. "Oh!"

She bent to retrieve the fan, but Morecombe had already scooped it up. He did not offer it to her, just smiled at her, his dark eyes sparking with laughter. Thea didn't know whether to reach for the fan, so she just twisted her hands together awkwardly and turned once more toward the Countess. Remembering that she had not curtsied to the older woman as she should have, she did so now, thinking miserably that she must look even more gauche.

The corner of the Countess's mouth twitched, whether from irritation or amusement Thea was not sure. She gave a small nod to Thea and said, "Allow me to introduce you to Mr. Morecombe." The Countess turned toward the young man. "Mr. Morecombe, my cousins, Mrs. Latimer Bainbridge and Miss Althea Bainbridge."

"Ma'am." Gabriel executed a perfect bow over Thea's mother's extended hand, then turned to bow to Thea. "Miss Bainbridge. 'Tis a pleasure to meet you. May I ask for the honor of this dance?"

Thea gaped at him. "Me?"

She heard the Countess emit a little sigh, and Alice Bainbridge said quickly, "That sounds lovely. Go ahead, Althea, it was good of you to keep me company, but I shall be fine here by myself."

A flush spread across Thea's cheeks. She was being thoroughly graceless, and she knew that Mr. Morecombe was laughing at her. Though his smile could be mistaken for polite interest, the light in his eyes could be nothing but laughter. She supposed she should be grateful that he was reacting in such good humor. He could have been sullen about Lady Fenstone's dragging him across the room to ask the wallflower cousin to dance—for Thea was well aware that that was what was going on here—but he did not betray even the slightest disdain. Still, Thea could not help but surge with resentment that he found her ineptness comical; it made her doubly irritated because she knew she did, indeed, look comical.

"Very well." Thea knew her words came out grudgingly, but she could not manage to twist them into anything else.

Morecombe's brows went up just a little, but he said nothing, only offered her his arm. Thea put her hand on his arm, praying that he would not feel the trembling in her fingers, and walked with him toward the dance floor. It made her a trifle breathless to be this close to him. She could feel the warmth of his body and smell the trace of cologne that clung to him, tinged with a hint of brandy and smoke. She imagined him in the smoking room with his friends, a glass of brandy in one hand, bringing a cigar to his lips with the other. Thea wondered if his lips would taste of tobacco and alcohol, too, and she blushed yet again at the wayward turn her thoughts had taken.

"You might give me back my fan," she told him crossly.

He chuckled and flipped the fan in his hand, catching it neatly by the other end. "Oh, no, I think I shall hold it hostage."

"Hostage! For what?" She glanced at him, frowning.

"A smile, I should think." He cocked a brow impudently at her. "I fear that will be the only way I shall gain one from you."

He was even more handsome up close, impossible as it seemed. His lashes were thick and black, deepening those already dark eyes until they seemed fathomless, yet light glittered in them, making them spark with life. Something coiled deep inside Thea, warm and twisting, and she had to look away. "Don't be absurd."

"You see? Already I have offended you." He let out a mock sigh as he handed back her fan.

"You haven't offended me. You simply talk nonsense."

"But isn't that what we are supposed to talk?" Gabriel grinned. "Everyone does at a party."

"I can't imagine why anyone wishes to go to them, then." Thea kept her voice tart even though his grin did even more peculiar things to her insides.

"I am sure we should not if we were all so serious. But a little nonsense can make the time pass pleasantly, especially if it can make a lady smile. Come, Miss Bainbridge, cannot I wrest even one small token of appreciation for saving your fan?"

"For saving me from the ignominy of being a wallflower, you mean." She cast a sharp sideways glance at him and caught the surprise that flickered across his face. "Come, Mr. Morecombe, surely you don't think I am naïve enough not to realize that you were pressed into service by Lady Fenstone to make sure all the young women had a chance to take to the floor."

"Clearly you don't know me well, Miss Bainbridge, for I am rarely pressed into anything. It is one of my many faults, as I'm sure a number of people would be happy to tell you."

"You did *not* ask Lady Fenstone to introduce us," Thea said flatly. She was not sure why she was pressing the matter, but somehow it was important to her pride to let him know that she was undeceived about his act of courtesy.

He cast a long look at her, then said, "No, I did not." He paused. "But neither did I hesitate."

Thea looked away, not sure what to say. Fortunately, they had reached the dance floor, making it unnecessary to speak. She took her place in line across from him, relieved to see that they would be participating in a country dance rather than one of the waltzes that had become all the rage in London. Veronica had learned the waltz, of course, and insisted on teaching it to her sister, but it was still considered a bit scandalous in the country, so Thea had never actually danced one before. At least she had stood up at a County Assembly a time or two in a country dance so she would hopefully not disgrace herself.

She was also grateful because the dance was both too active and too intricate to allow for conversation between her and her partner. Thea concentrated on executing the proper steps and tried to look at Morecombe as little as possible. Unlike her, he moved with ease through the steps, which Thea found irritating. What was even more annoying was that whenever she glanced over at him, she felt that same little flutter of excitement. And when they moved closer in their movements and their hands reached out to touch, palm to palm, it left her breathless, her heart pounding.

It was only the exertion of the dance, she told herself, that made her cheeks flush and her blood hammer in her veins. But, deep down, Thea was too honest to let herself believe such a lie. It was Gabriel Morecombe's nearness that made her feel so strangely wobbly and fizzy, so hot and cold, all at once.

The dance ended, and they made their polite curtsy and bow to one another. Gabriel offered her his arm, his eyes sweeping over her flushed face, and as they walked off the floor, he guided her through the open French doors onto the stone walkway beyond. Startled, Thea could think of nothing to do except go with him. She glanced around and saw that a number of other couples were strolling out onto the terrace to escape the heat of the ballroom, so she supposed that it could not be a scandalous thing to do. Again tingling with that sense of unease and excitement that Gabriel seemed to call forth in her, Thea strolled with him along the terrace. The garden below was illuminated with lanterns placed strategically along the paths between the flowers. A few bold couples even walked there, at least as far as to the fountain.

"I—why are we out here?" Thea asked. It sounded graceless—again—but she could think of no other way to put it. Gabriel might have asked her to dance as a courtesy to his hostess, but she could see no reason why he would extend the experience by taking her for a stroll.

He glanced at her, the same expression of mingled surprise and amusement in his eyes that she had seen there several times since Lady Fenstone had introduced them. "It was warm in the ballroom. I thought the fresh air might be nice." He stopped, half turning to her. "Would you rather return?"

Thea thought about going back to the chair beside her mother. "No."

He smiled faintly. "Good. Neither would I."

They continued past the steps down into the garden and stopped finally at the stone balustrade beyond. Thea looked out across the garden, very aware of Gabriel's presence beside her. She played with her fan, not quite sure what to do with her hands. She was certain she should say something. Veronica would doubtless know what to say, but the only things that came to Thea's mind were inane comments on the beauty of the garden or the refreshing quality of the evening breeze.

After a moment, she glanced over at Gabriel. He was leaning back against the balustrade, watching her. The muted light from inside the house slanted across his lower face, leaving his eyes in shadow, unreadable, and illuminating his chin and mouth. Her eyes flickered to the shallow dent in his chin, so curiously appealing, then moved up to the firm lips, which were, she had to admit, even more appealing. She should not be having such thoughts, she knew. She was not the sort, like Veronica, to daydream about husbands or wax rhapsodic over the handsome face of this man or the broad shoulders of that one. Veronica was a feminine girl, all ribbons and lace and smiles, like their mother. But Thea had always been more like their father, studious and well-read, a person who valued thought above emotion. A person's brain was what interested her most, not the curve of a man's lip.

She turned away, hoping the dim light hid the blush that she could feel flooding her cheeks. "I'm sorry."

"Sorry? For what?" He straightened and moved a bit closer, sounding honestly puzzled.

"I am not much of a conversationalist, I'm afraid. I am not used to"—she made a vague gesture toward the rest of the terrace and house—"to any of this. You must find this terribly . . ."

"Terribly what?" he asked when she did not go on.

"Boring." She faced him squarely then, for she refused to shy away from difficulties.

He let out a short bark of laughter. "Boring? My dear Miss Bainbridge, boring is definitely something you are not."

"I don't know how you can say that," she retorted somewhat

crossly. "There is really no need for you to be polite. I haven't said any of the things I should. I have been blunt and no doubt impolite. I have never danced before with any man I haven't known since I could toddle. And now I cannot even come up with the most commonplace remark."

His chuckle was low and warm and made something curl deliciously deep within her abdomen. "It may surprise you to learn that I am happy *not* to hear the most commonplace remark."

"Oh, you know what I mean." Really, the man was maddening. "You shouldn't laugh at someone who is admitting their grievous social ineptitude."

"What else should I do?" His teeth glinted in the darkness. "Let me assure you that I have danced with a great many girls whom I have not known since childhood. And I have heard a great many commonplace remarks. It is, quite frankly, a relief to enjoy the quiet and cool of the garden without hearing that the weather is quite nice this evening or that the breeze is most refreshing or that the party is so enjoyable."

"I thought of saying all those things, but I could not bring myself to do it."

"And for that, I thank you." He leaned forward, surprising her by taking her chin between his thumb and fingers. "How old are you, Miss Bainbridge? I daresay you haven't made your come-out yet."

"No." Thea could barely get out the word. His movement was startling and, at the same time, thrilling. She was certain that this was not the sort of thing she should be doing, but she was not about to pull away. "I am seventeen."

He smiled. "I think the bachelors of London are in for a surprise."

It occurred to her that his statement could be taken in a way that was less than complimentary, but then all thought flew from her head as he bent and kissed her.

His kiss was neither long nor deep, but it was the only kiss she had ever received from a man, and Thea felt it all through her. Her lips tingled, and her heart thumped against her ribs. His mouth was soft and warm; his scent filled her nostrils. Thea was shocked to feel a sudden, strong desire to throw her arms around his neck and press her body up against his.

Gabriel raised his head and stepped back. Sketching a bow, he offered Thea his arm to lead her back to her mother. Thea could do nothing but accept. She had not seen Gabriel Morecombe since.

Until tonight—when he had not remembered her.

Thea reached up and realized for the first time that tears had trickled down her cheeks. Annoyed, she dashed them away with gloved fingers. Really, she told herself, it was beyond enough to be mooning about here in the dark, feeling sorry for herself because some rake from London thought her beneath his notice. A saving anger began to rise in Thea, pushing back the hurt that dwelled like a rock in her chest. She was clearly guilty of the sin of pride in thinking that Lord Morecombe would remember her from their meeting so long ago. But Gabriel Morecombe had been rude and arrogant. It was not just that he had not remembered her or that he had not even bothered to call her by the correct name a few seconds after Mrs. Cliffe introduced her. It was that he obviously found the people here quite beneath his touch. The man's eyes had been glazed with boredom, his expression etched in lines of condescension. Clearly he wished himself somewhere else—no doubt off at the tavern drinking! Simply because he was an aristocrat, he thought that he was superior to the good, honest people of Chesley. It was no wonder Lord Morecombe had forgotten her; he had probably considered her not worth his interest even when he met her.

Thea straightened in her chair and smoothed down the front of her skirt. She ought to return to the great hall. She was not the sort to hide in a dark room, licking her wounds. However, she could not bring herself to go back and watch Lord Morecombe dance with Damaris and the Cliffe girls. Worse, what if Mrs. Cliffe decided to press him into dancing with the wallflowers, such as Thea? Thea was not about to risk that embarrassment.

She found a candelabra and lit it, illuminating the room with a soft glow. She was pleased to find a bookshelf on the wall behind the door, and soon she was settled down in a comfortable chair out of sight of the open doorway, engrossed in a book. A few minutes later, there were steps in the hallway, and Thea looked up to see her brother peering cautiously around the door. His expression brightened.

"Ah, Thea! So you stole away, too? Too noisy by half in there, I thought." Daniel came farther into the room. "You found a book?" She pointed toward the bookshelf, and he turned. "Ah, excellent."

He examined the shelves and chose a tome, then sat down on the chair closest to Thea, the candelabra burning on the table between them. The two of them remained there through the rest of the ball, reading in companionable silence, as they so often did of an evening. Thea glanced over at her brother and smiled fondly. She had a good life, she reminded herself. It was foolish to grow downcast because one arrogant rake had not recognized her. Her life was orderly and unhurried and had purpose. She did not want for anything, and she had friends and family. She could do as she pleased—within the bounds of propriety, of course. There was no reason to be discontented or sad over the behavior of Gabriel Morecombe, whom she would probably never see again, anyway. She would simply forget about him.

"*Lord, what a bore!*" Alan Carmichael declared as he and Lord Morecombe entered the drawing room of the Priory, followed closely by Sir Myles. Gabriel went straight to the decanters of liquor on the sideboard, and Alan flung himself into one of the armchairs flanking the fireplace, letting out a dramatic groan. "I should have listened to you, Ian, and stayed here."

Ian, Lord Wofford, who was stretched out in the other chair, his feet propped on the hassock and a snifter of brandy in one hand, merely lifted an elegant eyebrow. "Told you."

"It wasn't so bad." Sir Myles propped his elbow on the mantel and grinned at the other men. His eyes, usually twinkling with merriment, and his close-cropped curls were almost the same golden-brown color. Though not as tall as Gabriel, he was powerfully built, with the wide chest and muscular arms that denoted his devotion to the gentlemanly art of pugilism. "There was dancing. Young ladies. And the Squire served a damned fine hot punch back in his smoking room."

"Yes, but did you look at the ladies?" Alan countered. "All those Cliffe girls! There must have been ten of them."

"Four, I believe," Gabriel Morecombe offered as he poured healthy amounts of brandy into their glasses. "It only seemed like more because they were so uniformly alike in looks, dress, and general silliness."

"I have to endure that sort of rural festivity whenever I am home," Ian said. "I had no intention of subjecting myself to it here. I shall be eternally grateful that Father sold this place—though I cannot conceive why you agreed to buy it, Gabriel."

"Come, now." Gabriel made an expansive gesture, a smile lighting his handsome features. "Look around you." He turned and handed their drinks to Alan and Myles. "Where else can I obtain such peace and solitude as I have here?"

"And such lack of civilization," Ian drawled.

"Civilization is overvalued. I far prefer owning a house to which I can retreat without having to deal with tenants and my estate manager or worry about whether I offend my stepmother's sensibilities."

"Well, if you didn't want obligations, why'd you go to the Squire's Christmas ball?" Ian asked.

"A good question." Gabriel grimaced. "One which I asked myself as Mrs. Cliffe dragged me across the room, introducing me to every single woman who lives in the area. In truth, I suspect she imported a few from another village. After the first five minutes, I could scarcely have told you *my* name, let alone any of theirs."

Ian let out a crack of laughter. "I warned you! I knew every marriage-minded mama in the county would be there to introduce you to their eligible—and stultifyingly boring—daughters."

"Since you are already married, Ian, that would have presented no problem for you," Myles pointed out.

"True. Wouldn't have kept me from perishing from ennui, however."

"Well, I think you are all too harsh on the fair village of Chesley," Myles said lightly. "I, for one, enjoyed the evening of dancing. And while the Cliffe sisters were trying on the ears, it was more than made up for by the treat to the eyes that is Mrs. Howard."

"She *is* a beauty," Gabriel agreed.

"D' you mean the black-haired lovely?" Alan asked. "She was a peacock among pigeons, wasn't she?"

"Who?" Ian asked as he stood up and went to the sideboard to set down his glass. "A beauty here in Chesley? Sounds like a Banbury story to me. I would have remembered a raven-haired temptress."

"She moved here only a few months ago, I believe," Gabriel said.

"Good heavens. Why?"

Gabriel laughed. "Perhaps she was looking for peace and solitude, too."

"She'll get an ample amount of that," Ian retorted sardonically, turning and leaning back against the sideboard. "Now, gentlemen . . . are we going to proceed to any actual entertainment this evening?"

"What did you have in mind?" Gabriel asked.

"Loo, whist, vingt-et-un—whatever suits your fancy. Your butler told me he found several bottles and casks in the cellars. Lord only knows when they date from. I thought I'd go down and see if there was anything we might want."

Gabriel shrugged. "Be my guest."

"I'll go with you." Alan took a candlestick from the sideboard and the two men left the room.

Gabriel poured another drink for himself and Myles, and they settled down in the chairs in front of the fire, stretching their legs out toward the warmth.

"Hope the evening wasn't too much of a bore," Gabriel offered. "I thought it would be good to meet the locals."

Myles chuckled. "I didn't mind. Clearly I do not require the level of sophistication Ian does. When one grows up with five sisters, one becomes accustomed to attending such affairs. It helps make it more bearable, I suppose, that a *sir* is not as coveted a marriage prospect as a *lord*."

"Do you ever think about marrying?" Gabriel asked thoughtfully.

"As little as possible." Myles grinned. "Why? Don't tell me some girl's caught your fancy?"

"No. Not at all. I suppose I shall one day, but . . ." Gabriel shrugged. "It doesn't seem a very alluring prospect."

"Not if you look at Ian's marriage."

Gabriel glanced over at his friend. "Do you think Ian is terribly unhappy? He doesn't say anything, but . . ."

"But it's almost Christmas, and he is here with us instead of at the Park with his wife," Myles finished. "That must mean something. I've never asked him. I don't suppose he seems particularly *un*happy."

"But neither does he seem particularly happy."

"Everyone knows they weren't a love match."

"I'm not sure that makes any difference." Gabriel's voice had a bitter tone, and his friend shot him a quick sideways glance. But before Myles could speak, Gabriel went on, "I doubt Ian ever expected a love match ... or cared to have one, really."

"He's not a romantic."

"But there could have been a better match, someone more suited to him, if his father had not been so intent on gambling away Ian's future."

"Fenstone thinks of no one but himself." Myles sighed and drained his drink. "Always has. But it's done now. At least marrying Emily took care of his father's debt."

Gabriel snorted. "For the time being. Naturally the Earl's gone back to trying to run the estate into the ground."

"Do you mean Fenstone's run off his legs ag—" Myles stopped and sat up straight, staring at Gabriel. "Is *that* why you bought this place? So Ian's father would have enough cash to pay off his latest debts?"

Gabriel shrugged. "I wanted a house in the country besides the family seat."

"Of course you did." Myles gave him a knowing look. "Well, I hope you've managed to hold off the Earl's creditors for a while. Bad for Ian if his father landed in the River Tick."

They broke off at the sound of footsteps in the hallway outside. A moment later, Ian appeared in the doorway, a bottle cradled in each arm.

"What did you find?" Gabriel asked.

"A lot of spiderwebs and dust," Alan responded, brushing at the sleeves of his jacket as he came up behind Ian.

"And a cask of excellent Armagnac," Ian added. "Too big to bring up; you'll have to get the footmen to haul it up tomorrow. I did, however, find some bottles of passable cognac to tide us over."

"Very good." Gabriel stood and shrugged out of his jacket as Ian and Alan went to the table on the other side of the room. "Get out the cards, Myles. Cigars?" Gabriel picked up a box from the sideboard and passed it around as Ian opened the first of the bottles.

The men settled down around the table, and Myles began to shuffle the cards. Gabriel raised his glass. "Gentlemen! Here's to a short memory and a far merrier evening ahead."

# Three

*In the days after the* Squire's party, Thea was caught up in the whirl of activities that always preceded Christmas. Not only did she pitch in to help their housekeeper clean and cook for the upcoming festivities, but she also had the usual parish business to attend to. For years before her father's death, Thea had acted as his secretary, not only copying out his sermons in neat, legible ink, but also totting up his books and acting as a sounding board for his views on various parish matters. The parishioners had become accustomed to taking their problems to Thea first, to be relayed by her to the vicar, and when the living had been given to Daniel after Latimer's death, the church members had continued to go to Thea. Unlike Latimer, Daniel had little interest in hearing the matters Thea brought to him, so that she had grown used to simply handling them herself.

She did her best not to think about Lord Morecombe, but her mind stubbornly continued to return to that moment when he had looked at her with such a bored lack of recognition. It did not help that almost everyone who came to call on her for the next few days wanted to talk about little except the Christmas ball and their exotic new neighbor.

Mrs. Cliffe dropped by two days later, ostensibly to discuss the Ladies Auxiliary, but in reality to relive her social triumph. Thea, who had been working on Daniel's sermon for Christmas Day, did her best to hold her tongue as the Squire's wife and her sister, Mrs. Dinmont, extolled the many virtues of Lord Morecombe.

"Such a fine gentleman, don't you agree, Althea dear?" Mrs. Cliffe rarely needed an answer, so she did not notice Thea's lack of assent. "Even the Squire's mother admitted that he is a fine figure of a man."

"So handsome," Mrs. Dinmont added, playing her usual role in the conversation.

"Such an air of address! And a more finely turned leg I have never seen. Not, of course, that a high-minded young lady such as yourself would have noticed."

"Oh my, Maribel!" Mrs. Dinmont tittered into her hand. "The things you do say! Not, of course," she added after a look from Mrs. Cliffe, "but what you are absolutely correct. I am sure none of the gentlemen looked nearly so elegant on the dance floor."

"His friends were all very well, too, of course," the Squire's wife went on magnanimously. "Sir Myles is most charming. But he cannot compare to Lord Morecombe."

"No, indeed." Mrs. Dinmont bobbed her head. "No comparison at all."

"I vow, I was so pleased when he stood up with my own Daisy."

"Only after he had taken you out onto the floor," her sister pointed out archly.

"Now, Adele . . ." Mrs. Cliffe playfully slapped at her arm, laughing. "He was only doing what was polite."

"But, still, you moved quite smartly through the cotillion with him."

Mrs. Cliffe smiled and gave a little toss of her head. "I haven't yet forgotten how to dance a few steps. But it was clearly Daisy in whom his lordship was interested. He danced with all four of the girls, even little Estella, who was over the moon about that, I can tell you. But I know it was Daisy who caught his eye. I would not be at all surprised if we see Lord Morecombe at the manor again, you mark my words." Mrs. Cliffe nodded in a knowing way.

Thea deemed it unlikely that the supremely bored and arrogant Lord Morecombe had any interest in Daisy—unless he was drawn to giggling, combined with a lack of wit. If he had been attracted to anyone at the party, she felt sure it would have been Damaris, who was both beautiful and capable of carrying on an intelligent conversation. An inner devil tempted Thea to point out that the rakish lord whose misdeeds Mrs. Cliffe had been gossiping about for almost three weeks now would scarcely be a fit suitor for an innocent young maiden such as Daisy, but Thea refused to give in to her baser nature, merely smiling and nodding until Mrs. Cliffe and her companion finally left.

But if Thea had hoped to escape further tales of Lord Morecombe, she was doomed to disappointment, for the following day at the bakery she was treated to an account of the lord and one of his friends racing their curricles on the main road and nearly oversetting Colonel Parkson in his gig. That afternoon, paying a call on one of the sick of the parish, the old woman's daughter spent much of the afternoon regaling Thea with a description of the young lords at the Priory having a number of casks hauled up from the cellars, just so they could sample some old brandy.

It was a relief to finally escape the house and return to her own home. There, at least, she knew she would be safe from any discussion of Lord Morecombe, for Daniel had no interest in the occupants of the Priory. She could spend a nice quiet evening reading in front of the fire, the silence broken only by Daniel's occasionally reciting aloud to her a passage he found particularly interesting about the Roman ruins at Cirencester.

Thea let out a little sigh. Well, perhaps it was not an especially exciting prospect, but at least it was familiar and would not irk her as all conversations about Lord Morecombe seemed to. It was silly to let herself grow so irritated about the man, who was, of course, nothing to her. His attitude had stung a little, but it meant nothing. She would forget all about it as soon as Gabriel Morecombe and his friends went back to London.

And, she reminded herself, she had a great deal to look forward to. The Christmas celebration was her favorite time of the year. Tomorrow she would go out early and cut down evergreen and holly branches to decorate the house and church, an activity she always enjoyed. And in only a day or two her sister would arrive with her niece and nephews, and the house would then be filled with all the noise and activity she could wish for.

*The sun was not yet* peeking over the eastern horizon when she left the vicarage the next morning in search of greenery. Dragging a small wagon behind her, Thea headed across the bridge and past the church. There she cut across a field toward the woods beyond, where she knew she would find plenty of red-berried holly and fragrant fir trees. As she crested a small rise, Thea spotted a man riding up the road toward her. Even at this distance, she recognized the tall frame and the tousled dark hair. It was Gabriel Morecombe, heading from the village toward his house. She came to a dead stop.

Quickly Thea stepped back so that she was hidden in the shadows of the trees. The horizon had started to lighten, and she was able to make out the details of the horse and rider. He wore a fashionable greatcoat with multiple capes at the shoulders, opened carelessly down the front to reveal an unbuttoned jacket and a neckcloth hanging untied around his neck. He was bareheaded, his hair uncombed, and his jaw was shadowed with dark stubble. As he rode, he yawned widely and rubbed a hand down his face.

This was no man out on an early-morning canter. Clearly he was returning to his house after spending the night in the village. Thea could imagine what sort of place he'd spent the evening. The tavern for a while, no doubt, and after it closed . . . She drew herself even straighter, her jaw setting and her mouth thinning into a straight line. It did not matter to her, but if she had needed any proof that Lord Morecombe was exactly the sort of drunken, licentious . . . *libertine* that people said he was, here it was, right in her face.

The rider did not glance in her direction as he rode past. Thea waited, scarcely daring to breathe, until he was out of sight. Then she blew out a pent-up breath and hurried forward, the wagon bumping along behind her. Indignation fueled her steps, so that she strode faster and faster. The man was so bold! So brazen! Obviously, he cared little who saw him riding home at such an hour. He practically flaunted his wicked behavior in front of everyone. He had not even bothered to slip out under the cover of darkness. Not that it would make his activities any less reprehensible, but one would think the man could exhibit some shame, at least. She should have known what sort of man he was from the very beginning; he would not have kissed her that night so long ago if he was any sort of true gentleman. She had simply been too naïve to realize that he was a roué—well, perhaps not a roué, for she thought of them as being old, but certainly he was a rake. A rake and a libertine and a cad, too, no doubt.

It was fortunate that she was much older and wiser now. Not that he was likely to make any sort of advance to her—indeed, she could not imagine why he ever had. But, still, it was reassuring to know that now she would be able to withstand his charm, to see him for what he was. She would not allow herself to be maneuvered into such a situation nowadays, and certainly she would not simply stand there, stunned into silence, if he tried to kiss her. No, she would . . . well, she wasn't sure what she would do. Slap his face, she supposed; that seemed appropriate.

Occupied by such thoughts, Thea hacked away at the evergreen branches with the small hatchet she had brought, quickly loading the garden wagon. When the wagon was nearly full, she added several branches of holly loaded with red berries among their waxy green leaves. She could not find any low-hanging mistletoe, so, after a quick glance around to make sure no one was around to see her, she kilted up her skirt and tucked the end into the sash, then climbed up into the oak tree and knocked down several pieces. Satisfied with her haul, she turned and headed for home. Her stomach was rumbling with hunger, and she wished that she had eaten more than just the single slice of bread she had taken from the kitchen. However, even if Daniel had finished eating, Mrs. Brewster would have set aside a plate for her.

*In fact, when Thea parked* the wagon behind the vicarage and went inside to wash up, she found that her brother was still at the breakfast table, drinking his tea and perusing a letter. He looked up at her and smiled when she entered the dining room. "Hallo, Thea. Mrs. Brewster wasn't sure where you had gotten to."

"I went out early to gather evergreen boughs for the church."

"Ah. Excellent. It always makes the old girl look quite festive."

"Yes. I think I'll go over later and decorate."

"Mm." Daniel turned his attention back to the letter.

"Have you gotten the mail already?" Thea nodded toward the paper in his hands as she loaded her plate and began to eat.

"Yes. I took a little stroll before breakfast, so I picked it up. There's a note from Veronica."

"Oh, really?" Thea glanced up at him. "Did she say when she would be arriving?"

"That's the thing. Apparently she's not."

"What?" Disappointment formed in Thea's stomach like a rock, and she set down her fork. "What do you mean? She's supposed to be here any day now."

Her brother shrugged. "She wrote to say she won't be able to make it after all. Her husband came home unexpectedly. Apparently his ship had to return for repairs or some such thing." He continued to read the rest of the letter. "She says the Commander is well, as are the rest of them, and, of course, they are delighted to have him home. Then there is something about a dress she's going to wear to a Twelfth Night ball. She sounds quite excited about it."

"The dress or Commander Stanton coming home?"

"I'm not entirely certain." Daniel handed the letter across the table to Thea. "I have to say, I am disappointed not to see Veronica. Although it will certainly be more peaceful without the children here."

"Yes, I suppose so." Thea skimmed through the note and handed it back to her brother. The days ahead seemed suddenly much emptier.

"Well…" Daniel took a final drink from his cup and rose to his feet. "I should go work on my sermon."

Thea nodded. "I made some notes about your topic, if you'd like to see them." It was their polite fiction regarding the sermons she wrote for him.

"Of course, of course. I'll be in my study." Daniel nodded pleasantly and walked off.

Thea pushed away her plate, no longer hungry. The silence that her brother would treasure this holiday seemed to her an echoing emptiness. With a sigh, she left the room and started up the stairs. A cold loneliness was centered in her chest. She retrieved the sermon she had written from the small oak secretary in her bedroom and laid it on Daniel's desk. Work, she knew, was the best cure for unhappiness, so she put on her cloak and gloves and went out to the laden wagon she had left behind the house. Picking up its handle, she started toward the church.

St. Margaret's was an old building, built of the same native stone as much of the town. It was plain and squat, yet had a beauty in its simplicity. It did not strive to be anything it was not. Centuries ago, in the heyday of the wool trade, there had been talk of tearing it down and building a grander edifice, but the citizens of Chesley, ever a practical lot, had decided not to do so.

The church building had once been the chapel of Astwold Abbey, a convent established by Eleanor of Aquitaine. During the Dissolution, the abbey had been given to an ancestor of Lord Fenstone's. Most of the buildings had been torn down, leaving only two complete structures standing: the chapel and the priory. The priory, which stood at the opposite end of the abbey premises from the church, had been restored and added onto, becoming a residence for the earls of Fenstone. The chapel had been given to the village to use as its church almost three hundred years ago. The ruins of the rest of the abbey lay between the two buildings. If Thea looked in that direction, she could see the fallen stones and half walls that remained.

She did not spare a glance for the familiar sight today, however, as she pulled the wagon to the church door and carried a load of evergreen branches into the nave of the church. Walking down the main aisle past the intersecting arms that formed the cross of the church, she laid the branches on the steps leading up to the altar. She turned and skirted the raised sanctuary to open the door at the back of the church, which led into a short corridor containing the sacristy and a couple of storerooms.

Thea picked up a small oil lamp and carried it down to the farthest storeroom. There she made her way through the collection of churchly odds and ends that had wound up in there. In the back, she found the manger she intended to use for the living Nativity scene on Christmas Eve and hauled it out. It was a simple feed box that stood on X-shaped legs, and though it had not been used in a few years, it seemed to still be in good condition. Grabbing a few tools, she blew out the lamp and set it back in the sacristy, before carrying the rest of the things to the outer vestibule of the church, near the front doors. Later, when she was finished decorating the church, she would take the manger outside and clean it.

Now, however, she went back into the sanctuary and began to adorn the church for Christmas. She made her way down the left wall, cutting and arranging the fragrant branches on the sills of the stained-glass windows. When she reached the short intersecting arms of the church, she turned into the left one, which contained the small chapel devoted to St. Dwynwen.

Separated from the main part of the church by a decorative wrought-iron screen, the chapel held only a few rows of pews facing the main altar in the center of the church. Against one wall was a prie-dieu, flanked by a small stand of votive candles. On the other side of the prie-dieu stood a statue of a female saint, the Dwynwen for whom the little side chapel had been named. At the far end of the chapel, on either side of the single window, were stone sepulchres of a knight and his lady, their effigies carved on the top of the stone slabs.

This part of the church had always been Thea's favorite. It was dimmer than the rest of the church because it had only one stained-glass window, and the few flickering candles in their red-glass votive holders cast only a small, atmospheric light. The statue of St. Dwynwen, somewhat smaller than life-size, stood on a short, square pedestal of stone. The statue itself was simply, even crudely, carved out of wood, and it was faded and fissured with time. The saint looked out and down, smiling sweetly, her arms held out to the side.

From the time she was a child, Thea had liked to sit in the chapel. She loved the quiet, the light and scent of the candles, the aged statue. St. Dwynwen, she thought, looked to be a kind and understanding soul, not pretty perhaps, but loving. It was said that the knight entombed in the rear of the chapel had carried the statue back with him from his campaign in Wales. The story went that he had stopped at a small shrine to St. Dwynwen to pray for success in Wales, and afterward he had won not only the battle but also the heart of a beautiful Welsh lady. In gratitude, he had pledged his devotion to the saint and brought the statue back to his home, where he had given it and the funds for building the chapel to the convent as a gift in the name of his Welsh wife.

The tale had caught Thea's imagination, and she had pored through her father's books until she found the story of St. Dwynwen. Dwynwen, it was said, had been the daughter of a Welsh king and had fallen deeply in love with a man named Maelon. Her father would not let her marry Maelon, but insisted that she marry a wealthier lord. In a rage at being denied his love, Maelon forced himself upon Dwynwen. Heartsick, she fled into the forest, where she prayed for help. An angel appeared and, moved by her plight, gave her a potion for the treacherous Maelon to drink. When Maelon drank it, he was turned to ice as punishment for his cruelty. The angel told Dwynwen that God would grant her three prayers. From the deep love and purity of her heart, Dwynwen asked that Maelon be released from his punishment, that she herself not ever have to marry, and that God look after all true lovers. Maelon was restored, and Dwynwen retreated to Llanddwyn Island and spent the rest of her life in solitude, becoming over the years the Welsh patron saint of love and lovers.

Over the years, many people had prayed before the statue, both at its original shrine in Wales and here in Chesley, and a local legend had sprung up around it. The legend was, of course, romantic. It was said that whoever prayed with a truly loving heart to St. Dwynwen here in her chapel would have his or her prayer granted. Some argued that only prayers for love were granted, but others said that the kindly saint would answer even prayers of broader scope.

Now and then Thea had said prayers here, and as best she could tell, few of them had been granted. Still, it was her favorite place to pray or just to sit and think. She loved the quiet and the solemnity of it, the beauty of the sanctuary and the marble baptismal font that centered the arm on the opposite side of the church.

She lit a candle and knelt to say a brief prayer beside the statue, then went to the end of the chapel to decorate the lone window with evergreen and holly. Afterward, she sat down in the front pew and began to wire the boughs into garlands to string across the front of the church. The peace and solitude of the chapel surrounded her, and the heady fragrance of the evergreens filled her nostrils. But sitting here in the quiet, she found it hard to ignore the cold lump that lay in the center of her chest. For a while her activity had masked it, subdued it, but now the coldness seemed to grow and spread.

Thea told herself the hard lonely feeling would pass. After all, though she loved her sister and her niece and nephews, they were not really part of her life. It was disappointing that they would not be here for Christmas, but the next few days would be much like her days always were. This was her life—her brother, this church, the vicarage, the town.

Except that none of it was really hers. Her brother was the vicar; it was his house, his church, the people his parishioners. She only shared in that life as he allowed her to, and if he died, it would all go to some other pastor, some other family, and she would no longer have even a home. Thea shook her head—what a morbid and foolish way to think! Daniel was young and healthy; he was not about to die. But, she reminded herself, he might very well marry one day. He had given no sign so far that he had any interest in marrying, but it could reasonably happen. If he did marry, Thea would no longer be needed. Daniel was too kind to make her leave, but Thea knew that she would not have a real place in the vicarage. It would be another woman's home, not hers.

Tears pricked at her eyelids, and she was swept by an overwhelming loneliness. It seemed suddenly that she had no real place in the world, no home, no spot of her own, as if all her life were merely borrowed from others. This feeling had come over her before, a stark and cold thing that pierced her soul. Usually Thea could shove the emotion aside, fill her life with work, but suddenly she could not. With awful clarity, she saw the truth: she did not have a place, a life, of her own. She lived on the edges of other people's lives—writing sermons that would be her brother's, spending a week once a year with children that were her sister's, living in a house that belonged to the church, busying herself with the affairs of a church that was not hers. She was twenty-seven years old, unmarried, and childless. And so utterly invisible that a man who had kissed her ten years ago did not have even the slightest twinge of recognition when he saw her.

She would never have a real life. There was no likelihood that she would marry. Whom would she marry in this village? She had known everyone here all her life, and clearly no husband for her was among them. Even if she could somehow magically live somewhere else, she had little chance of capturing any man's heart. She was plain, and she could not even make up for her plainness with a sweetness of spirit. She was often opinionated—some would even say bossy—and she could be sharp-tongued. She had trouble asking for someone else's advice or help when she knew what she should do. It was difficult for her to flatter and smooth and soothe. The combination of her looks and personality was, she was well aware, a deadly obstruction to marriage.

Her life seemed suddenly so empty and pointless that it took her breath away. Something close to panic swept through Thea, and she knotted her hands together tightly in her lap. She was afraid she might cry out, might weep. Abruptly she dropped down onto the kneeling rail that fronted the votive-candle stand. Her clasped hands on the wooden rail, she closed her eyes. The imprint of the dancing candle flames still burned in her vision.

"Please . . ." She dropped her forehead to her hands, her mind too overset to know what to say. Intercessions, prayers, pleas, tumbled through her head. "Please help me." What did she want? "Give me a life. Please, give me a life of my own." She remained bent over, pain and fear storming through her. For once she could not push it away, could not ignore it, could not superimpose work over it. She could only feel the desperate, lonely longing.

Thea was not sure how long she knelt that way before a noise outside in the church brought her back to awareness of her surroundings. She raised her head and noticed that her cheeks were wet; she knew that she must have been crying. With hands that trembled a little, she wiped away the tears and sat back on her heels, listening.

Again a noise came, something like a squeak. She rose to her feet, frowning. She wasn't sure what the first sound had been. Perhaps a footfall or a door closing? She wondered if someone had come into the church. Thea wiped her cheeks and eyes again, thinking with embarrassment that she must look a mess. She walked out of the chapel and glanced around the church. It was silent and dimly lit, as empty as when she had entered it.

Then she heard an odd sputtering noise. It seemed to come from the vestibule, and Thea took a few steps in that direction. In the next instant, an angelic little face framed by pale gold curls popped up over the side of the wooden feed bin. Thea stopped, her mouth dropping open in astonishment.

A baby was in the manger.

# Four

For one horrified instant, Thea thought that she had gone quite mad. The baby let out a high-pitched squeal and grabbed the side of the manger with one hand, pulling himself into a sitting position. He grinned as he latched onto the manger with his other hand and shook it as he produced a series of bubbling, blowing noises. If this was a figment of her imagination, she thought, it was incredibly real.

Thea came out of her frozen state and hurried down the aisle, her mind tumbling with questions. She could not imagine who the child was or where he had come from. She was sure there must be a rational explanation for his sitting in the manger, but at the moment she had no idea what it was. Thea half expected to find the child's mother in the vestibule, but when she stepped into the area, it was empty except for the baby and the manger. She rushed over to the door and opened it to peer outside, but there was no sign of anyone there, either.

Turning back around, she stared at the child. He gazed back at her with lively interest. Up close, she could see that he was truly lovely. He had a softly rounded face with pudgy, rosy cheeks and an adorable tiny dimple on his chin. His blue eyes were enormous and his hair a soft tumble of feathery blond curls. Though she could not pretend to know every infant in the village, Thea was certain that she had never before seen this boy.

"Who are you?" she murmured, coming over to the manger.

He seemed delighted at her movement, and he banged both his hands down on his legs, smiling and releasing a crow of delight. Thea chuckled at the noise.

"Where is your mother?" she asked, bending down toward him.

He grinned and held his hands up to her, and something melted inside Thea. She picked him up, and he latched onto the shoulder of her dress with one hand. With the other, he reached out to pat her cheek, his gaze steady on her face.

He wore the customary white baby gown, with knitted bootees on his feet and a knitted sweater atop the gown. He had been sitting on a small blanket in the manger, and a tiny knitted blue cap was beside it. Thea wondered if he was warm enough. Even though they were inside the stone church, it was still quite cool. Thea had taken off her cloak as she worked, but she realized that now, after doing nothing but sitting for a while, she was chilled.

"Are you cold?" Thea picked up the little blanket and wrapped it around the baby, tucking the little knitted cap in her pocket. "It's a shame you aren't old enough to talk."

She went back into the church, which was warmer than the vestibule, and sat down in one of the pews to think. Try as she could, she could come up with no reason for his being in the manger unless someone had purposely abandoned him. She had heard stories of babies being left at a vicarage or a church. However, it seemed unlikely that someone could want to get rid of this child. He was utterly angelic in appearance, and he looked not only well fed, but was dressed in clean, new clothes.

Still, clearly, he could not have gotten into the place on his own, and whoever had put him in the manger had immediately fled. The other thing that was quite obvious was that Thea had to do something.

The first task was to get him out of this cold church. Thea set the baby down while she put on her cloak, then she pulled the knit cap onto his head. He did not seem to appreciate this, for he shook his head and grabbed at the cap, pulling it off. Thea persevered, pulling it on again and this time tying it quickly beneath his chin. She wrapped the blanket tightly around him, pulling up a flap of it to cover his head, and carried him out of the church and across the bridge to the vicarage.

She went in the side door into the kitchen, generally the warmest room in the house. Their housekeeper stood at the table, rolling out dough. She turned to look at Thea, and her eyes went wide.

"Miss Althea! What do you have there?"

"A baby." Thea took off the blanket and draped it over one of the chairs.

"I can see that 'tis a baby. But why are you carrying him? And who is he?"

"I wish I knew." Thea untied the cap and pulled it off as well, exposing the cluster of shining curls.

"Oh, my! Look at that; he's just like an angel, ain't he?" Mrs. Brewster came over to look at the child more closely, wiping her hands off on a towel.

"I thought the same thing myself." Thea stroked her hand across his head, the silky curls soft beneath her fingers.

"But how—"

"I found him. He was in the church."

"'The church?" Daniel's voice sounded from the door. He walked in, his eyes on the piece of paper in his hands. "Who was in the church?" He lifted his head when there was no answer. "Good God!"

Thea couldn't hold back a chuckle at her brother's stunned expression. "*He* was in the church. I haven't a clue what his name is." The baby made a rude noise with his mouth and bounced in Thea's arms, and Thea laughed again. "Isn't he beautiful?"

"Yes, I suppose so. But, Thea, I don't understand."

"I don't either. I was decorating the church with the boughs I got this morning, and I heard an odd noise. When I went out to check, I found this baby in the manger."

"In the manger!" If possible, Daniel looked even more astonished.

"Yes. It seems like Providence, don't you think?"

"It seems like a bad jest to me," Daniel retorted. "You have no idea whose he is?"

Thea shook her head. "I've never seen him; I'm certain of it."

"Aye," Mrs. Brewster agreed. "Me either. You wouldn't forget this one."

"But what are you going to do with him?" Daniel asked. "We can't possibly keep him."

Instinctively Thea tightened her arm around the baby. "I could scarcely leave him in the church!"

"No, no, of course not. But, I mean, well, he can't stay here."

"Why not? Mrs. Brewster, surely we must have something he can sleep in."

"Oh, aye. There's that big basket I carry the laundry in. It's long and deep. We can put a pillow in it, and he'll be snug as a wee bunny."

"That's perfect."

"And I've got a little bit of oatmeal left over from breakfast. We'll add some milk, and that'll fill him up. I'll get that basket." The housekeeper bustled out of the room.

Daniel turned back to his sister in some exasperation. "Thea, have some sense! You cannot simply keep a child as though it were a stray dog or cat."

"Of course not. But we cannot turn him away, either."

"I wasn't suggesting that. We should take him to the foundling home in Cheltenham." He nodded, pleased with the solution.

"The foundling home!" An icy fist closed around Thea's heart. "Daniel, no."

"But that is where he belongs, surely. He's been abandoned— an orphan or a child whose mother cannot take care of him or, well, I don't know what, but it's clear that he is a foundling."

"But we cannot abandon him, too."

"Thea." Daniel's face fell into puzzled lines. "I don't understand. You cannot mean that you and I would—would raise him?"

"I—well, I had not thought that far ahead. I suppose we cannot."

"There. You see?"

"But there's no need to rush to take him to the foundling home, either. I am sure you have no desire to drive our pony trap in the cold all the way to Cheltenham." Thea knew her brother well enough to know that such an argument would strike home with him.

"Well, no, but . . ."

"It may be that someone around here knows who he is, or to whom he belongs. We shall ask around, and Mrs. Brewster can ask, as well. Perhaps there is someone else in his family who will care for him. Or his mother might have second thoughts and return to get him. Maybe . . . maybe he was even stolen from his home. He looks quite well cared for, and his garments are nice. You see?" She brought the baby closer.

Daniel backed up a step. "Yes, well, if he was abducted, why was he left in the church?"

"I don't know. They might have gotten frightened or felt remorseful. It doesn't really matter. The point is that someone might turn up here looking for him soon. And then the whole problem would be solved."

"Yes, but what about in the meantime?"

"We shall take care of him—Mrs. Brewster and I. You needn't worry yourself about it. You will hardly know he is here."

Daniel looked doubtful, but he was a man accustomed to letting his sister take charge of things, and he said, "All right . . . if you really wish it. Though I don't understand . . ."

"I'm not sure I do, either," Thea murmured, but she was careful to wait until after her brother had headed back to his study.

By the time Mrs. Brewster returned, the baby had started to fuss, wriggling and squirming and sticking his tiny fist in his mouth. Thea tried patting him, then jiggling, but he screwed up his face and let out a plaintive wail.

"What's the matter with him?" Thea asked, anxiety rising in her. If he cried a great deal, Daniel might decide it was worth it to drive to the foundling home, even in the cold weather.

"Why, the wee mite's getting hungry, I'll warrant." Mrs. Brewster bent over him. "Look at him, trying to eat his own hand. I'll dish up some of that oatmeal right now."

Thea walked around the kitchen, jiggling the baby and distracting him by showing him various objects while Mrs. Brewster warmed up the oatmeal and thinned it with milk.

"We need to call him something, don't you think?" Thea mused. "I was thinking Matthew. It means 'gift of God'. That seems a proper name for someone found in a church."

"Oh, aye, miss." Mrs. Brewster cast a glance at Thea and smiled a little. "'Tis a fine name."

"What about you?" Thea asked the baby, leaning her forehead against his. "Are you a Matthew?" She had thought more than once before that people said the silliest things to babies. But holding him now, she found herself wanting to do the same. She wanted, she realized, to see that joyous smile again.

"Here we go. Shall I feed him, miss?" Mrs. Brewster set down the bowl and held out her hands for the baby.

Thea felt curiously reluctant to hand him over, but she did so.

The housekeeper, after all, was far more familiar with this sort of thing than she was. Thea watched as Mrs. Brewster sat the baby on her lap and curved one arm around him, then popped a spoonful of oatmeal into his mouth. Matthew's fussing stopped immediately, and he eagerly took a second bite. Thea ate a light luncheon of cheese and bread while the housekeeper fed the baby, then she went up to her room to get a pillow and bedding for the basket.

With care, she lined the basket with a blanket and sheet to make sure the baby would not come into contact with the rough weave. Then she laid in two well-stuffed pillows, one on top of the other. The light throw she had taken from the foot of her bed would do, she thought, for a cover, in addition to his own little knitted blanket.

"Why, look at this!"

Thea turned at the housekeeper's soft exclamation. Mrs. Brewster was bending over the baby, who was lying in the seat of the chair next to her. He was cooing contentedly as he wrapped his hands around his feet.

"Look at what?" Thea walked over to them.

"Well, I decided I'd diaper him with some of that muslin we tore up from your old dress, and look what I found pinned to his swaddling band." She handed a brooch to Thea and returned to the task of diapering the baby.

Thea took the brooch in her hand. The small, elegant piece had an oval of onyx with a gold, ornate scrollwork letter *M* in the center. Thea stared down at the brooch in surprise. She had seen just such a letter *M* the other night. Lord Morecombe had worn a signet ring with an engraved letter exactly like that.

Lord Morecombe. In that moment, Thea understood. The beautiful baby was Lord Morecombe's child. He even had the same little dimple in his chin! Matthew was a by-blow brought here by his mother, doubtless hoping that his lordship would acknowledge him. Had she taken the boy to his lordship and been turned away? Or had she simply left Matthew in the church, hoping that the brooch attached to his clothing would bring him to Morecombe's attention?

It certainly was not an uncommon story—a lord who dallied with some girl and got her with child. He went on about his careless, hedonistic way while she was left to face the consequences. Whether a seduced maiden or an immoral drab, the mother was in a terrible position, without the means to support a child if the father did not acknowledge the boy and provide her with funds. If she made it through the difficulties of pregnancy and childbirth, she could not find employment with a baby in her arms. Usually, she had to resort in the end to giving the child to a foundling home.

And Lord Morecombe certainly fit the part. Thea recalled the reports of his scandalous behavior; the way she had seen him riding home early this morning from what had obviously been a bed other than his own; his sinfully handsome features and devilish smile. He was the kind of man who kissed so many girls at dances that he could not even remember them a few years later!

Thea closed her hand hard around the brooch, her face setting in grim lines. Lord Morecombe was not going to get away with this.

She whirled around and picked up her cloak, throwing it

over her shoulders and tying it. Mrs. Brewster, who had finished diapering the baby and now sat with him on her lap, looked up in astonishment as Thea marched over and slipped the knitted cap and sweater back on the baby. He giggled with delight and reached his hands for Thea as she bent over him.

"Whatever are you doing, miss?" Mrs. Brewster asked, her voice tinged with some trepidation. "Why do you look so? Where are you going?"

"I am going to set things right." Thea swept the baby up and once again wrapped the blanket around him tightly. Then she marched out the door, leaving the housekeeper staring after her blankly.

Thea's anger carried her swiftly over the bridge and through the graveyard behind the church. Though it took some time to reach the Priory if one went by the road through town, it took no more than twenty or thirty minutes if she struck out through the grounds of what had once been the abbey. The December day was cool, but the vigorous walk kept Thea warm enough inside her cloak, especially since the weight of the child she carried added a good bit to the exercise.

Carrying a child, she discovered, was not the same as carrying a package weighing the same amount. In one way, it was easier, for Matthew held on to her with a grip like a monkey's and wrapped his little legs around her. But packages did not squirm and wriggle, nor did they reach up to explore one's features or spectacles or hair with their hands. The baby soon managed to work his head and shoulders free of the blanket, and no matter how many times Thea tugged it back up to cover him, he knocked it off his head again. He appeared to be fascinated by the glass lenses of her spectacles, and he reached for them time and again, often catching them and trying to jerk them from her head.

She tried pulling up the hood of her cloak to thwart him, but he was happy to grab the hood, as well, dragging it back and forth across her hair. She tried wrapping her cloak around Matthew, too, in an effort to keep him warm since he was so persistent in shrugging off the blanket. But then he was able to grab the front of her frock and the frilled fichu she wore tucked into the neck of the dress to add modesty and warmth. He liked to hold on with both hands and bounce, she discovered. At one point, she decided, he even seemed to be trying to climb up the front of her dress. To add to her difficulties, it began to mist, not heavily but enough to spot the lenses of her spectacles and to cling to her hair, now exposed by the hood that Matthew had finally succeeded in shoving off her head. The cloak ties had come loose as well, so that her cloak was inching back on her shoulders.

Thea finally had to take off her spectacles and thrust them into her pocket because they had become so bedewed that they were more an obstruction to her vision than an aid, but fortunately she was close to the Priory by that time and could make her way to its front door. She brought down the knocker with a force that made Matthew jump in her arms, alarmed, but in the next moment he decided that the noise was simply another fun thing and shouted back a loud sound of his own.

A footman answered the door, and his eyebrows shot up when he saw Thea standing on the doorstep, baby in her arms. "Miss?" He glanced around as if unsure what to do. "Can I, um, help you?"

"Yes, indeed, you can, by letting me inside," Thea retorted in some irritation, and she stepped into the house, forcing the young man to either physically block her progress or step back.

He chose to step back, spluttering, "But—miss—what—"

"I wish to see Lord Morecombe."

"I'm sorry, miss, but—"

As he began to speak, a man's voice shouted, "Bravo! Direct hit, Gabriel!"

Another, indistinguishable shout came in a male voice, as well as the sound of feet stamping and of metal clashing against metal. The noises all came from the room to the right of the entryway.

"Thank you, I can find my own way." Thea started past the servant, thrusting her rapidly slipping cloak into his hands.

That gesture stopped him for a moment as years of training made him hang the cloak on the stand by the door, but then he scurried after her, saying, "Miss . . . no, miss."

Thea ignored the footman as she strode up to the half-closed double doors. Thea stopped abruptly, staring at the scene before her. The large room had obviously once been the great hall of the medieval house. The long rectangle had a vaulted ceiling of heavy, blackened wood beams. A vast fireplace stood at one end of the room. The room was largely empty of furniture, containing only a long table and chairs, as well as a sideboard at the opposite end and a few chairs against the walls. The scarcity of furniture left a lot of empty stone floor, and two men were now moving up and down that emptiness, facing each other and wielding fireplace utensils like swords. Lord Morecombe advanced rapidly on the other man, whom Thea recalled was named Sir Myles something-or-other. Morecombe's fireplace shovel parried and thrust against the poker the other man used.

The men had taken off their jackets and thrown them across the table, along with their brightly colored waistcoats. Their faces were flushed, and their boots resounded on the floor as they darted back and forth, the metal instruments clanking and scraping against each other. A third man, Morecombe's other companion at the party, sat in a chair near the sideboard, a large tankard in his hand, cheering the others on. Two more tankards and a punch bowl stood on the sideboard.

"Miss . . . miss!" The footman came up behind Thea, hissing and wringing his hands. "You mustn't go in there. It isn't proper!"

Thea whirled on him, fixing him with a fiery look that stopped his speech immediately. She turned back and shoved on one of the half-open doors. It slammed into the wall with a satisfying crash that brought all movement in the room to an immediate halt. The baby in her arms made a little hiccup of sound and went very still, his hands curled tightly in the front of her dress. All three men swung around to face her. She could not see clearly enough to gauge their expressions, but she suspected with a sense of satisfaction that astonishment was on their features.

"Who the devil are you?" Morecombe asked. He tossed his little shovel carelessly onto the table and came closer to her.

As he came into focus, Thea realized, with a little skip of her pulse, how intensely masculine he was without his jacket, his lawn shirt damp with sweat and sticking to his chest, the sleeves rolled up almost to his elbows. His black hair was mussed from the strenuous activity as well, and it flopped down across his forehead, thick and shining. That she noticed these things—and that they made her breathe a little faster—simply fueled her irritation. This was precisely the sort of reaction this man caused, and that was why some poor woman had gotten into trouble.

"Well?" he asked when Thea did not immediately answer. "What are you doing here?"

"I am here about this child." Thea's anger shot the words out of her like bullets, sharp and fierce. "*Your* child. And your duty to him."

One of Gabriel's eyebrows rose quizzically, and he ran his gaze down her in a slow, obvious way, rudely taking in every bit of her from the top of her head to the tip of her toes.

"*My* child?" he drawled, his voice thick with amusement. "My dear girl, I have been drinking, I admit, but I am not that befuddled. I am quite certain that I have never lain with you. I would remember it if I had."

Thea's cheeks flooded with red as she realized two humiliating things. The first was that he had, once again, entirely forgotten her. He not only had not remembered their kiss ten years ago, he did not recall meeting her just the other evening at the Squire's ball. She was that forgettable! He was that arrogant!

The second, equally embarrassing realization was that Lord Morecombe thought that the baby was hers, that she was accusing him of having gotten her with child. He thought she was a loose woman. A doxy! A lightskirt! Even worse, it occurred to her exactly how she must look. The baby had tugged and pulled at her so much that her ruffled white cotton fichu was all twisted and half pulled out, leaving more of her chest exposed than was entirely proper, especially at this time of day. Indeed, on the side where the baby sat on her hip, he had gripped her dress so tightly that it was pulled almost off her shoulder. Her face was flushed from the exertion of her walk, and her hair and skin were coated with mist. Several strands of her hair had come tumbling down during the tussle with the baby over her hood and were hanging loose and curling wildly in the moisture. Morecombe could hardly be faulted for assuming the worst about her, she thought, but that did not make her any more inclined to like him.

A lazy smile curved his lips, and he came even closer, stopping right in front of her. She could see his face quite clearly now—the square jaw and chin, stubbled by a day's growth of beard that for some reason made her feel all warm and loose inside, the dark, intense eyes shadowed by thick, black lashes, the shallow cleft in his chin that made one want to touch it. She remembered how he had moved closer to her that evening ten years ago, his lips coming to rest on hers, and she recalled, too, the shock of pleasure that had run through her at the feel of his mouth. Her knees went a little weak, and she was scared that he might see her trembling.

"Of course," he said in a low voice, running his knuckles lightly down her cheek, "I would be happy to change that situation at any time."

Thea felt a sharp, visceral tug at the touch of his skin on hers, and her response appalled her, making her almost as angry at herself as she was at this bold, arrogant man. She jerked her head back, her eyes blazing, and snapped, "You may jest all you wish, but I can assure you that it is no laughing matter for this child, abandoned and cold and hungry."

His eyes went down to the child, and to Thea's annoyance Matthew dimpled and smiled at the man and ducked his head down to Thea's shoulder, looking back up at Morecombe in a charming way. Gabriel chuckled and reached his forefinger out to Matthew, who immediately wrapped one pudgy little fist around it.

"He scarce looks hungry to me. Or cold." Gabriel cut his eyes toward Thea, glinting with a charm of his own. "Indeed, he seems to be in a sweet place that any man might envy."

Thea ground her teeth. "Pray do not attempt to ply your wiles on me. I am not this baby's mother, but you are his father." She pulled the brooch out of her pocket and held it up to him.

"The devil!" Lord Morecombe stiffened, his eyes widening, and he snatched the piece of jewelry from her hand. He gazed at it for a long moment, then his hand curled around it tightly and he turned back to her, his eyes as hard and dark as the stone in the brooch. He wrapped his hand like iron around her wrist. "Who are you? What kind of game are you playing?"

Thea's heart pounded, and she tried to jerk her arm away from him, but she could not. She was suddenly, deeply aware of how large and strong he was. But she refused to show any indication of the leap of fear in her chest. "Pray, do not think you can frighten me into silence. It is you who are playing games, not I."

His fingers tightened, biting into her flesh, as he loomed over her, holding out the brooch in his palm. "What is the meaning of this? Tell me, blast it!" Behind Morecombe, she saw the other two men, who had been lounging at the table and watching the show with amusement, suddenly straighten and take a few steps forward.

Thea swallowed, but she tilted her face up defiantly to him. "Until you change your attitude, I have no intention of telling you anything. You may act like a savage with other women, but I am not going to wilt at your feet."

"I have no doubt of that. Still, I will have my answer." He set his jaw.

Thea glared back at him, adopting an equally stony expression. "Let go of me."

"Not until you tell me what is going on. Where did you get this? Where is Jocelyn? Is it money you're after?"

"Jocelyn!" Sir Myles exclaimed in astonishment, glancing at his companion, then back at Morecombe.

"Money! No! I don't know what you're talking about!" Thea tried once more to pull away from him, then gave up and faced him with haughty contempt. "I am not here seeking money from you. All I want is for you to assume responsibility for your child, and—"

"Blast it, woman! Stop yammering about 'my child.' I don't have a child, and I have never seen this lad before. And do not think that you can slip out of this by flaunting your admittedly tempting wares at me. Tell me how you got this brooch. Did you take it from Jocelyn?"

"Flaunting!" Thea's cheeks flamed with color, and she was so furious that for a moment she could not speak. Finally she gasped out, "I assure you that 'tempting' a man like you is the last thing I wish to do. I do not know anyone named Jocelyn. If she is your paramour, she—"

Morecombe let out a low, harsh noise that was similar to a growl, and Thea's voice died away.

"Jocelyn is my *sister*." He leaned forward, his eyes boring into hers, and the cold threat in his voice was more frightening than his earlier anger. "And you are going to tell me how you obtained this brooch if I have to pull it out of you word by word."

Thea gaped at him, her earlier certainty draining out of her in a rush.

"Tell me." He dropped her wrist and grasped her shoulder, giving her a little shake. "How did you get my sister's brooch?"

"I—it was on the baby when I found him. It was pinned to his clothes."

"Pinned to—" He stopped, his hand falling away from her shoulder. "You *found* him?"

"Yes. He was abandoned. I took him home, and my housekeeper found the brooch when she was changing him."

Morecombe looked at Matthew. He took a step back, raking his hand back through his hair. "Bloody hell."

The room was utterly silent. Thea shifted Matthew to her other side. Her anger had evaporated, and indeed, she now felt rather foolish for having jumped to the conclusion that Lord Morecombe was the baby's father. She thought about the obvious implication of their conversation, that the baby belonged to Morecombe's sister. That would certainly explain the quality of the child's clothes and that he had been well cared for, not to mention the resemblance in his cleft chin. Doubtless his sister would have had the money to spend on him. But why would she have abandoned Matthew? Could he have been abducted from her?

No, that made no sense, either. Lord Morecombe had not recognized the child—and while Morecombe was clearly not the best at remembering faces, surely he would know his own nephew. And why had he asked where Jocelyn was? He had acted as if he thought she had done something to his sister, as if Thea were trying to get money from him. Thea would have liked very much to find out more, but every question that came into her head sounded far too prying.

There was the sound of the front door opening and footsteps in the entry. A moment later, an exquisitely dressed, brown-haired man stepped into the doorway. It was her cousin Ian. He came to a dead stop as he saw the scene in front of him.

"What's going on? Gabriel?" He turned his head to Thea and his eyes widened. "Cousin Althea?" He peered at her more closely. "Is that you?"

Thea blushed, suddenly remembering the state of her clothes and hair. She had, she realized with chilling clarity, just made an utter fool of herself in front of these men. She must look like— and had acted like—not a dull spinster, but a raving shrew. No doubt Ian would now be the butt of rude jests about his "mad cousin Althea."

"What's happened?" Lord Wofford went on, coming farther into the room. "Who is that child?" He turned toward the other two men. "Myles? Alan? Gabriel! What the devil is going on?"

Lord Morecombe shook his head, seemingly coming out of his stupor. He cast a glance at Wofford. "Tell you later." Reaching out, Morecombe grabbed Thea's wrist and strode out of the room, pulling her after him.

"What are you doing? Let go of me!" Thea protested, trying in vain to wrest her arm from his grasp. She turned toward the other men and saw that they were all three staring after them, mouths agape in astonishment.

"Don't just stand there," Morecombe snapped at the footman, who was also goggling at them. "Fetch her cloak."

"Yes, my lord. Of course, my lord." The man jumped to retrieve Thea's cloak and advanced toward them, holding out the garment with some trepidation.

"Good God, man, she won't bite." Morecombe grabbed the cloak from the servant's hands and draped it around her shoulders. "At least," he added as he tied the strings at her throat, looking down at her with—unbelievably!—a small smile playing at the corners of his mouth, "I don't think she would bite very hard."

"Really!" His smile managed, somehow, to both light her indignation and at the same time wipe out her spurt of fear. "If that isn't the outside of enough! Clearly, you must be accustomed to dragging ladies off into the night."

He let out a chuckle as he grabbed his many-caped greatcoat from the hall tree and thrust his arms into it. "Oh, but I rarely drag off *ladies*," he countered provocatively, taking her by the arm again, this time with a less bruising grip, and steering her out the front door.

He guided her across the yard toward the stables, shouting to his grooms to saddle his horse. It was still misting, and Thea pulled up her hood and wrapped her cloak protectively over the baby as well. For his part, the baby seemed to find this latest trip great fun and kept squirming until his head was once again free of the enveloping cloak.

"Your friends are utterly useless," Thea grumbled. "They just stood there as you *abducted* me."

"I would say they were quite useful to me," he pointed out, and grinned, showing white, even teeth.

"Scarcely gentlemen," she countered.

"In their defense, my friends, being rational men, were not afraid that I was about to run mad and slaughter you. Though given your behavior, I can certainly understand why you might expect that sort of reaction from men."

"It will no doubt surprise you to learn that I have never before been threatened by a man."

Again came that slashing grin. "It does, indeed. But let me reassure you on that score. All I want is for you to show me where you found this child."

They had reached the shelter of the stables, and a groom hurried forward, leading a splendid roan gelding. As Thea looked at the animal, wondering exactly how they would ride, given that there was only one horse and she was holding a baby, Gabriel took the baby from her and handed it to the startled groom, then lifted Thea onto the horse. She was so shocked she could not speak, just took Matthew as Gabriel handed him up to her. Morecombe swung up into the saddle behind her and took the reins from the groom, and they started off.

"You might have at least asked," Thea snapped, struggling to hold the baby and manage to stay perfectly upright and not let her body touch his even though his arms were around her on either side.

"Asked what?" He glanced down at her.

"If I wished to go or whether I wanted to get on this horse. Or—or anything."

"Did you wish to remain at my house?"

"No, of course not."

"Would you have preferred to walk back to town?"

"No. That's not the point."

"What is the point?"

"That you are arrogant and unmannerly, and you treat people as if they were your servants."

"I beg your pardon." His tone implied that he did not mean those words in the slightest. "I did not order you to do anything."

"No, you didn't even speak, just grabbed my arm and pulled me along behind you."

He grimaced. "Holy hell, are you going to continue to natter about this all the way into town? I need to see where you found my sister's brooch. My manners were not the first thought on my mind. And would you quit squirming about? What are you doing?"

"Trying to stay upright. It's a trifle difficult when one is holding a baby and has no purchase and is riding sideways in front of another."

"Oh, the devil! What is the matter with you?" One arm tightened around her, pulling her flush against him. "Relax and you'll be fine. I won't let you fall off. Tempting as it might be to jettison you, I have to keep you."

Thea would have liked to make a sharp retort, but her brain would not work. She was sure a blush must be spreading over her entire person. She had never had her body pressed against a man's this way. Even with his coat and her cloak and all their clothes between them, it seemed positively immoral to be leaning against him. But the motion of the horse worked against her; it *was* much easier to sit this way, letting his body support hers.

However, she could not say that she was comfortable. She was far too aware of Gabriel's body. His coat was unbuttoned, and as they rode, the sides fell apart, so that even the protection of that heavy cloth between them was gone. He was hard and muscular. She could feel his chest slide against her side with the rhythm of the horse, and the tightening and relaxation of his thigh muscles as he guided the animal. His arms enveloped her. Her nostrils were filled with the scent of his skin and the faint trace of shaving soap, the tang of spiced wine on his breath. Thea shivered at her immediate response to his nearness.

"Cold?" he asked, reaching down to draw his coat around her and the baby. He tightened his arms around her to hold the coat in place, literally wrapping her in his warmth.

Thea closed her eyes and lowered her head to rest against the baby's. He was nestled against her, his small body relaxed, and she realized that Matthew was falling asleep. He made a soft noise and rubbed his head against her chest, sinking more deeply into sleep. Her throat closed, and she found herself blinking back tears. It seemed so sweet, so right, to hold the precious weight of this small body against her, to be cocooned in Gabriel's embrace, his heat and strength all around her, protecting and sheltering her.

It was silly, she told herself. Gabriel's gesture had been only a gentlemanly move, done more to protect the baby than anything else. It meant nothing. She did not want anything from him anyway. But she could not deny the way emotion surged in her, warming and opening her, a variety of sensations tangling through her in a most confusing way. How could she experience this maternal tenderness spreading through her chest and at the same time have an altogether different sort of stirring lower in her body? It seemed perverse and a little wicked, yet she could not deny that she felt both things.

She shifted fractionally, and something stirred against her hip. She realized that Gabriel's body had moved in response to her own movement, and her cheeks flamed. Was he . . . had he . . . Thea could not even think the words; in truth, she could not really put words to what she instinctively knew. It was embarrassing, scandalous, and even worse was that she wanted, perversely, to feel that movement again. She was tempted to shift once more and see what happened, to press herself more firmly into his body, or to rub her cheek against his hard chest.

She knew that was wrong. It had to be wrong. She shouldn't be wanting such things, thinking such thoughts. Thea squeezed her eyes even more tightly shut, concentrating on willing away her errant emotions. That was something she had mastered long ago, shoving aside that which did not fit or was not right or hurt too much. But it was rather harder, she realized now, to deny sensations that she was continuing to feel. How was she to stop thinking of the strength of his arms when they were hard around her? It was impossible, surely, not to notice the muscles that bunched in his thighs when the horse skittered a little to one side. And when his torso rubbed against hers with every step their mount took, causing the most intriguing friction, well, her mind simply could not seem to maintain control. She was a jumble of nerves, a confusing mixture of hot and cold and fear and eagerness.

With relief, she saw the first houses of the village in front of her. She straightened, putting a little distance between her and Gabriel, and glanced up at him. He turned his eyes down to look at her, but she could read nothing in his countenance. It was almost completely dark now, and his eyes were shadows in the planes and angles of his face.

She wondered what he had felt earlier, what he had thought. Had that physical reaction meant anything? She had no way of knowing. The male mind was a mystery to her. The only men she had ever known well were her father and brother, and she was certain that they were a world away from a man like Gabriel Morecombe.

"Well?" he asked, and Thea jumped, startled. For an instant, she thought he had been asking her about the direction of her thoughts, but then he went on, "Where are we going?"

"Oh. Yes. Turn left in the center of the village and go almost to the edge of town." When they neared the vicarage, she pointed to it, saying, "There."

"You found the baby here?" Gabriel pulled the horse to a stop. He dismounted, then reached up to lift Thea from the horse and set her on her feet. "What is this house?" He glanced toward the church looming past the house as he reached down to tie his mount's reins to the low iron fence. "The vicarage?"

"Yes. I mean, yes, this is the vicarage. But it's not where I found the baby." She started up the walk, curving around to go in the kitchen door.

He fell into step beside her. "Then why are we going here? I thought you were going to show me where you found him."

"I live here," Thea answered simply.

He stopped abruptly. "You what?"

"I *live* here." She turned to face him. "I am the vicar's sister."

His gaze narrowed, and he reached forward to push her hood back from her face. He stared at her for a long moment. "The devil you say. I met you at the dance. Miss Falbridge."

Thea rolled her eyes. "Bainbridge," she snapped at him. "My name is Althea Bainbridge." She whirled and stalked away.

# Five

Gabriel stood for a moment, looking after Thea, then followed her as she stepped into the kitchen. The warmth of the kitchen enveloped them, the air redolent with the scents of cooking. Mrs. Brewster turned at their entrance, and her eyebrows sailed upward at the sight of Gabriel Morecombe. She cut her eyes toward Thea.

"I was just about to take your brother an early supper on a tray to his office, Miss Althea. We wasn't sure when you'd be back. You want me to change to the dining table, then?" Her gaze flickered back to Gabriel. "Should I set more places?"

"No, it's fine." Thea kept her voice low so as not to disturb the sleeping baby. "Go on. I have something to do. I'm just putting the little one to bed first."

Thea squatted beside the basket and eased the baby down into it. No one moved or spoke as Matthew squirmed, then let out a tiny sigh and continued to sleep. Thea arranged the blanket over him and stood up.

"I shall return soon," Thea promised the housekeeper, and Mrs. Brewster nodded as she picked up the tray of food. With a last glance back at Gabriel, she left the room.

Thea lit the candle, then turned and started toward the out-side door, all without saying a word to Gabriel. Gabriel opened the door, grinning, and followed her outside.

"I didn't recognize you earlier," he said in an explanatory way.

"That was obvious," Thea snapped. "Since you accused me of being a lightskirt!"

He let out a laugh. "I didn't accuse you. I merely assumed. You did not, um, look like a vicar's sister."

"You are impossible." Thea whirled to face him. "Any decent man would be embarrassed at making such a mistake. He would be appalled to have insulted a gentlewoman in that manner. All you can do is laugh."

He grinned. "I suppose I am not a decent man. I have been told so before."

"You needn't seem so pleased about it."

She whipped back around and started toward the church. Gabriel came up beside her, saying conversationally, "In my defense, you did not look like the woman I met the other night."

Thea reached beneath her cloak and dug her spectacles out of her pocket. She put them on and once again turned to face him. "There. Is that better? Am I Miss 'Falbridge' now? Or perhaps Miss 'Dandridge'?"

He studied her, his head a little to one side. She had meant to shame him, but, she realized, she herself was beginning to feel uncomfortable beneath his gaze. He reached out and smoothed his hand over her tumbled and wayward hair. He picked up a curl and twined it around his finger thoughtfully. Heat slithered through Thea, and her mind went blank for a moment. Gabriel placed his other hand on the opposite side of her head, shoving her hair back and holding it tightly behind her head. Thea tried to suppress her shiver. She had never had a man's hands on her so. Strangely, she found it excited more than affronted her.

He nodded. "Yes, I can see it now, Miss Bainbridge." He released her and executed a bow. "Pray accept my abject apologies."

Thea grimaced, pulling away and once more walking toward the church, shielding the flickering candle with her hand. Gabriel strode along beside her. As they approached the bridge that led across to the church, he asked, "Exactly where are we going?"

Thea lifted her chin in the direction of the church. "Over there. I found him in the manger in St. Margaret's."

Her words were met with a moment of silence. Then Gabriel said, "You're not serious."

Thea glanced at him. "I am not the sort of woman who makes jests, Lord Morecombe."

"No. I can see you are not."

"We have a manger that we plan to use Christmas Eve. It was sitting in the vestibule. As I was decorating the sanctuary, I heard a noise, and when I went to investigate, there was Matthew, peeking over the edge."

"Matthew?"

Thea shrugged, looking a little uncomfortable. "That is what I decided to call him. I had no idea what his name was, but I could hardly keep calling him *the baby*, now, could I?"

"I imagine many would."

"Well, I did not."

"And why did you choose *Matthew*?"

"I would have named him after the church, but it is St. Margaret's, so that wouldn't do. The name Matthew means 'gift of God.' So it seemed appropriate, given the circumstances."

"It's a very good name," Gabriel said with a smile. "It suits him."

"Oh. Well . . . thank you."

Gabriel opened the door, and they stepped into the church. The candle's flame cast a small circle of light, barely illuminating the vestibule. The sanctuary lay like a dark cave beyond the second set of doors. Thea moved over to the manger and held the candle over it.

"This is where he was. I'm afraid there's little enough here to see."

He joined her at the small wooden manger. "There was nothing else with him? No note?"

Thea shook her head. "Only the little blanket and his cap. I didn't see the brooch until later at the vicarage. It was attached to his swaddling band beneath his baby gown."

"Hidden, then."

"Yes, I suppose so. I'm not sure why. Maybe she thought if she left it pinned to his gown, someone might steal it without taking the baby. At least if it was beneath his clothes, whoever found it would have been kind enough to take care of him."

"That would make sense. I wonder if she meant it for payment for the baby's needs—or did she hope someone would identify the child and bring him to me?"

"I'm not sure it would be obvious that the brooch was yours. I assumed it only because I noticed your ring the other night."

"A note would be more certain," he agreed. "Damn it, why wouldn't she have left some word?"

"My lord! You're in a church!"

"What? Oh. Yes. Sorry." He said the words absently, turning away and looking around him. He took the candle from Thea's hands and squatted down, searching the floor around the manger. "I had hoped there might be footprints."

"We keep the church clean. There's no dust. And it's been too dry recently for anyone to muddy their shoes walking in."

He straightened and set the candlestick down on the small table by the door. "You said 'she.'"

"What?"

"You referred to whoever left the baby as 'she.' Did you see her? Maybe a glimpse? Something that made you think it was a woman?"

"No." Thea shook her head. "I didn't see anyone. I just assumed that the person who left him was his mother. I don't know who it was at all. I'm sorry. I wish I could tell you more."

Gabriel sighed and leaned back against the wall, rubbing one hand across his forehead. "No doubt this all seems most peculiar."

Thea shrugged. "There is no need to explain."

He cast a sardonic look at her. "After having a baby thrust on you? After being dragged over here to show me where you found him? Surely you must want an explanation."

"Well, yes, of course I do. But it would be rude to pry."

His mouth quirked up appealingly on one side. "Since we have established that I am a man without decency, I think there's little need to avoid rudeness, don't you?"

He straightened up and began to pace the length of the vestibule, his hands shoved into his pockets. "My sister, Jocelyn, is eleven years younger than I. My father remarried after my mother died, and Jocelyn is their child. I wasn't raised with her, really, since I was off to school when she was only two or three years old. So we were not close in that way, but I loved her. Our father died when she was only sixteen, so I was her guardian as well. I tried to look after her and protect her; I wanted what was best for her. I was glad when she became engaged to a good friend of mine. I thought she would have a happy marriage. But then, suddenly, Jocelyn ran away." He stopped and turned to face Thea. "She left a note saying that she could not marry Lord Rawdon. She said she was going to a 'better life' and that we should not try to follow her."

"And did you . . . not follow her, I mean?"

He shook his head. "Of course not. She was only nineteen. She had never lived on her own. It was absurd. I went to all her friends, our relatives. But she had not run to any of them. I checked at all the inns to see if she had hired a post chaise. I even inquired about the mail coaches, though I could not imagine Jocelyn taking one. So I brought in a Bow Street Runner, but he had no better luck. I searched everywhere I could think of, but there was nothing. Nothing! That was over a year ago. In all this time, this"—he held up the brooch—"is the first sign I've found of her."

"But what does Matthew have to do with your sister? Is the baby hers, do you think?" Thea stopped abruptly, realizing the implications of what she had said. "I'm sorry. I should not ask such a thing."

He shook his head. "It doesn't matter. 'Tis the obvious question. The truth is, I have no idea. Why would her brooch be on the child if he were not hers? But if he is hers, why did she not come to me for help? Did she think I would turn her away? That I would not help her? I would never have done that."

Moved by his obvious distress, Thea reached out and laid a comforting hand on his arm. "I am sure she must know that." She smiled. "If your sister is the one who left Matthew here, I am sure she was counting on you. I don't know why she did not come to you herself, but I suspect it may have been more that she felt embarrassed. Ashamed. But she knew she could trust in your generosity."

He gazed down into Thea's face for a moment, a faint smile forming on his lips. "Thank you. You are good to say so, considering that I have been less than gentlemanly toward you." He covered her hand with his. "I truly am sorry that I did not remember you this afternoon."

Thea stepped back, shrugging. "It was not the first time."

As soon as the words were out of her mouth, Thea wished she could have them back. They revealed far too much. Quickly she turned away, trying to think of something to stop the questions she could see forming in his eyes. Unfortunately, her mind was an utter blank.

"What did you say?" Morecombe asked. "It wasn't the first time? What do you mean?"

"Nothing, really. We had best get back to the house now. I'm sure Mrs. Brewster will be ready to leave soon, and—"

"No. Wait." He circled around to face her again. "I am sure that was not 'nothing.' You said that it was not the first time I didn't remember you?"

"Don't be absurd. How many times could you forget me?" That had not come out well, either, she thought. There had been the echo of hurt in the words. Why could she not say something light and airy? She had had years of practice at telling polite lies—assuring someone that her new grandson was handsome or thanking a skinflint for his generosity in making a pitifully small donation to the church or declaring that she much preferred to sit and chat with the matrons than dance with the other young people. Why was it proving so difficult to conceal what she felt from this man?

"I would have said I wouldn't forget a woman even once," he retorted. "Particularly not one as . . . um, forthright as you."

"You mean as shrewish as I."

He chuckled. "You will not allow one even a sop, will you? My dear Miss Bainbridge, you—" He stopped, narrowing his eyes. "That's right. You are a Bainbridge. Ian called you 'cousin,' did he not? I *have* met you before. Sometime with Ian, no doubt."

"Do not belabor your memory. It was years and years ago, at a wedding."

"What wed—" Thea saw the light begin to dawn in his eyes. "Yes! Of course. Sweet Lord, that must have been over ten years ago. How could I not have remembered you at once? You were the girl who tried to talk me out of dancing with her." His eyes glinted with the same dark mischief they had shown back then, and Thea was sure, her heart sinking, that he remembered everything about that evening, including their kiss.

She turned away again sharply, her cheeks heating up. It just went from bad to worse with this man. Now he would think that the kiss had meant a great deal to her or she would not have remembered it so long. Of course, it was the truth, but it was humiliating that he was aware of it.

"It was nothing, really," she said, striving for an airy tone. "I cannot think why I would have remembered it myself. I'm sure I must have recalled you only because you were utterly lacking in decorum at the time."

He reached out and wrapped his hand around her wrist, whirling her back around to face him. Grinning, he said, "Ah, but I am still utterly lacking in decorum."

He reached out and took her spectacles from her nose, dropping them in the pocket of his coat. Before she could so much as protest or even blink, he wrapped his other arm around her waist and pulled her to him. And, once again, he kissed her.

But this kiss was nothing like the first one. Ten years ago, his mouth had been light on hers, gently pressing into her lips, then pulling away, leaving behind the tingling awareness of him. Now his kiss was hot and searching, his arms enveloping her. She could feel the hard tensile strength of his body all the way up and down her. His scent filled her nostrils, his heat surrounded her. And his mouth . . . she could not even describe what his mouth did to her, the pandemonium of sensations that flooded through her, igniting her nerves and melting her muscles. His lips caressed and teased; they entreated her to taste the full pleasure of his mouth even as they demanded her response. His tongue invaded her, startling her into a little jerk of surprise. Then, as he caressed and explored, Thea was even more stunned to find her own arms curling around his neck, her tongue twining with his.

He deepened their kiss, his hands sliding down to brazenly cup her buttocks, lifting her up and into him. She felt again, as she had on the ride over, that pressure against her, this time harder and more insistent, and she wanted, wildly, to rub her hips against him just to discover his response. That would be madness, she knew, utter wantonness, but even so she had to firmly clamp down on her desires to keep herself from moving. It was equally difficult to restrain the whimper that threatened to bubble up from the throat, and she had to curl her hands into the cape of his coat to stop them from sliding up into his hair.

Gabriel pulled away from her finally, raising his head and staring down into her face with something like shock in his eyes—mirroring, she suspected, the astonishment in her own face. His hands fell away, and he took a step back, turning aside. Thea's mind was a jumble of thoughts, chaotic and vivid—no, not even thoughts; they were too illusory and tumbling to be called that, only sensations and emotions. She yanked up her hood, hiding her face in the shadows of it. Picking up the candle, she mumbled, "I must—the baby ..."

Throwing open the door, she rushed out into the evening, not looking back to see if he followed her. The candle blew out as she hurried along, but Thea needed little light to walk the familiar path. She did not spare a thought for whether Gabriel could find his way without it—the man was the devil himself and sure to see perfectly in the dark.

She flung open the door to the kitchen and swept inside, stopping short as she took in the familiar sight of Mrs. Brewster drying a pot.

"Ah, there you are," Mrs. Brewster greeted her cheerfully. "Did you find what you were looking for? Where did you go, now, the church?"

"Yes, um, that's it, exactly." Thea turned jerkily away and hung up her cloak. She took her time, wondering guiltily if her lips looked as if they had been kissed. They felt swollen and tender, and it seemed to her that surely they must be reddened and bruised as well. What if Mrs. Brewster guessed what she had been doing? The housekeeper's eyes had always been sharp as a hawk's. Thea pressed her chilled fingers against her lips; she could feel the trembling in them, the same trembling that vibrated all through her body.

The door opened behind her and Lord Morecombe stepped in. Thea could not even glance at him; she was sure her face would give her away.

"No, we didn't find anything," she said to the housekeeper. "I must, I must look a mess—there was such a wind."

Thea slipped out of the room, not looking back at either of the other occupants. She heard Gabriel greet Mrs. Brewster, his voice smooth, with none of the nerves or strain that afflicted her. Of course, *he* would not feel anything. Stealing kisses in the church vestibule was doubtless commonplace to him—well, perhaps not commonplace in the church vestibule, but the kisses, yes, the kisses themselves were something he was most familiar with. No one could kiss like that without a great deal of practice. She felt sure Gabriel did not experience this weakness of the knees or the heat that burst low in her abdomen or that odd ache flowering between her legs.

Thea ground her teeth; she had to stop thinking about this. She faced the mirror in the front hall. She hardly recognized herself. Bright color stained her cheeks, and her lips were a deep red and fuller, softer, than usual. Her eyes seemed huge and dark, vivid. And her hair—oh, sweet heavens, her hair was almost entirely down, tumbling around her shoulders and curling wildly. She looked like a mad thing. Hastily, she skinned it back, combing through the tangles as best she could with her fingers, and began to braid it into one fat braid.

"Ah, Thea, there you are." Her brother came toward her down the hall, a book in his hand. "I missed you at supper. Mrs. Brewster couldn't remember where you had gone. To see Mrs. Howard, I imagine, eh?"

Thea nodded dumbly. Was it a lie if she did not deny the untruth he assumed? Her life, it seemed, had suddenly become a veritable cornucopia of sins—lies and lust and who knew what else springing up like weeds in a garden.

"I—" Her voice cracked, and she had to clear her throat. "I hope you were not bored by yourself."

"Oh, no, you know me." He smiled and waggled the book at her. "As long as I have a book, I am never bored."

"Of course not."

"I am going on up to my room. Read a bit before I go to bed." He glanced vaguely in the direction of the grandfather clock. "Early yet, I suppose, but on winter nights, it seems I get sleepy early."

"Of course. Good night, Daniel." Thank goodness he was retiring. The last thing she wanted was for him to go into the kitchen and see Morecombe. Even Daniel would want an explanation for the man's presence in the house, and she simply did not feel up to that at the moment.

As he climbed the stairs, she turned back to the mirror, winding her braid into a quick knot at the base of her neck and pinning it with the few hairpins she had managed to retrieve from the tumbled mess of her hair. It was still a wreck, of course, with a number of stray hairs around her face still slipping free and curling. But at least it was a more organized wreck.

The same could not be said for her dress, which was still in the ragged state the baby had left it. She tugged and tucked at the fichu, working it back into its proper place so that it modestly covered most of her chest above the neckline of the dress. Satisfied that she looked vaguely presentable and that her lips and cheeks had lost at least some of their deep color, she returned to the kitchen.

There she found Lord Morecombe, his coat off, seated at the end of the old, scarred kitchen table, a bowl of stew in front of him and a slab of bread, spread with pale, creamy butter, in his hand. A second bowl rested on the table in the place at his right, a slice of bread beside it.

"Well, I see you are staying to eat," Thea said crisply. She was pleased that she was able to speak without her voice trembling, though she could still not quite meet his eyes.

"Yes, Mrs. Brewster took pity on me. She doubtless saw how I was eyeing that bowl she'd left out for you."

Mrs. Brewster smiled benignly at Lord Morecombe, and Thea thought sourly that it should come as no surprise he had worked his wiles on her housekeeper. The man was obviously a menace to womankind. Just to prove that she herself was unaffected by him, Thea sat down next to him and began to butter her slice of bread.

"Mrs. Brewster, you are a superb cook. If I was not certain that Miss Bainbridge would stab me through the heart for it, I would steal you away to cook for us at the Priory," Morecombe went on, earning an almost girlish giggle from the middle-aged housekeeper.

Thea rolled her eyes and stabbed a piece of potato with her spoon, cutting it in two. "I should warn you that Mrs. Brewster is immune to flattery."

"Ah, but 'tisn't flattery when it's true, now, is it?" Gabriel countered, his eyes dancing.

Thea could not keep her lips from twitching into a half smile. "You are far too skilled at cutting a wheedle, you know. It implies regrettable things about your character."

"Only implies?"

Thea took a bite of the stew to cover her chuckle. It seemed most unfair that the man should be not only as handsome as he was but also possessed of charm; it made it terribly hard to dislike him.

"Well, miss, I'll just be on my way." Mrs. Brewster set the big black pot back on the stove, ready for the next day, and reached behind her to untie her apron. "The mister'll be wondering where I am. I made a bit of beef broth for the babe. Just mash up some of the potatoes in that."

"I will. Say hello to Mr. Brewster," Thea told her.

"Aye, I will." The housekeeper put on her jacket and knitted cap, then wrapped her bright scarlet scarf around her neck.

"Good night, Mrs. Brewster. And thank you for the stew." Gabriel stood and nodded to her politely.

Mrs. Brewster was actually blushing, Thea thought in astonishment, as the housekeeper sketched a little curtsy back at him before hurrying out into the night.

"Must you instantly win over *every* female you meet?" Thea asked sourly as he sat back down.

He gave her a droll look. "Obviously I have not succeeded with you." He pulled a chunk from his slice of bread and leaned back, taking a thoughtful bite. "I wouldn't say that I must win over anyone, really, but I find life is pleasanter that way. What is your preferred manner of getting through life—charging in and taking the bull by the horns?"

"I don't believe in ignoring wrongs, no." Thea lifted her chin.

"And those wrongs include bachelors living too . . . freely?"

"If living 'freely' means fathering children indiscriminately and leaving them about the countryside like old shoes, then yes."

He smiled. "I have tried never to leave even my old shoes about the countryside, let alone babies."

"You may laugh at me all you want, but that doesn't mean I am not right."

"Never." He reached out and ran a lightly caressing hand down her arm. "Never would I laugh at you, my dear Miss Bainbridge. But I confess that I find you . . . interesting."

Well, that was certainly damning with faint praise, she

thought, and her cheeks warmed as she kept her gaze on her bowl. She ate mechanically, very aware that he continued to watch her, and her stomach tightened with nerves. She hated that he could make her uneasy simply by staring at her. She hated even more that she could not help but wonder what he thought when he looked at her.

Thea made herself raise her eyes. She was not one to hide from reality. Gabriel was studying her, absently twirling the crust left over from his bread. Thea shifted under his gaze and cleared her throat. She had to fight an urge to make sure her hair was all in place.

"Have I sprung a third eye, Lord Morecombe?"

"No, not that I see, Miss Bainbridge," he responded evenly. "Is there a danger of that?"

"I meant that you are staring."

"Am I?" A faint smile touched his lips, mysterious and warm. "Do you expect me to apologize?"

"I do not expect anything from you." Thea kept her voice tart and refrained from shifting again in her seat. His smile did peculiar things to her insides, things that were both delightful and vaguely terrifying. He made her feel not quite herself, and Thea was not sure whether she liked that. She had the suspicion that she should not. "However, I fail to see what can be of such interest about my face, which you have been staring at since I sat down."

" 'Tis your hair, actually, that I am watching." The smile turned into a grin, quick and flashing, lighting his eyes. "I am wondering exactly how long it will be before your braid tumbles free."

"My braid?" Instinctively, Thea's hand went to her head, feeling for the coil of hair secured by only a few hairpins. It was, indeed, loose, the weight of it dragging the coil down the nape of her neck, and when she touched it, the braid slipped completely free, draping down over her shoulder.

Thea grimaced and started to re-pin it, but Gabriel reached out to stay her hand, saying, "No, leave it."

"Don't be absurd." Thea's voice came out more shakily than she intended. "'Twill come undone. It's inappropriate."

"No more inappropriate than sitting alone in the kitchen with a man."

"Then no doubt you had better leave."

He shrugged. "I have little affinity for propriety." He paused, then added quietly, "I like the way your hair looks down."

He raised his hand and tugged the end of her braid. She had not tied it, only slipped the end into the center of the coil, and at the little pull, the braid began to unravel, the curls slipping free.

"I'll look like a savage," Thea muttered, but she did not move to braid it back up.

"I *do* have an affinity for savages." The faint smile came again, touching his eyes more than his lips. "Your curls are beautiful."

Thea was painfully aware of how close Gabriel was, his hand resting on the table only inches from hers. She thought of the way he had kissed her earlier. Surely he would not do so again. Would he? Her breath hitched in her throat. She knew she ought to say something, do something. She should pull back from him. Yet she could not make herself move.

A little hiccuping cry broke the silence.

"The baby!" Thea jumped up and hurried over to the makeshift bed in the basket, not sure whether relief or disappointment was uppermost in her feelings.

She bent over the basket. Matthew's feet and hands were moving restlessly, and he rubbed his head against the pillow beneath him, his mouth twisting up and his face turning red. Quickly she bent and picked him up, and his face cleared a little. But then he jammed his fist in his mouth and closed his eyes, his face screwing up once more, and he began to cry. Thea bounced him a little and patted him on his back, but he opened his mouth and let out a wail.

"Good God!" Morecombe shot to his feet. "What's the matter with him? Is he all right?"

"I think he's hungry. Here, hold him, and I'll get his food."

"Me?" Gabriel's dark brows vaulted upward. "But I don't know what to do with him."

"It isn't as if I am an expert."

"You are a woman."

"An unmarried, childless woman," Thea retorted. "Of course, I could hold him if you would prefer to prepare his broth."

Morecombe looked askance at the fireplace. "The devil. Here, give him to me."

He extended his hands and Thea thrust the baby into them. Gabriel took the child, holding him out and looking at him warily.

"He won't bite you." Thea didn't bother to hide the amusement in her voice.

"Are you entirely certain?" He sighed and settled the baby into the crook of his arm, holding Matthew up against him.

To their amazement, Matthew's cries ceased immediately

and he stared up at Gabriel, his eyes wide. It was, Thea thought, entirely vexing; apparently the man's charm worked on infants as well. She went to the fire and picked up the small iron pot that sat near the embers. She dipped a ladle of the thin broth into a small bowl. As she turned back to the table, the baby left off his fascinated study of Gabriel's face and began to cry again, his little sobs building. Thea could not deny that she was small enough to feel some satisfaction at the event.

"Hurry." Gabriel cut his eyes toward Thea as he began to jiggle and pat the baby. "I think he's working up to something worse."

Thea forked a couple of pieces of potato from her bowl into Matthew's broth and quickly began to mash it up. She stirred it and tested a spoonful with her finger.

"I'm not sure it's cool enough."

"Put some blasted milk in it, then."

She tried that, testing it again, then nodded. No sooner had she done so than Gabriel handed her a squirming, red-faced Matthew. Thea set him on her lap, as she had seen Mrs. Brewster do, but the baby kept squirming and arching his back, his cries increasing, making it difficult to keep him in place. Thea wrapped her arm more tightly around him and dipped up a spoonful of the potato mixture with the other hand. As she held it toward his mouth, the baby's waving arms crashed into the spoon and sent its contents flying upward and outward, splatting against Gabriel's spotless white neckcloth.

Thea gasped. "I'm so sorry!"

"Doesn't matter. Just get something in him."

Thea managed to grab one of the baby's arms with the hand

she had around his waist, then she quickly thrust the spoon into his mouth. Matthew smacked his lips together several times, and half the spoonful rolled back out and down his chin.

"Does he not know how to swallow?" Gabriel peered down at the baby.

"He must. He ate earlier when Mrs. Brewster was feeding him. I think some of it got in."

How had Mrs. Brewster done this? It had all looked so much easier when she was feeding Matthew. But at least he stopped crying, even though his arms continued to wave—more in excitement now, Thea thought, than anger. The next spoonful again went flying, struck by the other arm, and this time it hit her face and dress. Thea continued to spoon the mixture into his mouth, dodging and holding his arms. She quickly learned to shovel the food that spilled out onto his chin back into his mouth. As he ate, his arm-flailing stopped, and Thea let out a sigh of relief. Adjusting him on her lap, she released his arm. But then Matthew decided to grab the spoon, and the potatoes plopped onto the front of her dress. A few bites later, the baby took a bite, then blew it back out with bubbles. He laughed, clasping his hands and looking up engagingly at Thea.

Thea let out a groan.

"I think he might be full," Gabriel offered.

"Really?" Thea commented drily, and leaned back in her chair. She was exhausted. The baby had bits of potato mixture in his hair, and on his hands and gown. A bit was even on one of his feet. And where had his little bootees gone? She had just as much food on her, all over her fichu and gown, and she could feel one spot drying on her cheek and another on her forehead. Several small spots were on the lenses of her spectacles. She could only hope there were none in her hair.

She looked down at herself and the baby in some disgust.

"I think perhaps we should have covered him with a rag," Gabriel said mildly.

Thea looked up, a tart response on her lips, but when she took in the sight of Lord Morecombe, his hair disheveled and his fashionable jacket and snowy-white shirt daubed with spots of potato, she could not keep from laughing. Gabriel glared at her for a moment. Then a smile quirked up his mouth, and in another instant, he began to laugh, too. The baby, seeing their laughter, grinned and let out one of his high-pitched crows. This only made the two of them laugh harder, and every time they were about to get control of their laughter, they had only to glance at each other, and it set them off again. By the time they finally stopped laughing, Thea's sides ached and there were tears running down her cheeks.

"Oh." She drew a long breath. "Oh, my."

Gabriel stood and cast a look down at himself. "The devil. Barts will ring a peal over my head."

"Who?"

"My valet." He glanced around. "I think I need a rag."

"You're scared of your valet?" Thea said as she handed the baby to him and went over to pull out a couple of rags and wet them.

"Any sane man would be. Barts is a veritable tyrant."

Thea rolled her eyes as she handed him a damp cloth. "Since

you are his employer, I would think there is an easy solution to that." She reached out and took the baby back to clean his face and hands.

"Let him go?" Gabriel gave her a horrified look. "He has been my valet since I was sixteen, and he was my grandfather's valet before that. The butler would see to it that I paid for it the remainder of my days. Not to mention my aunts and grandmother."

Thea chuckled and set the baby down on the hooked rug. "What a fearsome employer you are."

"I fear I am twelve years old to all my staff. That's why I bought the Priory. Entirely new staff. Well, except for Barts, of course."

Thea stared at him. "What a bag of moonshine! You did not buy a house just to get away from your servants."

He smiled. "No—or, at least, not primarily. But it is a pleasant benefit, I find." He tilted his head thoughtfully. "Though I must say, the new staff's service does leave something to be desired."

Thea shook her head, smiling a little, and removed her spectacles to wipe her face clean.

"Here, you've missed a spot." Gabriel reached out and took the rag and gently dabbed at her cheek, taking her chin in his other hand.

Thea went still, her breath suddenly shallow. He was so close that she could see him clearly, even without her glasses. It was, she thought, decidedly unfair that a man should have such long, lush eyelashes. His hands dropped away from her face, and he moved back, handing her the rag. Thea was aware of a distinct sense of disappointment, and to cover it she began to busily tend to the other spots on her clothes.

On the rug, the baby had gotten up onto his hands and knees. Thea looked at him, wondering if he could crawl yet—there were a great many things she must learn!—but he only rocked back and forth, making an *m-m-m* noise, clamping his mouth shut in a look of intense concentration.

Gabriel, following her gaze, watched him, too. "He looks as though he's about to launch himself forward."

Matthew rocked back onto his heels and peered up at Gabriel, letting loose one of his pleased-sounding crows and grinning gummily at him. Gabriel leaned down and picked him up, setting him on his knee facing him. His dark eyes searched the baby's face. Holding Matthew steady with one hand, he reached up with his forefinger and touched the little dimple in Matthew's chin that was so reminiscent of his own.

"Does he look like your sister?" Thea asked. It was far too intrusive a question to ask someone who was virtually a stranger, but she could not hold it back. And as Gabriel himself had said, he was scarcely a man wedded to propriety.

"I don't know." He shook his head. "Jocelyn had a little indentation here. I remember when she was young, she was pleased with it, saying it proved we were brother and sister. Otherwise, we did not resemble each other much. Her hair and eyes are lighter than mine." He smoothed his hand over the child's soft blond curls, and his face darkened. "But I do know one person who looks very much like this."

His eyes flashed, the softness of a moment before replaced by a hard, fierce light. Thea, watching him, realized with a start that Gabriel could be rather frightening if he chose. She wanted to ask who Matthew reminded him of, but she decided it was wisest not to.

"I think you are right," Gabriel said. "I will take responsibility of the baby, at least until we find out who his mother is."

Panic welled up in Thea's chest as she realized the implications of his statement. "No! You cannot take him home with you!"

Gabriel turned to look at her, surprised. "But I thought that was your purpose in bringing him to me."

"I didn't think. That is, well, when I thought you were his father, I wanted you to take responsibility, but you must see that your home is not the place for a baby. It would be better to leave him here, surely, until we know for certain who he is."

He looked at her oddly. "That seems rather a burden for you to take on, given that he is no relation to you—at least we are certain of that much, if nothing else."

"I don't mind. Truly. And Mrs. Brewster will help me."

"If he is my sister's child, my home is where he belongs."

"Yes, but you don't know that for sure. After all, someone could have stolen that brooch or ... well, I don't know how it came to be with him, but I am sure there could be other explanations."

"None come to mind at the moment."

"But it would be too cruel to take him in and later find out he was not your nephew and give him back. You should wait until you know."

"It would not be unkind to take him from your home later, after he has become accustomed to it?"

Thea ignored his question, saying, "Anyway, your house is not a fit place for a baby."

His expression iced over, and he looked very much the aristocrat he had appeared the other day at the Cliffes' ball. "I beg your pardon."

Thea just gazed back steadily at him. "You need not get on your high ropes about it. You know as well as I do that it's the truth. You cannot expect to raise a child in a home full of bachelors."

"I have servants."

"The ones whose service leaves much to be desired?"

"*Something* to be desired, not much," he argued, but the corner of his mouth twitched and the hauteur drained from his voice.

"You don't have any female servants, except for the cook, and that is only because she is married to the gardener and goes home every night to his cottage."

"I can hire maids."

"Can you?" Thea raised one eyebrow. "Perhaps you do not realize it, my lord, but the reason you have no women servants is because no self-respecting female would take up residence in a house filled with drunken men and women of loose morals."

His eyebrows shot up at that description, but before he could speak, Thea charged ahead. "And you need more than a few maids before you can hope to properly raise a child. You must have a nursemaid to take care of him, for one thing. And a proper nursery. You need a father who does not come home at dawn from drinking and carousing. You need a real home, not some great, half-empty stone pile where people ride their horses into the hall and jump the table on a bet!"

Morecombe stared at her, astonished. "Good gad, do you have spies in my house?"

Thea cast a disdainful look at him. "A new gentleman in the area, especially one who lives as you and your friends do, can hardly expect to go unnoticed. Every aspect of what goes on at the Priory is examined in every house in the village."

"Doubtless the vicar's sister gets all the latest gossip."

"Of course I do," Thea retorted somewhat smugly. "I also have access to the advice of a great number of mothers and grandmothers. Not to mention a very able housekeeper and a day maid. And a bed already made up for him." Thea gestured over at the basket. "Besides, Matthew knows me. He will be happier here."

As if on cue, the baby twisted around to look at her, then smiled and held out his arms to Thea.

"You are a traitor to all mankind," Gabriel told the baby sternly as he handed the child back to Thea. Matthew laid his head on Thea's shoulder and turned to gaze coyly back at Morecombe. Gabriel leaned toward the baby, saying softly, "In faith, if I had the same choice of where to spend my night, I believe I would take it, too."

Before Thea could react to his outrageous statement, Gabriel stood up. "Very well. I am not fool enough to continue arguing with you on this matter. I will leave young Matthew here until I find out exactly who his mother is."

He walked over to the door and shrugged into his coat. Thea trailed after him, carrying the baby. Gabriel chucked a finger under the baby's chin, saying, "Good night, young man. Sleep well." He turned to Thea, his dark eyes sharpening, though Thea could not read the emotion there. "And you, as well." He hooked her chin between his thumb and forefinger and tilted her face up, bending down to plant a soft, lingering kiss on her lips. "May your dreams be ... delightful."

With a half smile, Gabriel turned and was gone.

# Six

*Gabriel scarcely noticed the cold* as he rode home. He was too much occupied in thinking about what had happened this evening. Could that child really be Jocelyn's? The thought was staggering. He could not even decide whether his hope was that young Matthew was his nephew or that he was not. A faint smile touched his lips as he thought about the blond-haired baby. In general, Gabriel was rarely around children; indeed, he usually did his best to avoid them. But he had to admit that something about this one was quite winning. He chuckled as he remembered the angelic smile on the child's face after he had splattered his porridge all over Miss Bainbridge.

Something about her was curiously winning, too. He could not put his finger on it. As a rule, he was not fond of women who rang a peal over his head. Nor would he have thought that her accusing him of fathering an illegitimate child would have endeared her to him. But something about her tickled his sense of humor. He could not resist teasing her. Perhaps it was the way her eyes lit with fire or her pale cheeks flushed rosily when she was taking him to task. Or maybe it was simply that he very much wondered what it would feel like to sink his hands into her wild curls. The thought sent a tendril of heat curling through his abdomen ... and made him also consider exactly how those long legs would feel wrapped around him.

He shifted a little in his saddle, and his mind went to the unmistakable physical reaction his body had demonstrated during their ride to the vicarage. Her firm bottom had fit nicely between his legs, and the friction of it against him as the horse moved had added a distinct fillip to the ride. How could he have forgotten that he had met her? Even after she had reminded him that they'd met at the Squire's ball, he had had trouble remembering exactly what she had looked like at the party. He had only a vague impression of someone rather colorless and quiet. That seemed unlikely, given her behavior this evening. But try as he might to dredge up a memory, he could not recall seeing her dancing at the ball or even talking to anyone after that first introduction. Of course, he had primarily been intent on getting out of the place as soon as he politely could, but Miss Bainbridge did not seem like someone who was easy to ignore.

He remembered her better from that night so many years ago. He was not even sure which of Ian's sisters had been getting married, so it was little surprise that he could not recall Miss Bainbridge's name. But once she had needled him for forgetting, he had remembered her rather clearly. She had been so young, so awkward and overawed that his slight irritation at the Countess's maneuvering him into asking her to dance had quickly given way to sympathy. And then she had been so unexpectedly tart that he had found himself actually enjoying their dance and prolonging it with a stroll on the terrace afterward. He had even intended to stand up with her for a dance or two when she came to London to make her come-out, but he had not encountered her the next year, and she had soon slipped his mind.

It occurred to him that Miss Bainbridge could be a help in looking for his sister. Who better than the vicar's sister to ask questions of the locals? Sparring with her would certainly make his search more entertaining. Perhaps he would drop by the vicarage first when he set out to find the person who had abandoned Matthew at the church.

Gabriel found his friends waiting in the great hall when he returned. The three men were seated at one end of the long table, drinking port and halfheartedly playing a game of loo, but Gabriel had little doubt they were primarily waiting to discover what had transpired after he'd left the house with Althea Bainbridge. As soon as he stepped in the door, all three swung around to stare at him. Gabriel sighed inwardly. He would have liked to keep this evening's events to himself, but even a moment's reflection told him that it would be impossible. Out of friendship for him, his friends might swallow their curiosity about Miss Bainbridge and the baby and the possible connection to his sister, but he had little hope that news of this scandal would not get out. After hearing Althea comment on the doings in his household, he knew that soon the whole village would be gossiping about the baby found in the manger as well as Althea's tumultuous visit to the Priory.

"I presume the three of you have been hashing out my visit

from your cousin," he said to Ian, going over to the sideboard and pouring himself a glass of port before sitting down with the others.

"I told Ian what happened before he came home," Myles agreed. "Though Alan and I might have missed some of what was said. What was that thing Miss Bainbridge showed you? Was it Jocelyn's?"

Gabriel nodded, taking a sip of his drink. "It was her brooch." He pulled the brooch out of his pocket and tossed it onto the table in front of them. "I gave it to her on her twelfth birthday because she admired my signet ring." He sighed and ran his hand back through his hair. "I never checked to see if she took it with her. I presume she must have."

"But that baby—" Ian said, shock apparent on his face. "It can't be, I mean, it's not—"

"Hers?" Gabriel asked flatly. "The devil of it is that I have no idea. There is nothing else to identify him, one way or the other. Miss Bainbridge apparently discovered him in the manger."

Myles spluttered, choking on his drink. "The what?"

"The manger. Yes, I know—it's absurd. She had hauled it out into the church for some Nativity scene they are going to put on Christmas Eve and someone stuck Matthew in it."

"Matthew? That's his name?"

"The name Miss Bainbridge gave to him."

"No insult to your cousin"—Myles nodded toward Ian—"but are you sure this Miss Bainbridge isn't a bit touched in her upper-works?"

Ian shrugged. "She's only a second or third cousin. And God

knows, anything is possible amongst our family. My great-uncle Rupert was a cursed rum touch."

"Miss Bainbridge is anything but mad," Gabriel said flatly. "And there's no getting around Jocelyn's brooch. But there was no clue in the church as to who left him there. Miss Bainbridge saw no one besides the baby."

"It's my opinion it's all a hum." Ian gestured with his glass of port. "Someone got hold of that brooch somehow—found it, stole it, I don't know—and now they're trying to convince you the child's related to you. Hoping they can trick you into taking care of their by-blow, that's all. I say stick it in a foundling home and wash your hands of the whole affair."

"He's a baby, Ian, not an 'it.'" Gabriel sighed. "And I can't just shrug off the incident. Someone just happened to find Jocelyn's brooch? Or stole it out of her room? And then they happened to have a baby they wanted to abandon, so they stuck him in a manger in a church in Chesley, hid the brooch inside his clothes, and trusted he would find his way to me?"

"Does sound a bit convoluted," Sir Myles agreed.

Alan tugged at his lower lip thoughtfully, a frown on his face. "But, Gabe . . . you don't think . . . I mean, do you really think this baby is Jocelyn's?"

"He doesn't resemble her much. Though he's got a bit of a—" He touched the cleft in his own chin.

"Babies don't generally look much like anyone that I can see," Myles put in.

"This one does." Gabriel's voice was grim. "He looks like Rawdon."

The others all went still. Finally, Myles said softly, "Bloody hell."

"Exactly." Gabriel took a healthy swig of his drink and set it down on the table. "You saw him. Blond hair. Blue eyes."

"Any number of people have blond hair and blue eyes," Myles pointed out. "Why, Jocelyn's hair was blond."

"Dark blond. His hair is pale."

"Still. Hair often darkens as one gets older, doesn't it? Doesn't mean it was necessarily Alec's."

"What the devil is wrong with you?" Ian glared at Myles across the table. "Why do you defend that bastard?"

"I am not defending him. I am simply pointing out there are other blond-haired, blue-eyed men in the world."

"How many of them were engaged to my sister?" Gabriel's words came out hard and flat.

Myles flushed and looked away. "Yes, you are right. I'm sorry. Of course, if the baby is Jocelyn's, it wouldn't make sense that the father was anyone but Rawdon."

"But . . ." Alan frowned. "If the babe was Rawdon's, why the devil would Jocelyn have left? Wouldn't she want to marry him even more then?"

Gabriel nodded. "Exactly. Think about that: my sister ran away rather than marry Alec. One would assume that a woman who is carrying a man's child would be *more* likely to marry him, not less. Obviously Jocelyn didn't love the man, didn't want to be with him, didn't want him raising their child. Otherwise she would not have left."

Myles stared at Gabriel. "What are you saying?"

"I am saying that it makes no sense for a woman to run away

from a man she had given herself to freely. But it makes a great deal of sense if he had forced her."

There was another shocked silence around the table.

Myles pushed back from the table, looking troubled. "Gabe, no ... surely not."

"I don't know what else to think." Morecombe's dark eyes were hot and hard. "Would any of your sisters have run away from their husbands two weeks before they were supposed to marry them?"

"God, no. They were all over the moon about it, could hardly wait for the day."

"Obviously Jocelyn was not, and there must have been some reason for that. The note she left said she would be happier this way. It would have to be a pretty miserable life she was facing if bearing a child out of wedlock, all on her own, seemed a more attractive option than wedding an earl."

"I think you're right," Alan agreed. "Only thing that makes sense. Get a girl pregnant, and they're yammering for you to marry them. No woman wants her child to be a side-slip."

"Nor do they want to be considered a trollop themselves," Gabriel added. "Her leaving indicates more than that she simply preferred not to be married to Rawdon. She would have had to have hated—or feared—him."

"Yes, I understand that," Myles agreed. "But still ... Rawdon?"

"Why do you find it so hard to believe that the man is a villain?" Ian burst out.

"Why do you find it so easy?" Myles retorted. "Alec was our friend!" He glanced around at the others. "Am I the only one who remembers that?"

"Oh, no, I am well aware of it," Gabriel retorted with some bitterness. "I am the one who befriended him, who brought him into our circle. I am the one who introduced him to my sister. Indeed, I practically shoved her at him! I'll never be able to forget that."

"I'm sorry, Gabe. You know I mean you no disrespect. And it makes sense that Jocelyn ran away because he mistreated her. But, bloody hell, it's hard to believe that Rawdon would have forced himself upon anyone, much less your sister."

"We obviously did not know him nearly as well as we thought," Gabriel replied.

"You know what his family is like, Myles," Ian pointed out.

"Yes, I know his father was a proper tyrant, from the few things Alec told us about him. But Alec despised the old earl; that was clear. And just because the Staffords have a . . . a dark history—"

Ian snorted. "They were a bloody violent group—literally. If I remember correctly, the first Earl of Rawdon kidnapped his heiress bride."

"Several hundred years ago," Myles shot back. "Those Northern lords were all practically brigands. But it isn't as if they are carrying out border raids these days."

"No, but I've heard rumors that Rawdon's grandfather came into the title by helping his older brother to an early grave," Ian went on. "And wasn't there a Stafford who had to flee to the Continent because he killed his man in a duel?"

"It was the same chap—Rawdon's great-uncle," Gabriel said. "It was swords back then, of course, and he was reputed to be a master swordsman. He killed the man, fled the country, and proceeded to drink himself to death, living in style in Paris. Whether his brother helped him in pickling his innards, I've no idea."

"They're a cold-blooded bunch," Alan added.

"God knows his sister is." Myles made an expressive shudder. "Lady Genevieve may be a diamond of the first water, but her gaze would freeze a man."

"As I remember, you braved that wintry atmosphere a few times." Gabriel smirked at Myles.

"The devil!" Alan stared at Myles. "Did you really dangle after the Ice Maiden? You are a braver man than I." Alan shook his head reflectively.

"I did not *dangle* after her. I danced with her a few times. We did not suit, as they say."

"All the Staffords are cold. And high in the instep. It was doubtless foolish of us to become friends with him," Ian said, then shrugged. "But we were young then. I don't know why you are still so soft on him, though, Myles. I cut all ties with the man after he and Gabe had that mill in White's."

Alan let out a soft chuckle. "That was quite a sight. I was afraid White's would bar you."

"It was a devilish good fight," Myles mused. "But I presumed it was just the heat of the moment. That eventually you and Rawdon ... well." Myles shrugged and tossed back the rest of the alcohol in his glass. "Devil take it. I didn't think Rawdon was actually wicked. It looks as though I shall have to change my position." He sighed. "I'm sorry, Gabe ... about all of it."

"I know. I thought Rawdon was the sort of man I'd want at my back, too." Morecombe's face hardened. "Until I found out differently." He stood up. "Go on with your game, gentlemen. I am retiring early tonight. Tomorrow I have to find whoever left that baby at Miss Bainbridge's church."

Myles and Alan nodded to Gabriel, watching as he went to the sideboard to pour himself another glass and left the room with it. Ian tossed his hand down on the table and followed Morecombe out of the room.

The viscount caught up to Gabriel on the stairs. "Do you really think that child is Jocelyn's?"

"The truth? I don't know. That's why I have to find out who left him there. I cannot imagine that Jocelyn would do such a thing. But if the baby is not hers, how did they acquire that brooch? If someone took it from her, I can make them tell me where she is. After all this time, maybe I can find her."

His friend nodded, frowning.

Gabriel glanced at him. "What is it? You don't seem very enthusiastic."

"I should love for you to find Jocelyn, of course. It's just … I can scarce believe it. I think it must be some sort of hoax. Someone is toying with you."

"I can't believe you think your cousin is part of a hoax."

"Cousin Althea?" Ian let out a crack of laughter, his face lighting for a moment. "There's a picture. No. She's a female version of her father, who was a pious old stickler. I doubt she has ever had an indecent thought in her life, and if she has, I am certain she hasn't acted upon it."

"Mm," Gabriel said noncommittally.

"No, I believe that Cousin Althea found the baby just as you said. Nor am I surprised that she immediately assumed the worst about you."

Morecombe's lips lifted at one corner. "Am I so obviously a sinner, then?"

"No, but she is a bluestocking and a spinster—not the sort who thinks well of men in general, I'd say."

"She certainly thought ill of me."

"I have to wonder if Rawdon is behind this child suddenly showing up here."

"What?" Gabriel stopped and turned to stare at Ian. "Are you serious? Why would Rawdon want me to believe that he had his way with my sister?"

"I don't know. But the only person the child resembles is him. Maybe it is some by-blow of his by another woman."

"What purpose does it serve to make me think the baby is Jocelyn's?"

"Maybe to convince you that she is alive."

Gabriel looked at him sharply, then shook his head. "I know what you think. But I cannot believe it."

"Are you like Myles? You cannot believe Rawdon is a villain?"

"No, of course not. And you mustn't blame Myles. He does not know the things about Rawdon that you and I do."

Ian shrugged, and Gabriel continued, "It is not that I cannot believe it about Rawdon—that was hard, but I have accepted it. But I do not believe, I refuse to believe, that my sister is dead." Gabriel turned his intense, dark gaze on his friend. "And I am going to prove that she is not. This baby is going to lead me to her. I am going to find Jocelyn."

*Thea hummed to herself as* she buttoned the top button of her brown wool dress. She glanced down at the baby in his basket beside her before she turned to her mirror. She had just finished pulling a comb through her hair, and it was, at least, no longer tangled, though it did flare out from her head in a wild mass of curls. Raking it back tightly, she began the familiar braiding of it into a long, fat plait, which she then wound around the crown of her head, securing it with pins. It was soon tightly fixed, unlike the slapdash braid she had coiled up last night, though the fine, short hairs around her face slipped out and curled as they usually did. It was her custom to dampen them and slick them straight back, fixing them with pins.

But today, she found herself idly twisting them around her forefinger until she had several delicate curls clustering around her face. Gabriel had said he liked her curls. Had he meant it or was he joking? She tilted her head to the side, considering. Perhaps it did soften the outlines of her face, which was bonier and starker than the feminine ideal. But perhaps that was simply because she had not yet put on her spectacles. She picked the lenses up from the dresser and placed them on her nose, securing them behind her ears.

Thea looked at her reflection and sighed. It was foolish vanity, she thought. She reached for the water bowl, but at that moment Matthew left off his patient blowing and cooing and began his little hiccuping cry.

"Are you tired of waiting?" she asked. "You have been a terribly good boy this morning."

And he had, really. Aside from the adventure of diapering him last night and this morning—she still could not understand how a baby could twist and turn and roll so much, and the diaper was, admittedly, rather bulky and odd-looking—he had been happy and quiet, sleeping through the night and awakening her this morning with a series of coos and soft noises rather than the piercing cries he had emitted last night when he was hungry.

She was, she thought as she picked up his basket and started downstairs, going to have to find out from Mrs. Brewster how the housekeeper had kept him from splattering food everywhere yesterday when she fed him. As Thea stepped off the last stair into the hall, she met her brother. Daniel glanced at the basket she carried, then peered into it more closely. His eyebrows rose.

"Is he still here? I had forgotten about him."

"That's because he is so good." Thea set down the basket and reached in to pick up the baby. "I've named him Matthew. Would you like to hold him?"

A faint look of horror crossed Daniel's face and he took half a step back. "No, that's fine. I—why have you named him? You cannot mean to keep this child?"

"Of course not. Only until we find out where he belongs."

"Thea . . . he belongs in a foundling home." Daniel began to frown.

"No, truly, I think he does not." Thea began to explain the possibilities of the baby's parentage to Daniel, and with every word, his frown deepened.

"Oh, my," he said finally. "I—well, are you sure that this is what you should do? I mean, it does seem there's rather a lot of scandal attached to the boy." He cast a doubtful look at Matthew, who responded by blowing bubbles.

"That's hardly his fault," Thea said reasonably. "In any case, once Lord Morecombe gets everything in order, I shall be turning Matthew over to him." The words left her with a hollow feeling, but she ignored that. "Bring his basket, would you? I'm going to take him into the kitchen for Mrs. Brewster to look after while we have breakfast."

"Excellent." Daniel looked relieved. "I thought you were going to be holding him all through the meal. I read something very interesting last night about the excavation of the ruins of the Minerva temple at Bath, and I wanted to discuss it with you."

"Of course."

Mrs. Brewster grinned broadly at the sight of the baby and promised to feed him as soon as she dished up breakfast for Daniel and Thea. They left the baby in his basket with the day maid, Sally, cooing over him, and went to the dining room. Daniel was soon happily expounding on his readings, but Thea found it harder than usual to keep her mind on his words. The layout of the Roman baths had much less appeal than wondering what Lord Morecombe was going to do today about finding a nursemaid for Matthew, and how he intended to go about discovering who had left the baby at the church. It was most annoying to have to sit about and wait for someone else to take care of things, and Thea wished she had thought to offer help—not, she had to admit with an inward sigh, that he would have been likely to accept her offer. Men seemed to be stubbornly reluctant to allow a woman to help them.

Fortunately, Daniel did not notice that Thea's attention wandered, and she got through the meal with only a few vague responses when he paused for her opinion. Once breakfast was over, Thea took Matthew and sat down in the sitting room in front of the fire to tie evergreen boughs into the garlands she would tie on the staircase railing. Matthew seemed content enough to sit or roll about on the hooked rug at her feet. He picked at the rug and sometimes rose onto his hands and knees to rock back and forth as he had the night before. She had to smile, watching him; it was as if he wanted to crawl but had not figured out quite how to make his limbs move. It occurred to her that he needed some toys to play with. She would have to look in the attic.

After a while, when Matthew grew fussy, she sat down with him in the rocking chair. Soon his eyes began to blink, and he dropped his head onto her shoulder. His eyes closed and his little body grew heavier and limper. Thea closed her eyes as emotion welled in her, so sweet it was almost painful.

Thea was reluctant to lay the sleeping child down in the basket, but she thought that it was both foolish and idle to simply sit there holding him when there was work to be done, so after a few minutes she set him down in the basket and took the garlands she had made, as well as the mistletoe ball, into the entry. She tied the garland to the newel and went up the stairs, tying the garland in strategic spots so that it hung in shallow loops along the banister. Next, she picked up the mistletoe ball she had made of two hoops wrapped in red ribbon. In the center of the open ball, she had attached a cluster of mistletoe, the white, waxy berries and green leaves a dramatic contrast to the red frame.

She usually coaxed her brother into hanging the eye-catching decoration in the hallway, but she had heard him leave the house a while ago. She was tugging the hall bench out to the middle of the floor so that she could hang the ball herself when the front door knocker sounded. Thea opened the door to see Gabriel Morecombe standing on the other side.

"Lord Morecombe!" Her heart sped up, and she smiled, realizing a moment too late that her smile had probably been too bright. What if he assumed she thought he was courting her, which was, of course, absurd? She could hardly explain that she was *not* interested in seeing him, which would not only be rude but would doubtless make him think exactly the opposite.

"Good day, Miss Bainbridge." He paused, then added teasingly, "Have I displeased you already?"

"What? No. Why do you say that?"

"You smiled when you answered the door, and now you are frowning. Nor have you invited me in. Were you expecting someone else, perhaps?"

"Oh. No. My mind was elsewhere. Please come in." Flustered, Thea stepped aside, gesturing for him to enter.

He glanced down at the mistletoe ball in her hand and back up at her face, his eyes beginning to twinkle. "Why, Miss Bainbridge, do you usually greet your visitors this way come Christmastime? I scarce know whether you offer an invitation or a dare."

He was only teasing, Thea knew, yet she felt herself begin to blush. It was completely infuriating. What if the blush made him think she *was* wanting to kiss him? It only made it even more appalling to realize that she would not at all mind a repetition of the kiss he had given her last night.

"Don't be nonsensical." Thea closed the door a bit more forcefully than was necessary. "I was simply about to hang it."

He glanced at the ceiling, then back at her. "By yourself?"

"I was going to stand upon the bench."

"Please. Allow me." Plucking the decoration from her hand, he lithely stepped onto the bench and tied the mistletoe to the large nail.

"Thank you. You are most kind." Thea strove for the proper formality of tone. It would be extremely embarrassing if he realized that her lips kept wanting to smile.

"So prim and proper, Miss Bainbridge." He reached out a forefinger and touched one of the soft curls at her temple. "I like the way you did your hair."

Thea's stomach fluttered, and she looked away quickly. She was filled with such a tumbling rush of unusual feelings—an undeniable pleasure that he liked her hairstyle combined with the horrifying prospect that he might think she had arranged it that way in an attempt to please him, and sprinkled over it all a sizzling physical response to his touch—that she could not seem to find her mental footing. "I am sure you are an expert on such matters," she replied tartly, then was washed with embarrassment that she had responded with such a lack of social grace.

He chuckled. "Whether I am an expert is questionable, but I am definitely an interested observer."

She could not hold back a little smile at his words, though, again, she had no idea how to respond.

Gabriel leaned down toward her. "It seems foolish not to take advantage of the fruits of our labors."

He glanced up significantly, and Thea followed his gaze to the ball of mistletoe above them. Before she could move or speak, he kissed her. She threw her hands up against his chest as if to ward him off, but her arms had no strength to push him away. She felt limp and wobbly all over, her head light, as if she had been spinning, and Thea found herself curling her fingers into Morecombe's jacket and holding on to steady herself.

She had told herself that their kiss last night had not been as pleasurable, as shattering, as she remembered. Clearly, however, she had been lying to herself. His mouth was delicious, intoxicating. She was avidly alive to every sensation. Even the air against her cheek or the scent of the evergreen garlands or the sounds of pots rattling in the kitchen was suddenly sharper and clearer. Thea knew she was trembling a little, and it embarrassed her that he must feel it, but she could not seem to control her own body. She wanted to drink Gabriel in, to wrap her arms around him and press her body into his. Her body thrummed, something hot and dark and liquid growing deep within her.

The strange sensations shook her, and when Gabriel raised his head and looked down at her, she could not move, could only gaze back at him in stunned pleasure. His lips were dark and full, his eyes black under the shadow of his thick lashes. Thea wanted to touch him, to trace the lines of his face with her fingertips, feeling the warmth and texture of his skin, the hard lines of the bony outcroppings of cheeks and jaw and brow. The very forwardness of her longings shocked her.

Gabriel smiled a little, but his expression carried no hint of mockery or teasing, only a faint, almost sweet, hint of surprise. "Miss Bainbridge," he whispered. "You have a way of leaving me all a-sea." He brushed his lips against her mouth, soft and brief as the touch of a butterfly's wings. "I think I know you, and then I find . . ." He kissed her on the lips again, punctuating his words, the kiss growing in heat and length with every repetition. "You're . . . never . . . what . . . I expect." His mouth settled on hers with a hungry finality, and he kissed her as deeply as he had the night before.

Of their own volition, Thea's arms twined around his neck, and she moved onto her toes, pressing her lips into his. He let out a low groan deep in his throat, and his hands slid down her sides, his palms brushing the soft edges of her breasts before traveling farther down and around to curve over her hips. He dug his fingertips into the soft, rounded flesh, squeezing and pushing her into him.

Thea knew it was mad to be doing what they were. They were in the middle of the house in the middle of the day. She should pull away; she should be indignant, insulted. She should probably slap his impertinent face. But she could not bring herself to do what she should. She wanted only to taste more, feel more. She relished the surge of heat within her, the unaccustomed throbbing that started between her legs, the tightening of her nipples into small, hard points. Last night, when he'd kissed her, she had thought the feelings that had blossomed inside her must be the peak of desire, the height of sensation. But now, with every movement of his hands, each deepening of his kiss, the pleasure grew, her own hunger pulling her in further so that she wanted even more. Thea sensed that there must be still more awaiting her along this path. Gabriel, she was suddenly sure, could lead her beyond anything she had ever known, and she wanted, with a deep, physical ache, to let him take her there.

At that moment, the baby's wail arose from the sitting room.

With a gasp, Thea broke away from Gabriel. She stared at him, the full realization of what had just happened dawning in her eyes. Her fingertips came up to press against her full, damp lips, her eyes huge above her hand. He gazed back at her without a word, his chest rising and falling in quick pants. Gabriel took a step forward, one hand going out to her, and Thea whirled and ran for the sitting room.

She closed the door behind her and leaned back against it, trying to regain her senses as well as her breath. What had she done? What had she been thinking? Her face flooded with color as she recalled how wantonly she had responded to him—not just now but last night as well. He would be justified in believing her a hussy. Thea had never considered that she might have such loose, immoral behavior in her. She had never been silly over men or indulged in daydreaming about courtship and marriage. She had always considered herself practical and unromantic, the last sort of woman to feel the pull of desire.

But she could scarcely deny that her blood was running like a fever in her right now. Nor could she ignore the hot, empty ache deep within her that made her squeeze her legs together tightly in the vain hope that it would disappear. Clearly she was just as vulnerable to temptation as anyone else. And just as clearly, she would have to guard against it. Just as she would have to guard herself against Gabriel Morecombe.

Matthew's cries had not ended, and Thea pushed away from the door and went to pick him up. She held him to her, murmuring softly and patting him on the back, and his squalls diminished, then, after a final little hiccuping sob, stopped altogether. She looked down into his face and smiled. His wet lashes were stuck together into points like stars around his bright blue eyes. How, she wondered, could he look so utterly beautiful after crying like that?

She leaned her head against his, forehead to forehead, and he giggled, which meant that she had to do it several more times, and with each repetition, his giggles erupted into greater and greater laughter. If only she could stay in here playing with Matthew, she thought, and never have to go out to face Lord Morecombe. But obviously that would be impossible. She wasn't sure how she could face the man after the way she had just acted. Of course, last night she had felt the same way—was it always going to be this way around Gabriel Morecombe?—but eventually she had recovered enough to act normally. The happy thought occurred to her that he might just leave if she stayed in here long enough, but right after that the door opened and Gabriel stepped into the room.

"Do you always just walk into closed rooms wherever you find yourself?" she asked him crossly, grateful at least that her annoyance overcame her embarrassment.

"Only if I wish to see what's behind them," he answered imperturbably. His eyes went to the baby in her arms, and he smiled. "Well, Master Matthew, you seem to have changed your tune."

Matthew began to thrash his arms and gurgle in the way that meant he was happy, and he held out his hands to Morecombe in clear invitation.

"Traitor," Thea breathed, and walked over to hand him to Morecombe. She had no desire to meet Gabriel's eyes, but she made herself do it. She refused to be a coward.

"I don't pretend to know why you have decided to—to act in this way."

"In what way?" He looked puzzled.

She shot him a quelling look. "Please, my lord, I think we both know what occurred in the entry. There is no need to spell it out."

"Ah. What happened in the entry. I see. You want an explanation?"

"No! There is no need for that. But I must point out that you seem to have acquired a very incorrect notion about me and my...my standards of conduct."

The baby was squirming in his arms, and Morecombe lowered him to the floor, then turned back to Thea. "Indeed, Miss Bainbridge? And what notion is that?"

She glared at him. "That I would be open to—to your advances."

Again that engaging little smile tugged at the corners of his mouth. "I believe you *were* open to my advances...at least a bit."

"My lord, I am not a woman of easy virtue. Doubtless you are so accustomed to being with such women that you do not realize the difference."

"I never thought you a woman of easy virtue. Indeed, I suspect that your virtue is as hard as Cotswold stone. That does not mean I can't choose to chip away at it."

"This is not a laughing matter!" Thea's temper flared. "My reputation may mean nothing to you, but it is very important to me."

"Your reputation means a great deal to me, I assure you. I would never try to damage it, my dear—may I call you Althea? *Miss Bainbridge* seems a bit formal for two who have shared as much as we."

"No. You may not."

"You see? Hard as stone."

"While you may not *try* to damage my reputation, you certainly have no care for it. A true gentleman would not go about stealing kisses."

"Stealing? Seems fair payment for hanging the ornament, wouldn't you say?"

"One does not pay for a favor. That is not the issue, anyway."

"What is the issue? I thought we were talking about kisses."

"We are! Or rather, we are talking about the fact that you acted in a way that was not only improper but quite reckless. It is the middle of the day, and we were standing in our entry!"

"Ah, I see. You prefer your kisses at night and in some more secret place." He smiled, his eyes lighting. "Believe me, I shall be happy to oblige."

"No!" The scraps of composure Thea had pulled together were rapidly slipping away. The merry gleam in his eyes, the tempting curve of his mouth, the sheer enjoyment that stamped his face, all beckoned her. She was aware of a rather frightening impulse to forget her upbringing and throw herself back into his arms. But that would be sheer madness. "I am not saying you should kiss me at some other time and place. I am saying you should not kiss me at all!"

"I don't see why I would agree to do that. I quite enjoyed kissing you."

"Anyone could have walked in on us at any moment! My brother. Mrs. Brewster. Sally."

"I passed your brother on the street as I came over, so I knew he was not here. I could hear Mrs. Brewster in the kitchen. And I haven't the slightest idea who Sally is or why I should worry about her."

"She is the girl who comes in to help Mrs. Brewster, and she could have walked in on us."

"But she did not."

"That isn't the point!" She looked down and found that the baby had managed to roll and squirm his way over to the footstool. "How in the world did you get over there? No, dear, don't chew on the fringe." Thea swooped down and picked Matthew up, relocating him on the rug a few feet away. Turning back to face Gabriel, she straightened her shoulders. Putting some distance between them helped, she found. "Never mind. I can see that it is useless to try to reason with you."

"No doubt."

Thea clasped her hands together and adopted a polite expression. "Now. What brings you here today? I presume you had some reason for calling."

"Other than kissing you?"

"Lord Morecombe!" She gritted her teeth. The man was impossible. And it was difficult not to laugh.

"I apologize. I could not resist; I enjoy the sparkle in your eyes when you get in a temper."

Thea crossed her arms and waited, her expression grimly patient.

"Very well. I came to ask for your help."

Thea's brows shot up. "My help? In what way."

"I considered what you said, and I cannot deny that you have a point. I must employ a nursemaid for Matthew and acquire some other female servants as well. But I haven't the slightest idea where to begin, and the butler is someone I hired in London, so he has little knowledge of the area, either. It occurred to me that someone who had grown up in the village, who knew everyone, and who was, as well, a pillar of rectitude and morality would be the perfect person to help me in such an endeavor."

"Are you asking me to hire servants for you?"

"Well, I would hire them, obviously. But your advice on who might be a likely candidate would be a great help. And if you were to perhaps join me in interviewing said candidates, I would be most grateful. Also, and perhaps more important, I need to discover whether anyone in the village might have seen or even spoken with whoever left young Matthew in the church. Who could be more valuable in that regard than the vicar's sister, the woman who clearly hears all the latest gossip?"

"Oh. Well." Only an hour ago she had been wishing she knew what Lord Morecombe was doing to find Matthew's mother, and now here he was, offering to include her in it. She could not suppress the grin now. "I suppose we could ask Mrs. Brewster who might be available to act as a nursemaid. My knowledge of the village pales by comparison with Mrs. Brewster's, I assure you."

"Excellent." Gabriel smiled back at her, his eyes warm with approval, and Thea could not help but wonder how many other women had hastened to do as he asked, just to win that smile again.

She did not plan to be one of them, Thea told herself firmly as she turned and whisked Matthew up from the floor. It was her own curiosity and her desire to help the baby that drove her to join Lord Morecombe in his search, not any hope of pleasing Morecombe.

They found Mrs. Brewster in the kitchen, beating egg whites in a bowl. She pursed her mouth thoughtfully as she whipped the whisk through the whites, pausing to inspect the foam, then launching into another attack as she talked. "Well, there's Maggie Cooper; her youngest is old enough that her oldest girl could take care of him, but she wouldn't do if you're wanting to have her stay through the night."

"I would prefer that," Lord Morecombe told her.

Mrs. Brewster eyed him for a moment before saying carefully, "Are you talking 'bout taking the little one to your house, then?"

Humor lit Gabriel's eyes. "I assure you, I intend to make the place fit for female servants. Miss Bainbridge has informed me already that my household is generally regarded as a den of iniquity."

"And until such time as the Priory is suitable," Thea added, "the baby and his nursemaid will stay here. She can sleep in the extra bedroom at the end of the hall."

The housekeeper nodded. "Lolly Havers might do."

"Ned Havers's girl?" Thea asked. "Why, she's not even eighteen yet."

"Aye. But she's looked after the younger ones most her life. And I reckon as she'd be glad to have a room of her own and make a mite of money for minding the one baby."

Thea nodded. "True. And she does seem to have a level head for a girl her age."

It was soon arranged that Mrs. Brewster would send for the girl while Lord Morecombe and Thea started their search for the missing mother. Leaving Matthew in the housekeeper's care, Thea and Gabriel set out. The day was crisp, but the sun was shining down weakly, and it was, Thea thought, a beautiful day. She glanced up at the man beside her. She wondered what he was thinking, how his mind worked. He was completely foreign to her, unlike any of the other men she knew. Did he find her hopelessly provincial and naïve? Thea could well imagine the sort of sophisticated, beautiful women he must be acquainted with. They would know how to flirt and bedazzle him—not that she was interested in doing those things, but still, it must be nice to know *how*. The ladies he was used to would have gone to plays and operas and seen all sorts of places that Thea could only dream about. Glittering with jewels, dressed in the finest silks instead of a serviceable wool walking dress, such women would know all the latest on-dits and be able to discuss the events of the city.

What did she know? How Mrs. Gathers's daughter-in-law was recovering from her bout with catarrh or how many years it had been since old Mr. Adams had graced the church with his presence because he and Thea's father had had a falling-out over a certain Sunday sermon? Oh, and books; Thea had consumed a number of them over the years. But somehow she suspected that Lord Morecombe was not a bookish man.

As if feeling her gaze on him, Morecombe turned his head and raised his eyebrows quizzically. "What? You look as if you are contemplating very deep thoughts, indeed."

Embarrassed at being caught staring, Thea shrugged. "I was wondering what your plans are. How do you intend to set about finding Matthew's mother?"

"The Blue Boar seems the likeliest place to start."

"I wouldn't have thought you would need any introduction to anyone at the tavern," Thea commented drily.

He chuckled. "You have me there. I do know Malcolm Hornsby well enough to ask him a few questions, and I shall do so. But it is the visitors to the inn that interest me more than the ones in the tavern. And there *Mrs.* Hornsby reigns supreme. I feel sure that you will be able to get a great deal more out of her than I. She looks at me in a decidedly disapproving way—much the way you do, actually."

"She has three daughters," Thea explained, ignoring his comment about her. "And while that makes mothers of eligible girls like the Squire's daughters view you with great hope, it makes mothers of ineligible ones want to keep you far away—if they value their daughters' happiness and virtue, that is."

"You make me sound like a most despicable man. I really am not such a lecher, you know. I don't make it a habit to go about seducing innocent maidens."

"Then what do you call kissing me?" Thea shot back.

"I call that an unexpected delight." A slow smile curved his lips, his eyes lighting with an unmistakable warmth. "One I wouldn't mind experiencing again. But, trust me, it was not a seduction."

Whatever thoughts Thea had had in her head immediately fled. Her mouth was suddenly dry and her lips tingled. She was aware that she should give him a sharp setdown, but all she could think of was the heat that blossomed deep in her abdomen at his words. What would a seduction by Gabriel Morecombe be like?

Thea looked away, afraid of what he might read in her face. She cleared her throat. "This is scarcely a suitable topic of conversation."

"I know. Fun, isn't it?"

Thea closed her mouth on a gurgle of laughter. She would have liked to have retorted an unequivocal no, but she was not given to lying. In truth it *was* fun to be bandying words back and forth about such an illicit subject. It was exciting, even just a bit dangerous, and just beneath the surface bubbled the remembered heat and temptation of Gabriel's kiss—that slow turn of heat and desire, the hunger and ache that opened within her, the messy, tumultuous mix of emotions.

He bent his head a little, craning to see her face. "Have I offended you, Miss Bainbridge?"

"Your words would offend any decent woman."

"A curiously ambiguous reply."

Thea could hear the smile in Gabriel's tone. Try as she might, she could not keep from shooting a quick, challenging glance at him. "Well. Then I suppose you will just have to discover what I mean."

# Seven

*The wife of the inn's* owner was a short, slender woman who looked as if she had never indulged in eating her own rich cooking. Possessed of a seemingly unending well of energy, she drove her family and staff to perform with the same tireless perfection she achieved. The quality of her meals and the cleanliness and comfort of the inn's rooms were indisputable, and it was said that some went out of their way to spend a night at the Blue Boar.

She bustled forward to greet Thea, bobbing a curtsy and saying, "Miss Bainbridge, 'tis a pleasure to see you. Can I help you?" She cast a brief, curious glance toward Lord Morecombe. "My lord."

"Mrs. Hornsby." Gabriel nodded to her politely. "Perhaps we could have a cold collation in one of the private rooms. And if you would be so good as to join us ..."

The woman's brows rose with each statement, but she only nodded and led them to the best private dining room before hurrying off to see to their meal. Thea turned to face Gabriel, crossing her arms and regarding him coolly. "A cold collation? I thought we were here to ask questions, not eat."

"I was feeling a mite peckish, and quite frankly, Mrs. Hornsby's food surpasses my cook's. Though pray don't let that get back to Mrs. Cutledge or my bread will be soggier and the soup colder than ever. Besides, I have found that people are more apt to give one information if one has remunerated them in some way."

A serving girl entered the room, bearing a tray of food, followed by Mrs. Hornsby with a smaller tray containing cups and pitchers. The first few minutes were occupied in arranging the collection of cold meats, cheeses, and breads on the table before them, with a tureen of soup as the centerpiece.

"Now, then, my lord, how can I help you?" Mrs. Hornsby asked, pouring wine.

"I am looking for someone who might have stayed here in the past few days. Probably a woman, maybe a man or a couple. They would have had a baby with them."

"A baby?" The innkeeper's wife set down her pitcher and looked sharply at Thea. "Are you talking about that babe you found in the manger, miss?"

"You know about him?" Lord Morecombe paused in lifting his glass. "Was he here?"

The middle-aged woman shook her head. "Oh, no, my lord, I just heard about it. A miracle, that's what Liza Cooper says—little Lord Jesus himself appearing."

"Well, I don't think Matthew is our Lord and Savior," Thea replied. "Just a baby abandoned in a place where they knew he would be warm and soon found."

"That's what I said." Mrs. Hornsby nodded. "A miracle for the baby, though, you coming on it right away. Even inside like that, it can get powerful cold at night without a fire."

"The thing is," Thea went on, "we are trying to find out who left the baby there."

"I see." Mrs. Hornsby nodded, though she stole another curious glance at Lord Morecombe. "Well, there wasn't anyone with a babe spending the night here, miss. I can't remember last time someone came through with a wee one, must have been weeks."

"Do you think it's possible the child belongs to someone who lives around here?" Thea asked.

"I can't see how. Hard to keep a secret like that in Chesley. There's been a few babies born here the past year—how old is it, do you think?"

"Mrs. Brewster said she thought he was probably six or seven months old. So he would have been born in the late spring or early summer, I suppose."

Mrs. Hornsby nodded. "The Johnsons' wee one died right after it was born, you know. The Stouts' baby passed on two months ago. And Dora Potts would cut off her right arm rather than give up that child of hers."

"I have never seen the baby before. I can't believe that he is from Chesley."

"Another town maybe," Mrs. Hornsby suggested. "Bynford or Nyebourne. Or it could have been a stranger just passing through—left the baby and kept on walking."

"What if the person did not stay at your inn?" Morecombe asked. "Could they have rented a cottage? Or a room in someone's home?"

"Not so as I've heard." Mrs. Hornsby paused, considering. "I can ask around, get the mister to ask in the tavern. Mayhap somebody saw them on the road going or coming."

"I would appreciate it," Gabriel told her, and smiled.

Mrs. Hornsby smiled back, ducking her head, and bobbed another curtsy before she left the room.

Gabriel settled back with a sigh and tore a piece from the loaf of bread. "Doesn't sound promising, does it?" He looked at Thea. "Is she right? Is there nowhere else for someone to stay?"

"I suppose the mother could be staying at a local house. I haven't heard of anyone having visitors. Now and then I've heard of someone renting a room out, but not lately." Thea paused. "We can visit Mrs. Williams after this if you'd like. She's the greatest gossip in town. If anyone would know whether there has been a stranger staying in town, it would be she."

Mrs. Hornsby returned a few minutes later with the news that no one in the inn or tavern had seen anyone with a baby either in town or on the road. Nor had anyone noticed a stranger (or an unknown carriage) in town, except for the two people who had stayed at the inn the night before, who had not, she was certain, had a baby with them. She assured them, however, that she would continue to ask.

With their meal finished and having gathered all the information they could, Thea and Gabriel left the inn and started toward Mrs. Williams's cottage. As they walked, Thea said, "I was surprised, watching you talk with Mrs. Hornsby."

"Why?" He looked at Thea curiously.

"You were at ease with her. Quite nice."

"Did you expect me not to be?"

"I wasn't sure. You said you wanted me along to help you with her. I thought perhaps you were unused to talking to ordinary people. And I thought you might act . . ."

"Like an arrogant aristocrat?" he suggested.

"Let's just say, more like the man at the Squire's party."

"I must have been a terrible guest that night."

"No, not terrible. You just seemed very much the lord of the manor. Like my cousin."

"Ian? Oh, he's a good enough fellow. He is not fond of rural pastimes."

"It seems strange he would be here then."

"I think it's more a matter of avoiding Fenstone Park." Gabriel gave her a quick, rueful grin. "Pray ignore that remark. As for my behavior, I have little excuse. I am often bored by such events. Had I known that you were there to provide more scintillating conversation, perhaps I would have paid more attention. But, as I recall, when Mrs. Cliffe introduced you to me, she had already run the gauntlet of every eligible—or slightly eligible—female in the surrounding countryside, beginning with her own four giggling daughters. When I met you, I was doubtless numb with boredom."

His words surprised a laugh out of Thea, and she covered it with her hand. "You are a terrible man."

"Because I made you laugh? You should do it more often. You have a charming laugh—your eyes light up and your nose crinkles just so."

"Oh!" She let out a little wail, clapping her hand over her nose. "Do not say so! I have always hated that. I look like a rabbit."

"What is wrong with that? I have it on the best authority that rabbits are adorable."

"What nonsense you talk."

"Nonsense makes the most agreeable conversation, I find."

She could not help but chuckle again and shake her head. "I shall have to stop talking; it is only encouraging you."

They fell silent for a moment as Thea turned down the narrow lane leading to Mrs. Williams's cottage. Out of the corner of her eye, she could see Morecombe glance at her and then away. He thrust his hands into the pockets of his greatcoat.

Finally he said, "I do apologize most earnestly for not recognizing you that night. It was not that I had forgotten you—or at least, the memory was still there, just pushed to the back of my mind. I recalled it quite clearly when you mentioned it. I confess that I had forgotten your name or that you were Ian's cousin. But it had been ten years or more since that night."

"Of course. It's perfectly understandable."

"I would not have wounded your feelings for the world. I am not that careless or callous a man, I hope."

"I can see that you are not." Thea turned her face up to look at him, and she smiled. "I do not hold it against you." She realized with some surprise that she actually meant the words. Somehow the sting of his not remembering her had faded over the last day. "However," she added rather saucily, "that does not excuse your forgetting me a week later."

"Ah!" He laid a hand on his chest, wincing with mock pain. "A fair hit, Miss Bainbridge. But even you must admit that there were extenuating circumstances. I saw you only briefly at the party." He held up one hand, ticking off the excuses finger by finger. "I would never have expected you to show up in my house, taking me to task. You were not wearing your spectacles. And your hair was tumbled most delectably about your face. Not to mention the fact that you were carrying a baby. And swooping down on me like a Fury."

Thea rolled her eyes. "You exaggerate."

They had reached a neat little cottage, its warm stone almost completely covered with ivy. Thea turned up the walk, with Gabriel on her heels. She had barely had time to knock when the door was opened by a plump, white-haired matron, beaming at them.

"Come in. Come in." Mrs. Williams practically pulled Thea into the room while managing to give a little curtsy to Lord Morecombe at the same time. She ushered them into the tidy main room of the house, offering them luncheon—and when that was politely refused, tea and cakes.

Thea did not have to worry how to subtly bring up the topic of Matthew, for the older woman immediately began to ply Thea with questions about the child.

"Is it true that you found him in the manger, miss?" Mrs. Williams shook her head in wonder. "Can you imagine that? Is it a little boy? I heard he was beautiful as an angel."

"Yes, he is a handsome young man." Thea could not keep from smiling as she thought of Matthew.

The old woman nodded. "I thought as much. Only fitting, really, him being found in the church and all." She cast a glance over at Gabriel, as she had all through their visit. "It's very good of you, my lord, to be helping Miss Bainbridge look for the mother."

"It seemed the least I could do."

"I hear there was a bit of a stir at the Priory yesterday after Miss Bainbridge found him," Mrs. Williams went on, watching Gabriel brightly.

"Um, well . . ." He glanced over at Thea, obviously at a loss for words.

She suppressed a smile and came to his rescue. "The vicar and I hoped that Lord Morecombe or one of his friends might have some knowledge of the child, being new to town themselves." Her reasoning, she knew, made little sense, and she doubted that Mrs. Williams believed a bit of it. But for politeness' sake, she would have little choice but to accept Thea's explanation. "I was certain that if anyone knew whether someone who was visiting in Chesley had brought a baby with them, it would be you."

Mrs. Williams took the bait, straightening and beaming with pride. "Indeed I would, miss, you can be sure of that. But the truth is, I have been racking my brain since I heard the news, trying to think who the babe might be. The fact is, I don't know of anyone with a lad that age in Chesley, except, of course, for the Potts, and the poor wee thing couldn't be him."

"No. It's not."

"There's no visitors with one, either. Old Mr. Jonas's daughter and her family are here with him, but that babe is a newborn." Mrs. Williams chattered on about every family she could think of that had children, rejecting each of them in turn. Clearly, she had nothing to add to their store of knowledge.

After a few more minutes of polite conversation and some-times less than polite questioning from Mrs. Williams, Thea and Gabriel extricated themselves from the conversation and started back toward the vicarage. Gabriel, walking alongside Thea, shook his head and let out a short laugh.

"How the devil could she know all about that child already?" he wondered. "I am surprised she did not describe the brooch you showed me."

Thea smiled. "I told you, she knows every ... ing about every-one. Between her husband's family and hers, she is related to half the people in the village by blood or marriage, and she spent much of her life in the apothecary's shop with her husband, chat-ting to everyone who came in. She would have made an excellent spy if there were anything worth discovering in Chesley." Thea paused. "I apologize for causing a scene yesterday at the Priory. I should have thought about the gossip it would start, but, frankly, I was too incensed at that time to care whether I set tongues to wagging about you."

Gabriel shrugged. "People talk. It makes little difference to me."

"That must be a pleasant way to live."

He glanced over at her. "If people whisper about me, I don't hear it. It does not hurt me."

"Mm. It's different for a woman, I fear. What people whisper means a great deal—especially when you are the vicar's sister."

"Ah. So now we are talking about duty. You have a duty to live a blameless life or it will reflect badly on your brother."

"Yes, of course." She sighed unconsciously.

"I know a bit about duty."

"You do?"

He laughed. "You needn't look quite so surprised. I am not entirely lazy and self-indulgent."

"I didn't mean that." Thea flushed.

"Now, Miss Bainbridge, don't start telling me bouncers. I rely on your candor."

"Very well. I have seen little in your actions to indicate otherwise. Well, I mean until now."

"You mean your opinion of me has changed?" he asked wryly.

She gave him a stern look. "Not entirely. But I do see that you are concerned about Matthew, that you have a sense of duty toward your nephew . . . and your sister."

"I love Jocelyn," he replied with simple honesty. "How could I not try to find her? Help her?"

"There are some who would turn their backs on someone who caused scandal to their name."

"My name means little to me compared to my sister." He was silent for a moment, then said quietly, "I remember when she was born. My governess told me I had a baby sister, and later the nurse took me in to see her in her cradle." A faint smile touched his mouth. "She was so tiny and so red. I thought she was not nearly as cute as the puppies in the kennels. But when I put out my finger, Jocelyn wrapped her fingers around it, and I felt . . ." He shook his head. "I'm not sure what it was, but I knew that I had to protect her, that she was mine. I fear I did not look after her well enough."

"We all make our own choices. And in the end, no one else can bear the consequences for us. I am sure you did your best."

"Did I? Sometimes I wonder. Perhaps it was only the easiest. The most convenient for me." They walked on in silence for a moment, then he said, "I was happy that she was going to marry Lord Rawdon. He and I were friends. Good friends. I thought it would be pleasant . . . fun . . . for me. *I* wanted it. Obviously I wasn't thinking about my sister; I didn't even realize that she did not want to marry him."

Thea laid her hand on his arm. "You must not blame yourself. Who would not want one's sister to marry a good friend? I think that I would be happy, surely, if my brother told me he was going to marry my friend." Of course, the thought of her studious brother marrying the vibrant Damaris was a bit ludicrous, but in principle the theory held true. "It would ensure that you continued to be close even after she was married. You thought that he would be a good husband, that he would care for her and protect her."

"I thought he loved her."

"Then how can you say it was wrong to be happy she was engaged to him?"

"She ran away from him. Obviously she did not wish to marry him."

"Sometimes people change their minds. Surely she wanted to marry him in the beginning or she would not have accepted his proposal. I mean, you did not arrange the marriage between you and him, did you?"

"No, of course not. He came to me and asked my permission, naturally, and I was happy to give it to him. But she accepted his proposal. She seemed eager to marry him, I thought."

"No doubt she was. People can have doubts later. They might decide they made the wrong decision."

"But why did Jocelyn not tell me that she had changed her mind?" Gabriel frowned. "She must have believed that she could not, that I would be angry with her, even insist she marry him."

"You must not think that. Perhaps she simply could not face the scandal she knew it would cause if she broke off the engagement. Things can seem frightful, even unbearable, when we are young. Or she may have felt too embarrassed or ashamed to tell you. Sometimes, silly as it seems, the people we love the most are the ones to whom we are most afraid of revealing our foolishness. That does not mean she was afraid of you or did not trust you."

They walked on in silence for a moment, then Gabriel said, "Thank you. Whether that is true or you are merely being kind, I confess it does make me feel better."

"You sound surprised."

"I am a bit surprised that you should make an effort to ease my mind. You have not appeared to like me overmuch."

She gave an eloquent little shrug. "The truth does not have anything to do with liking or disliking."

The grin she was coming to know well flashed briefly. "So you are saying that you still do not like me overmuch."

"I would not think you would care what one spinster in an out-of-the-way village thinks of you. No doubt you are very well liked by any number of women."

"Sometimes the challenging course presents the more appealing prospect."

Thea glanced at him sharply. She was not sure what to make

of such comments from him. They seemed, well, flirtatious, yet she could not imagine why a man such as Lord Morecombe would flirt with a woman such as her. Perhaps he was simply too much in the habit to stop. Or maybe he disliked the thought of any woman not succumbing to his charms, even when he had no real interest in her.

Whatever the case, Thea did not fool herself. She prided herself on not believing in nonsensical daydreams. She was not the sort to stitch a few words from an eligible man into a pattern of romantic interest, especially when the man was someone as handsome and charming as Gabriel Morecombe. His flirtation meant nothing; his kisses even less. Still, she could not deny that his words warmed her. She found herself wanting to smile at him, and she had to clamp her lips together to keep from doing so.

Fortunately, they were almost to the vicarage, and Thea was able to simply avoid his comment, instead picking up her pace and heading toward the low gate leading into her yard. Inside the kitchen, they were greeted by the sight of a blond girl seated on the rug with the baby, playing peekaboo with his blanket. She scrambled up as Thea and Gabriel stepped into the room and stood gazing at Lord Morecombe in awe.

The baby, upon seeing Thea, raised his hands toward her and let out a stream of babble. The smile she had been able to restrain with Gabriel burst forth undeniably now, and she bent to pick him up, swinging him up to settle him on her hip in a gesture that was already seeming quite familiar.

"Good afternoon, Lolly," Thea greeted the girl.

"Miss." Lolly bobbed a little curtsy toward her and a deeper one to Lord Morecombe, blushing and ducking her head.

Thea sighed and glanced at Gabriel. He looked faintly amused.

"Lolly, Mrs. Brewster tells me you might be interested in acting as a nursemaid for young Matthew here," Gabriel began gravely.

"Yes, sir." She ventured a quick upward glance at him but seemed unable to say anything else.

"Did you ask your parents, Lolly?" Thea asked. "Will they allow you to take care of the baby?"

"Oh, yes, miss." The girl turned back to Thea, looking a little relieved. "They said as long as it was for you, miss, and I'd be staying here."

"Yes, well, for the time being, that is certainly where you will be staying. If that should change in the future, we would address it then. But do you think that you will be able to adequately take care of the baby?"

Lolly smiled. "Oh, yes, miss. I look after all my brothers and sisters at home, leastways all the little ones. One baby'd be that easy."

"Your mother would not be here to supervise."

"I know what to do, miss."

As long as she was not looking at Lord Morecombe, the girl seemed confident enough, Thea thought. The only way to tell if she could do the work would be to let her try. Thea looked over at Gabriel questioningly.

"Why don't you look after him for a few days?" Morecombe suggested, echoing Thea's thoughts. "Then we can decide what to do for the future."

"Oh, yes, sir, thank you, sir." Lolly bobbed a curtsy, then another for good measure, beaming. "Miss, I'll do a good job. You'll see."

Lolly was eager to start her work, even offering to begin right then, but Thea assured her that the following day would be soon enough. Lolly left, promising to return early the next morning with her things. Thea turned to Gabriel, feeling suddenly awkward. It occurred to her how strange it was to be standing with an aristocrat in her kitchen, a baby in her arms, and Mrs. Brewster cooking at the fire behind them. Gabriel should have looked very out of place here, Thea thought, in his elegant clothes, the top of his head nearly brushing the low ceiling. However, he did not seem ill at ease, and Thea was aware that the awkwardness lay more in herself than in him. They had done what they set out to do today, and there was no reason to see him again. The idea disappointed her, and the sheer foolishness of that emotion made her even more awkward.

"What will you do now?" she asked.

He shook his head. "I cannot think what else to do here."

"No. It seems unlikely that she is staying in Chesley," Thea said.

"If she did not spend the night here, it seems that she might have stayed at a nearby village."

"Yes. Bynford is east of us, on the road from Oxford."

"That seems the likeliest place to try next." He paused. "I—if you wouldn't mind, perhaps you could accompany me?"

Thea glanced at him, startled, and saw that Morecombe himself appeared faintly surprised.

"We worked rather well together, I thought," he went on in the silence that followed his invitation. "Unless, of course, well, it might be a bit chilly. I brought only my curricle with me to the Priory—but I promise to provide a lap robe and a hot brick for your feet."

"Yes," Thea said quickly, afraid that if he went on speaking, he might talk himself out of the offer. "I mean, I would be happy to help you. And since Lolly will be here now, I won't have to worry about overburdening Mrs. Brewster with the baby." Thea thought she heard a soft grunt from the direction of the fireplace, but Thea ignored it.

Morecombe smiled. "Very well. Thank you for your help. I shall see you tomorrow morning."

Thea nodded and watched him leave, her stomach dancing in a mix of excitement and nerves. Behind her, Mrs. Brewster clanked a long wooden spoon against the edge of a pot.

Thea turned, uneasily sure that her housekeeper had something to say about the scene she had just witnessed. She expected disapproval, for Thea knew that going with Lord Morecombe to Bynford the next day was skating perilously close to scandal. She was a little surprised, however, to see not disapproval, but a frown of worry forming between the housekeeper's eyes.

"Are you sure what you're doing, miss?" was all she said.

"'Tis an open carriage," Thea pointed out. "And we will simply go there and come back. Bynford's not far. We shall be gone only a few hours. And it isn't as if I am a young girl in need of a chaperone; I am quite past marriageable age. I believe my reputation is good enough to bear up under spending three hours in an open vehicle with a gentleman."

"'Twasn't scandal I was thinking of," the housekeeper

retorted. "I know you're not the sort to lose your head even over a man who looks like sin walking, which his lordship does." She paused, then added softly, "It's your heart I'm worried about, Miss Althea."

"Nonsense. I didn't cut my eyeteeth yesterday, you know. I'm not likely to lose my heart to any man, much less an arrogant wastrel like Lord Morecombe. My heart is firmly under lock and key and has been for years."

Matthew chose that moment to let out a coo and reach up to pat Thea's cheek. She looked down at his cherubic face, and the organ in question seemed to swell in her chest. She was lying, she knew. She could hold her heart secure from Gabriel Morecombe, she felt sure of that, but it had already been lost to this young man.

Smiling at him, she bent to kiss his head. His soft curls tickled her cheek. What would she do if Matthew did turn out to be Gabriel's nephew? She would have to do the right thing and let him take his place with his family. But how would she be able to give him up?

*Gabriel strode down the street*, heading back to the inn where he had stabled his horse this morning. He had not really meant to ask Miss Bainbridge to accompany him tomorrow on his search for Jocelyn, but somehow the words had slipped out. He had already spent the better part of a day in her company, and in general he was disinclined to call on any lady two days in a row. It was not a wise practice to visit a woman frequently, for they (or their relatives) were likely to begin to have hopes about the possibility of marriage—and Gabriel had no interest in marrying, at least not anytime soon. Someday, of course, when he was older and ready to raise a family, to fulfill his duty as Lord Morecombe, he would find a suitable lady and ask her to marry him.

But that day was far away still. There were still too many things to do and enjoy to shackle himself to a wife. Being a man who enjoyed the company of women, he certainly did not avoid them, but he was careful to keep his attentions to eligible girls brief and light. He might flirt and dance and escort women to a ball or a play now and then, but he avoided young girls just making their come-outs, and he made sure that he did not pay too much attention to any eligible woman. There were, after all, plenty of willing widows as well as actresses and opera dancers who understood the rules of the game and with whom he could spend all the time he chose.

Althea Bainbridge was definitely not one of those women.

He had to smile to himself. Althea was the daughter and sister of vicars, and she was unmarried. Not just unmarried, but a spinster of several years, a veritable ape leader. Such a woman was exactly the sort to stay away from, the kind who would start spinning dreams out of moonlight, turning a flirtatious exchange into an incipient proposal of matrimony.

And yet . . . he had not been able to stop himself from asking her to spend the next day with him. It had been so easy with Althea today. Not awkward or boring. They had fit well together in the way they had questioned the innkeeper's wife and the town gossip. It was odd how frequently she spoke the same thought he had or asked the question he wanted answered.

When he had thought about riding over to Bynford by himself, the idea had not appealed. He liked her dry wit and her intelligence. She never seemed to fear offending him or to strive to please him. Being with her, he realized just how often other young women molded their conversation to his, echoing his opinions or asking what he thought instead of making a statement of their own. Not often could one talk with a woman who would give back as good as she got. And some who did, such as Rawdon's sister, were far too icy for his taste. He could not imagine a woman like that reaching out to put a soothing hand on his arm and reassure him that he was not to blame for his sister's fleeing her nuptials.

Another thing was odd about his time with Miss Bainbridge. He had never told anyone, even his closest friends such as Ian or Myles, about his fear that he had pushed Jocelyn into marriage with Rawdon. Yet, after knowing this woman for less than two days, he was confessing the doubt that had ridden him for the past year. She did not seem the sort to whom he would want to tell his thoughts or secrets—she was starchy in manner and vaguely defiant in her speech. Nothing in her manner was especially warm or sympathetic. Indeed, she seemed more inclined to berate a man than to offer him comfort. Yet she had done exactly that, and her words had made all the more impression on him because of her no-nonsense manner.

He reached the yard of the inn, and the ostler hurried to saddle and bring out his mount. Gabriel tossed the boy a coin and swung up onto his horse, turning him down the road toward the Priory. As he rode, he continued to think about Althea.

He felt sure that any of his friends would be amazed to find he had any interest in her. But, given that he had given in to impulse and kissed her three times now, he could scarcely deny that he was drawn to her. She was not beautiful, it was true. But he found something in her looks intriguing. The unruly curls that kept pulling free of her pins and tumbling around her face tugged at him. They were neither red nor brown but something in between, the color of glossy mahogany, warm and inviting. He wanted to reach out and touch them, to feel their softness, to coil them around his fingers. Nor could he keep from wondering what she would look like with all her hair hanging loose around her shoulders. A man could sink his hands into that mass of curls. Bury his face in it and drink in the sweet scent of her. He had thought of doing exactly that thing more than once today as they went about their business.

She was thin and spare and tall, not a woman to cuddle, but he could not keep from picturing her long legs wrapped around him, her slender form beneath him. Beauty was in the lines of her long body. And beauty was in the solemn depths of her gray eyes. Althea Bainbridge was not soft and winsome; she had no dimples and flutters and soft sighs. But something in the sharp, high lines of her cheekbones and the stubborn set of her chin appealed to him. And something more was inside her, some heat that glimmered now and then in her glance, like the wildness in her curls . . . and the passion of her kiss.

Gabriel smiled sensually as he recalled kissing her this morning under the mistletoe, the way she had risen up to him, wrapping her arms around his neck. Without artifice or guile, she had kissed him back, the desire pure and sweet in her mouth. She had obviously been inexperienced, but the passion had flared hot in her, as swift and intense as a flame.

The response in his own body had been equally fiery. Gabriel shifted a little in his saddle as he thought of the moment. An affair with the vicar's sister in a small village was unthinkable. He could not give in to the temptation—he would not only be acting the cad but also embroiling himself in a scandal. There would be no hope of her behaving as a sophisticated London woman might. Still . . . he was no longer a raw lad. He could spend time with a woman, enjoy her company, and not give in to temptation. Althea seemed to be a sensible woman; she was mature and not at all fanciful. She would not assume that he was courting her just because he asked for her help in regards to the baby.

A little warning voice sounded deep in his brain, pointing out that he was lying to himself. He was mad to even think of spending any more time with Althea Bainbridge. Gabriel grinned, kicking his horse into a trot. He could not deny it. Perhaps he *was* mad. But if he was, he intended to enjoy his madness to the fullest.

# Eight

*Thea frowned at the three* dresses she had laid out on the bed before her—one dark blue, one brown, and one gray. They were all hopelessly dull. How, she wondered, could they be so uniformly dark and plain? She had once worn sprig muslin dresses, white as befitted a girl and patterned in pretty pastels. But that had been years ago, and those gowns had long since been consigned to the rag bin. Still, it did seem that she could have replaced them with something a bit … prettier.

Why hadn't she purchased some ribbons or lace from the traveling draper the last time he had come through town? Perhaps when she was in Bynford she could pick up a length of pale blue ribbon for the dark blue wool or a bit of blond lace to perk up the neckline of the brown serge. While Lord Morecombe was talking to the tavern owner, she could slip away and—

Thea turned and sat down on the bed beside her dresses. What in the world was she thinking? That would be an entirely vain thing to do, running off to buy such fripperies when he was engaged in the serious matter of searching for his sister. Besides, he would be bound to consider it foolish for a spinster such as her to be thinking of dresses and trims and such. It was one thing for a young girl, but quite another when it was a woman of her age and station. That was the very reason, after all, that she had stopped purchasing girlish materials and colors years ago. When one was twenty-seven years old, it hardly seemed appropriate to be concerned with ornamenting oneself, particularly if one was the vicar's sister. And most particularly if one had never been a beauty to begin with.

Stifling a little sigh, Thea picked up the gray dress. She held it for a moment against her breast, picturing for an instant going downstairs in the light blue merino wool that had once been her favorite. It had been a sweet dress with a soft ruffle around the neck and cuffs and a flounce just above the hem of the skirt. It was hopelessly outdated, of course, and she had stopped wearing it several years earlier, but she had been unable to give it away or put it in to be torn into rags. It still lay, folded, in the bottom of the cedar chest at the foot of her bed. No doubt it was some sort of sin to be so attached to a material thing, but Thea had always thought the color looked quite good with her skin and hair and gave her gray eyes the faintest bluish tinge.

With a shake of her head, Thea dismissed the mental image and stood up to pull the gray dress over her head. She hooked it up the back and looked at herself in the mirror. This gown, of course, made her gray eyes look, well, gray. And the color did little for her skin. But it was silly to be concerned with how she looked. It was not as if she were accompanying Gabriel on a pleasure jaunt. Her cloak would cover up her dress most of the time, anyway. Still, she took down the better of her two bonnets from the shelf. After all, a woman had some pride.

Downstairs, Thea ate breakfast with her brother. He did not ask how she intended to spend her day, and she did not offer the news. She would not have lied to Daniel, but it was just as well that he did not know she was riding in Lord Morecombe's curricle to the next village. It would only worry him, and with any luck no one would see them and comment on it to Daniel. If they did—well, it would be all over by that time and nothing to be done about it.

After breakfast Thea went into the kitchen looking for Matthew. Lolly had taken charge of the baby as soon as she arrived this morning, carrying him off to change and dress and feed him. It had been easier getting ready and eating without the baby, but Thea had missed him, and it made her heart swell with happiness when he grinned and raised his arms to her as soon as she stepped into the kitchen.

She picked him up and carried him to the sitting room, where she sat down to play with him on the rug in front of the fire. Last night she had made a rudimentary doll for him out of pieces she'd found in the rag bag, and she had also dug out an old set of wooden blocks that had been tucked away in a chest in the attic. When the maid let Lord Morecombe into the house an hour later, that is how he found them, with Thea "walking" the doll across the rug toward Matthew and bouncing the doll up to "kiss" him as a finish. The "kiss" never failed to elicit a round of giggles from the baby.

Thea did not hear Gabriel enter, but the baby turned his head and, catching sight of him, let out a little shriek. Thea turned to see Gabriel standing there watching her, and she felt suddenly warm all over. She scrambled to her feet.

"I'm sorry. I didn't see you there. You should have said something."

"I enjoyed watching."

"Oh. Well." Thea wasn't entirely sure what he meant by that statement, so she made no reply, just busied herself with brushing a bit of lint from her skirts. "I, um, let me give Matthew to Lolly, then we can leave."

"Certainly." Gabriel crossed the room in a few easy strides and swooped Matthew up, raising him high above his head. Matthew let out another shriek of sheer glee, so Gabriel lowered and raised him once more before he settled the baby into the crook of his arm.

Watching them, Thea could not keep from smiling. "He likes you. You're quite good with him."

"Am I?" He glanced at her with an expression of faint surprise. "I would not have thought so. I have never been around babies, really. But this one seems an easy chap to entertain."

"He's quite happy," Thea agreed. "And very healthy, too, it seems to me. He must have been well cared for. That makes it even odder ..."

"That someone left him in the church? I agree." Gabriel nodded, a frown forming between his eyes as they walked back into the kitchen to turn the baby over to Lolly.

A few minutes later, they were in the curricle and headed down the road away from the village. The day was cool and gray, without the pale sunshine of the day before, but, as promised, Gabriel had provided a heavy, fur-lined traveling rug and even a wrapped warm brick for her to put her feet on. With her bonnet and gloves, as well as her cloak, Thea was toasty warm. She brushed her hand surreptitiously over the soft fur; she had never seen a lap robe this luxurious. It would keep her warm even if it were a good bit colder.

Gabriel drove a matched pair of grays, and the well-sprung carriage and the smooth gait of the horses was far different from bouncing along in her brother's trap or even the Squire's roomy, old-fashioned coach. It was immediately apparent that Gabriel was an excellent driver—as well as a swift one. Thea felt a thrill of excitement as they moved down the road, the cold air rushing against her cheeks. She glanced over at Gabriel and grinned. He caught the look and returned her smile.

"You don't mind the speed?"

"No! It's exciting," Thea answered honestly.

"Ah, a girl after my own heart."

He turned his attention back to the road to neatly maneuver past a farmer's slow-moving wagon without breaking the rhythm of the team. But after a few minutes, he pulled the pair back to a slower pace.

"How is Lolly doing with young Matthew?" he asked.

"Very well, so far. Matthew seems to like her. He is a pleasant child, I admit, but still, I think that speaks well for her. And she seemed quite competent at feeding and diapering him. She even brought some diaper cloth from her house, which I must say was sorely needed. I searched our attic the other day and came up with a few little dresses for him, but no diaper cloth."

"We should purchase some cloth today. Is there a draper's in this village?"

"It is rather too small for that, but there is a haberdashery there, and he carries a small selection of cloths and some sundries." It was where she had thought of going to purchase the ribbons and lace, though she did not add that.

He nodded. "Very well. We shall add the haberdasher's shop to our list of stops."

The trip passed quickly, for they talked all the way over to Bynford. It was, Thea discovered, amazingly easy to talk to Gabriel. He asked her questions about Chesley and made her laugh with his observations about the town and its citizens. He told her about the village near his own estate and the people with whom he had grown up. Thea found herself revealing far more about her family and her life than she would ever have imagined telling someone she had known for only days. Their conversation strayed to books and from there to plays, and Thea was both surprised and elated when Gabriel related to her his most recent visits to the theater.

He glanced at her and laughed. "I think I should be insulted by your look of astonishment. I am not completely a barbarian."

"No. Of course. I mean, I did not think you were. It is just, well, I have always heard that gentlemen …"

He raised a brow, waiting, then prodded, "What? That gentlemen attend the theater only to ogle the actresses?" When color filled Thea's cheeks, he let out a whoop of laughter. "Really, Miss Bainbridge, I thought you were a naïve vicar's daughter. That seems a remarkably cynical viewpoint."

"Just because I have been in Chesley all my life does not mean I haven't read anything about the world at large."

"Mm. Sounds to me as if you've been reading London scandal sheets."

"Certainly not." She gave him a look of disdain.

"Well, I confess: I have gone precisely to ogle the actresses a time or two. But I have been known to actually attend a play for the play itself. I have even been to the opera to listen instead of eyeing the opera dancers."

"Really, Lord Morecombe, it is scarcely appropriate to be discussing your *conquests*."

"How unkind—I was discussing the times I was *not* looking for conquests."

"It's an inappropriate subject altogether."

"And yet you brought it up."

"I did not! I stopped before I said anything."

He chuckled. "You thought it."

Thea shot him an exasperated look. He was watching her, laughter lurking in his dark eyes, and she realized that she wanted, quite badly, to kiss him. She remembered the way his mouth had felt on hers, the honeyed heat, the fierce hunger. She froze, suddenly breathless, her nerves tingling all over with memory and anticipation. Something changed in his face, and his eyes went to her mouth.

"You are excessively tempting." His voice was low and soft, no longer laughing. He shifted the reins to one hand and reached out to hook his forefinger under her chin. "How is it that that Quakerish bonnet makes me want to pull it off and kiss you?"

Thea sucked in a quick breath. "Lord Morecombe..."

"Miss Bainbridge . . ." His smile was slow and did peculiar things to her insides. "Don't you think we could address each other a bit more informally? Is it your custom to call a man you've kissed *Lord Morecombe?*"

"Only when that is his name," she tossed back.

He roared with laughter.

"Oh!" Thea clapped a hand to her mouth. "I should not have said that. It was most . . . most . . ."

"Inappropriate? It was clever, my dear girl." He picked up one of her hands and brought it to his lips. "And that is exactly why I find it so enjoyable to talk to you."

She could not really feel his lips; after all, a glove was between his mouth and her skin. But her hand tingled nevertheless. Thea pulled her hand back and folded it with her other in her lap. She should really make a protestation against his familiar gesture. She should explain that her wit had carried her away, that she had never kissed other men, as her tart retort had implied.

Instead she said only, "You do?"

"Enjoy talking with you? Of course. I would not, otherwise. You are quite right in what you thought of me from the beginning. I am a thoroughly selfish man, and I am given to my pleasures. I rarely do anything that does not please me."

"I do not think that is true." Thea met his gaze. "If you were a selfish man, you would not be driving through the cold, trying to discover who left a baby at the church."

He looked at her oddly. "In what way do I not act in my own interest? It may be my sister's child."

"There are a number of men who would not try to find their

sister in this instance, knowing the possibility of scandal it could bring. Who would not want the child."

"No, I am not one of those men. If that raises me in your estimation, then I am fortunate." He paused, then his mouth quirked up again. "Has it raised me enough to call me Gabriel?"

Thea could not help but chuckle. "You are a most persistent man. It would be terribly forward for me to call you by your given name. I have known you less than a week."

"Not true. Not true at all. By your own admission, you have known me for over ten years. It seems to me that I should be considered an old friend."

Thea rolled her eyes. "What a complete hand you are! We met almost eleven years ago and have not spoken since. Scarcely a friend."

"A family friend, then. I have been friends with your cousin since we were boys."

"My *second* cousin. Whom I have seen only little more often than I have seen you the past ten years."

"You are a most difficult woman. Call me Lord Morecombe, then, if you must. But I shall call you Althea."

"Pray, do not. No one calls me Althea except for older ladies who have known me my whole life and do not know me at all."

"Ah. Well, I shouldn't like to belong to that category. So what should I call you? Let me think . . ." He studied her for a moment.

Thea shifted under his scrutiny and turned her face away, aware of a vague fear that he would somehow see too much in her.

"I think I shall call you Thea."

She whipped back around to gape at him. "How did you know?"

"Is that what you are called?" He smiled. " 'Twas only a guess. But it seemed to suit you better."

She shrugged. "It is what my brother and sister call me."

"Thea." He tried the name again. "I like it."

She should not warm to the sound of her name on his tongue, Thea knew, but she did. How could her name seem so different when he said it? So warm and intimate? And why was it that all the inappropriate things Morecombe did were enjoyable?

"So when I say, 'Thea,' will you reply, 'Lord Morecombe'?"

"You are being absurd."

"Not I. I think it is the *Lord Morecombe* that will be absurd."

"Perhaps I shall endeavor simply not to call you anything."

"Clearly you haven't the least concern about wounding my feelings."

Thea tried to glare at him, but she broke into a chuckle before she could even begin to level a stare at him. "Oh, all right. Gabriel. Gabriel, Gabriel, Gabriel. There. Are you satisfied?"

He smiled. "Yes. I believe I am."

*Bynford was slightly larger than* Chesley, but it also boasted only one inn and tavern. Gabriel and Thea were greeted by the innkeeper, a middle-aged man of substantial girth who beamed as he invited them into his best private room.

"Will you be dining with us, sir? We have a very nice rack of lamb. Perhaps a cup of mulled wine to take away the chill?"

Gabriel agreed to both food and drink and added that he would like a word with the innkeeper, as well.

"Of course, sir. What may I do for you?"

"I hope you can provide me with some information. I am looking for someone who may have come through Bynford, perhaps even stayed here at your inn."

"Indeed? Well, I will be happy to help you if I can. When did this person pass this way?"

"Perhaps two days ago. I am not sure whether it was a man or woman or a couple, but they would have had a baby with them. The child has fair hair and blue eyes." Gabriel turned toward Thea.

"He's about six months old, and about this tall." She gestured with her hands. "A beautiful child."

The man's eyebrows sailed upward. "A babe, you say?"

"Yes." Thea took a step closer. "Have you seen him? Was he here?"

"No, ma'am. I am afraid there has been no wee one in this place since ... well, months."

"Oh." Thea sighed. "You looked—I thought you recognized the description."

"I'm sorry. I did. That is—what I mean to say is I have not seen a child like that, but I have heard that description. Just yesterday it was—a fellow was in here asking me about a woman and a little boy."

"Really? Are you certain it was the same child?"

He shrugged. "Since I never saw him, I can't be certain, but the man asked about a woman with a child of such an age who would have been here in the last few days. Terrible eager to find them, he was, but, like I told you, there hasn't been a baby staying here in a long time."

"Did the man mention any names?"

"No." The man thought for a moment, then shook his head and repeated, "No. I'm certain not."

"This man who was asking you. Did he say who he was?"

"No. He was closemouthed, that one. Not a friendly sort, either, I'll tell you."

"Did he say anything about the woman with the baby? What she looked like?"

"No. Truth is, I'm not sure he said that much about how the baby looked, just how old he was and that he was a boy. He said . . . I think he said the lad was blond, but that was all."

"What did he look like, this man who inquired after the woman and baby?" Gabriel asked.

The innkeeper tilted his head to one side, thinking, then said, "He wasn't very noticeable. Average, you might say. Not tall, not short."

"His hair?"

After much thought, the innkeeper decided that it was brown, though he had kept it covered most of the time with a cap. "Sorry, don't know the color of his eyes. I didn't notice. I didn't think that much about it until you came in asking for the same baby."

"How was he dressed?" Thea asked. "I mean, was he dressed like a gentleman?"

"Oh, no, he wasn't a gentleman. Didn't talk like one, neither. He looked—well, like a worker, I'd say. Not wearing livery, like a footman, say, but maybe like a gardener or a gamekeeper. A heavy jacket and a cap."

"You said he didn't talk like a gentleman. How did he talk?"

"Not like anybody around here." Once again the man thought for a moment. "I'd guess he was from the city."

"London?"

The innkeeper nodded. "I've only been there a few times, you understand, but that's how he sounded to me."

Gabriel nodded, then went on, "Have you seen a lady recently, even one without the child? She's about this tall." Gabriel gestured at his shoulder. "Her hair is dark blond, and her eyes are blue. She's very pretty. About twenty years old."

The man regretfully shook his head. "There's been no lady traveling alone, sir. There was one woman, but she had a companion with her, and both of them were up in years. A man and wife, a few men. A schoolboy and his tutor." He paused, thinking. "That's all I've seen, sir."

Gabriel asked him a few more questions about anyone in the area who might have a baby of the right age, but the man could think of no one except the solicitor and his wife, who had a brown-haired, brown-eyed child under a year of age. Gabriel thanked him, pulling out a gold coin to hand to him.

"If you see or hear anything else about this woman and child," Gabriel went on, "I would appreciate it if you could get word to me. I'm at the Priory, near Chesley."

"Of course, sir. I'd be happy to. I shall keep my ears open, you can count on that." The innkeeper bowed more deeply than Thea would have thought possible for a man of his size and left the room, pocketing the coin.

"What do you make of that?" Gabriel turned toward Thea.

"Someone else looking for Matthew's mother? I have no idea."

Thea frowned and sat down. "I suppose he could have been look-ing for someone else entirely, although that seems unlikely."

"It would stretch my belief in coincidence too far." Gabriel began to pace. "It could be the woman's husband or father, I sup-pose. She has run away, and he is searching for her."

"In that case, Matthew would have nothing to do with you or your sister."

Gabriel nodded. "But if so, why would the baby have had Joc-elyn's brooch with him?"

Thea agreed that it made little sense, but she could offer no other possible explanation for another man inquiring after a woman and child. She could come up with a few tales fit for the pages of a lurid novel—kidnappings and lost heirs and such, but all ended in the same impasse. Why would the baby have had Joc-elyn's brooch pinned to his underclothes?

They ate the hearty luncheon that the innkeeper brought to them, and the warm spiced wine did much to rid them of the chill from the winter drive. Afterward, they visited a few nearby shops, asking the owners the same questions they had posed to the inn-keeper. No one recalled any stranger with a baby, though the apothecary said that someone had been in the shop asking the same questions the day before. His description matched that of the innkeeper, even down to the man's not having been "from around here."

Their last stop was the haberdashery, where Gabriel bought a number of pieces of cloth, not only for diapering, but also for making more clothes for the baby. Thea knew a widow in Chesley who would be grateful for the money to sew up a few little gowns.

Thea had decided to crochet another blanket for Matthew, and so, while Gabriel was sidetracked by the haberdasher into a perusal of quality neckcloths, she looked at the shop's yarns. She wound up purchasing enough not only for a blanket but a little sweater, as well. Finally, she could not resist adding a few ribbons and a length of blond lace. It was foolish extravagance, she told herself, but even that knowledge could not dampen her pleasure over the purchase.

The return trip to Chesley was quieter. For some time Gabriel drove, his eyes intent on the road, without saying anything. Thea, watching him, did not wish to disturb his thoughts. It was, she found, surprisingly enjoyable to simply look at his profile. His black lashes were absurdly long, his chin and jaw strong. She could see the beginning of a shadow over his cheeks and jawline as the day wore on. She was aware of an urge to reach out and trace his straight black eyebrow with her forefinger or to slide her finger along his jaw. Just imagining it made her shiver. Thea looked away, tucking her hands under the lap robe.

"Cold?" Gabriel looked over at her and reached out with one hand to pull the traveling rug higher, tucking it in more firmly against her side.

Thea smiled at him, that same treacherous longing fluttering in her insides. "Thank you. I'm fine, really." She paused, then went on, "What are you going to do now?"

He shook his head. "I'm not sure. Frankly, I don't know what to do. Clearly, if Jocelyn is Matthew's mother, if she left him here, she does not want to be found."

"I'm sorry." Thea could hear the hurt in his voice. What must it feel like to know that one's sister, missing for over a year, had been so near and would not even contact him? "It very well may not be her."

"I know. But it is hard to think otherwise, with her brooch pinned to his clothes."

"The brooch could have been stolen. Or perhaps she sold it."

"But why attach it to a child and then place that child only minutes away from where I live? I cannot believe in such a coincidence. If he is not Jocelyn's child, I think it is very clear that someone wants me to believe he is. But why?"

"She might hope it would insure her child's future. If someone could make you believe the child belonged to Jocelyn, perhaps you would take the baby in. Even if you did not accept him as your nephew, you might very well provide him with the necessities of life, maybe even more—an education, a start on some sort of career when he is older. If I were starving and alone and I had that brooch, that would seem a much better use than selling it for a few coins."

Gabriel looked at her. "I did not think of that."

"You doubtless do not have people turning up at your door homeless and hungry, the way a man of the cloth does."

"No. I suppose not. But how did she get her hands on the brooch? And how would she know that much about Jocelyn?"

"I don't know. She would have to know something about you, as well—that you are at the Priory, for example. And that you are the sort of man who would care about such an obligation. There are many gentlemen who would not lift a finger to help such a baby." Thea hesitated, then asked somewhat hesitantly, "Do you think there is any possibility that what I suspected at first might have some truth in it?"

He glanced at her, his expression wry. "What? That Matthew is my by-blow?"

Thea felt her cheeks warm, but she nodded, staring back at him with her clear, straight gaze.

Gabriel made a small shrugging motion. "I cannot deny there is a possibility. As you were quite vociferous in pointing out, I have hardly lived the life of a saint, though I have tried to take care ... well." He stopped, casting another little glance at her, and cleared his throat. "At any rate, Matthew's coloring is very different from mine. My mother was dark; Jocelyn's was fair. That would not preclude his being my son, of course. But I would think that any woman I have, um, known, would come to me straightforwardly and ask for my help. I do not think that I seem a cold, uncaring brute, at least not to, ah, people who have been around me." Now it was he who looked embarrassed. "I think I am generally accounted a generous man."

Thea suspected that he was. Gabriel could be arrogant and annoying, and more than once, she had felt a most unchristian urge to hit the man. While it would be silly to pretend that he was anything but a virile man who enjoyed the company of women and the pleasure that it entailed, she had realized that he was not the selfish sort of hedonist she had first imagined him to be. She did not think he was the sort to take his pleasure without any thought to what happened to the woman who provided it. He could be kind, and she had no doubt that he could be generous.

So why then would a woman not ask him for help if she was carrying his child?

Thea sighed. "No. I think Matthew is not yours."

"I can see that it distresses you to give up that idea." The corner of his mouth twitched in amusement.

"Don't be absurd. It isn't as if I want you to be Matthew's father."

"No?"

"Of course not. It is just that it would explain someone bringing the baby here and putting the brooch with him. There is little reason for a complete stranger to do so."

"Which makes it difficult to believe that he was left by anyone but my sister."

Thea nodded. "I am sorry. I know it must be upsetting."

"To think that my own sister would not even come to me? Talk to me? Ask me for help?" He stared off into the distance, his jaw hard. "Bloody hell! I don't know what to think. I cannot understand why she would care so little, trust me so little. It makes me furious to think that she would stay away this long without even contacting me or her mother—that she would not write to let us know she was not dead. But at the same time, I am elated to think that Jocelyn might still be alive. I had almost given up hope. And then you showed up with that brooch in your hand ..."

Thea drew in a sharp breath. "You had assumed she was dead?"

He nodded. "I did not want to believe it. There was no reason to think so from her note. She just said that she could not marry Lord Rawdon, that she wanted to be happy. My first thought was that Rawdon had done something to upset her, that he had made her so unhappy she ran away. I thought she would turn up in a few days, contrite and tearful over the scandal she had caused. I tried to find her, of course, hoping I could get us out of the incident with as little scandal as possible, but I could not. It was as if she had vanished into thin air. I could not imagine where she went. I still cannot."

"What about her fiancé? Did he have no idea?"

"Him!" Gabriel's lip curled, and his face turned as hard as stone. "I could not see that he even cared that she had left. He went to his clubs and sat about drinking, doing all his usual things. I asked him how he could sit there so calmly, and he said, 'Am I supposed to gnash my teeth and wail because a girl decides to cry off?' That was when I hit him."

"Oh, dear."

Gabriel's grin held no humor, and his eyes had a feral glint as he admitted, "There was a bit of a mill. The club tossed us out. Ian said it was a near thing that there wasn't a challenge."

"A challenge? You mean to a duel?"

He nodded casually, as if duels were an ordinary part of one's day. "But Myles kept it from going forward. I haven't talked to Rawdon since."

"I am sorry. It must have all been very difficult for you."

His gaze was bleak as he said, "I lost my sister and at the same time I lost my best friend." He shrugged. "But how I felt wasn't really important. All I cared about was finding Jocelyn. But she had disappeared completely. She never wrote to tell us that she was all right or to explain why she had left. It is like living in limbo, not knowing whether someone is alive or dead, half the time angry with them for leaving you in ignorance, the other half grieving for them. The more time passed, the more I believed she must have passed on."

Thea's heart squeezed in sympathy. "And then I found Matthew."

He nodded. "Now I have hope. When I saw that brooch, for the first time in a long time I thought I would see Jocelyn again. I thought maybe she was waiting to see what I would do, that she feared I might reject her and the child. So I hoped that she would be nearby, that if I looked for her, I would find her. But now . . ." Gabriel sighed. "It seems clear she does not want me to find her. She was careful to stay at a distance, to bring the baby to Chesley only to leave him. Jocelyn—or whoever left Matthew—seems to be rather adept at keeping out of sight. I think I shall write to my businessman in London, get him to hire a runner to look into it. I am, frankly, a little at a loss here."

"What about Matthew?"

"There is scarcely anything I can do but provide for him, is there? If there is the slightest chance that he is Jocelyn's child, I cannot turn him away." Gabriel smiled faintly. "And he is rather engaging, isn't he?"

Thea thought of the baby's sunny smile, the silky texture of his curls, the way he fell asleep so trustingly in her arms, and her heart melted all over again. "Yes. He is very engaging."

"Perhaps our time would be better spent making a home for Matthew." He glanced at her. "I should not say *our,* should I? You may not wish to help me. I need to make the Priory inhabitable for an infant—hire a staff, get a housekeeper, reassure everyone that I am not operating a house of ill repute. And, well, whatever else needs to be done. I fear I am woefully ignorant. That is a good deal to ask of you, I know—"

"Don't worry about that," Thea assured him quickly. "I should be very glad to help you. Is there a nursery area in the Priory?"

He looked at her blankly. "I'm not sure. I don't remember seeing a room with a cradle. I haven't the slightest notion how to get a cradle, either."

"There might be something you could use in the attic, at least temporarily. Tom Bryson is a good woodworker; he could probably make you one."

"Perhaps you could go through the place with me, see what we have, where to put the bed, what we need to do to put everything in order for a baby."

Thea knew that she ought to refuse. It would not be proper for a single woman to call at the Priory with only single young men in residence. It had been bad enough to do so the other afternoon when she had impulsively stormed over to confront Gabriel. But to plan to go there, to do it with the full realization of what she was doing, was truly flouting convention. She must tell him no.

"I would be pleased to," Thea said.

# Nine

*The next morning Thea took* the baby and went to call at Damaris's house, where she persuaded her friend to accompany her on a visit to the Priory. While it would be a bit out of the ordinary for them to do so, the presence of a baby and a widow would provide enough mundane respectability to keep from spelling doom for Thea's reputation.

They drove to the Priory in Damaris's stylish enclosed carriage, which made the ride warm and pleasant despite the gloomy gray winter day, and Thea regaled Damaris with descriptions of the preparations for the living Nativity scene.

"We shall have our final rehearsal this evening, with costumes and all."

"And how is Amelia Cliffe?"

Thea closed her eyes as if in pain. "Hopefully she will suffer enough stage fright that she will not giggle. As long as she is still and silent, it will all go off smoothly enough. But it has been difficult to convince her that Mary should be gazing down at her child in wonder rather than staring all around to spy her family and friends. Poor Mr. Millwood is determinedly long-suffering."

"That seems apt enough for Joseph."

"Yes. And while Jem's collie may be somewhat unrealistic in the manger scene, Jem assures me that he is necessary to keep the sheep in their place. Fortunately the cow is quite placid and has no tendency to wander off."

Damaris laughed. "Is it worth it?"

"Oh, yes. When it is over, all the arguments and mistakes will be forgotten. Everyone will remember it as absolutely perfect. They missed it the years we did not have one. Father found them rather frivolous, but Daniel is quite happy to have one, and the parishioners enjoy it. It is, after all, a celebration; people should have fun."

"Of course they should. And you, I think, should qualify for sainthood for doing all the work to make it happen."

"I would not go that far. Thank goodness Mrs. Cliffe has a whole brood of girls, so we will have an undisputed Mary for a few more years. At least everyone acknowledges that the Squire's daughters should be first in line for that honor."

"I had not expected the Christmas season in Chesley to be so lively," Damaris said. "Did I tell you that I have decided to give a Twelfth Night party?"

"Really? A masque ball?" Thea looked at her friend with interest. Thea supposed it was telling that she enjoyed masques as much as she did, but something about donning the elegantly decorated masks was deliciously freeing, especially on Twelfth Night, when one could play a role.

Damaris nodded. "I know we are not a large society here, but don't you think it would be fun? I ordered a set of character cards from the stationer's last time I was in Cheltenham."

"Yes, indeed. I have never attended one with an actual stationer's set of cards, only homemade ones—you shall think us sadly provincial, I know."

"Don't be silly. I have made do many times with ones I lettered myself." Damaris smiled. "I plan to open up the doors between the drawing room and the music room to create enough space for dancing. I shall have cards in the library, which should satisfy Squire Cliffe and the Colonel."

"It sounds delightful."

They were soon at the Priory. The footman who answered the door was better trained than the one Thea had encountered when she came here before, and he took their coats and bonnets with quick efficiency before showing them to a sitting room that was much smaller and more comfortably furnished than the half-empty great hall Thea had visited last time. Still, she noted, many of the softer, more elegant touches that bespoke a woman's hand were missing.

Gabriel was seated at a table near the window, paper and ink in front of him, and he looked up when the footman announced the women. A smile began in his eyes, warming their dark depths, before it spread to his lips. He rose and started forward. "Miss Bainbridge. And Mrs. Howard. I am pleased to see you."

He bowed formally to the women, keeping his voice grave, but he found it difficult to maintain his formal demeanor when the baby let out a happy crow at seeing him and held out his hands. Gabriel laughed and took Matthew from Thea, lifting him up in the air.

"And how are you, young man?" He jiggled the boy above his

head, and Matthew erupted with gales of laughter. Gabriel lowered him, tucking him into the crook of his elbow.

Across the room Thea's cousin had stopped in his lazy tossing of the dice with another young man and was staring at Gabriel in astonishment, as was the man opposite him. A third man was seated on the other side of the table where Gabriel had been sitting, obviously in the midst of cleaning a gun, with rags and various implements lying beside a disassembled pistol on the table before him. Gabriel introduced his friends, and the other men bowed in polite greeting, but only Sir Myles came forward to look at the baby.

"I believe I have not been formerly introduced to this young man." He reached out a playful hand to the baby.

"This is Matthew," Gabriel told him.

"Matthew. An excellent name," Myles said as Matthew wrapped one of his pudgy little fists around Myles's finger. "I can see that you and I are going to be fast friends."

"Miss Bainbridge has kindly offered to help me get my household in order," Gabriel said, guiding the group back toward the sofas and chairs that centered the room. "Make it habitable for a baby."

"You mean, you're bringing him here?" Alan's voice rose, panic-stricken.

"Not just yet," Gabriel temporized. "We need to do some things first."

"What do you mean?" Alan glanced around vaguely.

"Add some rugs, I should imagine." Gabriel nodded toward the floor, where a rather faded Persian rug lay under the central seating group of furniture. "The great hall hasn't any, and there's not enough in here, either. Not very good for a baby to crawl on, especially when it's cold."

The talk turned to a discussion of such things as housekeepers and maids, the state of the rugs in the house, the presence or lack of a nursery, and the possibility of such items as toys, cradles, and child chairs in the attic. Alan's face grew more alarmed with each statement, and Ian kept shooting sidelong glances at Matthew, who was sitting in Gabriel's lap and leaning over to chew on the arm of the chair. The only one of the men who seemed at ease was Sir Myles, who divided his time between flirting with Damaris and entertaining the baby by dangling his watch on its chain.

Damaris offered Gabriel the services of her housekeeper in hiring a housekeeper and maids, then followed it with an invitation to all the men to attend her Twelfth Night ball. Gabriel and Sir Myles were quick to accept the invitation, though Thea thought that neither her cousin nor Mr. Carmichael seemed nearly as eager. She suspected that they were rather disgruntled at having their weeks of unfettered male activity infringed upon by the arrival of a baby ... not to mention two interfering females.

When Gabriel suggested that the two ladies might look about the place to give him ideas as to what should be done, Sir Myles was quick to offer to show Mrs. Howard about the kitchens and serving area downstairs, and when Matthew let out a wail of displeasure at seeing the shiny watch he had been reaching for suddenly removed from his sight, Myles good-humoredly scooped him up and took him along.

Gabriel smiled and turned to Thea. "Myles is obviously

charmed. I cannot decide if he is more taken with Mrs. Howard or the baby. Shall we go up and try to locate the nursery?" He turned toward the other men. "I assume you would prefer to stay here with your game?"

Alan nodded mutely, still looking faintly confused.

Ian frowned, saying, "The devil, Gabe! Surely you don't really mean to do this ..."

Gabriel stiffened almost imperceptibly. "I am not usually given to saying one thing and doing another."

"Of course not. I didn't mean that. It's just—I am not sure you've really thought this through." Ian glanced at Thea. "Cousin Althea, you must know some worthy group who takes in abandoned infants. A church society or such."

Before Thea could respond, Gabriel said, "We're talking about my blood here."

"You don't know that," Ian retorted. "You know nothing about the child. He doesn't even resemble you."

"I know who he looks like." Gabriel's voice was as brittle as glass now, and his face was as unyielding.

"Of course. Not my place, needless to say." Ian backed off quickly, giving a shrug and moving away from them.

Gabriel offered Thea his arm, and they left the room. His arm was like iron beneath her hand. She was not sure what to say, so she said nothing as they climbed the stairs. At the top of the staircase, they turned, and Gabriel glanced out the window toward the drive in front of the house. He stopped abruptly and strode over to the window.

"Bloody hell!"

"Gabriel?" Thea's heart turned cold at the expression on his face. His eyes were black and hard as stone, his face set in lines of fury. He looked, she thought, ready to kill. She took a step toward him. "What is it?"

He did not answer, merely whirled and ran back down the stairs. Thea hurried after him. They had gotten halfway down the stairs when there was a thunderous knock on the front door. The footman sprang to answer it, opening the door to reveal a tall man whose broad shoulders in the caped topcoat seemed to fill the entrance.

The man barged in, rudely shoving past the footman. He swept off his hat and thrust it at the astonished servant, saying peremptorily, "Where is she? I am not leaving until she speaks to me."

The visitor had a lean, angular face. His cheekbones were soaring and sharp, his nose narrow, with a small outward bump toward the top, as if it had been broken. His mouth, above the square, ungiving chin, was a straight line. The eyes beneath the ridge of his brow were a pale, startling blue, and the hair that fell around his face was a trifle longer and shaggier than was entirely fashionable, and of a blond shade so light it looked almost white in the light through the open door. He appeared sculpted from stone and removed from emotion, his pale, aristocratic face revealing no sign of what he felt.

"Rawdon!" Gabriel growled, and rushed down the remaining steps and across the entry, throwing himself at the man.

They slammed back into the opened door, which crashed into the wall under their weight. Thea winced at the loud crack that sounded as Rawdon's head hit the wood, but he was clearly not stunned for long, for he shoved back hard against Gabriel. They staggered, barely missing the astonished footman, who quickly shut the outer door before retreating to the farthest corner of the room.

The two men reeled around the entryway, knocking over a chair and bouncing into the walls as they grappled and punched. Gabriel landed a flush hit to the other man's jaw, and Rawdon fell back against a narrow table against the wall, knocking over a tall candlestick and sending it rolling off onto the floor. Gabriel pounced on him, but the other man slid to the side, quick and lithe as a cat, and brought up his hands to latch onto Gabriel's jacket and pull Gabriel with him as he fell to the floor.

"Stop!" Thea cried, appalled. She whirled toward Ian and Alan, who had come running from the sitting room at the crash and now stood, tankards in hand, watching the fight. "You have to stop them."

Alan cast her a derisive glance. "You must be mad! More than my life's worth to get between those two."

Thea stared at him. "You can't be serious! Cousin Ian?"

Lord Wofford gave a little shrug. "Carmichael's right. Might as well try to stop a runaway horse." He turned toward Alan. "I'll put a gold boy on Gabriel. Rawdon's gloves soften his hits."

"Done. Gabe's a bruiser, but I'd never take anyone in a mill over Rawdon. Man never gives in."

"You're *betting* on them?" Thea's own temper spiked, and she reached out and grabbed the large tankard from Ian's hand.

"What the—" Ian stared, astonished, as Thea marched across

to where the two men were rolling across the floor, punching and wrestling.

"Stop that this instant!" she ordered, and flung the contents of the tankard squarely into their faces.

They broke apart, spluttering and gasping. She had hit Gabriel more fully in the face, and he rolled away, his hands going to his eyes. Rawdon, who had caught the ale more on the side of his face and head, pushed back his wet hair and staggered to his feet, not even glancing toward her as he started toward Gabriel again.

Thea dropped the tankard and swooped up the tall candlestick that had fallen to the floor earlier. The fat candle atop it had broken and fallen off when it hit the floor, leaving the sharply pointed end naked. She stepped in front of Gabriel, lying on the floor, and faced his opponent, the long candlestick thrust out toward him threateningly.

"Stop right there!"

The blond man halted abruptly, staring at her. "Who the devil are you? Get out of my way."

"I am Althea Bainbridge, and I am not moving until the two of you stop behaving like wild animals."

He blinked at her, nonplussed. One side of his hair was wet and plastered to his skull, and the liquid had dripped down his neck and spotted his coat. A raw, reddish patch spread along his high cheekbone, and his lip was cut, a thin line of blood trickling down from it. And still he managed to look haughty and aristocratic.

Behind Thea, Gabriel rose to his feet, cursing. "Bloody hell! My eyes! What the devil did you throw on me?"

"Whatever was in Cousin Ian's tankard. Ale, I assume."

"Did you have to use something that stings?"

Rawdon's lip curled. "Oh, stop whining, Morecombe. No doubt she was merely trying to save you from your own wretched judgment." He flicked a cool glance toward Gabriel, then turned the full force of his ice-blue eyes back on Thea. With a stiff nod that managed to in no way lessen the arrogance of his demeanor, he said, "I apologize for disturbing your peace, ma'am."

Thea had no idea what to say in reply, but at that moment a voice sounded from the hallway behind them. "Hallo, Alec."

Lord Rawdon glanced past Thea and Gabriel to where Sir Myles now stood with Damaris, who was holding Matthew. Rawdon nodded. "Myles." His gaze slid over to Ian and Alan. "Wofford. Carmichael. Gathered for Christmas, I take it."

"I don't know why you are here, Rawdon, but I want you out of my house. Now." Gabriel came up beside Thea.

She lowered the candlestick to her side, but decided to keep it in hand as she stepped to the side, her gaze going from one man to the other.

"I am here to see Jocelyn," Rawdon said.

"And you came *here?*"

Rawdon's eyes blazed a fierce pale blue, like the center of a flame. "I intend to talk to her. I am not leaving here until I get some answers."

"Answers?" Gabriel's voice rose dangerously. "You think you can demand answers—that you can demand *anything* from my sister after what you did to her?"

"Holy hell! Are you still prating about that?" Rawdon said contemptuously.

"You bloody bastard!" Gabriel took a step closer to the other man, his fists clenching at his sides. "You dare to say that? As if what you did to her was nothing? You take my sister! You force her! You make her flee from her family and home in shame? And then you dare to come here and demand to see her? You're damned lucky I haven't put a bullet through that rock you have in place of a heart."

"*Force* her?" Rawdon went as taut as a bowstring, and he, too, stepped forward, his hands curling into fists. "You are accusing me of *raping* Jocelyn? You bloody, arrogant son of a bitch!"

Thea tensed, her heart pounding, certain she was watching murder forming on the two men's faces. She raised her candlestick with both hands and edged toward them. She had the uneasy feeling she would not be able to stop them even if she started swinging the candlestick.

Fortunately, quick footsteps came from behind her, and Myles snapped, "Alec, wait! Dash it, Gabriel, you don't know that. You don't even know for sure Rawdon's the father."

Gabriel ignored Myles, focusing only on the man before him. "Yes, I'm accusing you of raping my sister. There's the proof!" He swung around, his hand shooting out to point at the baby in Damaris's arms, gazing with wide, solemn blue eyes at the scene before him.

Rawdon followed the direction of Gabriel's finger. His eyes widened, and for an instant he looked like a man who had just taken a blow to the stomach. He walked past Gabriel, stopping a few feet from Damaris. Damaris did not step back, but she tightened her grip on the baby, keeping her eyes on the tall man's face. Almost as one, Myles, Gabriel, and Thea moved after Rawdon, coming up beside him. Thea looked from the baby to Rawdon and back again. The similarity in their coloring was undeniable. Could that fierce, almost gaunt visage have once looked like Matthew's sweet, rounded face?

"This is Jocelyn's child?" Rawdon's voice was soft, barely above a whisper. "Truly?"

"And yours," Gabriel replied flatly. "The resemblance is difficult to deny."

Rawdon turned his head to look straight at Gabriel. "And of course you would leap from that to the idea that I raped Jocelyn. Did Jocelyn say that?"

"She told me nothing, but it's not very hard to follow: Jocelyn fled our house rather than face the shame of bearing your baby. For a woman to choose that path instead of marrying the father of her child, she would have to despise the father."

Rawdon's blue gaze was glacial. His tone matched it as he said, "If the child is mine, then perhaps I should take him with me."

"No!" Thea gasped, and Gabriel stepped in between Matthew and Rawdon.

"You won't touch that child while I'm still breathing!"

"Really? I would be happy to change that state."

Matthew, who had been watching the scene unfold before him with wide eyes, started to cry at this last outburst of angry voices. His face screwed up, turning red, and tears gushed from his eyes as he let out a high-pitched wail. Even the two furious men flinched at the sound and turned to look at the boy.

"Now see what you've done!" Thea snapped, and went over to take Matthew. "I think it's time you leave, sir." She jiggled Matthew and patted his back, murmuring in a soothing voice.

"The hell I will! I intend to find out—"

Matthew ratcheted up his screams a notch, and Thea swung around to face Rawdon, her face fierce. "You are upsetting the baby!"

At that moment, with a loud clearing of a throat, a woman's voice called across the room, "Excuse me, please!"

Everyone turned to look at the front door. A small woman in a fashionable bonnet and velvet pelisse stood framed in the open doorway. Her hands were encased in a huge sable muff that matched the trim at the neck and cuffs of her coat. She stepped inside, followed by a maid carrying a small case.

"Oh, sweet Christ!" Thea heard Gabriel murmur under his breath.

"Emily," Ian said weakly.

"I apologize for just walking in, but no one answered my knock." She glanced around, her eyes widening as they went from Gabriel to Rawdon and then to the baby in Thea's arms. "I, um, am sorry to interrupt."

For a moment, no one spoke. Then Gabriel broke the motionless tableau and stepped forward, saying, "Lady Wofford. Please accept my apologies. Come in." He made a sharp motion at the footman, still hovering in the far corner of the room, and the man hurried forward to shut the door behind the two visitors, then came up to take Lady Wofford's pelisse and bonnet.

Without her coat and bonnet and the enormous muff, Lady Wofford looked even smaller—the sort of woman often deemed *dainty* and the kind who never failed to make Thea feel as if she were looming over her. She was pretty, with eyes of a faded blue and light brown hair, but her much ruffled and beribboned dress and the complicated rolls and curls in which she had styled her hair rather overwhelmed her, making her seem, perversely, less attractive than she was. A tiny frown marred her brow as she surveyed the group before her. Her gaze stopped on Thea and Damaris, and the small frown deepened.

Thea realized with a blush how odd they must all look to Ian's wife. Gabriel and Rawdon shouting at each other, each of them still wet about the head and shoulders. Her own husband and their friends standing about watching this scene ... and, worst of all, two women she did not know, one holding a screaming child, here alone with the men. Thea had little doubt what the other woman would assume about her and Damaris.

"No, please, Lord Morecombe," Lady Wofford went on with a stiff smile. "It is I who should apologize to you. I know that a wife is scarcely a welcome guest at a man's hunting lodge." Her gaze swept down Thea. "Obviously you are engaged in the sort of male pursuits from which ladies are better excluded."

Thea's color deepened as a swift rush of anger replaced her embarrassment.

"Not really a hunting lodge, my lady," Myles said, smiling. "Just Morecombe's second house."

"And you are always welcome here," Gabriel added, though

his wooden voice detracted somewhat from the impact of his words.

"Emily, my dear." Ian moved forward finally. "Of course you are not excluded. Please, allow me to introduce you to our guests. You remember my cousin Miss Althea Bainbridge, don't you?" He put a faint emphasis on Thea's last name, the same as his own. "And her friend, Mrs. Howard. Cousin Althea and her brother live here in Chesley, you know. He is the local vicar."

"Ah. I see." Lady Wofford's brow cleared a little, and she gave a carefully measured smile to Thea. "No doubt things are done differently in the country."

Thea returned the same sort of smile to Lady Wofford and made a brief curtsy. "Yes, I am told that Chesley is a pleasant relief after being in the city."

"Lord Rawdon." Lady Wofford's faint nod served as nothing more than an acknowledgment of the man's presence.

"Lady Wofford." He nodded to her, and Thea could not decide which of the two looked haughtier and less giving. Rawdon turned toward Gabriel. "I'm not done here, Morecombe."

"Alec . . ." Myles made a casual move that placed him between the two men. "Lady Jocelyn is not here, I swear to you."

"Jocelyn?" Lady Wofford's eyes widened. "Jocelyn is here?"

"No, my dear, of course not. That is just what we were discussing."

"But—" Ian's wife glanced back at Lord Rawdon. "My goodness," she finished awkwardly.

Lord Rawdon shifted as if to step around Myles, and Damaris came forward, hooking her hand in the crook of his arm and more or less compelling him to turn with her toward the door unless he wished to be blatantly rude. She strolled toward the front door as she talked. "Why don't I show you the way to the village? I was just about to go there myself. There's a quite passable inn in Chesley, unless, of course, you mean to travel on this afternoon."

"I don't plan to travel anywhere else, believe me." Rawdon let Damaris propel him along, but he stopped now and turned back to look at Gabriel. "We are not finished here." He gave a general nod in their direction and swung around to open the front door. Damaris started to follow him, but he stopped her with a single chilled glance. "I am quite capable of finding the inn on my own, I assure you."

Grabbing his hat from the hovering footman, he strode out the door. Damaris stood for a moment, staring after him, before she turned and rejoined Thea. "Well, I don't understand what that was all about, but he is certainly a rude man."

Thea nodded. Matthew's cries had subsided into little shuddery breaths. He rubbed his damp face against Thea's shoulder, then released a sigh and laid his head down. Something about the gesture made Thea's throat close up with emotion, and when she glanced over at Damaris, she saw her friend watching Matthew with a faint smile, tears glinting in her eyes.

Damaris blinked and her smile widened to include Thea. "They are so sweet when they're like that, aren't they?"

Thea nodded. Once again the thought flashed into her head, as it had several times the last couple of days: what would she do when Gabriel decided to take Matthew? At some point he and his entourage, now including this baby, would leave Chesley to return to London. As Thea had every other time the thought had occurred to her, she pushed it firmly away.

"I cannot think what Lord Rawdon was doing here, and just before Christmas, too," Lady Wofford said. "Why did he think Lady Jocelyn was here? Have you heard from her, Lord Morecombe?"

Gabriel, who had been glowering at the door through which Lord Rawdon had left, forced a smile onto his face. "No, my lady, I have had no word from my sister. Nor do I know why Lord Rawdon chose to come to the Priory. Clearly, for some reason he believed Jocelyn to be here."

"I see." Lady Wofford's tone indicated that she did not, in fact, see at all, but she did not pursue the matter. Her gaze flickered curiously to Thea and the baby now nestled against her shoulder. "Well, no doubt you are surprised to find me on your doorstep. I do apologize." She smiled at Gabriel before turning toward her husband. "Your father is most upset that you have not joined us at Fenstone Park, my dear, so I told him I would come try to change your mind. Of course, I know that the last thing gentlemen wish when they gather at a lodge is a wife's presence." She made a droll moue as she said the words. "But since you say that this isn't a hunting lodge, I hope you will not turn me away."

"Of course you are welcome here," Gabriel told her. "If you cannot persuade Ian to join his relatives for Christmas, you must stay with us and celebrate the day here. We shall be all the merrier for having a woman's touch at the feast."

"You are always such a perfect gentleman." Lady Wofford smiled.

Ian wrapped his hand around his wife's arm. "Why don't I show you up to my room, Emily. You must be tired after your journey today."

"I did not travel it in one day—you know me, I am such a poor traveler, I'm afraid. But I am a little tired, I will admit."

She let Ian whisk her away up the stairs, motioning to the maid to follow. The others watched them until they disappeared. Alan swung around and let out a heavy sigh. "Well, that sets the cat among the pigeons, doesn't it?"

"Yes, I would say our carefree bachelor days are gone," Myles agreed, though his smile showed little concern over the matter. "There is always the tavern in town."

Alan grimaced and swung around, heading into the great hall. "I am going to enjoy a glass of port and a cigar while I still can. Anyone else?"

Gabriel shook his head. "As soon as I clean up a bit"—he threw a wry glance in Thea's direction—"I plan to look at the nursery. Ladies? Would you care to join me?"

"I would love to," Thea replied. "But Matthew has fallen asleep." She smoothed a hand over the sleeping baby's back.

"Here, leave him with me," Myles offered. "I'll watch over him down here." He cast a smile at Damaris. "Perhaps Mrs. Howard will stay to help. After all, I shall doubtless need a woman's expertise if he should wake up and start crying again."

Damaris chuckled, shaking her head at him. "Don't think you can gull me, Sir Myles. It is quite apparent that you are more knowledgeable about babies than any of us. But I shall be happy to help you watch over him."

While Gabriel went off to wash away the residue of the ale Thea had flung at him, the others made a makeshift bed for the baby in the sitting room by positioning two cushioned armchairs together, and Thea laid Matthew down upon it. Gabriel appeared a few minutes later in a clean shirt and neckcloth, his hair still damp from his hasty face-washing.

"Couldn't you have just tossed some water in my face?" he teased Thea as they made their way up the stairs. "Did it have to be ale? It's so sticky."

"It was the closest thing at hand," she retorted. "Better than bashing you with something."

"I'll never forget looking up and seeing you there, facing down Rawdon with that candlestick." Gabriel let out a laugh. "You are a woman of great worth. Next time I face a duel, I shall bring you as my second."

Thea rolled her eyes. "Thank you, but I believe I'll decline the honor."

They turned left at the top of the stairs and walked along the hallway to where a double set of closed doors led off to the right. "I have never been in this wing of the house," Gabriel admitted as he opened one of the doors. "But since there is no nursery in the main portion of the house, I assume it must be here—if, of course, there is a nursery at all."

They walked along the corridor, which was narrower than the one they had just left, opening doors on either side and peering into the rooms. Several of the rooms were empty, though one or two contained some minimal furniture. Clearly, this section of the house had not been used in some time.

"Why do you think Lord Rawdon came here?" Thea asked. "Why did he think your sister was here? He seemed very intent on speaking to her."

"I know. I can't help but think he had some reason to think so. Of course, clearly she did come to Chesley if she is the one who left Matthew in the church. But how did he know?"

"He did not seem to know about Matthew," Thea pointed out. "He looked quite astonished when you pointed out the baby."

"True." Gabriel nodded, frowning. "I wish now I had asked him a few things before I hit him. But at the time it just made me so bloody furious to see him standing there, demanding to see Jocelyn, after everything he'd done."

He pushed open a door to reveal another room. This one had a low set of shelves along one wall, as well as a short table with four small chairs. Doors on either side of the room led into three smaller rooms, all empty.

"Ah, I think we've found it." Gabriel wandered around, peeking into the other small rooms. He picked up one of the books from a shelf and glanced through it before replacing it.

"Yes, it looks like a nursery."

"Rather far from the rest of the rooms," Gabriel commented.

"Mm. That's rather the point, isn't it? So the adults aren't awakened by nighttime crying, and the children are not kept up by the adults staying awake hours later."

"I suppose so. Of course, the nursemaid is here to see to them.

Still…" Again he frowned, leaning back against the low bookcase, his legs stretched out, bracing him against the floor.

Thea smiled and nodded. "I know. It seems to me that one would worry with the baby being so far away. I have kept Matthew's basket beside my bed. I am afraid he will cry and I won't hear him."

"Perhaps I should have him in a room in the same wing." He paused. "But you're right—we might wake him up late at night. Babies turn everything upside down, don't they?"

"Yes, I suppose they do."

Gabriel was silent for a long moment, staring out at the floor in front of them. Finally he said, "We were very good friends, you know."

Thea glanced over at him, surprised at the sudden switch in topic. "You and Lord Rawdon?"

He nodded, crossing his arms in front of him. "I met him at Eton. He was … not well liked."

"I'm shocked," Thea said drily.

Gabriel smiled faintly. "His family has a reputation."

"What sort of reputation?"

He shrugged. "They're very proud, even arrogant. One of those old Northern families that were accustomed to ruling their lands almost absolutely. They came over with William the Conqueror, but it's said that even farther back there's ancient Norse blood in them. Rawdon's father is a harsh old bas—um, man. And they say his grandfather was even worse."

"They don't sound pleasant."

"No. That's why others tended to stay away from him."

"But not you?"

Gabriel shrugged. "I got into a mill one afternoon. There were three of them and one of me, and Rawdon came to my aid." Gabriel grinned faintly, thinking of it. "He throws a sweet right hook. Can't say we beat them exactly, but in the end they were the ones who ran."

"So you became friends."

"It was the first time I had really talked to him. And, well, we just got along, it seemed. I introduced him to the others. Ian and Myles and Alan and I had been friends since we were lads. There was another, Gerald Lacey, but he's married now so we don't see so much of him."

"Marriage doesn't seem to stop my cousin from joining you."

"No. Ian is not, um, uxorious."

"Mm."

"Rawdon was my friend for fifteen years. It has been odd the last year. Have you ever felt like that? Remembering all the years you were close as kin to someone, maybe closer, yet despising them now."

"I'm sorry." Thea stepped closer to him, reaching out her hand impulsively and taking his. She covered it with her other hand, holding it warmly between hers as she looked up into his eyes. "I have not ever felt it. I can only imagine how awful it must be."

The smile warmed Gabriel's dark eyes before it touched his lips. "Whenever I am certain that I know you, you surprise me yet again."

"I surprise you because I express sympathy for you?" Thea asked teasingly. "Am I such a shrew the rest of the time?"

"Not a shrew. I'd say . . . a warrior, perhaps. A Boadicea, wielding your candlestick as you guard your fallen and less capable soldier."

Thea could not help but laugh at his description. "Boadicea? Now I fear that you must have suffered a blow to the head when you and Lord Rawdon fought. I hardly think I qualify as a warrior queen."

"Oh, but you do. You are all strength—rescuing abandoned children, facing down the wicked, saving those of us who have strayed from the path."

He smiled at her, and Thea could not look away from his well-formed mouth. His upper lip was sharply defined, the bottom one fuller and softer. She remembered well the way they had felt upon her own lips, soft and almost velvety, yet firm as they sank into her. She was aware of how much she would like to feel his mouth on hers again, and unconsciously her lips parted a little.

Something flared in his eyes, and he straightened. He raised her hand to his mouth and pressed his lips against her skin. Thea's heart fluttered, and she feared that he must see the sudden frantic beating of her pulse in her throat. He turned her hand over and laid another kiss in her palm. A tremor ran through her. She had never known the warmth that flooded her now, that swept over her whenever he touched her or looked at her in that dark, languorous way. She wanted him to kiss her, to put his hands on her as he had the other day.

And as if he knew her very thoughts, he slid his arms around her, settling her into his body, and bent to take her mouth with his.

# Ten

As it did whenever Gabriel kissed her, the world seemed to spin away from Thea, leaving her breathless and clinging to him. The taste of his mouth was darkly intoxicating, at once sweet and heady. The yeasty odor of ale still clung to him, mingling in her nostrils with the warm scent of his body and the spicy hint of cologne. Her hands slipped up and over his shoulders. Thea was amazed at her own boldness. She had daydreamed many times over the past few days about how Gabriel's hair would feel upon her skin, and she indulged her curiosity now, sinking her hands into the thick, silky mass. The strands twined and curled around her fingers.

His breath shuddered against her cheek as he lifted his head to change the angle of their kiss. He swept his hands down to cup her buttocks, pressing her up into him, and she felt the swift surge of his passion against her body. His skin was suddenly flaming as he turned her, and moving back blindly, she came up against the low bookcase. He lifted her onto the bookcase, stepping in between her legs so that his body was flush against her, only their clothes separating them.

Thea would not have thought the fire in her veins could have flared any hotter, but it did so now, flashing through her and centering in the ache between her legs. She wanted to squeeze her legs together against the sudden, insistent hunger, but she could not because Gabriel stood between them. Instinctively she wrapped her legs around him, seeking ease. He jerked, making a noise low in his throat, and ground his body into hers. His mouth consumed hers, drinking her in even as it filled her. He moved his hands up her sides, cupping her breasts in his long, supple fingers. Thea shivered, startled by the intimate touch and equally surprised by her reaction.

Her breasts were full and aching, the nipples suddenly hard. His thumbs brushed over them, lightly abrading them with the soft cloth of her dress. He continued to play with her nipples through the fabric, gently pulling and rubbing, and with each movement, the ache inside Thea grew stronger and more demanding. Even as she thrilled to the sensations Gabriel was creating in her, she wanted something more.

He slipped his hands over her breasts and delved down inside, pushing aside the modest fichu and dragging down the neckline of her dress and chemise beneath. She could feel the cool air on her breasts as they were exposed, and the hard central buds tightened even more. Gabriel pulled his mouth from hers. His eyes were blazing, his face flushed and heavy with desire as he gazed down at her breasts in his hands.

"Beautiful. You are so beautiful."

He bent and brushed his lips over the trembling soft top of one breast, and Thea let out a choked sound of pleasure. She could feel his lips curve in a smile against her skin, and then, amazing her yet again, he traced the tip of his tongue in lazy circles across the sensitive flesh. Thea jerked and squeezed her legs more tightly around him. With a soft groan, Gabriel took her nipple into his mouth and began to suckle.

Thea leaned her head back against the wall, lost in the pleasurable sensations running through her. One of his hands slid down her body, skimming over her side and waist and down onto her legs. His fingers slipped beneath her dress and petticoats, inching upward over her leg. His touch seared her even through the cloth of her pantalets as his hand moved from the outside of her leg over her knee and onto the soft line of her inner thigh. He lifted his mouth from her breast, ending the bone-melting things he was doing to her there, and buried his face in the crook of her neck. His breath sounded in her ear, harsh and rasping, as he softly kissed the sensitive flesh of her neck, teasing her with lips and teeth and tongue.

His fingers meanwhile crept ever closer to the hot, moist center of her passion. She could not move away, for she was pressed too tightly against the unyielding wall, but Thea knew that she had no desire to move, anyway. If she shifted her body, it would be simply because it was becoming harder and harder to keep still under the exploration of his hand.

Then his thumb was on her, pressing through the damp cloth of her undergarments and touching the swollen, aching point in which all the sensations besieging her seemed to gather. She gasped. It was outrageous . . . wicked . . . appalling . . . and unbelievably pleasurable. Thea could not hold back a whimper as she moved beneath his caress, squirming and lifting. She dug her fingers into his shoulders, embarrassed at the way moisture flooded her, knowing he must feel it and sure that this must prove her overriding wantonness, yet reveling in the pleasure, too, and aching to feel even more.

Gabriel obliged her, stroking his thumb against her, light as a feather. She could not hold back the noises that rose from her throat, soft moans that seemed to be pulled from her. Her head rolled against the wall as her hips began to move in time with the rhythm of his stroking thumb. Thea heard his own harsh breaths, felt the heat and tension that permeated his body, and she knew she was not alone in this maelstrom of passion.

Something coiled and twisted inside her, building and building until it was as if she were running, straining to reach it even though she had no idea what it was. Amazingly, pleasure exploded deep in her abdomen, and she cried out, clapping her hand over her mouth to still the sound. But nothing could stop the heat that rushed through her, the pleasure that pounded in waves to the outermost reaches of her body.

He braced his arms on either side of her against the wall, struggling to control his breath, his body taut as a bowstring. "Thea . . ." Her name escaped his lips—she wasn't sure whether as a prayer or a curse.

Thea sagged limply against the wall, floating in the warm, buoyant sea of pleasure. She was not sure if she would be able to stand, or even move at all. Her legs were like jelly. But at the moment, she could not bring herself to care.

Gabriel moved away from her, and she felt the loss of his heat and bulk. She roused herself as best she could, opening her eyes and saying, "Gabriel? Are you—am I—" She realized that she had no idea what to say.

He was at the window, turned away from her and staring out, one arm raised to lean against the wall. He shook his head. "Just give me a moment. I must think, for just a bit, of—well, of anything but you."

It occurred to her, horrifyingly, that he was angry with her, displeased, that this flood of passion that had stormed through her had not touched him at all. Even worse, what if he had been disgusted by the exhibition of her base desires? Thea sucked in her breath, her hand flying to her mouth and tears starting in her eyes. She slipped off her perch and found that she could stand, after all, though her knees seemed amazingly weak. She shook her dress and petticoats down, smoothing and tucking and rearranging until everything was once again in modest order . . . though she rather doubted that inside her anything would ever be in order again. She did not understand how she could feel so wonderfully good and at the same time so scared and embarrassed. Her body had become a stranger to her, a delightful, perplexing, maddening stranger.

"I'm sorry," she said, her voice barely a whisper. "I should go."

He whirled to face her. "No! I mean, yes, perhaps you should go. But don't be sorry." His voice was low, but sharp and hard. He came over to grasp her arms and leaned his forehead against hers, closing his eyes. "There is nothing to feel sorry about. You are . . . a delight." He kissed her forehead softly, carefully, then released her and moved away again. "But right now it is very hard for me to remember that I am a gentleman. Or, at least, pretending that I am one."

"Oh." She paused. "Perhaps I should go look at the rest of the wing."

He smiled faintly. "That would be an excellent idea."

Thea walked into the corridor outside the nursery and strolled aimlessly along it, glancing into the rooms. Her thoughts skittered about like fireflies, unwilling to stop or coalesce into anything coherent. She wished she had a mirror and wondered if she looked as flushed and hazy as she felt. She glanced down at her dress again and straightened the row of decorative buttons down the center of the short bodice. What was the state of her hair?

She stood for a moment, gazing out the long window at the end of the hallway without really seeing anything. At the sound of a heel scraping on the floor, she turned and saw that Gabriel was walking toward her. His face was still a trifle flushed, but aside from that and a softness to his mouth, he looked much as he always did. She could only hope that she did, as well, but she rather suspected that her face revealed much more than his. Of course, he was more experienced at this sort of thing.

Thea was surprised at the flash of jealousy that stabbed her when she considered Gabriel's previous dalliances. It was really none of her business; the man's previous life had nothing to do with her. But she could not help but feel a burning resentment at the thought of him sneaking into and out of other rooms in other houses with beautiful, sophisticated women on his arm.

Why, she thought, her heart squeezing in her chest, was he dallying with her? He could have almost any woman in the kingdom; it was absurd that he would be interested in a plain spinster in a little village. The answer, of course, was simply that she happened to be there. Chesley offered few women to choose from—only Damaris would qualify as a sophisticated beauty of the sort Morecombe was accustomed to. Damaris, she knew, must appeal to him more, but he scarcely knew her. It was Thea with whom he had been thrown together.

That was the only reason. Proximity. Convenience. He was a virile male who enjoyed women, and if no suitable lady was around, Gabriel would dally with one less suitable . . . in short, herself. To think anything else would be vain and foolish. Thea prided herself on being neither of those things.

So she pushed aside the spurt of jealousy and, fixing a pleasant smile on her face, went forward to meet him. As soon as he offered her his arm and she slipped her hand into the crook of his elbow, she felt the same tingling tendril of heat she experienced whenever she touched him, and it was difficult to keep at bay the memories of what had happened between them only minutes before.

As luck would have it, as they stepped back through the door into the main bedroom wing of the house, they met Ian and his wife walking out of their room. Emily's eyes widened as she looked at Gabriel and Thea, and Thea felt a telltale blush spreading up her throat into her face. It was inappropriate, even shocking, she knew, for a female visitor to be roaming about upstairs alone with a man. That she had just been engaged in precisely the sort of activity that such social restrictions were designed to thwart only increased Thea's feeling of awkwardness.

"Gabriel." Ian nodded at Morecombe, his gaze sliding curiously over to Thea. "Cousin Althea."

"Miss Bainbridge and I have been searching for the nursery. It seems there is one, to my surprise."

"Nursery?" Emily repeated blankly. "Oh—for the, ah, child downstairs?" Courtesy obviously kept her from inquiring any further, but Thea could see the questions forming in the other woman's eyes.

"I see." The curiosity was missing from Ian's eyes, but his neutral voice held no approval. "Well, then ..."

"I am sorry," Thea said with a brittle smile. "But I am afraid I must be going now. Mrs. Howard and I have tarried far too long. It was nice meeting you, Lady Wofford. Thank you for showing me the nursery, Lord Morecombe." She gave them a brisk general nod and started toward the stairs.

"Pray, allow me to see you out." Gabriel caught up with Thea before she reached the staircase, and they walked together down the steps, though Thea was careful not to take his arm again or even look at him.

She managed not to look directly into his face until he was handing her up into the carriage after Damaris, but when she did look up then into his dark, fathomless eyes, her heart did a lazy roll within her chest and she involuntarily clutched his hand harder. The feelings she had successfully been repressing for the past few minutes rushed back in on her, and she was once again breathless and warm, her entire being so aware of him that she could scarcely focus on anything else.

Thea found herself stammering her good-byes, and she

eagerly took the wriggling Matthew, whom Sir Myles handed up to her, and bent her head to fuss over him, to avoid meeting Gabriel's eyes again. The baby was not happy, for it was past his feeding time, but Thea was frankly grateful for his whining and restlessness, as it afforded little chance for conversation all the way back to Damaris's house. Thea suspected that her friend's sharp eyes had missed nothing, but Damaris made no comment and asked no questions.

When they reached town, Damaris directed her coachman to drive Thea and the baby home first, though it was out of the way, so Thea could get Matthew inside to eat before his cranky fussing turned into full-scale wails. Thea handed the baby over to Lolly to feed, then hurried into the entry to remove her bonnet and cloak.

Daniel popped his head out of his study down the hall. "Thea! There you are." He came toward her, frowning. "Where have you been? Was that Mrs. Howard's carriage?"

"Yes. I told you I was going to call on her this morning."

"I did not expect you to be gone all day," her brother retorted rather plaintively. "Mrs. Stedman was here about the Ladies' Guild tea in January, and I hadn't the faintest idea what she was talking about."

"I'm sorry. I didn't realize she was dropping by today."

"Yes, well, I would have had Mrs. Brewster tell her I was not here, but unfortunately, I was walking down the stairs when she came in, and she saw me." He shook his head at the thought of his bad luck.

Thea smiled. "I will call on her and find out what she wanted."

But her brother was not through with his litany of grievance.

"Then Mrs. Cliffe dropped by just as Mrs. Stedman was leaving, so I could not help but talk to her, as well. She was all up in the boughs over something about this Nativity scene, and I had the devil's own time trying to calm her down. She kept asking me questions, and when I told her that you had gone to call on Mrs. Howard, she told me she had just been at Mrs. Howard's and Mrs. Howard was not there. I think she believed I was fibbing her."

"That *is* too bad," Thea commiserated. "Mrs. Howard and I went to pay a call on Cousin Ian and Lord Morecombe at the Priory."

"Cousin Ian? Mercy sakes, why did you go to see him? Really, Thea, I don't think it's a good idea for you to spend so much time with Lord Morecombe. It doesn't look good, a single woman like yourself jaunting all over the countryside with a known rake like Morecombe. A woman's reputation is a precious thing; it is easily damaged and almost impossible to repair once it is ruined."

"It is hardly like you to sound so . . . so pious. I am scarcely jaunting about the countryside. I have simply helped Gabriel look for Matthew's mother."

"Matthew? Who is Matthew?" Daniel asked crossly.

"The baby who was left in the church. Daniel, really . . ."

Her brother scowled. "That baby. That's another thing. I don't understand why you are fussing over that child. The foundling home is the place for him, not the vicarage. It's bad enough that you are spending time with Lord Morecombe—and, really, Thea, you should not call him by his given name, you know; it simply does not look right—but the fact that the two of you are carrying this baby about only makes it that much worse. People have begun to talk. I have already heard the whispers—why is Morecombe always hanging about here and where did the baby come from? There have been hints that perhaps the baby itself is the connection between the two of you." He looked at her significantly.

"Of course it's the connection between us," Thea began reasonably, then stopped, staring, as she caught the implication of his words. "Wait a moment. Do you mean—are you saying that people are implying that Matthew is mine?" Her voice slid upward as it grew in volume. "That I am his mother and Lord Morecombe is his father?"

"It's ridiculous, of course, and it's only just whispers and sideways glances now. But you must realize how such things grow and become rumors, and then before long everyone is talking about it."

"But it's absolutely absurd! How could it even be possible? Lord Morecombe only arrived in Chesley a few weeks ago! I had not even met him before the Squire's party! And exactly how could I have carried this baby for nine months, then delivered it six months ago, all without anyone in the village knowing about it? Or even suspecting anything? How could I possibly have kept such a thing secret for the past year? When would I have carried on some mad affair with a London nobleman? I mean, really, I ask you, when would I have delivered a baby in secret? I never go anywhere. I have never lived anywhere but this village. When have I ever done anything but take care of all the little problems of St. Margaret's and its parishioners? Everyone in Chesley knows everything there is to know about me. They have seen and remarked on each detail of my life down to what shoes I wore to church last Sunday and to whom I nodded on the street yesterday. I have no secrets! In short, I have no *life!*"

"Thea!" Daniel hissed, casting a pained glance in the direction of the kitchen. "Have a care! Keep your voice down. Everyone in the house can hear you. Mrs. Brewster is the soul of discretion, of course, but that nursemaid is bound to gossip."

"What does it matter?" Thea shot back. "According to you, everyone in the village already thinks I'm a doxy! Why should I care if they decide I'm a shrew as well?"

With that parting shot, Thea whirled and stomped up the stairs, leaving her brother staring after her in slack-jawed amazement.

The afternoon turned grayer and the clouds more lowering as the day wore on, and the main topic of conversation at the Nativity rehearsal that night was the possibility of snow for Christmas. The rehearsal consisted of little except putting on their costumes and being placed in the positions in which they would stand on Christmas Eve, for there was no dialogue, but it seemed to take an inordinately long time and a great deal of conversation. Thea was greatly relieved when the whole thing was over and she was able to go home to the vicarage and sit down with a nice cup of hot tea in the kitchen. Mrs. Brewster had already left, but the kitchen was still warm and spicy with the aromas of her holiday baking. The next day was Christmas Eve, and Mrs. Brewster would be baking and cooking more or less without pause.

The house was quiet. Matthew was sleeping in Lolly's room

tonight since Thea had been out for much of the evening, and the two of them were already upstairs fast asleep. Daniel was, of course, in his study reading. Thea thought about going in to talk to him, but she was still feeling a trifle ruffled from their less-than-amicable discussion this afternoon. Instead, she finished her cup of tea, thinking idly about the list of things she had to do the following day. Christmas Eve was always busy at the vicarage, what with the arrival of the Yule log and the poor of the parish coming to the door for gifts of food, not to mention making the plum pudding and other dishes for the feast the next day.

When Thea went upstairs to her room later, she could not resist walking quietly down to the small room at the end of the hall and peeking inside. Lolly was asleep in the narrow bed, the covers pulled up to her ears. The baby's basket lay between her and the door, and Thea tiptoed the few steps to the basket to peer down at the baby sleeping inside. The sight of him tugged at Thea's heart as only sleeping babies can, and she stood for a long moment, simply looking at him.

Finally she turned and slipped back down the hall to her bedroom. She undid the ties of her dress in back and pulled it off, then untied the ribbon of her chemise and removed it as well. As the material slid across her bare breasts, she could not help but remember this afternoon and the way Gabriel had touched her breasts, his fingers expert and sure. Her nipples grew taut just at the memory. Thea curved her hand over one of her breasts as he had done, and she wondered how it had felt to him. Had he found her small and unsatisfying, or had the weight of her breast in his palm sparked desire in him as it had in her?

Thea turned to the mirror and studied her naked chest. She wondered how her body would appear to Gabriel, and she feared that he would find her narrow and unwomanly. She felt a little guilty to be gazing at herself naked. No doubt it was a sin. But she did not turn away. Instead, she untied her petticoat and pantalets and slid them down so that she stood fully nude. She stared at her long, slender legs and the swell of her hips, the flat plain of her abdomen. Her curves were womanly though not lush. If Gabriel saw her this way, would he think her desirable or would he find her lacking?

A shiver ran through her at the thought of Gabriel looking at her naked, and her nipples tightened perkily. She thought of his dark eyes gliding slowly down her body, aglow with passion as they had been when he kissed her today. Thea closed her eyes as she raised her hands and let them drift down, smoothing over her breasts, her fingers circling her nipples and feeling them tighten into hard little buttons in response. There was pleasure there, but not the same as it had been when Gabriel touched them. She moved downward, sliding over the bony outcroppings of her ribs and onto her waist and stomach, her fingers slipping ever nearer to that magical center that Gabriel had found and ignited into passion. She stopped as her fingers touched the springing curls there, and she pulled her hand away quickly.

Whatever was she doing? Thea whirled away from the mirror and picked up her nightgown, pulling it over her head and thrusting her arms into the long sleeves. She buttoned it up to the very top, then pulled her dressing gown on top of it as if she were donning armor. However, the clothes did not stop the persistent little ache that had started between her legs. She was shamefully aware that the only thing that would ease it was the touch of Gabriel's fingers there again. Thea blushed at the thought and began to take down her hair. She brushed it out, feeling it crackle and curl around the brush, wild as it always was in the winter.

Normally she would have plaited her hair into two thick braids to keep it from tangling as she slept, but tonight she did not. She was too restless, too unsettled. Even that restraint seemed bothersome. Finally, she simply tied it back with a ribbon at the nape of her neck.

Blowing out her light, she knelt on the little steps beside her bed to say her nightly prayer, finding it both lengthier and far more jumbled than usual, before she climbed into bed. It was dark and she was tired; she should have gone to sleep easily. But tonight sleep was a long time coming. As soon as she closed her eyes, thoughts of this afternoon flooded her mind, with nothing to distract them or pull her away. She remembered each kiss, each touch. The sounds and scents and tastes teased at her senses again, tempting and taunting her.

Scold herself as she might for the wanton thoughts and hungers that surged in her, Thea could not rid herself of them. She turned her face to her pillow, cool upon her heated skin, and wished that she did not feel the things she did. No . . . she was honest enough to correct her thought. The problem was not that she wished she didn't feel the way she did. The problem was that not only did she enjoy this feeling, she wanted to feel it all over again. And more.

Thea let out a groan and turned over, pulling the pillow over her head as if she could block out her thoughts. It did not work, and finally she simply gave up and turned her mind over to the rush of memories.

She was unaware she had finally fallen asleep until she awoke. Groggily she blinked, then glanced around her room, making out the shapes of the furniture in the darkness. She wasn't sure what had awakened her. Clearly it was still nighttime; no trace of light seeped in around the draperies. Thea tried to snuggle back into sleep, but something nagged at her, and finally she slipped out of bed, throwing on the dressing gown that she had laid across the foot of her bed and thrusting her feet into her soft house slippers. Putting on her spectacles, she padded over to the window and pushed back the edge of the drape, peering out into the night.

"Oh!" She sucked in a sharp breath of wonder.

Moonlight lit the landscape gently, and in the light she could see the falling flakes of snow. She leaned her head against the edge of the wall, gazing out at the softly swirling, floating snowflakes. It could not have been falling long, for only a frosting of snow was on the ground and along the bare, dark branches of the trees. Thea smiled, thinking how perfect it would be to have snow for Christmas. She hoped that it would continue to fall long enough to last through the next two days.

A faint thud sounded, jerking her out of her dreamy contemplation of the snowfall. She turned around, frowning, and crossed the room to stick her head out into the hall. Something pricked at her consciousness, some memory or thought that was gone before she could grab hold of it. She glanced up and down the dark hallway, seeing nothing unusual, and for a moment she contemplated simply going back to bed. However, she knew that she would be unable to find sleep unless she had gone downstairs and found what caused the noise. Turning, she went to the fireplace and lit a twist of paper from the still-hot coals. She used it to light the small oil lamp on her dresser and carried the lamp out into the hallway.

It was cold downstairs, which was always true, but tonight a distinct breeze curled around her ankles beneath her dressing gown. Holding up the lamp, she turned toward the front door. It was standing open a few inches.

She stood frozen, staring, and as she did so, a little gust of wind pushed the door open and it swung back to thump lightly against the wall and rebound almost closed again. Snowflakes drifted in and landed on the floor, melting almost instantly. Thea shivered, and the movement seemed to wake her from her trance. She hurried forward and pushed the door closed. Her heart was hammering in her chest, though she told herself there was no reason to be afraid. No doubt the door had simply not been well shut and the wind had blown it open. After all, no one would be out creeping into houses on a night like this, would they?

For her peace of mind, Thea made a quick tour of the downstairs, looking into each room to make sure it was empty. Then she started back up the stairs. Halfway up the stairs, she paused, looking at the little wet spot on the stairs, illuminated in the light of the lamp. She moved the lamp back and forth, peering down more closely at the stairs. Here was another little damp spot on the wooden stair beside the cloth runner. And a drop of moisture was trembling on the stair rail. As she stood there, staring, something dropped into place in her brain, and she realized what thought had eluded her drowsy mind earlier when she left her bedchamber. She had stepped through her open doorway when she left the room—and she was certain she had closed her door last night before she went to bed.

Her pulse began to race, and Thea ran up the remainder of the stairs. The corridor stretched out in front of her, and she hurried down it, making as little noise as she could. An indefinable fear clutched her chest, driving her straight to the nursemaid's room at the end of the hall. Lolly's door, too, stood open, and Thea had to swallow hard to hold back a choked whimper. She knew she had closed the door to Lolly's room, as well, after she had checked on the baby.

At a glance she saw that Lolly still lay in the bed, snuggled deep in her covers. Thea tiptoed to the basket, holding the lamp up. There was nothing there but the pillow that formed Matthew's bed. The baby was gone, blanket and all.

# Eleven

"Lolly! Lolly!" Thea shook the girl's shoulder. "Lolly, wake up! Where is Matthew?"

"Wha—" Lolly sat up groggily.

"Where is the baby? What's happened to Matthew?"

Lolly blinked at her. "What? Miss? Why—he's in his bed." She pointed over at the basket.

"No. He's not."

Lolly scrambled out of bed and ran to the basket, then frantically searched the rest of the small chamber, babbling as she looked, "Matthew! Matthew! Oh, miss, where could he have gone?"

Thea's mind was racing. Matthew could not have climbed out of his basket and crawled away. He had not even started crawling yet. And it was utterly absurd to think he could have opened the front door.

Clearly someone had entered the house and taken the baby.

Still, she had to make sure he was not in the house. Thea turned to Lolly, saying, "Check everywhere in the house. Look in any room he could have crawled into. I'm going for help."

Thea hurried back to her room and threw a dress on over her night rail, thrust her bare feet into boots, and topped it all with her cloak. Grabbing a knitted cap and gloves, she spared a moment to check with Lolly.

"No, miss. I've checked them all!" Tears stained the girl's face. "Except the master's room, of course, but his door's closed. Oh, miss, I'm so sorry. I don't know what could have happened!"

"I have a fairly good idea. If I am right, Matthew is warm and safe enough, I think. But I will need help to get him back. You keep searching, just in case. I shall return as soon as I can."

"But, miss, it's snowing!"

"I know."

Thea ran downstairs. In the kitchen, she lit the lantern, tugged on her gloves and cap, pulled up the hood of the cloak, and took off into the night.

The moon and lantern gave her light enough to see her way, but the snow was falling harder now, making it difficult to see any distance in front of her. Fortunately, the path was as familiar to Thea as the village. She had grown up playing with her siblings around the church and old convent grounds.

The bridge was a little slick, as was the flagstone path to the church, but once she turned off through the graveyard, the dirt path was not slippery despite the snow, and Thea took it at a fast pace, breaking into a trot whenever she could. Her heart was pounding, her breath coming in rapid spurts. She barely noticed the cold, but the trip seemed endless. After she passed the ruins, the landscape was less familiar, almost devoid of landmarks in the white storm, but she could still make out the narrow path immediately in front of her by the light of her lantern. It was eerie out here alone in the dark, with the snow falling around her, and for one panicky moment she felt disoriented and was afraid that she had strayed from the path.

But then she saw the dark bulk of the Priory ahead, and she rushed on with a renewed effort. When she reached the door, she crashed the brass door knocker against its plate with all her force, beating out a determined tattoo. She did not wait for someone to open the door, but reached out and pulled at the handle. Unfortunately, unlike her own front door, someone had locked it, and she could not make it budge. She returned to beating on the door until suddenly it swung open to reveal an astonished-looking footman, obviously roused from his bed.

Thea pushed past him, still carrying her lantern, and ran to the foot of the stairs, screaming, "Gabriel! Gabriel! I need your help!"

With the sound of pounding footsteps, in the next moment Gabriel appeared at the top of the stairs. His hair was tangled, and he was shirtless and barefoot.

"Thea!" He ran down the steps, pulling on his shirt as he came. "What happened? What's the matter?"

"He's taken Matthew!"

"What? Who—" He stopped on the bottom step, just above her. "The devil! Rawdon? He's taken Matthew?"

"I don't know! I didn't see it, but it must be he! I woke up and the front door was ajar and Matthew was missing! Someone came in and took him. And Lord Rawdon said—"

"That he should take his son away from me," Gabriel finished grimly. "I'll kill the bastard." He turned and pointed to the footman. "Get my curricle brought around. Immediately!" Gabriel swiveled back to face Thea, taking her hand in both his. "Don't worry. We shall get him back. I promise you. I'll just go dress, and we'll leave as soon as possible."

"Thank you." For the first time since she had found Matthew missing, Thea relaxed, letting out a deep sigh of relief.

Gabriel turned and ran back up the stairs, taking them two at a time. As he reached the top of the stairs, Ian and his wife appeared, wrapped in their dressing gowns, babbling questions.

"The baby's missing. I have to go." Gabriel pushed past them.

"What! What's happening?" Emily exclaimed, and they moved out of Thea's sight, following Gabriel down the hall.

She could still hear their voices, though she could not make out the words—the rapid flood of questions and Gabriel's terse replies, Emily's voice rising rather hysterically until finally Ian snapped at her to shut up. After that the woman began to cry, and all the voices quieted, followed by the sound of doors closing. In a few moments, Gabriel appeared again, dressed and booted now, though he had not bothered with a neckcloth. He was shrugging into his overcoat as he came.

"Gabriel, wait!" Ian came to the top of the stairs. "You can't just go storming over there!"

"The hell I can't."

"But you don't know what's happened. You don't know that it is Rawdon who took this child. You don't even know where the baby is."

"Who else would it be?" Gabriel countered. "I'll tell you what I do know: Rawdon said he would have his son, and now Matthew is gone. And I'm going to the inn to get Matthew back."

"I wish Myles and Alan weren't off drinking. Blast Emily for showing up and bringing gentility to the house. If they were here, we could hold you and keep you from going off half-cocked."

Gabriel shot him a cool look. "You mean, you could *try* to hold me here."

Ian sighed. "I'll go with you then. Just let me get dressed."

"No, stay with your wife." Ian rolled his eyes and started to protest, but Gabriel went on, "I can't wait. Rawdon may be leaving town; I have to get there as soon as I can. If I need help, Myles and Alan may still be at the tavern."

"Bloody domesticity," Ian muttered.

"Don't fret." Gabriel clapped Ian on the shoulder. "Go see to your wife. I have to leave."

Gabriel took Thea's hand and picked up her lantern with his other hand, but to her surprise he turned and went down the hallway behind them. She understood why he had turned that way when he strode into a room, pulled a box from a cabinet, and opened it to reveal a set of dueling pistols. Checking to make sure the guns were loaded, he stuck them into the great pockets of his coat, then led Thea out of the house by the back door.

"Good Lord!" he said as they stepped outside. "It's snowing." He looked at her. "You came here through the snow?"

She nodded. "I know it took a great deal of time. Perhaps I should have gone straight to the inn and confronted him myself."

"No!" He scowled. "You definitely should not do that. He is not someone you can count on to act like a gentleman." Gabriel started off toward the stables, putting his arm around her and pulling her against his side. "You were right to get me. But I hate to think of you tramping through this nasty weather."

"It isn't that far if you come through the ruins instead of round by the road."

"You struck out across the countryside?" He let out a little laugh and his arm tightened around her shoulders. "Ah, Thea, Thea . . . you are definitely a daughter of Boadicea."

The groom had worked quickly, despite being awakened in the middle of the night, and by the time they reached the stables, he had harnessed the pair of horses to the light open carriage. Gabriel gave Thea a hand up into the curricle, then hung the lantern from the front of it and climbed in to take the reins. The hood of the vehicle protected them in large part from the falling snow, but it did not keep the flakes from drifting in from the sides. Thea was grateful for the warm fur lap robe.

The snow had completely covered the road by now, adding to the difficulty of seeing it in the darkness, but much of the lane was lined on one side or the other by a hedge, which made it easier to follow. The matched grays seemed to have little trouble staying on the road, though Thea noticed that Gabriel drove them at a much slower pace than he had the other day.

"Tell me again what happened," he said after they had maneuvered out of the Priory grounds and onto the main road into the village. "Everything."

Thea described to him how she had awakened and looked out at the snow, then had heard the noise and gone downstairs to investigate. She explained the drops of water she'd seen on the floor and the stairs, adding, "I realized that it had to be melted snow that had dripped off someone who had come inside since it started snowing. And I remembered that I had closed the door to my bedchamber, but it was open when I awoke."

"He had been in your room?" Gabriel's hand clenched on the reins.

"I assume he must have been looking for the baby. Matthew has always been in my room before—though I can't imagine he would know that—but tonight Lolly took the baby to bed in her room because I was at the rehearsal. Oh, I wish I had brought his basket back to my chamber when I got home!"

"Don't blame yourself. Rawdon would have taken him no matter whose room he was in."

"But I might have heard him and awakened. Maybe I could have kept him from stealing Matthew, or at least raised an alarm."

"Yes, and you might have been hurt trying. Or you might have slept through it just as Lolly did. Don't worry; we shall get him back. Hopefully Rawdon wouldn't have been fool enough to set out for London in this snow. I don't know what he hoped to accomplish by doing such a thing, other than to cause me some bad moments. Of course, he seems to think Jocelyn is with me, so perhaps his purpose was to force her to talk to him."

"At least I was somewhat reassured when I realized that it must have been Lord Rawdon who took the baby. I mean, he would not harm his own son, would he?"

"I would not think so, though God only knows. I cannot understand his mind."

They reached the village sooner than Thea would have

thought possible, given the snowstorm. When Gabriel pulled the curricle into the yard of the inn, it took a moment for an ostler to come hurrying out to take the team from him. The lad gave Gabriel an odd look, but that changed quickly enough to admiration when Gabriel pressed a silver coin into his palm. "Pull them in and keep them warm, but don't unharness them just yet. Tell me, is Lord Rawdon still here? Has he ridden out tonight?"

The ostler's eyebrows went up. "That swell from London, sir? Nay, his black's still in the stable, right and tight. Beautiful piece of horseflesh, that one."

"Yes, he is. Good." Gabriel gave the boy a pat on the shoulder and turned to Thea, who had jumped down from the carriage while he was talking to the ostler. Gabriel took her arm, and they hurried into the inn.

Gabriel veered into the public room as soon as he stepped inside, and Thea peeked curiously around his shoulder into what constituted Chesley's main tavern. The fire in the great fireplace had burned down to embers, and a potboy was wrapped in a blanket, asleep on the rug in front of it. No one else was in the room.

"Sir Myles and Mr. Carmichael aren't here?" Thea asked. "Where could they be? We didn't pass them on the road."

"There's another place, ah, not too far away." He shifted uncomfortably and glanced around. "They, um, know some people there."

Thea looked at him blankly for a moment, then colored as she realized what subject Gabriel was dancing around. "Oh! You mean ... um, women. Of that sort."

"It's a possibility," he admitted, then turned quickly away and strode out the door. He walked to the stairs, bellowing, "Rawdon! Get out here!"

Thea flinched at the noise, thinking rather belatedly of the other guests who might be staying there. Still, she could think of no other way to find the man. Knocking on every door in the place would wake everyone as well. She started up the stairs after Gabriel, who continued to shout the other man's name. A door or two opened down the corridor, heads popping out to stare at them.

"Blast it, Rawdon, answer me!"

Two rooms down, a door slammed open and Lord Rawdon appeared in the doorframe. He was dressed in his shirtsleeves, waistcoat unbuttoned and his neckcloth gone, but he looked fully alert and not as if he had been in bed. Thea noted that he still wore his boots.

"Holy hell, Morecombe!" he growled, stepping out into the corridor. "What are you doing? It's the middle of the night."

"Did you think that would stop me? Did you really hope to wait out the snowstorm and leave tomorrow morning before I found out? Well, I know, and I'm here, and by God you will give him back to me or I'll tear you limb from limb."

"I haven't the faintest idea what you're blathering about."

Gabriel sneered and shoved past Rawdon into the room.

"What the devil?" Rawdon turned to stare after Gabriel as he went into the center of the room and turned all around, looking. A candle burned on a low table by the bed, casting a dim yellowish glow over the place. It was not much light, but the room was small, and even Thea could see, standing out here in the corridor, that no child was in the room.

"What the hell have you done with him?" Gabriel charged back out of the room.

"With whom? Are you foxed?"

"Of course I'm not foxed!" Gabriel roared. "Give him to me!"

"Leave me alone. You're bloody mad as a hatter."

"Gentlemen! Gentlemen!" The innkeeper came pelting up the stairs behind them. His bony frame was swathed in a florid dressing gown, and a nightcap was tilted rakishly on his balding head. "Pray what is the matter here?" He smiled at them and genially nodded beyond them at the other guests who had emerged from their rooms. "Whatever the problem, I am sure we can sit down and discuss this peacefully. Perhaps downstairs."

Both men shot a contemptuous look at the innkeeper before turning back to face each other. Rawdon started back to his room, saying, "If you have nothing intelligible to say, I am going to bed."

"No, you are not." Gabriel pulled one of his pistols from his pocket and aimed it at the other man. "You are going to tell me what you have done with Matthew."

Lord Rawdon crossed his arms in front of him and regarded Gabriel coolly. "No, I am not."

Gabriel drew back the hammer of the pistol with a click. The innkeeper let out a low moan and sagged against the wall. Thea thought he might faint, but she hadn't the time to pay attention to him now.

"Gabriel," she said in a low voice, taking a step closer. "If you kill him, we shall have no way of knowing where Matthew is."

"You're right." Gabriel kept his eyes trained on Rawdon but lowered the pistol, easing the hammer back into place, and stuck it into his pocket. "I shall have to beat it out of him."

Rawdon straightened, a light sparking in his pale blue eyes. "Come ahead, then." He brought up his fists, taking a boxing stance.

Gabriel began to peel off his coat. The innkeeper darted in between them, spluttering, "No, my lord, please, my lord." He looked pleadingly from one man to the other. "Surely this can be discussed civilly. Explained. Settled. There's no need to resort to fisticuffs. Come downstairs, I'll bring you a bottle of port . . ." He trailed off.

The innkeeper could see, Thea thought, just as she could, that both men were implacable. In another moment they would start circling each other like wolves, looking for an opening to jump in and rip one another apart. Thea slipped in between them, turning to look up at Lord Rawdon.

"Please, my lord, please tell me where Matthew is. He will be lonely and afraid. He's used to being with me. He does not know you, and wherever you have him, he could be cold or hungry." Tears welled in her eyes.

Rawdon drew back, for the first time looking faintly uneasy. "Madam, I don't know who you are or why you keep turning up in front of me, and I have no idea who Matthew is. If I knew where he was, believe me, I would tell you so that I could get this madman out of here."

"Matthew is your *son*, you bloody bastard!" Gabriel roared, and started to step around Thea, but she shifted to keep between them.

"The baby?" Rawdon stared at them. "You think I have Jocelyn's child?" He brushed a hand back through his hair, cursing softly under his breath. "All right. I shall talk to you. But I suggest we remove our conversation to a room downstairs, as the innkeeper suggested." He nodded toward Hornsby, saying, "And I think a bottle of brandy would be in order."

"Yes, my lord, right away." The innkeeper bowed with relief and hurried off down the stairs.

"I didn't come here to sit down over a bottle of brandy with you and chat!" Gabriel told him furiously.

Rawdon regarded Morecombe without expression. "Do you really want to have this conversation about the child here in the hall of the inn, in front of half a dozen people?" He gestured down the corridor, where every doorway held one or two guests, eagerly awaiting the rest of the drama.

Gabriel's gaze flickered to the onlookers, and he frowned. "No, of course not. We'll go downstairs. But I swear, if you are playing some sort of game here …"

"I don't play games." Rawdon closed the door to his room, then swung away and stormed down the stairs.

Gabriel and Thea followed him. The innkeeper was waiting for them at the door of the public room. "I know it's not proper, your having to go in here, miss, but everyone's gone, and the fire is still warm."

"It's perfectly all right," Thea assured him.

The innkeeper bustled about, bringing glasses and a bottle of brandy to the table closest to the fire, where Lord Rawdon already stood waiting.

"Thank you, Hornsby." Gabriel dismissed the innkeeper with a polite nod and waited until he had closed the door behind him before he turned to face Rawdon.

"I suggest we start by sitting down," Thea said, on the theory that it required more effort for seated men to get into a brawl than ones who were standing. She took a seat herself at the table, and after a brief pause and an exchange of measuring looks, the men followed suit.

"I don't have the boy," Rawdon said flatly. "Of course I do not expect you to believe me or to believe that I am not the sort of person who would abduct a baby. But if you would think rationally, there is no reason for me to take that child."

"You threatened to take him this afternoon at the Priory."

Rawdon made an impatient gesture. "I said that only because you had irritated me beyond endurance, as usual. I had no intention of doing so. Why would I take him? He is not mine."

"You have the gall to deny that he is yours?" Gabriel stiffened. "One need only have eyes to see the resemblance."

"I am not the only man with blond hair and blue eyes."

"Are you accusing my sister of being a trollop? Are you saying that she slept with other men?"

Rawdon shrugged lightly. "Obviously she slept with *one* other man."

With a low growl, Gabriel jumped to his feet, knocking over his chair.

"Gabriel, no!" Thea threw herself at him, grabbing his arm.

Rawdon, too, rose, his blue eyes blazing with pale fire. "That is ever your answer, is it not? I am growing tired of your taking a swing at me every time some uncomfortable truth arises and slaps you in the face. Believe me, if that boy were mine, I *would* take him from you. I would never allow anyone of my blood to remain in your hands. But I would not sneak into your house and steal him like a thief in the night. I would take him openly, legally, in a court of law. There would be no reason to do it any other way. You must realize that a father would win that battle. But he is *not my child."* He spoke slowly, each word falling with the thud of a hammer stroke. "And you are welcome to him."

The two men stared at each other for a long moment. Then Gabriel let out a low oath and half turned away. Thea sank back down in her chair, suddenly empty and sick. Lord Rawdon's words had the ring of truth. He was right in saying that a powerful and wealthy aristocratic father who claimed a child would likely win custody of a son in any court of law over the child's uncle—or even over his mother, in all likelihood. And if Rawdon had taken Matthew, what had he done with him? The baby had obviously not been anywhere in the man's room. Moreover, when she had looked more closely, she had seen that Rawdon's gleaming Hessian boots did not bear a drop of melted snow or mud on them. Most telling of all, she had seen the blank astonishment in Lord Rawdon's face when he had realized whom Gabriel was talking about. The man might be a villain and a liar, but she found it hard to believe he was that excellent an actor.

"But…then…who is it?" she asked, her words almost a moan. She looked up at Gabriel, who gazed back at her bleakly. "Who took Matthew?"

Gabriel shook his head. "I don't know. The person who left

him at the church, perhaps?" He sat down heavily and leaned his elbows on the table, shoving one hand back into his hair.

Rawdon glanced at him sharply. "The person who left him at the church? What are you talking about? Surely Jocelyn brought the baby here."

"No. I told you: Jocelyn is not here. I have not seen her."

"I found the baby," Thea explained. "He was abandoned by someone at the church—left in the manger."

Rawdon's brows rose at this news. "But then . . . how do you know the baby is Jocelyn's?"

Silently Gabriel reached into his pocket and pulled out the brooch Thea had found on the infant and held it out toward Rawdon. Some sort of emotion flickered in Rawdon's gaze and was gone too quickly for Thea to even identify it.

"Good God."

Gabriel shook his head. "This is enough chatter. Clearly we are wasting time here." He rose to his feet and began to button his coat. "We shall return to your house, Thea, and see if we can still find any tracks. Perhaps the snow will not have completely filled them in, and I can follow the abductor."

Thea stood up.

"Wait," Rawdon said. "I'll get my coat and come with you."

Gabriel turned to him, surprise clear on his face. "Why?"

Rawdon let out a snort. "I am sure you will come up with some sufficiently villainous reason for me to look for a baby lost in the middle of a snowy winter's night."

Gabriel did not speak for a moment, then said merely, "Very well. Let's go, then."

When they stepped outside, they found that the snow had increased, now covering the ground in a soft, thick blanket. It was a tight squeeze for three people in the curricle, but it was at least warmer, Thea acknowledged, being sandwiched in between two large males. The trip to the vicarage was short and silent, neither of the men saying a word.

Gabriel halted the vehicle before the vicarage, and the two men got out to look for tracks, moving slowly along the street and up the path to the front door, holding out the lantern to cast its yellow circle of light over the newly fallen snow. Thea went around to the kitchen door and entered the house.

Lolly sat huddled on one of the chairs at the kitchen table, a blanket wrapped around her, her tearstained face resting on her folded-up knees. She looked up hopefully when Thea entered, but her face fell when she saw that there was no baby in Thea's arms.

"Oh, miss! Did you not find him, then?"

Thea shook her head. "No. I assume you found no trace of him inside the house, either."

"No. I looked everywhere—twice! Who could have taken him, miss? Who would have done such a thing?"

"I don't know. I thought I knew, but apparently I was wrong, and now I haven't any idea. But whoever it was, the baby should not be out in this weather. We must find him. The men are outside looking for tracks. Why don't you make us some hot tea to ward off the chill? And maybe a bite to eat. I am going to get more properly dressed. We will have to search for him somehow."

Thea ran up the stairs and changed her clothes, pulling on

her warmest wool dress and, beneath it, flannel petticoats and woolen stockings. She grabbed some blankets and the baby's basket and carried them back downstairs to the kitchen. When she got back, Lolly had gotten the fire going and a pot of water was heating on its hook above it. A few moments later, the door opened and Gabriel and Rawdon entered, shaking the snow from their clothes.

"We couldn't find any decent tracks," Gabriel said as they came forward to stand in front of the fire, stripping off their gloves and holding their hands out to the heat.

"There were a few prints heading toward the church, but Morecombe said those would be yours, Miss Bainbridge," Lord Rawdon added. "There are one or two in the yard that appeared to be leading into the road, but we could not find any that indicated which way he went after he reached the road."

"We must find them," Thea said.

"I'll warrant I can catch him," Gabriel said. "I'll take my team over any mount he—or she—could be riding."

"She? Devil take it, do you really think it could be Jocelyn who took him?" Rawdon asked skeptically.

"I cannot imagine it, but I am reaching the point where I no longer know what to think," Gabriel admitted.

"It cannot be your sister," Thea said firmly. "Not unless she has run mad. The baby's mother would not have to steal her child out of my house. All she need do is claim it. In any case, I cannot think a mother would expose her baby to this weather. It is terribly cold and wet, and what if they were to get stuck in a snowdrift somewhere? I cannot believe she would do so."

"Nor can I, but if it is not Jocelyn, who is it?" Gabriel shrugged. "It does not matter anyway. I must go after him, whoever it may be. Since we cannot tell which way he went, I will take the road east. It seems the most likely to me. The vicarage and church are on the edge of town. If he went the other direction, he would have to ride through town, where there would be more chance of being seen. Logic says he would have come in from the east and left in the same direction."

"I am going with you," Thea said, standing up.

"What? No. It is cold and snowing even harder now. You just said yourself the weather was too bad to be out in."

"For a *child*. I think that I can bear the same amount of cold that a man can," Thea retorted. "And do not tell me I cannot go. Matthew is my responsibility. I found him and I vowed to take care of him, and he was stolen from under my roof. I refuse to sit idly by while he is out there in the snow somewhere! Besides, you could use an extra pair of hands—and eyes. There could be more than one person involved, you know, and if you think that I would not fight to get him back—"

"Oh, no, my dear." A ghost of a smile touched Gabriel's lips. "I would not dream of thinking that."

"Then it's settled. I will simply jot a note to Daniel explaining where I have gone, and we can be off."

"I shall take the road leaving the village in the other direction, then," Lord Rawdon said. "It won't take long to saddle my horse, and it would be wise to make sure that both ways are checked. No doubt there are other ways out of town, but if we can cover the main road, we should have a good chance of finding him."

Gabriel looked at Rawdon for a moment and gave a short nod. "Very well."

"Thank you, Lord Rawdon," Thea added, feeling that Gabriel's response had been less than adequate.

Rawdon nodded back to them, then turned and left. Gabriel stood, hands on hips, gazing at the door through which Rawdon had gone. "I don't trust him."

"I truly think he was surprised when he realized the baby had been taken." Thea finished her note, signing it briefly, and folded it. "Which would indicate that he was not the kidnapper." She wrote her brother's name on the note and propped it on the table for him to find the next morning.

"Yes," Gabriel agreed reluctantly.

"And given the fact that every time you see him, you try to pop him on the nose, it does seem that he is doing a good deal more for you than would be expected." Thea stood up and began to don her cloak and gloves.

"He isn't doing it for me."

"For who then?"

"I don't know."

"Well, as long as he is doing it, I suppose that is what matters." Thea jammed the knitted cap down over her wild tangle of curls and turned to Lolly, who sat on the hearth, watching them. "Be sure my brother gets that note tomorrow—well, I guess it's *this* morning. I trust we shall return with Matthew."

"Yes, miss, I pray you do."

Thea picked up the baby's basket and the blankets she had stuffed inside it and started for the door. Gabriel opened the door and followed her out, picking up the lantern as they went.

He once again attached the lantern to the curricle and went to his horses to give each of them a pat and a few words. Climbing into the vehicle beside Thea, he took up the reins, and they started off into the night.

Gabriel kept the horses to as fast a pace as was safe on the snowy road. Thea pulled up the heavy, fur-lined lap robe high around her, tucking it in on the outside. Her other side was flush against Gabriel—for warmth, she told herself. It was perfectly true, but she could also not help but be aware that his muscled leg pressed against hers. And that, she told herself sternly, was an utterly inappropriate thing to be thinking about at a time like this.

She fixed her attention on the road in front of them, peering through the falling snow. The circle of the lantern lit only a small area, and there was little to see but the falling flakes. Thea hoped that the horses would be able to stay on the road. Their pace was perforce slow, but before they had gone far down the road, Gabriel pulled the team to a stop and handed the reins to her, then jumped down and took the lantern from its hook. He carried it over to the side of the road and held the lantern up as he stared at the ground.

Thea could see that the snow was different there, far less deep and smooth—as though, she realized, the snow had been trampled and chopped up sometime recently, then a layer of snow had fallen on top of it, leaving odd valleys and peaks. There, at the edge, was a darker pile, just beginning to be covered by snow.

She leaned forward. "Is that—"

"Yes. Horse droppings." Gabriel turned and hurried back to

the carriage to rehang the lantern and hop in. He took the reins back from her and slapped them over the horses' backs, continuing to talk with an undercurrent of excitement in his voice. "It appears to me that a horse was tethered there for some time tonight—just as it would be if the fellow tied his horse out on the road and walked in to grab the baby. Quieter that way, I'd guess, and no one would see a horse waiting in front of your house and think it odd and come to investigate."

"Then we are on the right road."

He nodded. "I think so. Carrying a baby is bound to slow him to some extent, not to mention the fact that he was on foot till he got here, and I dare swear his horse cannot match my pair. We should make up time on him. The problem will be making sure we catch it if he's turned off. I don't want to run past him."

They were alone on the road in the snow, which was growing increasingly heavier. Thea thought of Matthew, wrapped in his blanket, carried by some stranger through this night, and her heart clutched in her chest. She prayed that whomever they were pursuing had thought to wrap an extra blanket around the baby.

The team forged on through the night as the snow grew deeper around them. Since Gabriel had to keep all his attention on driving through the treacherous conditions, Thea kept a sharp lookout on either side of the road, watching for some sign that the kidnapper had passed this way or that he might have turned off the road. The quiet, broken only by the sound of their passing, and the blur of the falling snow were enough to lull her into a daze, and Thea kept having to blink and shift around in her seat to maintain a sharp focus. It began to seem as if they had been driving through this cold, isolated landscape for hours, as if they might continue to do so forever.

"Gabriel, look!" Thea shot straight up, pointing out the right side as the lap robe slid unheeded down from her shoulders.

"What?" Gabriel hauled back on the reins.

"I'm not sure. But the snow was disturbed back there." She was already scrambling out the side of the curricle, and Gabriel quickly followed her.

Picking up her skirts, she ran through the snow to the spot she had seen a few yards back. She stopped and looked down at the area of churned snow. Gabriel stopped beside her.

"I think the horse stumbled here," he said, excitement tingeing his voice. "Probably not enough to fall, or at least not more than to his knees, but he is struggling. And look, there's only a light dusting covering it all. I don't think it has been very long."

"Oh, Gabriel!" Fear choked her voice. "It has been so long already. And he is so little!"

Gabriel took her arm, his grip hard and strong. Thea turned to look at him. A hard, bright light burned in his eyes. "We shall get him back. He is going to be all right."

Though she knew he could not promise that, his words reassured Thea. She swallowed back her fear and gave him a tight, hard smile. "Yes, we will."

The light of the lantern picked up the other horse's tracks now, at first faintly, then more and more clearly. The gap between them was narrowing. Thea clenched her hands together tightly in her lap as the team labored on. The snow grew deeper, their pace slower. Thea could feel the tension mounting in Gabriel's body beside her. Finally, he climbed down, taking the lantern, and went to the head of the team. He stroked their heads, murmuring to them, then hooked his hand in the harness and urged them forward, the lantern bobbing in his other hand.

They could not continue like this long, Thea knew. How could the kidnapper still be running? Where did he intend to go? It was impossible to tell where they were in the darkness and snow, but she felt they must be some distance still from Bynford, the next village on this road. Had the man managed to reach there? Would they be able to get that far? She could not imagine what they would do if the horses stopped, unable to plow on through the snow.

In the still night, Gabriel's sharp exclamation carried back to her. She straightened, peering out. Gabriel let go of the horses and carried his lantern to the left side of the road. He stepped off the road, and in the light of his lantern, Thea could see tracks leading off the road in front of him. He whirled around and came back at a run, sending snow spraying around him. He led the horses off the road and onto the lane.

Since the lane was somewhat sheltered by a hedge on one side, the snow was not as deep here. Gabriel returned to take up the reins again, urging his team to a last hard effort. The animals responded, picking up their pace. The hedge ended, and the snow became deeper again, but still they plowed through it. Finally, up ahead, at the farthest limit of her vision in the snow, Thea saw a small, dim glow.

"A light?" she asked, peering forward just as Gabriel slapped the reins and let out a cry, urging the team forward.

Gradually the light resolved into something faintly glowing and square in the midst of a low mass. A window, she thought, in a small house. The team pounded forward, the sound of their hooves muffled by the snow. Now Thea could see a dark lump of a figure trudging through the snow around the side of the house. The shape turned and let go of the load he had had in his hands. It was logs, she saw as they fell, bouncing and rolling, disappearing in the soft snow.

The figure turned and began to run clumsily back around the house. Gabriel pulled the team to a stop and jumped down from the curricle. He took off after the man, snow spurting up behind him. Thea scrambled down and started after him. Ahead of her, she saw Gabriel take the man down in a flying leap.

At that moment, Thea heard the thin, high wail of an infant. She turned and ran toward the house.

# Twelve

*The snow seemed to drag* at Thea's feet, slowing her steps. She slipped and fell, but scrambled back up and ran on. She flung open the door, revealing a small room. A lantern sat on the rough table to her left, and a fire had been started in the fireplace, casting a ruddy glow. A few feet from the fire was an armchair, and in it lay a squirming, kicking bundle, issuing forth a high-pitched, exhausted cry.

"Matthew!" Thea ran over to the chair and picked up the blanket-wrapped baby. He had kicked off most of the heavy outer blanket around him, and his own smaller knitted blanket had been worked into a wadded-up ball on his stomach. His face was screwed up in fury, his eyes squeezed shut and his mouth wide-open. He was trembling, though Thea was not certain whether it was from the cold or from his own panicked crying. As soon as Thea picked him up, murmuring soothing words, his crying hiccuped and stopped. He drew a shaky breath, his eyes opening to look at Thea, and a long shiver ran down his body. He began to cry again, but this time more softly and plaintively, shuddering out his breaths.

"There, there, hush now, I'm here. Gabriel and I have you now. It's all right."

She continued to murmur, holding him close and stroking her hand over his head and down his back. His head was hot and damp, as it got sometimes when he cried. She kissed him, and then she realized she was crying, too, the tension and fear of the last few hours seeping out of her in slow, silent tears. Matthew laid his head against her chest, letting out a little sigh as his crying sputtered to a halt.

The sharp report of a gun sounded outside, and Thea jumped. Gabriel! Wrapping the baby up again in the blanket and setting him down, Thea grabbed the poker from the fireplace and started for the front door. She was almost there when Gabriel appeared in the doorway. His eyes went to the poker in her hand, and a grin crossed his face.

"Don't hit me. I'm unarmed."

Even as he spoke, Thea dropped the poker in relief and flung herself across the room, throwing her arms around his neck. His arms went just as tightly around her, and he lowered his head to rest it against hers. They simply stood, clinging to each other, until at last the baby's crying pulled them from the moment. Gabriel's arms loosened around her, and Thea turned to go to the baby.

"Is he all right?" Gabriel asked, closing the door and following her.

"I think so. He was unhappy, but he didn't look as if he had been harmed." She picked Matthew up and the baby stopped crying almost immediately. Thea turned back to Gabriel. "What happened? I heard a gunshot."

"He got away from me. We were wrestling about in the snow, and he grabbed one of those logs he'd been carrying and sent my hat flying."

"Gabriel!" Thea's eyes flew to his head. The hat he had worn earlier was gone. "Are you all right?"

"I'm fine. Don't worry about me. But he stunned me long enough for him to run away. By the time I managed to go after him, he was on his horse. I fired at him, but with that snowstorm, I hadn't a prayer of hitting him." Gabriel paused, looking disgusted. "I didn't even get a good look at him. It was dark and he was bundled up, with a hat and some long, knitted scarf tied around his face. All I am certain of is that it was a man and he is smaller than I."

"I'm sorry he got away, but we have Matthew back, and that's what's important."

Gabriel nodded. "I have to see to the horses." He frowned. "I don't think we can make it back to Chesley tonight. The team has reached their limit, and the road is just getting worse. The snow is still falling. We can't risk getting stuck or breaking a wheel, not with the baby along."

"No, you're right. We were lucky to be able to make it this far. But what about your horses? Will they be all right?"

He nodded. "There is a shed behind the house. That was apparently where the kidnapper kept his horse. There's even a goat and its kid out there. The building is small, but they'll fit, and there's hay and a water trough. It won't be quite what they're accustomed to, but they should do well enough."

"Good. Then at least there will be milk for Matthew. I shall see what else is here."

Thea turned to explore the cabin. A door led into a small chamber, which contained a bed, a chest, and a small washstand with a mirror. She was pleased to see that the chest contained a few towels and sheets. At least she would be able to clean up and put new sheets on the bed.

She returned to the main room. Besides the chair in front of the fireplace, there was also a square, scarred wooden table and two chairs, as well as a low stool. On the counter was a jug of water, and a round loaf of bread wrapped in a towel. A door so low that she had to stoop to pass through it led into a small, dark room that was two steps lower than the floor of the house.

She brought the lantern closer and saw that it was a small pantry built out from the rest of the house. It was no more than a few feet square, with a roof that slanted down steeply from the cottage wall. The outer three walls were made only of planks, so it was much cooler than the rest of the house. Clearly it served as a place to store food, and Thea found a small jug of milk as well as a slab of bacon, a hunk of cheese wrapped in cloth, and a healthy piece of cold cooked roast. The kidnapper had obviously made sure he would not lack for sustenance.

Matthew was growing fussy, alternately sucking on his fist and rubbing his eyes against her shoulder. Thea kissed his head, saying, "Not sure whether you're sleepier or hungrier, are you, young man?"

She brought out the jug of milk and poured a bit into a cup she found in a cabinet, then tore off a chunk of the bread and sat down at the table to feed Matthew. Pulling off little pieces of the bread, she dipped them into the milk and popped them in the baby's mouth. Obviously hungry, Matthew gulped them down.

Gabriel came inside carrying the baby's basket from the curricle, still stuffed with the extra blankets. A smile crossed his face. "Looks as though you have mastered the art of feeding him."

Thea laughed and glanced down at the baby, whom she had tucked against her side, one of his arms pinned against her body and her arm looped around his other arm. "Yes. Mrs. Brewster showed me how to hold him—and I have had a bit of practice now. But I still have to be careful if it's something he doesn't want. I received a whole mouthful of mashed peas down my front yesterday."

Gabriel set down the basket and went to the fireplace. He stirred up the flames with the poker and stripped off his gloves to hold his hands out to the fire. "It's still snowing. I think the horses will do well enough in the shed. I rubbed them down as best I could and put out some hay."

"Good. We appear to have plenty of food in here, as well."

He came over and squatted down beside her, reaching out to take Matthew's chin between his thumb and forefinger. "And how are you, Master Matthew?"

"Eating like a trooper," Thea responded, smiling. "Honestly, he seems to be all right. The thief had the baby wrapped in an extra blanket, so I have to be grateful to him for that. And though Matthew was screaming madly when I came in, I think he was only scared and unhappy, not hurt."

"He doesn't feel as though he has a fever." Gabriel stroked his finger over the baby's soft cheek, and Matthew responded with a wide-mouthed grin that spilled his milk and bread back out onto his chin. Gabriel chuckled and stood up, pulling back on his gloves as Thea wiped the baby's chin. "I should bring in the firewood he dropped in our struggle. We shall need more than is sitting by the hearth."

Thea nodded. As Gabriel started to move away, she reached out impulsively and caught his hand, bringing it up to her cheek and leaning against it. "Thank you."

He bent over her and laid his lips tenderly upon her forehead. Then, giving her hand a squeeze, he left. Thea continued to feed Matthew. The room was warming up now, so she shrugged off her cloak and pulled the knit cap from her head. Gabriel made several trips bringing in more wood, and by the time he finished and dropped the bar down across the door to shut out the cold, as well as intruders, Thea had changed the baby, sending up silent thanks that she had thought to bring some of those necessary cloths with her.

Gabriel pulled off his many-caped driving coat and laid it over one of the kitchen chairs to dry. He settled down in the chair beside the fire and offered to hold the baby. Thea smiled her thanks and handed Matthew to him. Sitting down on the hearth next to the chair, she allowed herself to simply luxuriate in the heat for a moment. She looked over at Gabriel. Matthew's head was bobbing sleepily, and finally, with a sigh, he laid his head down. His big blue eyes were still open, but his stare was becoming glazed, and Thea felt sure that within a few minutes, he would be asleep.

She stretched and sighed, leaning back against the rock wall beside the fireplace.

"Tired?" Gabriel asked.

Thea nodded. "It's been quite a night. I'm happy and exhausted—and still my nerves are humming too much to be sleepy."

She pushed back her hair, which spilled down over her shoulders in curling profusion. She had not plaited it before she went to bed as she usually did, and in all the rush and excitement, she had left it as it was. The damp weather had turned it into corkscrews. Thea divided her hair as best she could without a comb or mirror and began to braid it.

"No," Gabriel said softly. "Don't do that. Leave it that way."

Thea raised her brows at him. "'Tis a mess. I look positively wild."

He grinned, and a light sparked in his black eyes. "Maybe I like you positively wild."

For some reason, his words reminded Thea of her actions the afternoon before, when he had touched her so intimately and she had responded with a shattering rush of pleasure. Color rose in her cheeks and she jumped to her feet, letting go of her hair. "I—I think I shall wash up a bit."

"There's a washbasin here?"

"Oh, yes, we have all the amenities," she tossed over her shoulder as she walked away, pleased that she managed to keep her voice light and seemingly unconcerned.

Inside her was another matter entirely. There she was a fizzing mass of emotions. Thea had been shaken by the events of the night, her nerves stretched almost to the breaking point, then flooded with relief at finding Matthew alive and unharmed. She felt at once vulnerable and amazingly strong, vital and surging with life even as her legs still trembled, weak and watery as if she had been ill.

Thea went into the bedroom and closed the door. Taking out a towel and a rag, she poured water into the basin and began to wash. Her gaze kept straying to the bed beside her. She tried not to think about their sleeping arrangements, but that effort proved to be remarkably unsuccessful. What was going to happen tonight? Gabriel would be a gentleman, she told herself. He would sleep in the other room, no doubt. But she could not help but wonder whether she really wanted him to.

That she would even consider such a thing took Thea's breath away. What was the matter with her? What had happened to her over the last week? She was the vicar's sister, for heaven's sake! She was virtuous; she lived as she should and did the things that she ought. She followed the rules.

Or at least she always had until she met Gabriel. Thea did not even want to think about all the conventions she had flouted since he came along. Still, she could not blame it all on him. He had provided the temptation perhaps, but every step she had strayed off the path had been willingly taken. The confusing tumble of sensations and emotions in her now was hers, not anything pushed on her by anyone else.

Thea could not help but think of all the years she had lived without feeling any of the things she had felt yesterday afternoon—the hours and days and months she had passed through without tasting the sweetness of Gabriel's kiss or the pleasure of his hands on her. She wanted . . . oh, she wanted so much more than she had ever known. All her life, she had been plain. Ordinary. But when Gabriel kissed her, when his arms went around her and his body pressed into her, she exploded with beauty. She felt anything but ordinary.

She turned away, knotting her hands together and pacing about the small room. It was foolish to be thinking this way. Nothing was going to happen between them. Just because they were alone here together . . . just because circumstances had thrown them into a situation where it would be easy to give in to temptation, it didn't mean that they were going to do so.

Afraid that her thoughts might show on her face, Thea decided to change the bed linens, too, before she returned to the other room. Finally, with no reason left to linger in here, she squared her shoulders and stepped out into the main room. Gabriel was slouched in the chair by the fire, his long legs stretched out in front of him and his dark head resting against the back of the chair, his eyes closed. Matthew lay on his chest, peacefully asleep. Thea came to an abrupt stop, an almost painful sweetness clutching at her chest.

Gabriel's eyes opened, and a sleepy smile turned up the corners of his mouth. "I think we can put him to bed," he said in a low voice.

Thea nodded and went to the baby's basket to take out the extra blankets and set them aside. Gabriel carried the baby over to the basket and bent to lay him down inside.

Thea let out a gasp. "Gabriel! You're hurt! There's blood on your head."

He straightened, his hand going to his head. "Oh, that. It's nothing. I told you, he gave me a thump with one of those logs."

"You said he'd hit you," Thea retorted in some exasperation. "You didn't say you were bleeding."

"I didn't really know it."

She took his arm and pulled him over to the table. Pushing him down into one of the chairs, she held up the lantern to take a closer look at his head.

"Well, I suppose it doesn't look too serious, just a scrape rather than a cut. But I should clean it."

Thea poured water from the jug into a bowl and dipped a rag in it. Squeezing out the rag, she dabbed gently at the wound. Gabriel winced, but remained still. The blood remained stuck in his hair, so she held the wet rag against his head, letting it soak. She could not ignore how close she was to him. She could feel the warmth emanating from his body. The side of his head was at the level of her breasts, and without thinking, she ran her other hand over his tousled curls. Gabriel stiffened, and Thea felt the sudden surge of heat in him. Quickly she dropped her hand away, embarrassed by her action, and finished wiping the wound clean.

"I saw a bottle of gin in that cabinet. Perhaps I should use it on the wound. I have read of using whiskey to clean wounds. Gin would be the same, wouldn't it?"

"I think I'd rather use it inside me," he retorted, but shrugged. "Why not? They say pain makes one a better person."

Thea pulled the bottle of liquor from the cabinet and poured some in a cup, which she set down in front of Gabriel. Then she poured a bit of it on the cloth and held it to his wound. He sucked in his breath sharply.

"What sort of books do you read anyway?" he asked. "Tales of cleaning wounds? Hardly sounds like what one would find in the vicarage."

"I read almost anything I can get my hands on," Thea answered honestly. She sat down at the table on his right. "I think I read that bit about whiskey in the memoirs of a traveling minister in the colonies." She gestured at the bottle. "What does that taste like?"

"Blue ruin? Pretty ghastly, actually, but it does the trick. Here." He slid the cup across the table to her. "Try it. It'll warm you up."

Thea picked up the cup and took a small swallow, making a face at the taste. "Oh! How bitter!" She shivered as it slid fierily down her throat and into her stomach. "It tastes like perfume."

Gabriel chuckled. "My dear Thea, is it your habit to drink perfume?"

"Well, it tastes the way I would think perfume tastes." She reached out and took another sip, then set the cup down with a shudder and slid it back to him. "Why does anyone drink that?"

"Cheaper than brandy or whiskey. And it has the result you want."

"What is the result?" Thea asked curiously, leaning forward and crossing her arms on the table.

He smiled and reached out to run his finger down the length of her nose, brushing it over her chin as it fell away. "You look at one in such a way—as if you would soak up every bit of knowledge you could find."

"Even Papa said I was an admirable pupil. I just . . . like to know things, to find out everything I can. I want to know why and how and where. I suppose it seems silly, living in a village out in the country as I do."

"I think that makes it all the more understandable. The way a man imprisoned would want to discover all he could about the outside world."

"Exactly!" Thea beamed, pleased and somewhat surprised at his understanding. "There is so much I have never seen or done. Those plays you were talking about the other day. The opera. Musicales."

He poured more gin into the cup and took a swig. "If we were in London, I would take you. Well, the plays and the opera, anyway. Not the musicales. Those are deadly dull. But I should like to show you the plays."

"And museums!" Thea exclaimed, her eyes shining. "I would love to go to a museum. My sister said her husband took her to Bullock's Museum, and she saw Napoléon's carriage. Oh, and the Tower—Traitors' Gate … the ravens … the tower where the little princes disappeared …"

Gabriel laughed. "I can see I would have my hands full, escorting you about the city. No doubt you'd want to see Astley's and Vauxhall Gardens, as well."

Thea nodded and let out a wistful sigh. "I should like to see them all." She glanced at the cup. "I think I know what you mean—about drinking that. I feel warmer and, I don't know, relaxed." She took off her spectacles and set them down on the table, running her hands back over her face and into her hair. Then she picked up the cup and took another drink.

"Careful." He reached out to take the cup from her. "You won't like it if you get foxed on daffy."

"Daffy." Thea smiled. "Blue ruin. It has such colorful names. But I don't think you need worry about me becoming foxed. It tastes much too nasty. I don't know how you have managed to drink what you have of it."

"It's an acquired taste." He paused. "Not the sort of taste the vicar's sister should acquire."

"The vicar's sister shouldn't do anything," Thea retorted, "except sit in the corner and knit."

"I cannot imagine you doing that."

"I can knit," she answered with some indignation, though she added honestly, "but I'm not terribly good at it. Veronica was always better than I at such things. Mama said that was because Veronica practiced whereas I always had my nose stuck in a book. Which is quite true, of course. But it was much more boring to knit."

"More entertaining to read about cleaning wounds," he agreed, his eyes twinkling.

"Well, it was!" Thea lifted her chin. "Father said it was too bad that I was born a girl."

A smile curled up one corner of his mouth, and his eyelids lowered a fraction. "I cannot agree with that sentiment."

His voice was low and rich with meaning, and it teased at something deep within Thea. She shifted a little in her seat. "Well, he meant it was too bad that I could not take advantage of the sort of education a man could. Rather a waste of intellect." She looked away, surprised by the hot sting of tears suddenly burning her eyes. "Though naturally he never meant to be harsh, I'm sure."

Thea started to rise from her seat, but Gabriel's hand clamped around her wrist on the table, holding her in place. "Nothing about you," he said, his voice hard, "is a waste."

She glanced at him, surprised. Gabriel's face was fierce and unyielding. Thea smiled, warmth spreading through her at his words.

"That's very nice of you to say," she began.

He shook his head. "Not nice. Just truthful." He lifted her hand and pressed a kiss into the palm, then held her hand against his cheek. Sighing, he let go of her hand. "Ah, Thea, I am not a good man."

The tingling from where his cheek had touched her palm spread up her arm and through her chest. Her insides were in a tumult, needs and wants tumbling around madly. "You must not say that. I think you are a very good man."

He looked straight into her eyes, and the heat she saw in them stunned her. "I would not be if I took advantage of this situation. Of you."

Thea gazed back at him, and her next words were barely above a whisper. "What if I wanted you to?"

His eyes widened. "Thea . . . no. You don't know what you're saying." He cleared his throat and turned away, rising to his feet. "I should not have given you that gin."

"I am not inebriated," Thea protested, jumping to her feet. "I hardly had two swallows of it." She moved around to stand in front of him, blocking his way and forcing him to meet her gaze. "Are you going to try to tell me that I do not know my own mind?"

He smiled faintly. "Never that. But you don't know what it will be like."

"I know what it was like the other day."

He swallowed convulsively, his face turning subtly warmer. "That was different. We were not alone."

"So there was more chance of discovery and gossip."

"You could have left then." His voice was rougher, a hint of desperation on his tongue.

"And if I do not want to leave?"

"Blast it, Thea, do not make this any more difficult. I have put you in a very precarious position, and to do anything—to behave in the manner I would very much like to—would be dastardly on my part."

"It certainly did not seem to bother you before now!" Thea told him tartly. "These compunctions came upon you rather suddenly."

"You're not being fair."

"No. You are right." She turned away abruptly. "I should not plague you. One cannot help it if one does not feel a . . . a certain way." Thea returned to the table, embarrassment burning in her stomach. Why had she said so much? Taken things this far? The alcohol must have loosened her tongue. She busied herself with the things on the table, putting the cork in the bottle and moving it back to the cabinet.

"You think I don't feel desire for you?" Gabriel rasped out behind her. "You think it's easy? That I don't care?"

"It does not matter." Thea shrugged, still not looking at him. "I think that—"

"Doesn't matter!" He crossed the room to her and took her arm in his hand, whirling her back around. "It matters to me!" He loomed above her, scowling, jaw set, his eyes glittering. He grabbed her other arm, and for an instant they simply hung there, staring at each other, scarcely breathing. Then he pulled her up hard against him and sank his lips into hers.

Heat rushed through Thea. She was suddenly intensely alive, every nerve ending tingling. Desire thrummed in her, warming her blood and stealing her breath. His hands slid down her back, sinking into her buttocks and pushing her up into him. He moved her hips against him, and she felt the unmistakable answering jolt of his desire. The message was clear, the hunger undeniable. Thea wrapped her arms around his neck and returned his kiss with all her fervor.

At last Gabriel released her and raised his head. His face was slack with desire, his breath rasping in his throat, his eyes wide and dark. "We shouldn't—"

"I am tired of people telling me what I should not do!" Thea shot back fiercely. "For once I intend to do as I please."

Cupping his face in her hands, she went up on tiptoe and pressed her lips against his, once, twice . . . and then, with a shudder, his arms clamped around her again, and he buried his lips in hers.

They kissed until she could not breathe and the blood was pounding through her veins. Thea thought she might faint, but when he released her, she let out a murmur of protest. However, he let her go only to bend and sweep her up into his arms. Thea sighed with pleasure and rested her head upon his shoulder, her arms twining around his neck. In his arms she felt small and precious. Wanted. Not an awkwardly lanky spinster passed over by every male eye, but a woman who stirred a man's blood, whose kiss could make him hungry with desire.

Gabriel carried her into the small bedroom and closed the door after them. He set her down, and as soon as her feet touched the floor, he was kissing her again. His lips moved over her face and neck and ears. He nibbled at her sensitive earlobe, then traced the whorls of her ear with his tongue, and Thea let out a small noise of surprise that soon turned into a soft moan as the things he was doing sent shivers through her. She felt as if she were melting deep inside, something low in her abdomen turning heavy and molten.

He sank his hands into her curls, his fingertips pressing into her skull, and his mouth came back to hers, claiming it in a deep, long kiss that left her shaken and speechless. Thea felt as if she might slide right down to the floor, her legs like jelly, and she curled her hands into the front of his shirt, holding on. His hands went to the back of her dress, expertly unfastening it. She had thrown on the easiest dress to don, one with only ties; it was equally easy to undo. Thea could find no fault in that as Gabriel's hand slid beneath the open sides of the gown.

She did not mind the cool air, for Gabriel's hand was deliciously warm in contrast. He trailed his fingers down her spine as he took her mouth in another searching kiss. Heat burned with a low, insistent throb between her legs, and Thea was almost overwhelmed by the flood of sensations his fingers and mouth awakened.

Thea wanted to feel his fingers on her bare skin, without all the layers of her clothes. She broke away, and Gabriel looked at her in faint surprise and question, his hand falling away from her. But when she pulled her arms out of her dress, letting it fall to the floor, a slow, sensual smile spread over his mouth. He reached out and took the ribbon bow of her chemise and tugged it loose. The thin cotton undergarment sagged, exposing the tops of her breasts, and his fingers teased in under it, opening the neckline wider and sliding it downward in torturously small increments.

His knuckles slid over the soft tips of her breasts and glided down, pushing the material before them until he hooked into the waist of her petticoats and pantalets. Releasing the material, he pulled open the drawstring of each garment, his eyes all the while remaining on her. Once more he began the slow journey downward, his fingers spreading wide over her skin as the material bunched and moved, exposing ever more of her flesh.

Thea's breath grew ragged, and she was filled with a strange, wild mixture of emotions as he revealed every inch of her body to his eyes and hands—anticipation, pleasure, and a growing hunger roiled and clashed with the anxious fear that he might find her displeasing. His hands moved around to her back and curved over the soft mounds of her buttocks, and she heard a low noise, somewhere between a moan and a growl, escape his throat. She smiled to herself, certain that whatever Gabriel was feeling, it was not displeasure.

He pushed the underclothes the rest of the way down, impatience ending his slow teasing of their passion. The garments caught at the barrier of her half boots, and he went down on one knee to unhook the shoes. He lifted her foot, tugging the boot off, and she put her hand on his shoulder to steady herself. Gabriel gazed up at her, grinning his enjoyment of her from this new vantage point.

The other boot came off as easily, and Thea stepped out of her clothes. Gabriel did not stand, however, but instead put his hands on either side of her leg to roll down a final bit of clothing Thea wore, her stocking. He did the same with the other leg, his fingers lingering over her curves. Then he slid his hand daringly higher, moving over her calf and thigh, toward the center of Thea's heat.

She let out a choked noise, remembering with vivid clarity the way his fingers had found her and caressed her there the other day. She knew she should feel embarrassed; no doubt it was weak and sinful to ache for him to touch her that way again. But she didn't care. All she cared about now was the trembling ache inside her, the heat. But his hands halted on their gliding path, and he stood up, leaving the hunger still burning within her.

"Hardly seems fair, does it, that you are the only one undressed?" he said huskily as he tugged his shirt out from his pants and untied the top tie. He reached down and grasped the ends of his shirt and pulled it off over his head in one swift motion.

Thea's eyes were fastened to his nakedness now as she examined the wide expanse of his chest, taking in every detail from the flat, masculine nipples and the ripple of muscle beneath his skin to the curling black hair tapering in a $V$ down his chest and disappearing into the waistband of his trousers. His body was hard and male, so very different from her own, and the sight of it stirred her. Her fingers itched to reach out and touch the firm pad of muscle and the bony line of his collarbone, the sharp points of his shoulders. She wanted to experience the texture of his skin, to run her hands over the ridges of his ribs.

Gabriel's hands went to the buttons of his breeches, and Thea sucked in a soft breath. Quickly he undid the top set, and the garment sagged down, revealing a tantalizing glimpse of his hipbones and the thin line of hair growing downward. He stopped and sat on the edge of the bed to pull off his boots, but Thea did not mind the wait, as she found it equally fascinating to watch the curve of his back and the play of muscles as he tugged off his boots and stockings. He stood up and unfastened the remainder of the buttons, skinning out of his breeches so that he stood before her as naked as she.

Thea's eyes widened as she took in the sight of a male's fully naked body. She had never before seen the sight; indeed, she had never expected to see it. While she had had a vague idea of what a man must look like—after all, looking at a fully clothed male, she knew his chest was wider, his hips narrower, his legs longer and more muscled than a woman's—she had not been prepared for the reality of it. The power, the size, the overwhelming *maleness* of him. Gazing now at Gabriel's lean body, she felt her own body tightening in response. Gabriel in the flesh was a little shocking … and more than a little exciting.

He came back to her, reaching out to take her arms in his hands. "Having second thoughts?" He slid his hands up and down her arms in a soothing way.

Thea dragged her eyes back up to his face. "It is a trifle, uh, what I mean is, you seem a bit—that is to say, I am not sure exactly what happens, but are you certain we shall, um, fit?"

He chuckled, a low rumbling sound that Thea found curiously comforting. "Indeed, my dear, we shall definitely fit." He bent to nuzzle his face into her hair. "And I promise I will do my utmost to make sure you discover what happens in a most enjoyable way. But if you are not sure, we can stop here and now."

"No!" Thea said quickly. "I don't want to stop." She looked up at him and smiled, unaware of the flirtatious glint in her usually serious gray eyes. "I want to know. I want . . ." She trailed off, not sure how to express the tumultuous feelings of desire, need, and frustration bubbling inside her.

Gabriel slid his hands up over her bare shoulders and onto her neck, bracing his thumbs on her chin. "Believe me, I want, too." Gabriel lowered his head and brushed his lips across hers. "I want very much."

His lips touched hers lightly again. He lifted his head, smiling down into her eyes, then bent to take her lips again. He drank her in, and Thea rose up on tiptoe to match his desire. It was wildly exciting to kiss him like this, their naked skins pressed together. She could feel the hard, insistent pulse of his need against her, and the heat between her legs throbbed in response, seeming to flower and open eagerly.

As they kissed, his hands went to her back and he trailed his fingertips lightly down her on either side, touching her skin so lightly and delicately that it was as if a feather had brushed over her. She shivered in response and kissed him back even more feverishly. His fingers moved in the same way over the curve of her bottom and down onto the tops of her thighs, sliding tantalizingly close to the cleft between her legs. The pulse within her deepened, her skin tightening and prickling with need. Moisture flooded between her legs, embarrassing her, and she ached to spread her legs apart. She wanted to feel his fingers on her there. She wanted, she realized with some shock, to feel the throbbing length of his manhood there.

Breaking their kiss, Gabriel picked her up again and deposited her on the bed, then lay down beside her. Propping himself up on his elbow, he began to kiss her again, first her mouth, then her ears and face and neck. His other hand went to her breasts, cupping and caressing them, rolling her nipple gently between his thumb and forefinger. He slid lower, his lips trailing over her chest and down onto the pillowy-soft flesh of her breast. The tip of his tongue drew tantalizing designs over the soft orb as he traveled still lower to take her nipple into his mouth. Thea drew in a sharp breath and her fingers clenched in the coverlet beneath her. His mouth pulled and released, each new suction sending a frisson of pleasure straight down through her to gather and twist in her abdomen. His tongue circled the tight, little bud, lashing then soothing.

As his mouth worked on her breast, his fingers slid down her body, gliding over the plain of her stomach and abdomen, creeping ever lower. Her legs moved restlessly on the bed, opening for him, inviting his touch. But he did not immediately touch her there, sliding instead onto her thighs and back, tracing the crease where her thigh met the trunk of her body, then coming back up onto her abdomen and curving down to the other side. Her hips moved as if of their own volition, seeking him, yet still he did not come to the burning core of her, but teased with a featherlight touch, advancing and retreating. All the while, his mouth feasted on her breasts, moving from one to the other, every velvety stroke of his tongue stoking the need inside her.

Thea could not hold back a moan, and she felt his pleased smile in the movement of his lips on her body. Finally, his hand slipped into the V between her legs, and Thea shuddered. But this time he did not bring her to that hard, fast peak as he had before. Now his fingers explored her, parting and stroking, even, startlingly, slipping inside her. But that, too, only added fuel to the flame of her desire.

She would never have dreamed that she could feel so much, want so much, that passion could build in her until it was a white-hot flame and her whole body tingled and yearned for satisfaction. Yet with everything he did, the passion only increased more until she thought that she must burst with the force of the desire inside her.

He moved between her legs, and she felt at last the full length of his maleness between her legs. But she knew that was not all she wanted, either. The gentle, throbbing press of his flesh against her was another teasing promise, not fulfillment. She let out a little sob, clutching at his back. He groaned, too, at her movement.

"We're almost there, my sweet," he murmured, kissing her neck. "I want to make you ready."

"I am ready." Her words were almost a growl, and it earned a breathy, little chuckle from him.

"All right."

He reached down to position himself, and she felt the tip of his manhood prodding against her. Thea opened her legs wider, tilting her pelvis, and then he was pushing into her, filling her. Panic seized her for an instant as she feared that he was too big, that something was wrong with her, that it would not work and she would be left with this spiraling need that would never be satisfied. Then with a hard thrust, he plunged deep inside her, and pain flashed through her.

Gabriel paused, panting, his body slick with sweat. She could see the fierce concentration on his face, the powerful stillness in him, and she knew that he held himself back, not wanting to cause her further pain. Thea moved, wrapping her legs around him and giving him deeper access to her body. He dropped his head, kissing her neck as he began to stroke in and out, slowly and gently at first, then with increasing speed and force as passion took control of him. Thea clung to him, her whole body trembling with the need that was building inside her. It coiled and twisted, arching higher with every thrust of his body.

She felt as if she was teetering on the edge of something. Her heart slammed in her chest, and each breath was a ragged sob. She wanted, she ached, to reach the summit she was driving toward. And suddenly, she was there ... falling over, sliding off the precipice into an explosion of pleasure. Thea cried out as passion surged through her, filling every inch of her. She shook with the pleasure and release of it, and against her she felt Gabriel shudder, too, as they fell, spinning, locked together, into the abyss.

# Thirteen

Thea awoke in a cocoon of warmth. She blinked, trying to draw her scattered thoughts together. It took a moment to remember where she was and why a hard male body was curled around hers, but when she did, a slow smile crept across her face. Gabriel lay snuggled up to her back, one arm draped over her waist. Her body was naked under the rough sheets, but she was not cold. Gabriel's naked body behind her was warm as a furnace . . . and much more pleasant to be lying against.

She felt a soft prod against her buttocks, and she realized with some astonishment that desire was running through him even in his sleep. Would he wish to do that all over again? Her face grew warm at the idea, then even warmer when she realized that despite the soreness between her legs, her body was already responding with anticipation to the thought of Gabriel's filling her again. Thea squirmed back against him just to see what would happen, and the length of his m...... leaped. She heard his low, warm chuckle above her ear.

"Minx," he said lightly, but with no discernible displeasure in his voice, and he further proved that by sliding his hand down onto her abdomen and pressing her back against him more firmly.

His hand roamed possessively over the curve of her hip and down the side of her thigh, then back up and over her front, moving languidly over her stomach and lingering on her breasts. Her skin prickled in response, as though his caresses the night before had made her flesh even more responsive to him. This, she thought, must be the trap of wicked behavior—that once ensnared, one wanted it even more. At the moment, however, she could not find it in herself to worry about it; it was far too enjoyable to have his hand caressing her so intimately.

"Do you want—I mean—are you intending—" She stumbled to a stop, unable to think of any way to express her question that was remotely ladylike.

"Yes, I want," he murmured, his breath tickling her ear. He took the lobe lightly between his teeth.

Thea let out a shaky little breath, already feeling her nether regions melting.

"I want very much," he continued, and traced the shell of her ear with his tongue. "In fact"—he nuzzled into her hair as his fingers toyed with her nipple—"there's nothing I want more right now than to lie here for a few hours and further your education." He pulled aside the veil of her hair and bent to press his lips against the tender skin of her neck before he lifted his head and went on, "However, I intend to play the gentleman and leave you to sleep."

With a sigh of regret, he pulled away and slipped out of bed. Thea turned and unabashedly watched him dress, glad that he was turned slightly away from her and did not see her eyes greed-ily taking in the pull and release of the muscles in his back and legs. She was aware of a shocking desire to sink her teeth into the fleshy mound of his buttock.

"But what are you going to do?" she asked, keeping her voice quiet. Last night, after they had made love, Gabriel had pulled out of his sleepy, relaxed state long enough to bring in the baby and place the basket at the foot of their bed, and she did not want to wake Matthew.

"I plan to check on the animals." Gabriel spoke in the same whispered tone. "And I have an idea—something I saw last night. If I am right, it might be just the thing you want."

Since Thea knew that the one thing she wanted at this exact moment was his body back in bed with her, she seriously doubted that he was right. However, she said nothing, just snuggled deeper under the covers.

"What about Matthew?" she asked, unable to hold back a yawn.

"Sound asleep. It's only been a few hours. 'Tisn't close to noon yet. And he had a hard night."

Gabriel leaned over the bed to kiss her softly on the lips. Her arms snaked around his neck when he would have pulled away, and their kiss turned into something deeper and longer. Finally he pulled away. "Vixen. You will make me forget my good inten-tions." He gave her a last hard, brief kiss, then straightened and tiptoed away, reaching down to pick up his boots as he left.

Thea smiled to herself as he sneaked out the door. She closed her eyes, thinking that it would not be so bad, after all, to sleep a little longer. It was sweet of Gabriel to think of her comfort—and to think, once she had thought him nothing but a selfish rake. On that thought, she slid back into sleep.

She had no idea how long she dozed, coming to vague consciousness now and then when she heard Gabriel rattling around in the outer room. Finally her eyes opened, and she knew that she would not be able to fall asleep again. She slipped out of bed, wondering what the clanking and other noises were that she had heard earlier.

The air was chilling, but she could not dress, she thought, without washing as best she could, so she picked up the water jug and rag and started to wash, wincing at the cold. By the time she was finished, she was freezing, so she pulled the cover from the bed, wrapping it around herself as she tiptoed over to the basket and peered in at Matthew. He was still sound asleep, his mouth open slightly.

Gabriel was right, she thought; the poor baby must be horribly tired after the hard, frightening events of the night before. It was not surprising that he still slept—why, it probably had not yet been as long as he slept on a normal night. Still, she laid a light hand on his forehead just to make sure he was not feverish. Reassured, she straightened and started to pick up her clothes.

She heard another thump from the outer room, followed by a soft curse, then another sound she could not identify. Curious, she wrapped the cover more tightly around her body and opened the door to peer out. Her eyebrows vaulted upward.

A large, elongated wooden tub sat in front of the fireplace, looking utterly out of place. It was the sort of thing she had seen for feeding or watering horses, but it appeared two-thirds full of water, and Gabriel was bending over it, pouring steaming water from a kettle into it. He glanced up and saw her and smiled.

"Ah, there you are. I thought I would have to come awaken you. It's just about the right temperature." He refilled the kettle from a bucket that sat by the table and hung the kettle back on its hook at the fireplace, swinging it in to hang near the fire.

Thea pulled the door shut behind her and came forward, her voice filled with wonder. "A bath? You've drawn a bath?"

He grinned, looking quite proud of himself. "I saw it, sitting empty there in the stables last night, and this morning when I woke up, it occurred to me that it would be exactly what you would enjoy this morning."

And it was, Thea discovered. It would be wonderful to soak in the hot water, letting the soreness melt away, the warmth heating her all through. "Thank you." Tears clogged her throat, making her words come out hoarse. "You're very—oh, blast!" She blinked away the tears that pooled in her eyes.

He chuckled. "An eloquent thanks, my dear." He grabbed her around the waist and gave her a vigorous buss on the mouth, followed by a little slap on her bottom. "Now, out of your blanket, and into the bath."

She hesitated, heat rising in her cheeks, embarrassed at the thought of dropping the cover and standing completely naked in front of him. He raised his brows in question.

"What? Surely you are not shy. Not after last night?"

"'Tis daylight now," she protested.

"I'll warrant you look the same. I tell you what." He shrugged out of his jacket, then tugged off his boots, balancing on one leg, then the other. "I'll get in it as well. So you won't be the only one naked."

"Take my bath?" Thea retorted indignantly. "I think not!"

"Not take, my dear. Share." He whipped his shirt off over his head and dropped it to the floor.

Thea looked at the tub. "You must be joking. We shan't both fit."

"Of course we will. It just takes putting the pieces together right. Like a puzzle. You like puzzles, don't you?"

She gave him an exasperated look, but found it difficult to maintain since he was sliding off his breeches, revealing his long, muscled legs and, well, everything else. He reached out and twitched the bedcover from her grasp, dropping it on the floor beside the tub.

"Gabriel!"

He ignored her protest as he stepped into the tub and sat down. He did fit, which she had rather doubted, though he had to sit with his knees jackknifed to do so. He reached his hand up to her, as debonair as if he were helping her over a threshold or into a carriage. She took his hand and stepped into the tub as well, placing her feet carefully between his legs, turning her back to him as his hand nudged her to. She sat down slowly, his hands sliding up her body to her waist to guide her.

They did manage to fit, she found, as she leaned back against his chest and propped her feet up on the end of the tub. In fact, they fit almost perfectly, the warm water rising up over their lower bodies and lapping lazily at her breasts. She reached up, pulling her hair back and twisting it to wrap it in a looped knot at the base of her neck.

"No." He reached out to still her hands. "I like it down."

"It is wild and a nuisance."

"Yes, it is wild, but not a nuisance at all." He took her long, thick hair in his hands and wrapped it around behind his neck, bringing it up across his face and drawing in the scent. "It's soft and smells like—like you. I could lose myself in your curls." He nuzzled the back of her bare neck.

"It will get all wet."

"Then I shall have to brush it dry in front of the fire." He kissed his way along her collarbone to her shoulder, and Thea gave up her protests.

His hands moved slowly over her water-slicked body, and Thea let her head loll back against him, her eyes closing, lost in the pleasure his touch brought.

"You are beautiful," he murmured, his teeth gently worrying the cord of her throat.

"Don't be absurd."

"You doubt me?"

Thea snorted. "Of course I do. You needn't use blandishments to woo me. I have already given you what you seek, and we both know that I am not the sort of woman who is ... pleasing to men."

"I beg your pardon. I am a man, and I find you quite pleasing." At the little twitch of her mouth, he went on, "I'm perfectly serious; I'm not trying to seduce you." He paused, then added, with a demonstrative stroke of his hand, "Well, I *am* trying to seduce you, but not with flattery. I find you beautiful."

Thea swallowed against the emotion that tightened her throat.

"Your wild curls captivate me," he went on in a low voice, his breath drifting tantalizingly over her hair and face. "From the moment I saw them tumbling all about your face, I wanted to sink my hands into them and kiss you senseless."

"To shut me up, no doubt," she shot back tartly.

He chuckled. "That would have been an added benefit, no doubt, but it was not the motivating force, I assure you. Why do you think I kissed you in the church? Not because I was trying to challenge the Almighty. I could not keep from doing it. I have not been able to stop myself from kissing you a number of times, as you may have noticed."

"I think that is more due to your nature. We have already established that you are ... shall we say, an expert with women?"

"I confess, I have enjoyed the charms of more than a few of the fairer sex. But that only serves to prove my point—I am clearly a judge of female beauty. An expert, as you say. 'Twould be foolish to gainsay me."

"You are an expert at wagging your tongue."

"That, too." He tickled her ear with the tip of his tongue, making Thea giggle. "Shall I tell you more? About how you enticed me?"

Thea shrugged, unwilling to admit that his words warmed her even more than the water around them, so that she felt as if her heart were blossoming inside her chest. Some part of her brain told her she was foolish, but she could not keep from soaking up his words.

"I am sure you will be surprised," he went on gravely, "when I say that it was not your sweet tone or compliant manner that made me dream of you the past few nights and wake stiff and sweating like a hard-run horse, my heart thundering."

Thea's breath caught in her throat, the now familiar ache beginning to pulse deep inside her, his words stirring her almost as much as the velvet touch of his lips on her neck.

"It was the thought of your breasts and how they would feel in my hands. I knew they would fit perfectly." He cupped her breasts in his hands to demonstrate, and his forefinger traced around the nipples, making them prickle. The heat in Thea's abdomen grew, swelling and throbbing and spreading out.

"And I dreamed of those deliciously long legs. I kept imagining what they looked like beneath your prim gowns. I could not see you walk without wanting to measure them with my hands." His voice deepened huskily as his hands slid down to her thighs. "Each step you took, I thought of the way your legs would feel wrapped around me."

His hand slipped into the crevice between her legs, gliding down her inner thigh and back up, teasing along the crease of her leg. She felt swollen and aching, yearning for his touch. His fingers were featherlight upon her, teasingly opening and exploring the intimate folds of her flesh. As his fingers stroked her, arousing her almost past bearing, he kissed her neck, using his teeth and tongue to draw shivers of arousal from her.

Thea's breath was ragged, and she braced her feet against the edge of the tub, widening her legs, inviting him wordlessly. He found the hard, bright center of her desire, the pulsing, vulnerable ache, and he pressed in, the rhythmic movement of his hand thrusting her pleasure higher and higher. Thea could feel the passion taking her, sweeping over her and cresting like a wave. It broke over her, and she could not hold back a thin, sharp cry. She shuddered as pleasure rippled through her, then relaxed with a deep, satisfied sigh.

She lay against him, replete, numb, her mind adrift. Thea felt the push of his member against her, and she knew that he, of course, was still unsatisfied, but she could not move. Her bones seemed to have all turned to molten wax inside her.

Gabriel kissed her neck and along her collarbone, his breath harsh and rasping. "I have to taste you," he muttered.

Surprising her, he stood up, hauling her up with him. She turned to him, but he was already stepping out of the tub and spreading her bedcover out on the floor before the fire. She could not tear her eyes away from his strong, lithe body or the hard, elongated maleness that thrust out from his body. Thea would have liked to touch him, but she was not bold enough, even in the warm, sated state she dwelled in now.

Gabriel lifted her from the old wooden tub and laid her down on the bedspread, then covered her with his body, propped himself up on his elbows. She opened her legs, luxuriating in the feel of his maleness pressing at the gate of her femininity. He gazed down at her for a long moment, his eyes hard and bright, the firelight glowing in them. Then he bent his head to take her mouth, kissing her as though he would consume her. He kissed her again and again, and when he pulled his mouth from hers, he moved down her body, kissing seemingly every inch of her.

He took her breast in his mouth, devoting his complete attention to it. Thea was shocked to feel her body respond to him, the heat and tension building in her once more. She would have thought that all the passion had been drained from her in that explosion of pleasure. But somehow it lurked inside her, curling and leaping and swelling with each touch of his lips.

Gabriel moved to her other breast, lavishing the same exquisite care on it. He made his way down her body, mumbling low, soft words she could not understand but the hunger and need of which was abundantly clear. His tongue dipped into the well of her navel, moving out to trace patterns over her skin. He moved ever lower, and Thea felt his hands slip beneath her hips, lifting her. Then, unbelievably, his mouth was on her in that most intimate of places, teasing and stroking, arousing her in a way she would never have imagined.

"Gabriel!" Passion roared through her even more fiercely, igniting her to a white-hot pitch. Thea curled her fingers into the spread beneath her, a groan escaping her clenched lips as Gabriel toyed with her, his tongue driving her higher and harder than anything else he had done before. She arched up, digging in her heels, her body taut, desperately seeking the release that dangled just beyond her grasp.

Then it crashed through her, and she trembled all over. For a moment she was beyond thought, beyond speech, her world narrowed down to the supreme release that carried her away. Gently he lowered her hips and lay down beside her. Thea could do little more than gasp for breath, her heart slamming inside her chest.

After what could have been hours or mere moments, for she felt utterly beyond time, Thea turned her head to look at Gabriel. He was watching her, his eyes still glinting between his narrowed lids.

"Gabriel . . ." She reached out and put her hand on his chest, not sure what she wanted to say. A hundred emotions were tumbling about inside her, and she could not even begin to straighten them out enough to give voice to them. "But you are still unsatisfied" was what she found herself saying.

"I enjoyed it, believe me. And it was your first time last night. I did not want to hurt you."

"Are you sure it would hurt?"

"No." His smile was wry. "I have little experience with virgins."

"I think I should like to try. You seem to want something more . . ." She looked down at the clear evidence of his unspent desire, and her hand drifted lower.

"Indeed." He sucked in his breath as her hand glided lower, but when she shot him a tentative glance, he said, "No, don't stop."

"Do you like it?" Thea smiled a little, sliding her hand farther downward.

"You know I do. I can see you grin like a fox."

She giggled. She had never before felt like this, so happy, so free and unfettered. "But, indeed, my lord, I thought you might find me too bold."

"I like a bold wench." Her fingers reached him and stopped, barely touching the base of his manhood. He let out a low groan, his teeth clamping down on his lower lip.

"I don't know what to do," she admitted, the teasing leaving her voice.

"I think . . . whatever you try . . . I shall find pleasing," he told her, his lungs laboring.

Thea skimmed her fingertips along the length of him, amazed and delighted by the satin smoothness of his flesh over the hard line beneath. Slowly she trailed her fingers up and down him, and the low moan her actions pulled from him stirred an answering heat in her belly.

She was not so surprised this time to find that desire could pulse in her again, and she let herself savor each moment along the way. She played with him, teasing and arousing him, her hand sliding farther down to cup the sac between his legs. Gabriel shuddered. His eyes were closed, his skin stretched taut across his facial bones, his breath harsh on his lips. Thea gently curled her fingers around him, and he jerked, but he shook his head when she paused.

"Don't stop."

She stroked him with slow, almost languid motions, feeling the slick glide of his skin against her palm. His pulse pounded in his throat, his chest rising and falling in pants, and the signs of his passion aroused her.

"I want you inside me," she whispered to him. "I want to take you inside me."

His eyes flew open, fierce and bright. He reached out, taking her hips in his hands, and tugged her toward his legs. "Ride me."

"What? Oh." Her eyes widened a little, but she moved quickly to do as he said, straddling him and lowering her body over him until she felt the springing thrust of his maleness against her. Reaching down, she took him in her hand once again, guiding him into her. The sensitive flesh throbbed at the touch of his hardness, and she moved the tip of his manhood against her, tormenting them both in the most delightful way. She eased down slowly, then pulled back up, exploring each new sensation she created. The exquisite friction tantalized, delighted, beckoned, and promised.

He moved beneath her, pushed almost to the breaking point, and then his hands clamped on her hips, and he lifted up, slamming into her with hard, fierce thrusts. Thea matched his rhythm, the dark, tumultuous pleasure driving her ever closer. At last it exploded, sweeping them both over the edge and into the dark chasm of pleasure.

*Thea was not sure how* long she lay there, her head pillowed on Gabriel's broad chest, half-asleep and utterly at peace, before a wail sounded from the bedroom, breaking the peace. She felt the rumble of Gabriel's laughter beneath her ear.

"At least we can rest assured that the cold did not harm his lungs." Gabriel eased out from beneath her and stood up, grabbing his breeches and pulling them on. "I'll get him."

Thea rose, too, wrapping the cover around her once more, and followed him into the bedroom. Gabriel picked Matthew up, and his crying stopped immediately, the tears turning to a smile. Thea had long since given up being astonished by Gabriel's seemingly magical effect on the baby. After all, she had experienced Gabriel's charm, as well. While Gabriel whisked the baby out into the main room of the cottage, Thea dressed.

She ran her hands through her hair, wishing she had a brush or comb. She started to braid it, but stopped, Gabriel's words going through her head, and she let her hair fall back down. She leaned in close to the mirror to look at herself. Could Gabriel really find her beautiful? Was that tumble of reddish-brown curls really appealing? Did he see something in her level gray gaze that other men did not?

Thea tilted her head to one side and then the other. She could not help but think that she did look different today—her skin had a glow, her features a softness, that she was not sure had ever before been there. Could happiness make one prettier? If so, she should be stunning, for she was certain that she had never before felt the singing joy that filled her now.

She supposed that she should feel guilty and sinful, but Thea could not. She had experienced something she had never thought she would, and it had been far more wonderful than she could ever have imagined. The joy might be brief; Thea was far too realistic not to admit that within a few weeks or even days, Gabriel would likely be gone from here—perhaps taking Matthew with him. But however short this happy moment was, Thea intended to enjoy it. And if sorrow followed, so be it. Good things rarely came for free, in her experience.

Gabriel was feeding the baby at the table when Thea joined them. She picked up the spectacles that she had left on the table the night before and settled them on her nose. Gabriel looked up at her and smiled, and Matthew followed suit. Despite the difference in their coloring, Thea could see the resemblance between them, and she could not help but think that the child must be his sister's. But she could not understand why his sister would have abandoned the baby. Knowing Gabriel as she did now, she could not think that Jocelyn would have thought Gabriel would be angry or punitive.

"Why did that man steal Matthew?" Thea asked, following the train of her thoughts. "Who was he?"

"I have no idea." Gabriel tore another piece of bread from the piece before him and dipped it in milk, then offered it to the baby. Matthew grabbed it and shoved it in his mouth, bouncing as if to some inner tune. "I did not get a very good look at him as we fought, but he certainly didn't look familiar. Why would anyone steal an abandoned baby?"

"It makes no sense," Thea agreed, reaching out and tearing off a little chunk of bread to pop in her own mouth. "Perhaps someone stole the baby from him and he was taking it back."

"But if he had a legitimate claim to the child, he wouldn't have crept in and grabbed it from your house in the middle of the night. Rawdon was right in saying that the child's father could take the baby legally. The argument makes even more sense given that Matthew was abandoned. Most people would happily turn a foundling over to anyone who appeared to claim him."

"True. So I would not think he is Matthew's father."

"No."

Thea looked at Gabriel. "Do you still think that Lord Rawdon is his father?"

Gabriel sighed. "I don't know what to think. I don't even know if my sister is his mother."

"I was just thinking that he looked a bit like you."

"Does he now?" Gabriel gazed down at the child, tilting his head consideringly. Matthew chose that moment to purse his lips and blow out milky air bubbles, making Gabriel and Thea laugh. "Obviously he has my sophisticated charm."

"Indeed."

More seriously, Gabriel said, "I feel as if . . . as if he is connected to me. But perhaps I am merely being foolish. If he is Jocelyn's, 'tis hard for me to believe the father was someone other than her fiancé. Obviously Rawdon was not the man who stole Matthew—still, I suppose he could have hired the fellow to do so."

"But you just said that he would not need to. He could take him from you in court."

"True." Gabriel sighed, obviously reluctant to give up the idea. "No, I think Rawdon must not have had a hand in taking Matthew. But that does not mean he is not the father. A large number of men have no interest in claiming their by-blows. Still, given the enmity between us, I would think he would take his child simply because I do not want him to."

"Perhaps the kidnapper took the baby from your sister—or whoever his mother is—and was asking for a ransom for him. But then somehow the baby wound up at St. Margaret's, and he was trying to steal him back."

"So he stole the baby from his mother, then someone stole it from him, and then that someone abandoned the child in the manger of an empty church?"

Thea made a face. "Well, if you put it that way . . ." She shrugged.

"I am not sure we are ever going to understand what happened with Matthew."

"You may be right." Gabriel wiped the baby's mouth and stood up, putting him to his shoulder and patting his back. He strolled over to the window as he talked. "But I intend to make certain that no one has a chance to steal him again."

"I will keep him with me in my room every night from now on. And I will make sure that not only is the door to our house locked, but also the door to my bedchamber."

"I shall have one of my men standing watch at night, as well. Not that one you bullied so easily. Peter, I think; he seems made of sterner stuff."

"A guard? Really, Gabriel, that won't be necessary, surely."

He shot her a hard look. "Do not fight me on this, Thea. I will not leave you and Matthew exposed to danger. What I would prefer is to be there myself to make sure nothing happens, but obviously that is not a possibility. And even if I take Matthew to the Priory with me, it would still leave you vulnerable." His face was a study in frustration. "The only thing I can do to protect you both is to put one of my servants there at night, and I will do so."

Ordinarily his peremptory tone would have been enough to make Thea argue, but she could see how much he disliked his comparative lack of power in this situation, so she only nodded her head. Rising, she went over to where he stood in front of the window, and he looped an arm around her shoulders, tucking her against his side. For a long moment they stood silently, gazing out at the snowy scene in front of them. Gabriel bent and kissed the top of her head. "I think I would prefer to stay right here instead of going home, frankly."

Thea smiled and rubbed her head against him. "It seems much more pleasant. But I fear we could not stay here forever. For one thing, we are getting low on milk."

"I think it comes from that goat out back."

Thea tilted her head back to look at him skeptically. "And are you planning to try to milk that goat?"

He looked offended. "You think I could not?"

Thea laughed. "I am wiser than to offer you such a challenge." She returned to her contemplation of the snow outside. She understood what Gabriel meant. It would be wonderful to stay here together, alone except for Matthew. She could smile at Gabriel whenever she wanted or reach out to touch his arm without worrying about what someone observing them might think. There were no rules here or gossip or other people, only the sweet excitement of his hands and mouth on her, the indescribable fulfillment as he plunged to his peak within her.

Unconsciously she let out a little sigh. Gabriel leaned down to whisper in her ear. "We could celebrate our very own Christmas here, you know."

She cast a teasing glance up at him. "Indeed?" She glanced around. "Here?"

"Of course. We have everything we need."

"Oh, really? And what do we have of Christmas?"

"First, and most important, we have the best present that either of us could have received." He held Matthew out to her. "We found Matthew."

Thea laughed and reached out to take the baby. "That is true enough."

"But it is only the beginning." Gabriel went over to the fireplace and dug amongst the wood piled beside it, pulling out the largest of the logs. Brandishing it triumphantly, he said, "We have the Yule log."

"Oh, and the Yule candles." Thea pointed to a low, fat candle sitting on a saucer on the counter.

"Indeed. And . . . we also have a feast."

"A feast?"

"Of course." Gabriel offered Thea his arm in his most courtly manner and escorted her back to the table, where he pulled out a chair for her with a flourish.

He went into the pantry, returning with a chunk of wrapped cheese and the piece of roast beef. He added the bread to the table and stepped back, his hands behind his back.

"My. What more could we ask?"

"Dessert." He brought his hand out from behind his back, presenting, with a flourish, a faintly withered apple.

Thea laughed. "It is a feast indeed."

She realized that she was hungry, and they both tucked into the food with a hearty appetite. It tasted, she thought, as good as any meal she had ever had. Whether it was her hunger which made it so or the company in which she ate, she knew that she would never forget the meal.

Afterward, she put Matthew down to play on the floor a little distance from the fireplace. Gabriel sat in the armchair beside the fire and pulled Thea into his lap. She leaned against his chest and watched the baby play. Gabriel's arms were wrapped around her and his head rested on hers. She felt cocooned in his warmth, his heartbeat steady and reassuring beneath her ear. Now and then he trailed his fingers down her arm or stroked his hand along her hip, and at his touch, heat blossomed. She was amazed to think that desire could rise up in her yet again.

"I think," she said, "that I must be a wanton."

His laughter rumbled in his chest. "I am very glad for that." He nuzzled her neck, sending bright little shivers running through her.

"A lady should not feel this way. I am sure of it."

"What way is that?" He slid his thumb up her arm.

"All fizzy and warm whenever you touch me."

"Ah. And what about when I do this?" He slipped his hand down her front, his finger circling her nipple.

"It makes me wonder when I can put Matthew down for a nap."

He chuckled, but she could feel the swift, pulsing response of his desire beneath her.

"And *that*," she added, shifting on his lap and feeling him leap beneath her again, "makes me think all sorts of sinful things."

"Mm. I like the way your mind works." He bent his head for a long, thorough kiss.

Finally Thea broke their kiss. "We must not. Not in front of the baby."

Gabriel cast a look at Matthew, who was busily clanking a wooden spoon against an overturned pot. "I don't think he will notice."

"I will know," she replied unarguably. "I am not *that* wanton."

He grinned at her wickedly. "Then I shall endeavor to make you more so."

She felt herself blushing a little at the look in his eyes, and he chuckled, running a finger along her cheek. "I love to see your blush. I should like to do a great many more things to bring that color to your cheeks."

"Gabriel!" Thea could not keep from adding a moment later, "What things?"

He roared with laughter and gave her a hard, swift kiss. "I will be happy to show you, once Matthew goes to sleep." He looked toward the baby again. Matthew had lost his spoon with a wild wave of his hand, and he let out a little bellow, reaching out and making grasping motions. Gabriel sighed. "Somehow I am not hopeful that he is going to sleep anytime soon."

"True. Perhaps we had best talk about something else."

"Tell me about Christmas in Chesley."

"Truly?" Thea looked up at him.

He nodded. "What do you like the best?"

"The morris dancers," she answered promptly.

"The morris dancers? I thought that was a spring event in villages."

She nodded. "It is. But they do it here on Christmas Day, as well. Do they not in your village?"

"I am usually in London. I remember them from the spring when I was little, back on the estate. But I do not think they are about as much as they are in the Cotswolds."

"We are not a people prone to change." Thea sighed, and after a moment, she said in a sad voice, "We should go back."

"I know." He sounded no more happy about it than she.

"Everyone will wonder where we are if we are both gone at Christmas. It will be a terrible scandal."

His arms curled around her more tightly, and he bent to kiss the top of her head. "Yes. You are right." He stood up, setting her on her feet. "I am going to look around, see what the conditions are."

Thea nodded and turned away, unwilling to let him see the tears that sprang to her eyes. She knew that they should go, but she did not want to. She wished—foolishly, she knew, for it would be her reputation more than Gabriel's that would be damaged by a scandal—that Gabriel had not acquiesced so easily, that he had tried to deny her assertion or argue it away or cajole her into staying.

To take her mind off the possibility of leaving, she went about the cabin, straightening up and putting the food back into the pantry. She glanced out the window and saw Gabriel walking through the snow toward the road, leading the two unharnessed horses. They passed out of her sight, and she returned to her work. There was little enough to do after that, though the baby began to fuss and she occupied herself for a little while in picking him up and walking about, patting and soothing him. When she felt him grow heavier in her arms, she knew that he had fallen asleep.

"Couldn't you have chosen to do that earlier?" she murmured to him, then laid him down in his little bed, tucking his blanket in around him.

Gabriel came in a few minutes later. She held up her hand

in warning, pointing to the sleeping baby. He nodded and came closer, taking her arm and leading her into the bedroom. Closing the door, he turned to her.

"I broke a trail with the horses to the road. That should make it easier for the curricle to pass through. The worst thing would be to break one of its wheels and leave us stranded on the road."

"Will we be able to make it?"

He grimaced. "If there were nothing else involved, I would say we should wait another day. If I did only what I wanted, I would wait another week." He came closer, reaching up a hand to cup her cheek. "But you are right. Your reputation will suffer if we wait. Just last night and today, perhaps we will be able to keep it secret. But if you are gone Christmas Day, I fear everyone will notice. And I have little faith in a vicar's ability to tell everyone a satisfactory lie."

Thea gave a rueful smile. "If you knew Daniel better, you would have even less faith in his lying."

"I will not have you hurt by village gossip. I think we can probably make it to Chesley. We did not come as far as it seemed last night. It took us over two hours, but I think we will be able to make it back in less time without the wind and falling snow. When I reached the road, it was clear that there had been traffic on it—a wagon or coach, perhaps more than that. It will not be as difficult on the road as it will be up to it. If we can make it there, we should be fine."

Thea nodded. "Very well. We are ready to go. All I have to do is put another blanket on top of Matthew."

"Wait." He reached out to cup her neck, a devilish grin spreading across his face. "We have something to do before we go."

A thrill ran out through all Thea's nerves. She cast a teasing glance up at him. "Really? And what is that?"

"Yes, really." He plucked the spectacles from her face. "I will show you."

# Fourteen

They made love sweetly this time, stoking the fires of their passion until they finally burned too hot to be denied and swept them to a shattering paroxysm of pleasure. But the sun was moving inexorably in the sky, so, reluctantly, they left their bed. While Gabriel went out to harness the team, Thea rose and dressed, plaiting her recalcitrant hair into two long braids and tying them with a piece of ribbon she cut from her petticoat. A look in the mirror told her that her hair still looked anything but orderly, but she comforted herself with the thought that no one would be able to see it once she pulled on her knit cap and the hood of her cloak. She folded one of the extra blankets she'd brought and tucked it around the sleeping Matthew, then wrapped up the remainder of the bread, just in case he grew hungry on the trip.

She cast a last look around the place, feeling the treacherous sting of tears in her eyes. She told herself it was nonsensical to feel this way over a nondescript little cottage that they had been forced to stay in because of bad weather. It was in no way a romantic trysting place, and she was not the sort to be foolishly romantic, anyway. But she knew, with a tug in her chest, that the night she had spent here had been the most wonderful time of her life.

They stowed the baby in his basket on the floorboard between them, the heavy lap robe across their laps hanging over his basket like a roof. Thea stuffed the other blanket between them in an attempt to cut off as much of the draft from the baby as was possible.

As Gabriel had predicted, the drive to the road was difficult, the snow still deep even after the horses had trampled it down, and Thea spent most of the time with her hands curled into fists, tensely waiting for the crack of a wheel hitting a hidden rock or rut. They had to stop once and get out to push when one of the wheels got stuck, but they persevered, finally reaching the road. Here a passing wagon or coach had created ruts and a more beaten-down path, and they were able to move more freely. Gabriel drove carefully for fear of hitting an icy patch, but they did not encounter any problems beyond Matthew's awakening and fussing at being left in his basket.

The trip was almost eerily quiet, and they passed no one on the way. The snow-covered trees and bushes were beautiful, broken only now and then by the darting flight of a bird. It was easy to feel as if they were alone in this pristine world. When, just as the last sliver of sun was passing over the horizon, the curricle approached the familiar grounds of the church and vicarage, Thea felt a distinct stab of disappointment. Her normal life was about to continue, the idyllic moment of time with Gabriel gone.

Gabriel helped Thea, who was now carrying the baby, down from the vehicle and carried the baby's basket into the house. Thea stepped into the kitchen and was at once engulfed in warmth and light and the wonderful aroma of spices. Lolly was sitting curled up on the hearth of the great fireplace, and she leaped to her feet with a loud whoop when she saw Thea.

"Oh, miss! The baby! You found him!" She rushed forward, and Thea handed Matthew over to her.

"Yes, and he seems to be all right, but I am sure he is in need of both food and a new set of clothes."

"Yes, miss, this is wonderful! I'm so happy!" Lolly jiggled the baby, kissing him all over his face and making him giggle. She practically danced out of the room, taking Matthew upstairs to change.

Thea turned to Gabriel. She smiled, forcing down the sudden onslaught of sadness. It wasn't as if he were going away forever, she told herself. She would see him again, no doubt soon. But she could not help but think how very different it would now be.

He reached out to take her hands and looked down at her, frowning. "Blast. I cannot even give you a proper good-bye for fear your brother or someone will pop in at any moment." He cast a wary eye at the door into the rest of the house, then bent to give her a quick kiss. "Oh, the devil with it." He pulled her into his arms for a deeper and much more satisfying kiss.

At last he released her. "I must get home. I cannot leave my team out there any longer."

"No. You should not. They deserve a nice warm stable and a good meal of oats."

"They shall get it, no worry there. And I shall doubtless receive a proper scolding from my head groom."

He hesitated, giving her hand a last squeeze, then turned abruptly and walked away. At the door, he pivoted back, saying, "I shall send a man over as soon as I get to the house."

Thea nodded, and he was gone. She let out a sigh and began to pull off her cloak and gloves.

"Thea!" The door opened and Daniel walked in. "Thank goodness you are back. I could not believe it this morning when Lolly gave me your note. Really, Thea, what were you thinking?"

"I was thinking about Matthew's safety."

"Who?"

"Matthew. The baby. Really, Daniel, you cannot be that forgetful."

"No, of course not, it's just—I don't know, things are all at sixes and sevens since you took up that child."

"What things?" she asked, reminding herself to be patient. Daniel was not an unkind man; he simply got fussy when his world fell out of its proper little order.

"I have been trying to write my sermon for tomorrow." He gave her an aggrieved look. "I searched all over for your suggestions, but I couldn't find them."

"I didn't have time this week, Daniel, but I am sure you were quite able to write the Christmas sermon without my help."

"Yes, of course, that is exactly what I have been doing today. But then there were all those people who kept coming by for food."

"We always give food to the poor on Christmas Eve."

"Yes, I know, but you take care of that. I am sure they all wondered where you were."

"What did you tell them?"

"I told them you were feeling under the weather, but that is not the point. I had to *lie* to them."

"I know you dislike lying, and I am very grateful, believe me." She paused, hoping that her brother would ask about Matthew, but when he did not, she said somewhat tartly, "We found the baby and brought him back. He seems to have not suffered from his ordeal."

"I see. Well, that is good." Daniel's voice showed a lack of conviction in his words. He started to say more, but at that moment Lolly came back into the kitchen, carrying Matthew.

"Here, I'll hold him while you get his supper ready," Thea offered, taking the baby and settling him on her hip with an ease of practice that had her brother frowning.

A knock sounded at the back door, and Daniel said crossly, "Now who in the world can that be? I thought the poor were all gone."

"Ah, but 'the poor are with us always,' are they not?" Thea reminded him with a grin, and went to open the door, preparing herself to look ill. Given the state of her hair, she suspected that a visitor could easily believe that she had just arisen from her sickbed.

But when she pulled open the door and saw the tall, blond man on the doorstep, she knew she would not have to pretend anything. "Lord Rawdon, come in."

"Miss Bainbridge." He stepped inside, politely sweeping off his hat. His gaze went to the baby. "I came to tell you that I was unable to track down anyone—apart from some poor peddler who got caught in the snowstorm, that is. But I see that you have found the child."

"Yes, we did. We caught up with the kidnapper at the cottage where he had taken refuge. Ga—that is, Lord Morecombe struggled with him, but he got away."

"Did he get any information from the fellow?"

"No, I'm afraid not. The man knocked Morecombe in the head with a log before he could ask him anything."

"Ah." The ghost of a smile touched Rawdon's face. "Then at least he didn't damage Morecombe much."

A giggle escaped Thea at his words. Behind her, Daniel cleared his throat ostentatiously.

"Oh! I'm sorry," Thea told Rawdon. "I have neglected to introduce you to my brother. Lord Rawdon, this is my brother, the Reverend Daniel Bainbridge. Daniel, the Earl of Rawdon."

Rawdon nodded politely to her brother, his gaze flickering over Daniel with a decided lack of interest before he turned back to Thea. "Well, I shall leave you to get on with your holiday, then. I am glad you recovered the boy. He, ah, seems unharmed."

Rawdon reached out awkwardly to touch Matthew's shining curls. Matthew regarded him solemnly for a long moment, then, as Rawdon pulled his hand back, the baby broke into one of his sunny smiles, startling a chuckle from the man.

"A pretty child. I can see Jocelyn in him."

The instant of bleakness in Rawdon's angular face touched something in Thea. She thought of the man spending Christmas by himself at the inn, and she blurted out, "We are having a few guests over for the Christmas feast tomorrow. Perhaps you would join us . . . if you are not otherwise occupied, I mean."

He glanced at her with faint surprise. "Indeed. Well . . . yes, I mean, that is most kind of you. I should be honored to join you. Till tomorrow, then." He nodded toward Daniel. "Reverend."

Thea closed the door behind Rawdon and turned to see her brother staring at her in astonishment.

"Who in the name of all that's holy was that?" Daniel asked, his voice shooting up almost to a squeak. "Are we to have any more lords tromping in and out of the house at all hours?"

"No, I believe I know only the two." Thea gave the baby back to Lolly and went over to take her brother's arm and nudge him from the room with her. "Really, Daniel, just think, an earl will be gracing our Christmas dinner. The Squire's wife will be green with envy."

"I don't give a fig about the Squire's wife and her envy. Dash it, Thea, you can't go about consorting with all these noblemen. You don't know what they're like. I do; I went to school with chaps like that. No doubt you think that they are gentlemen just because they're titled, but I can tell you that a greater group of frivolous-minded, hedonistic men you will never meet. They have no concern for a woman's reputation unless you are as highborn as they—and not always even then."

Thea smiled at her brother and reached over impulsively to give him a hug. "Why, Daniel, I do believe you are truly concerned that I will get hurt."

"Of course I am. What do you think I have been talking about for the past age?"

Thea decided it was best not to tell him that she thought he had largely been talking about the inconvenience she had caused him as vicar, so she simply smiled and said, "You need not worry. I am quite aware of the morals of highborn men, and I have no doubt that many of them do not deserve to be known as gentlemen. However, I can assure you that Lord Rawdon has no designs upon my virtue. I scarcely know the man."

"Yet you invited him to Christmas dinner."

"I felt ... sorry for him."

"Sorry?" Daniel goggled at her.

"He is alone. And, however much a villain Morecombe thinks him, no one deserves to be alone on Christmas."

"A villain?" If possible, Daniel looked even more distressed. "Really, Thea, I don't understand." He waved his hand hastily when she started to speak. "But that is not really the issue. It is this time you spent with Lord Morecombe that worries me."

"Lord Morecombe expressed an appropriate concern for my reputation," Thea told Daniel primly.

"That's all very well and good, but his concern will not shield you from gossip. Thea . . ." Daniel lowered his voice. "What if everyone knew that you were not here last night? That you spent the night in *his* company? I am sure nothing happened, of course, but your reputation would be ruined, anyway."

Thea suspected that Daniel's certainty regarding her virtue had more to do with the belief that Lord Morecombe would be uninterested in seducing her than in any staunch conviction regarding Thea's morals, but she said only, "That would happen only if word got out that I was not here last night. I have no intention of telling anyone, and I am sure that Lord Morecombe will not speak of it, either, so unless you plan to go about spreading the news…"

"No, of course not! But what about Lolly? And Mrs. Brewster? I told her you were ill and not to disturb you, but she gave me a decidedly odd look, and I know she suspected something. Unless I miss my guess, she went up to check on you, anyway."

"She probably did. But I do not believe Mrs. Brewster would say anything that would hurt me. And Lolly is too afraid of losing her job over the baby's disappearance to add to that by spreading gossip. I shall make sure she knows it."

Daniel frowned. "And that is decidedly odd, too, Thea. Why would anyone come here and steal a foundling?"

"I don't know. But Gabriel said he would send a servant over to stand guard so that it cannot happen again."

"We are to have another stranger living in the house now?" Daniel heaved a sigh, then held up his hands. "No. I don't even want to know. I am going to my study. I haven't had a moment's peace all day."

He trudged off. Thea watched him go, then turned and went to lock both the front door and the one into the kitchen. It took some time to find the kitchen key; she could not remember the last time it had been locked. The footman arrived from the Priory, looking cold but quietly determined. His name was Peter, and he was, he assured her, a good shot, having grown up as the son of a gamekeeper. He did not seem unhappy at the thought of putting down a blanket and sleeping on the floor at the top of the stairs, which was apparently what Gabriel had instructed him to do.

"His lordship's a generous man; he's doubling me wages," he confided to her in a boyish manner. "More interesting than serving food and polishing silver, anyway."

"Very well. My chamber is the first one after the stairs. Come and wake me if you encounter any trouble."

Thea went up to her room finally, grateful to wash and change out of the clothing she had worn far too long. Lolly brought both the baby and bed to Thea's bedroom, as Thea had instructed. Thea locked the door after the girl left. Matthew was already rubbing his face and tugging at his hair, and he was asleep before she blew out the candle.

She went to the window and parted the drapes, gazing out into the night. The snow cast back an almost bluish light under the glow of the moon. Thea looked past the trees to the church. Beyond it somewhere lay the Priory. She wondered what Gabriel was doing now and whether he thought of her.

It would not be the same for him, of course. The things she felt—the wonder, the pleasure, the aching sense of loss at his absence. It was not his first time; he was doubtless well accustomed to the pleasures that were so new for her. Anyway, she had always heard that it was different for men. They could feel desire and lust for a woman without any sort of affection. She was not fool enough to think that Gabriel loved her—not, of course, that she loved him, either. She did not.

Did she?

Thea moved restlessly away from the window, letting the draperies fall back together. She did not love Gabriel. She could not. It was absurd. She had known him only weeks, after all, and even though he was a far better man than she had first thought, even though he was charming and handsome and the three of them had seemed almost like a family back there at the kidnapper's cottage, none of that meant that she *loved* him. She did not.

Did she?

*Thea awakened to the pealing* of the church bells. She smiled as she lay there, her heart rising within her. The unease she had experienced the evening before was gone in the pale golden light of Christmas morning. Raising up on one elbow, she glanced over the side of her bed. Matthew was awake in his basket, all covers kicked off, babbling to himself as he played with his toes.

She slipped out of bed and opened the draperies and stood for a long moment, admiring the way the sun sparkled on the snow. Humming, she went to the dresser and pulled out a brown wool round gown. If she handed Matthew over to Lolly to feed and dress, she might be able to tack on the blond lace she had bought at the haberdashery in Bynford last week, which would make the gown look much more festive.

Thea left for the Christmas service an hour later, well pleased with her efforts. The color of the dress was still dull, but the bits of lace at the high collar and cuffs softened it nicely. She had not put her hair in its usual braided crown, but had pinned it up in a cascade of curls at the crown of her head, leaving the shorter curls in front to feather around her face.

A defiant imp inside her was tempted to take the baby to church, but after a brief struggle, her more reasonable nature won out. Matthew had already been exposed to a great deal of poor weather, and she was lucky that he had not fallen ill. It seemed to be tempting fate to drag him out in the cold again, just to show that she did not care about the village gossip. So, leaving him in the warm kitchen under the watchful eye of Lolly and Mrs. Brewster, as well as that of Peter, she donned her cloak and bonnet and sallied forth to join the other worshippers.

Thea felt rather proud of her brother, who had not only written a good sermon, but also delivered the words he had written with more feeling, she thought, than was his wont. Apparently Daniel was of the same opinion, for he was in a merry mood after church. He set himself to his traditional task of preparing the wassail bowl while Thea helped Mrs. Brewster and Lolly in the kitchen.

Sometime later, a knock sounded at the front door, and Thea opened it to find Damaris standing on the front stoop with Lord Rawdon. Her face must have registered her surprise, for Damaris smiled and offered an explanation: "Lord Rawdon and I met as I was coming up High Street. Imagine our surprise when we discovered we had the same goal in mind."

Damaris's large blue eyes were sparkling, and Thea wondered whether it was from amusement or irritation. As she remembered, Lord Rawdon had been rather rude to Damaris when they had met the other day. Of course, he had been rather rude to everyone, Thea reflected. She hoped she had not made a mistake in inviting him.

Daniel, too, appeared somewhat wary as he greeted Rawdon, but when the man offered him a bottle of the inn's best brandy, Daniel thawed a good deal and invited Rawdon back to his study to sample some of the drink. Thea took Damaris's pelisse and muff and led her into the sitting room, where the Yule log was still burning merrily.

"I nearly swallowed my tongue when Lord Rawdon told me he was coming here," Damaris said quietly, leaning in closer to Thea. "Whatever possessed you to invite him?"

"I'm not sure. Daniel was rather taken aback by it as well. But I—it just seemed the proper thing to do on Christmas. Was he rude to you?"

Damaris considered the idea for a moment, then shook her head somewhat tentatively. "Not rude, really. It's just—his eyes are so cold and, I don't know, watchful. I haven't the slightest notion what he's thinking, which is a bit annoying. There is something about him that makes me want to take him down a peg." She chuckled. "Terrible of me, I'm sure."

"He is arrogant, there's no denying that. But I think perhaps he may not be quite the villain Gabriel believes him to be." Thea related the story of Matthew's abduction and Lord Rawdon's attempt to help.

"He rode out in that storm to look for him?" Damaris raised her eyebrows. "That is impressive, especially given the way Lord Morecombe feels about him." She paused. "Do you think he is not the baby's father?"

"I don't know. It is hard to escape the similarity of their coloring, but, as he pointed out, there are other men with blond hair and blue eyes, and Matthew's hair is not quite as pale as Lord Rawdon's. Nor are his eyes the same shade of blue."

"Few are. Rawdon's are like ice." Damaris gave a little shiver.

"And, of course, babies' eyes often change color as they grow older."

"Last night, when Lord Rawdon looked at the baby, there was something in his eyes. Not affection, really, but more sorrow, perhaps, or loneliness. I'm not sure; it was quite fleeting, and perhaps I am refining too much on it. But I felt it would be wrong of me to let him sit at the inn alone on Christmas after he had tried to help us find Matthew."

"Quite right, I'm sure. But tell me the rest of it. I presume you must have found the babe."

"Yes, and took him away from the dreadful man who abducted him. But the man escaped."

"Thank heavens you were able to find him and bring him back in that storm."

"Yes, it was quite fortunate." Thea decided not to correct her friend's assumption that they had returned with the baby during the storm. She trusted Damaris to keep her secret; there was no one she trusted more. But she found that she did not want to reveal anything about her time with Gabriel, not even to her dearest friend. She simply wanted to keep this close to her heart.

The meal went off more smoothly than Thea had expected. While the two men had been sampling the brandy and the wassail, Daniel had discovered that Lord Rawdon's ancestral home was not far from Hadrian's Wall. There were, Daniel told them, his gray eyes sparkling, even remains of a Roman fort on Rawdon's property. That had been enough to establish the Earl as a valued guest in the vicar's eyes.

They had barely finished eating and were still sitting at the table, talking, when a cannonade of noises erupted in the street outside.

"What in—" Rawdon's eyebrows arched.

Thea chuckled. "I think the children must be parading."

"The children?"

"Yes. Do they not do this in your town? On Christmas, all the children go through the streets banging on drums—or pots or whatever they can get their hands on to make a fine noise. Usually they do it earlier in the morning. Perhaps the weather slowed them down."

She went to the window, and the others joined her to watch the children rattling by in a ragged procession. The boy in front carried a much-worn little drum strapped around his neck, and he beat it with more enthusiasm than rhythm. Behind him, in more or less a line, children hopped and skipped, some tooting little horns, others banging away on drums and pans with sticks or their hands or whatever they happened to have. They made their way down to the church and started back up the road.

"It is almost time for the morris dancers," Thea said.

"Do they dance here?" Rawdon asked.

"Yes, on the road in front of the church. There's room, you see, for people to stand and watch here by the churchyard," Daniel explained.

"Well." Lord Rawdon offered a faint smile. "We certainly should not want to miss this."

They all bundled up and went outside, including Lolly and the baby and their guard, Peter, who had been having their own Christmas feast in the kitchen with Mrs. Brewster and her husband. Outside they found a number of villagers who had already congregated in the area in front of the bridge to the church, and more people were arriving by the moment, gathering on either side of the road. Thea greeted several people she knew and waved to others who were too far away to speak to.

Thea glanced over at Lord Rawdon, who was standing a little apart from the rest of them, a faintly bemused look on his face. Thea wondered what he was thinking. Thea turned to check on Lolly and Matthew, as she had been doing every few minutes since the family came outside. She wondered how long it would take for her to get rid of the worry that Matthew would suddenly disappear.

A ragged cheer arose from the crowd, and Thea glanced up the road toward the center of town. A group of men were marching toward them along the road, all wearing white, full-sleeved shirts and bright green vests. Green ribbons were tied around their upper arms, the loose ends fluttering. More green ribbons, as well as a band of jangling bells, were tied just above the knees of their breeches. Each man carried a short staff. Despite the cold, none wore jackets. They had been, Thea was sure, fortifying themselves with alcohol at the inn and perhaps at homes along the way, and they were well warmed. When the dance was over, Thea knew that Daniel would offer them refreshment from his own wassail bowl.

The dancers acknowledged the crowd's cheers with friendly shouts and waves of their cudgels. They formed two lines, and as three of their compatriots played a lilting tune on pipes and a drum, the men started their traditional dance. They danced forward and back, stamping their feet and knocking their staffs against the ground and against each other's staff, all in an intricate arrangement of steps. The infectious enthusiasm in their movements, cheerful and noisy, was hard to resist. When Thea glanced at Lord Rawdon, she saw that even he was smiling.

She was glad she had invited him. The day was turning out better than she had hoped. If only . . . but, no, she told herself firmly, she would not take away from her happy mood by thinking about how Gabriel was not here to share the day with her.

Just as she thought it, Thea glanced up and saw an elegant carriage making its way down the street, driven by a coachman in full livery. Only one party around here could be arriving in such a fine equipage, she knew, and Thea's heart swelled in her chest. Gabriel was here.

*Gabriel awoke on Christmas morning* and reached for Thea before he remembered that he was back at the Priory in his own bed. He had spent only one night with her, yet it seemed unnatural that she was not there by his side, warm and soft. He closed his eyes, waiting for his heart to slow down and his blood to settle from the heated dream he had been having. It had involved Thea, of course, and it was better not to remember it too closely or he would find himself in a sorry state to start the morning.

He swung out of bed and rang for his valet, hoping that movement would help dispel his thoughts of Thea. Ridiculous as it seemed, he had been feeling as if something were missing ever since he'd left her at the vicarage the night before. He had gone upstairs to his room last night as soon as he returned, having no desire to see any of the others or explain what had happened. But once he had bathed and changed and lain down, he had found himself curiously unable to sleep. The problem, he knew, was that he missed having Thea in bed beside him.

Even stranger was that the feeling was still there this morning. He decided to drive over to see her after breakfast, then remembered that it was Christmas. She would be feasting with her family and friends. No doubt she would go to church this morning; she was the vicar's sister, after all. Any call he made on her would have to wait until this afternoon. He wondered if it would cause gossip in the village if he called on her on Christmas Day. He was beginning to think that almost anything he did would cause gossip in the village.

His valet brought tea and toast to ward off Gabriel's hunger until the feasting began. Gabriel ate, staring out the window toward the ruins of the abbey in the distance, then shaved and dressed in the clothes Barts had laid out for him. He glanced at his watch after he attached it to his vest and was appalled to see how little time had passed. The day was going to prove endless, he feared.

He had slept late, and dressing was a long process, made even more so by his valet's obsessive attempt to tie Gabriel's neckcloth in a perfect and intricate arrangement of Barts's own devising. Barts's earnest and heartfelt desire was to create a new style of tying a neckcloth, one that would equal or surpass all others, and which he would have the satisfaction of naming. Their visit to the country had allowed him the opportunity to experiment without having to expose his creations to the criticisms of the polite world, and he had indulged himself upon every occasion when

Gabriel did not balk at the lengthy procedure. Today Gabriel had given him free rein, intent only on passing the time until he could reasonably call on Thea.

Therefore it was almost noon when he made his way downstairs, and he found that his friends had already started imbibing their holiday cheer. He was immediately bombarded with questions about what had happened the other night when Miss Bainbridge had appeared in the middle of the night, forcefully pounding on the front door. Alan and Myles, having been absent during the scene itself, had heard about it in great detail the next day, and all of them, it seemed, had spent Christmas Eve speculating on what had happened to Gabriel.

Out of politeness, he delayed telling his story until Emily joined them, which had the practical benefit of allowing him to mentally tailor his story to expunge all mention of Thea's having accompanied him on the rescue of the baby. He regaled them with the tale over their Christmas dinner, describing everything from the visit to Rawdon at the inn down to his fight with the abductor.

"So you didn't recognize the chap?" Myles asked, frowning.

"No, though I would not guarantee that I haven't seen him before. He was wearing a hat and scarf wrapped round it to keep it on, and he had the scarf around most of his lower face as well. It was bloo—excuse me, Emily—it was black as pitch out there, too. I couldn't get a good look at him."

"But what did you do then?" Alan paused in cutting his meat. "I mean, where did you go after you found him?"

"We stayed in the cottage where I found the kidnapper. He had it well stocked."

"You mean, you and the baby alone?" Alan goggled at him. "What did you do with it?"

"The baby? I took care of him, what else could I do? We slept, mostly."

Alan shook his head, seemingly more impressed by the thought that Gabriel had managed to handle a baby for a day than he had been by Gabriel's chase through the snowstorm after the abductor.

"Well, at least you know now that Alec was not involved," Myles offered, pushing away his plate and taking a sip of wine.

"I wouldn't be so sure of that," Ian protested. "Rawdon could have hired this chap to steal the baby. That way he could whisk it away while establishing an alibi for himself at the inn."

"Really, Ian, that's a trifle convoluted, isn't it?" Myles replied. "How could he have been certain that Gabe would discover the baby missing and come storming over there in the middle of the night to find Alec all snug and safe in his bed? Gabriel only knew the child was missing because Miss Bainbridge awoke and came over here. Rawdon could scarcely count on that happening. The odds would be that Gabriel would not accuse him of kidnapping Matthew until long after it happened, and how could he have proved that he'd been there all night?"

"Perhaps he could not *prove* it, but he would be there, clearly without the baby, and that would establish his innocence."

"You mean to say he planned this and hired a man to steal the child all in the few hours after he came to the Priory—and in a village where he knew no one?" Myles scoffed.

"Perhaps he had it all planned before he came and that is why he came here to begin with."

Gabriel stiffened. "You're right. I had forgotten all about that in the excitement."

"You think he stole the baby?" Myles asked. "I thought you just said—"

"No. I don't believe he kidnapped Matthew. Or arranged it, either. I think he was probably telling the truth about that. He was right in saying that he could take Matthew away from me in court if he wanted, and he would be bloody minded enough to do it despite all the scandal that would ensue. But there must be some reason why Rawdon came here. He wouldn't just drop in to the Priory to say hello. I meant to discover the reason if I could, but the abduction drove it out of my head."

"What do you mean?" Alan asked. "He came here because of the baby. He must have heard that the lad was here."

"How would he have known?" Gabriel pointed out, and they all swung their heads toward Myles.

He made a face. "Why are you looking at me? I didn't tell him."

"Even if Myles had written to him, there wouldn't have been enough time for Rawdon to get the letter and come here," Gabriel said. "The baby hasn't been in Chesley that long."

"Besides," Myles pointed out. "I don't think Alec knew about Matthew. He was completely taken by surprise when he heard the boy was Jocelyn's."

"But that is just it." Emily's words took everyone by surprise, as she had been silent throughout the whole exchange, and all the men turned to look at her. She looked somewhat taken aback at the attention, but she lifted her chin a fraction and went on, "We don't really know that this child is Jocelyn's. The only 'proof' you have is a piece of jewelry that anyone could have pinned to his clothes. I, for one, don't believe it. I did not know your sister very well, Gabriel, but I found her to be a good, sweet girl. She was not the type to, well, you know ..." Emily trailed off, looking flustered.

"Quite right, my dear," her husband agreed. "We are making a rather large assumption. That baby could belong to anyone. It is my belief that someone is playing a trick on you, Gabriel. This boy is doubtless some lowborn child. His mother got hold of that brooch somehow and left it with him where you would hear about it. Obviously she hoped that you would react precisely as you did—assume the baby was your sister's and take him in."

"Ian's right," Alan agreed. "It's all a hum. You should send the boy to a foundling home."

"He can hardly do that if there's any chance Matthew is Jocelyn's child," Myles retorted. "What you ought to do is bring the baby to the Priory. Plenty of protection here. I don't think you'd have some chap breaking in and grabbing him, not with all of us around, not to mention the servants."

"Quite right," Ian agreed, making a toasting gesture with his glass. "Bring the little fellow over here. After all, we are perfectly respectable now that we have a woman in the household. I am sure Emily would love to have a baby about, wouldn't you, my dear?"

Gabriel had to press his lips together tightly to keep from laughing. Emily looked as if she had swallowed a fly. But she smiled gamely and said, "Yes, of course, that sounds like just the thing. It would be delightful, no doubt, to have a little one in the house. Of course, I do not know how much longer we shall be here. We have already imposed on your hospitality a great deal."

"Nonsense, you are always welcome here," Gabriel responded with automatic courtesy.

His statement had always been true in the past—at least as far as Ian was concerned. (Emily's presence tended to make any gathering rather tame.) However, he realized as he spoke the words that the open invitation was now a polite fiction. The truth was, the presence of his guests added an unwelcome complication to his life. It would be far easier to see Thea if he was alone at the Priory. He would not have to worry about keeping his friends entertained; he would not have to spend time here playing cards or chatting when he could be down at the vicarage talking to Thea. Right now, for instance, he could not simply ride over to call on Thea as he wanted to do. He was expected to celebrate with his guests, and if he managed to see Thea, he would have to maneuver it so that it fit in with the celebration.

He was far too well-bred to reveal such thoughts, so he uttered the smooth social fiction, then turned to Myles to address his friend's suggestion to move Matthew to the Priory. "Of course, I will bring Matthew to live with me at some point, but I think for the present it is better if he remains with Miss Bainbridge. He is familiar with her and happy there. And there is really no reason to move him just yet. I have set up a guard at the vicarage to make sure nothing happens."

Gabriel did not add what was uppermost in his thoughts, which was that he would not think of distressing Thea by taking

Matthew away from her. Besides, if the baby resided here, Gabriel would no longer have a handy excuse for calling at the vicarage.

"It would not be fair to the baby, in any case, to keep him here, as I will be gone much of the time. I want to get my hands on the man who abducted the baby. I can't help but think that he might lead me to whoever left Matthew at the church. I must know whether it was Jocelyn. And if it was not my sister, perhaps whoever did leave him has some knowledge of her."

"But surely that person has already left the village," Emily pointed out.

"Unfortunately, I imagine that you are right. But I have to keep trying, nevertheless. I cannot ignore any possibility that it will lead me to Jocelyn."

"No, of course," Emily agreed, nodding, though Gabriel could tell from the look of pity in her eyes that she suspected he was doomed to disappointment. "You must do whatever you can."

Everyone at the table fell silent for a time after that. Unsurprisingly, it was Myles who started a new conversation.

"What Christmas activities do you have planned for us, Gabriel?" he asked, grinning. "Charades, perhaps? Games?"

"You clearly spend too much time with your sisters' children," Ian told him dampeningly.

"Well . . ." Gabriel cast a glance around the table. "I understand there is morris dancing in the village."

"Morris dancing?" Emily asked, her nose wrinkling. "Truly? You want to watch men dance with sticks?"

Myles laughed and slapped a hand to the table. "Sounds like just the thing."

"Only if we have a glass of brandy before we go," Alan said.

"Or perhaps two," Ian added.

It took some time to get everyone clad for the outdoors and ready to go, especially given the round of brandy before they left. But finally they got into Emily's elegant carriage—the only vehicle in the stables large enough to house them all—and started out. Myles began singing Christmas carols as they rode, and Alan had consumed enough brandy by then to join him. Even Emily unbent enough to sing along with everyone else.

The village had an empty look when they arrived, but they followed the stragglers down the road toward the vicarage, and soon the crowd and the dancers came into view. The carriage stopped short of the crowd, and they disembarked. Gabriel was the last to emerge, and he paused before he stepped down, casting a quick glance over the crowd.

He spotted Thea immediately. The hood of her cloak had fallen back, and she wore no hat, so the sun gleamed on her thick hair, picking out the red highlights. Curls clustered around her face, and more curls fell from the crown of her head. She turned to look at the carriage, and her eyes met Gabriel's across the distance. Something warm and eager swelled in his chest, and Gabriel grinned. He stepped down from the carriage, and as he did so, his gaze fell on the man standing behind Thea.

*Rawdon.* Jealousy stabbed through him, as swift and sharp as a knife. Scowling, Gabriel strode toward them.

# Fifteen

*As Gabriel walked toward Thea*, Rawdon stepped up beside her, and the intimation of protection in the other man's stance infuriated Gabriel.

"What the devil are you doing here?" Gabriel stopped in front of Rawdon, his hands doubling into fists at his sides.

Rawdon raised his brows in his coolly annoying way. "Watching the village festivities. Much like you, I imagine."

"I invited Lord Rawdon to join us for Christmas," Thea put in.

"You *invited* him? When you know that I don't—" Gabriel stopped abruptly, realizing that his words were exactly the wrong tack to take with Thea.

"What I *know*," Thea began, crossing her arms and settling her level gaze on Gabriel, "is that Lord Rawdon went out into a snowy night to search for Matthew. I also know that Christmas is a time of peace and goodwill. I think it would be advisable if you remembered that, as well."

A number of furious retorts crowded Gabriel's mind, most of them about how he did not want Alec Stafford, Lord Rawdon, anywhere near Thea, but Gabriel had the good sense to keep the remarks to himself. Swallowing his anger, he unclenched his fists and said, "Of course." He smiled at Thea, but the glance he turned on Rawdon was far less mild.

Rawdon gave him a look of faint amusement, then turned toward the others in Gabriel's party, who had since caught up with him. "Lady Wofford." He sketched a bow. "Gentlemen."

"I would have thought morris dancing was a bit too common an entertainment for you, Lord Rawdon," Gabriel commented.

"Ah, but that shows how little you know me, doesn't it?"

Emily watched the dancers weave in and out in an intricate pattern, knocking their cudgels together, their feet all the while tapping out the jiglike steps. "How ... quaint." She gave Myles an amused smile. "Not exactly the Paris Opera Ballet, is it?"

"No, but somehow here in the country, we manage to make do with our trifling diversions." Thea gave the other woman a sharp, short smile.

Myles glanced from Thea's stony face to Emily's startled one and smothered a grin. Damaris moved in, saying in a pleasant tone, "The steps are handed down from generation to generation. When we look at them, I believe we are glimpsing an England from centuries past."

"Indeed, Mrs. Howard?" Myles was happy to play along with Damaris's peacekeeping lecture. "Do tell us more."

Gabriel turned to Rawdon. "I want to talk to you."

"Indeed." Rawdon eyed him thoughtfully for a moment, then moved closer to the house, stopping beyond the hearing range of the onlookers.

Gabriel followed him. As he moved, he cast a quick glance

around the crowd until he caught sight of Matthew in Lolly's arms, standing with Gabriel's servant on one side of her and the indomitable Mrs. Brewster on the other. He relaxed a little.

"No one has approached him," Rawdon said unexpectedly. "I have kept an eye on the nursemaid and his guard."

Gabriel glanced at him, faintly surprised. "Thank you."

Rawdon's only reply was a shrug. "You said you wanted to talk to me."

"Yes. I have been thinking about your arrival at the Priory the other day. Why did you come?"

If possible, the other man's face became even more remote. "Why does that matter?"

"It simply does. I am not trying to attack you. I just want to know why you chose to visit the Priory."

Rawdon's jaw set, and for a moment Gabriel was sure Rawdon was going to refuse to answer him, but then with a bitter twist of his lips, Rawdon said, "Because, fool that I am, I wanted to see Jocelyn. I wanted to hear it from her own lips."

"Hear what?"

"The truth."

Gabriel frowned, but decided not to pursue that avenue of conversation for the moment, instead going back to his original concern. "But Jocelyn was not here. Why did you think she would be?"

"Because she told me she was going to see you. I went to London first, but they said at your club you had come here."

"You talked to her?" Gabriel stiffened, staring at Rawdon.

"No, she wrote me."

"Jocelyn had been corresponding with you?" The world seemed to tilt around Gabriel.

"No, of course not. I haven't heard from her since she left last year. But a few days ago, I received a letter from her."

"Why? Why would she write to you?"

"Because, unlike you, Jocelyn does not hate me," Rawdon retorted acidly. "She wrote to ask my forgiveness, if you must know, and she said that she was traveling to see you."

Gabriel felt as if his former friend had punched him in the heart. "Did you know about the baby?"

"Not until I saw him."

"Then where *is* Jocelyn?" Gabriel flung his arms out to the side. "Why is she not here?"

"I have no idea. When I got here, I thought you must be hiding her from me. I stayed, hoping I would be able to catch her somewhere in the village alone. But then when the baby was stolen from Miss Bainbridge's house, well, it was clear that Jocelyn was not here."

"Sweet Jesus," Gabriel murmured. He looked at Rawdon. After all the time he had spent despising the man, it seemed unsettlingly familiar to be standing here talking to him once again. "Then Jocelyn did come here and abandon her child at the church—I cannot believe Jocelyn would do that!"

"Perhaps she assumed that if she left the brooch with the baby, someone would bring him to you. It seems exceedingly trusting, but then Jocelyn is a sweet, naïve girl." Rawdon paused. "Or at least she seemed so back then."

"Why would she not simply come to me?"

"Perhaps she was ashamed. If she was not married . . ."

"But surely she would realize that I would not turn her away. That I would not think ill of her. She must know I would never judge her."

Rawdon's eyebrow quirked up and he directed a long stare at Gabriel before he murmured, "Perhaps I am not the best person to respond to that statement."

Gabriel flushed. "You think I was too quick to judge you? How did you expect me to behave? It was obvious that my sister fled from you!"

"Obvious!" Rawdon stiffened, jamming his fists into the pockets of his coat. "How was it obvious that I was in the wrong?"

Gabriel's temper was beginning to rise again, too. He could see out of the corner of his eye that people were casting glances in their direction, but his anger was too hot for him to worry about the proprieties. "Because I knew that you had not behaved as a gentleman. I heard what you had done."

"You 'heard'? You 'knew'? Of course you would have believed anything you heard about me, any rumor or calumny. It would never have occurred to you to believe me, would it? Or even to ask!" Rawdon whirled and started away, then turned back. He unbuttoned the first two buttons of his coat and reached inside, pulling out a folded piece of paper. "Here. Read it for yourself. I don't care. I have nothing left of my pride, anyway."

He shoved the piece of paper into Gabriel's hand, then turned and strode away.

*Thea had been carefully observing* the confrontation between the two men, ready to intervene, and when Rawdon abruptly thrust something at Gabriel and left, Thea hurried over to Gabriel. He was still standing where the other man had left him, staring down at a folded piece of paper in his hand.

"Gabriel? Is everything all right?"

He looked up at her a trifle blankly. "She wrote him a letter. My sister—she wrote *him* a letter."

Thea reached out and took Gabriel's arm. "Come. Let's go inside. Better to read it there."

He nodded, letting her lead him back into the house. Thea took him to her brother's study in the back of the house, where they were less likely to be disturbed, and pulled him down onto the small sofa beside her. "What does her letter say? Is she here in England?"

"I don't know. I haven't read it. I'm almost afraid to." Gabriel gave Thea a wry smile. He returned his gaze to the paper, unfolding it. "It is Jocelyn's hand; I recognize it."

He began to read. When he was done, he simply sat for a moment, like a man stunned, then wordlessly handed the letter to Thea. She took it and read what Jocelyn had written.

> *Dear Alec,*
>
> *I pray that I may still call you that. It is my earnest hope that despite the transgressions I have committed against you, your generosity will yet extend to reading this note from me. I do not ask for your forgiveness nor do I expect it. But I would entreat you to accept my most heartfelt apology.*
>
> *You offered me the great and precious gift of your name, and I answered it with deceit and betrayal. I have no excuse.*

*I was young and foolish. I was in love, and I believed myself loved in return. That I was deceived in that regard is no excuse for the deception I dealt to you. In the end, I could not bear to continue to lie to you and everyone I held dear.*

*I thought all well lost for love, even my good name. I told myself that you would have a better life without me. I hope that this, at least, was true: that your life has been happier and that you have found another who will be the wife you deserve.*

*I am sorry, truly sorry, for the pain and shame I have brought to you, as well as to my family. I hoped that if I fled to the Continent, I could keep my scandal from tainting everyone else. But now I realize I must return. I can only trust in my brother's good nature to take me in with the same kindness shown to the Prodigal Son.*

*Yrs.,*
*Jocelyn M.*

Thea raised her eyes to Gabriel's still face. "Gabriel . . ."

"Have I been wrong about him all this time? I was so certain that she had run from him, yet here she is, begging *him* for forgiveness."

"It was understandable. What else would one assume when she left rather than marry him?"

"Even now, I don't know what to think," Gabriel admitted. "Everyone had always talked about the Staffords; they are that sort of family. I discounted most of the rumors. But after Jocelyn became engaged, there were more, and they weren't just vague.

They spoke of women Rawdon had hurt. Still, I could not believe it of him. I shrugged them off. But when Jocelyn ran away, I feared that I had been a fool to trust so blindly in Alec. That is when I learned about a lady on whom he had forced his attentions. The woman had no reason to lie—her honor would have been badly compromised if word of what had happened had gotten out."

"Then it would seem reasonable to assume that he had hurt your sister or at least frightened her enough that she ran away," Thea agreed.

"All that time, when I feared her dead, she had just fled to the Continent!" Gabriel shook his head in disbelief. "I had the runner check at the ports and he found no trace of her, but I didn't seriously believe that she would have gotten that far, anyway. I would never have dreamed she had such a well-planned scheme. Or the resources."

"Perhaps she was not alone."

"She may have had her maid with her. The girl vanished at the same time, but I was not sure if she accompanied Jocelyn or if she merely vanished because she feared being blamed for Jocelyn's running away."

"No, I didn't mean her maid. I meant another man. She says that she was in love, that she thought that she was loved in return."

"Of course." Gabriel shook his head. "I am a trifle slow today. If Rawdon is not the father—and I cannot imagine he was after this letter—then another man was."

"She said she was deceived. Perhaps he told her he loved her and would marry her, and they ran away to the Continent. Perhaps they even did get married."

"It makes sense. Jocelyn was engaged to Rawdon, but she didn't love him. Maybe it was because she thought I was pushing her to do so."

"Or perhaps she thought she loved him, then realized she did not. You said she was only nineteen, didn't you? Or maybe she heard the same rumors about him that you did, and she regretted her decision."

"In any case, she fell in love with another man—how, God only knows. She was always chaperoned."

"Still, she went to parties and balls, and there are always a number of young men there."

"True. She could easily have met a man and even imagined herself in love. But when would she have been alone with him enough to—" Gabriel stopped, catching the significant glance she sent him. "Yes, of course. One finds a way."

"You said her maid ran away, too. Perhaps her maid accompanied her on trips about town, to shop and make calls and such."

"Only, instead of that, Jocelyn was really meeting her lover. No wonder Hannah vanished when Jocelyn left. She had been helping her mistress deceive us all. So this fellow took Jocelyn to France or Italy or wherever. But then her dreams fell apart. I doubt he married her since she said she was deceived. My guess is that he was a fortune hunter. Perhaps he mistakenly thought Jocelyn had money of her own. She had a good dowry, of course, but that was in my control, and I would not have accepted a fortune hunter for her. Other than that, she did not have any money— at least, not until her mother passes on, which will probably be many years. When he found out she did not have a fortune, he abandoned her. And her child."

"So she came home. To you."

"Except she did not." Gabriel sighed. "And that brings us back to the crux of the matter. Why did Jocelyn leave the baby in the church?" He took her hand in his and sat for a moment, looking down at their linked hands. "Rawdon said Jocelyn might not have come to me because she was ashamed. Do you think that is true? That she was fearful of my disapproval?"

"It is hard for me to judge since I do not know her."

"But do I seem so unreasonable and unbending?" He raised his head to look at her, his dark eyes troubled. "Am I so puritanical?"

"*Puritanical* is *not* the first word that comes to my mind when I think of you," Thea said drily.

He grinned and leaned closer to her, murmuring, "That is because when I am with you, I feel anything but puritanical."

Thea felt her cheeks heat up, and he chuckled. He kissed her lightly on the lips. "I love to see you blush. I love to make you blush."

"You must, for you do it often enough," she pretended to grumble, but when he pulled her over into his lap and kissed her more thoroughly, she made no protest, just wrapped her arms around him and kissed him back. He nuzzled the side of her neck, murmuring, "I have missed you terribly. I've done nothing but think of you since I left this house last night." He raised his head and smiled down into her eyes. "How can that happen, Miss Bainbridge? How are you able to completely occupy my thoughts? I am inclined to think you are a sorceress."

"Hardly." Thea would have liked to make a clever retort, but she found it difficult to think when Gabriel's lips were roaming the soft flesh of her throat.

"Hello? Lord Morecombe? Miss Bainbridge?" A woman's voice came floating back to them from the front of the house.

Thea bolted from his lap, her pink cheeks flaming now. She straightened her spectacles, which had gotten pushed awry, and smoothed down her skirts.

"Emily!" Gabriel muttered, and let out a soft curse. "The woman has the most damnable timing." He stood up. "I am coming, Lady Wofford." He turned to Thea. "They doubtless want to leave. I don't believe the village offerings are quite Lady Wofford's notion of entertainment. I could stay and let them go back without me. I could walk home later through the ruins, if you will show me the way."

"I shall show you the ruins some other day," Thea assured him. "But for now, it is probably better that you go. My brother and Damaris and all the others are here. We would have no time alone in any case."

"Very well." He strode to the door and peered down the hallway, then turned back. "Lady Wofford must have gone into the sitting room." He pulled Thea to him and gave her a brief, hard kiss on the lips. "I will call on you tomorrow."

Thea nodded, not quite trusting herself to speak. She was afraid that if she opened her mouth, she might ask him to stay.

Gabriel strode out the door, and Thea heard him say, "Ah, there you are, Emily. I was looking at the vicar's library."

Ian replied, "Cousin Daniel always was a bookish sort. Well, that whole branch of the family, really."

"Yes, I do not mean to insult your family, dear, but your cousins are a rather odd group. So very ... well, I hesitate to use the word *provincial* ..."

"And yet you do," Gabriel said shortly.

"My." Emily let out a little titter. "I do believe you are in need of Christmas cheer. The sooner we get back to the Priory the better, don't you agree, Ian?"

"No doubt."

"You're right. I think everyone will enjoy the day more if we return to the Priory," Gabriel said, and the footsteps faded down the hall, the front door closing behind them.

*Thea spent the next afternoon* taking Boxing Day gifts to the butcher and other tradesmen the vicarage used. As she started back toward the vicarage, she was surprised to see Gabriel emerging from the inn's courtyard. He was frowning, but his face cleared when he saw her, and he swept off his hat to present an elegant bow.

"Miss Bainbridge, what an unexpected pleasure." His words were ordinary, but the smile in his eyes warmed Thea.

"Lord Morecombe. I am surprised to see you here."

"I was coming to call on you, actually. I left my horse in the inn's stable." He cast a glance down at her, adding, "I was hoping my visit would prove longer than I feel comfortable leaving my mount out in the cold."

"Indeed? People might talk."

"I suspect they already do," Gabriel retorted. "I am growing more familiar with life in Chesley. I wager that at this very moment, there are at least four pairs of eyes trained on us."

Thea laughed. "It is probably a low estimate."

They continued walking, and after a moment, Gabriel said, "I also dropped in to the inn to speak to Lord Rawdon."

"Really? Why?"

"To apologize. Whatever I heard about him, clearly he was not the cause of my sister's leaving. I wronged him."

"What happened?" Thea looked up at him. "Did he accept your apology?"

"He wasn't there. Hornsby said he paid his shot and left yesterday afternoon."

"Oh."

"I suppose he decided there was no reason to stay. He came here to see Jocelyn, and she is not here."

"I am sorry that you were unable to see him, though—to part on better terms."

"I doubt that we shall ever be on good terms again. After all that's happened—well, there's no love lost between us. Still, I won't feel right until I have apologized. But that will have to wait until I return to London."

A chill that had nothing to do with the weather crept through Thea at his words. How long would it be until he would be leaving? A man such as Gabriel would not want to stay away from the city long. Quickly, to keep from thinking about that idea, she said, "How are the rest of your party? Have they recovered from the holiday cheer?"

"I presume so. I have not seen that much of them—I have been a terrible host, I confess." He slanted his gaze down at her. "The truth is, I feel like saying to them, as Mercutio did, 'A pox on both your houses!'"

Thea chuckled. "Surely not!"

"They all seem a damned nuisance lately. I keep having to play the polite host when all I want to do is be with you."

Thea sucked in a breath at his statement, her heart suddenly tripping merrily in her chest. She should not take such hope from his words, she told herself, but she could not squelch the effervescent happiness bubbling up inside her. They had reached the vicarage, and she stopped irresolutely, glancing toward the house. If they went inside, there would be no chance of being alone. Someone could pop in at any moment.

"Let's continue to walk," Gabriel said, echoing her thoughts. "You offered to show me the abbey ruins."

Thea smiled. "Of course, if you'd like?"

"I'd like very much."

"Very well, then." She started toward the footbridge over the water. "You have been inside the church, of course."

"Not in daylight."

"Then we shall see it first. It will give us a chance to warm up a bit, anyway."

The snow was still deep enough to present a picturesque view of the church and graveyard. Gabriel pulled open the massive wooden door of the church, and they went through the vestibule and into the sanctuary beyond. As they strolled down the aisle, Gabriel reached down and took Thea's hand, lacing his fingers through hers. Even through their gloves, Thea was very aware of the contact, and though they touched nowhere else, her whole body tingled at the closeness, alive with anticipation.

She kept up a flow of talk as she showed him the church, relating the legend of St. Dwynwen and its connection to the abbey, more in an attempt to distract herself than anything else.

"And does it work?" Gabriel asked. "Praying to St. Dwynwen, I mean? Have you ever tried it?"

Thea blushed, thinking of her own heartfelt prayer in this chapel only a week ago and the way Matthew's little blond head had popped up moments afterward, followed soon by the tumultuous entrance of Gabriel himself into her formerly humdrum life. "Perhaps," she murmured, and slipped away.

She led him out the side door of the church and into the graveyard. It was pristine, the snow unmarked except for a few tracks of small animals and birds. The graves were mounds of white, the stones capped by snow.

"St. Margaret's was the chapel of the abbey. The remainder of the convent lay that way." She pointed behind the church toward the ruins, their stark, half-fallen walls softened by the blanket of white.

They started toward the ruins, their hands still linked. Despite the cold, their steps were slow, and they walked close together. In this moment, the world seemed far away, separated by the sea of snow all around them. There was no one to see, no one to hear. Gabriel slid his arm around her shoulders, and Thea snuggled into his side, leaning her head against him.

"It seems almost a shame to make a path here, it is so lovely," she said. "You see that low wall?" She pointed to their right. "These used to be convent buildings. They were almost completely dismantled and the stone used. This was the herb garden, and beside it, the room where they made their nostrums and tinctures and salves. And beyond that were the sickrooms. Closer, here was the chapter house. And up ahead were the cloisters, where the nuns used to walk."

She pointed to the arches of stone in front of them. The cloisters were a colonnaded walkway, open on one side except for the columns, and with a wall on the opposite side. A roof stretched across the walkway, and the whole thing was largely intact.

"There are rooms behind the walkway?" Gabriel pointed to a doorway in the midst of one of the cloister walls.

"Yes. The roof's gone now and some of the walls, as well." She led him through the doorway and into the partially collapsed room beyond.

Only two walls remained, but they sheltered the room somewhat from the weather. There was even a patch in one corner without snow. Grinning, Gabriel pulled Thea to him, wrapping his arms around her and smiling down at her.

"At last, a bit of privacy." He bent and kissed her. "I thought I was going to have to kiss you in the church again."

He kissed her cheek and took her earlobe between his teeth, worrying it delicately. "I keep trying to think of some way to get you alone. I was wondering this morning whether I could steal you away to that cottage again."

Thea smiled, her face turning dreamy and sensual. "I would not mind returning."

Gabriel let out a soft groan. "When you look at me like that, it's all I can do not to pull you to the floor right here." He pulled her back for another lengthy kiss, and when their lips parted at last, his breath was rasping hard and fast in his throat. "I'd like to send all my guests home."

Thea let out a little chuckle. "That would be rather rude."

"Frankly, I don't care. If I were alone at the Priory, we would have an entire house to ourselves."

"That sounds inviting." Thea linked her arms around his neck and went up on tiptoe to plant a light kiss on his lips. "However, I think 'twould be most improper for me to be in your house with you all alone."

"Propriety can go to the devil," he growled, and pulled her to him again, burying his face in the crook of her neck. "I do nothing but think of you all the time. I am sure my friends must think I have lost my mind. They talk, and I don't hear half their conversation, and when they ask me a question, I haven't the faintest notion what to reply. It is entirely your fault."

"Mine!" Thea laughed. "Well, I like that!"

"I like *this*," he retorted, and came back to take her lips again.

After a long moment, he raised his head, smiling down into her eyes. "I have something for you."

"What do you mean?" Thea tilted her head back.

He reached into a pocket of his topcoat, pulling out a small box, which he held out to her on his palm. Thea looked down at the box and took a step back, then turned her gaze back up to him. "What is it?"

He grinned. "Open it and see."

"But—"

"It is Boxing Day. You give presents on Boxing Day."

"To the grocer and the man who delivers the coal and such."

"Well." He shrugged. "I did not have it yesterday or I would have given it to you. I saw a shop in Bynford the other day, and I rode over there this morning to get you something."

"But I—I have nothing for you."

"You have already given me a far better gift than I deserve." He jiggled the box in front of her face. "Open it. I know your curiosity is too great to leave it alone."

Thea laughed and picked up the box to open it. Inside lay a set of filigreed gold earrings, each centered by a bloodred oval stone. Thea drew in her breath sharply. "Gabriel!" She cast an amazed look up at him. "You should not."

"Do you not like them?"

"Of course I like them. They are beautiful!" Thea traced her forefinger over one of the stones. "But they are too much."

"Nonsense. 'Tis only garnets. Mere fripperies, really. I would have gotten rubies, but this was the best they had. The jeweler in Bynford hasn't a very large stock. Indeed, I was lucky to find these; they were the only red stone he had, and I wanted something to match that touch of red in your hair."

"But, Gabriel, I cannot accept them!" Thea's hand clenched more tightly on the box even as she said the words. "A gift of jewelry? I could not accept jewelry from a man—well, obviously, a man other than my brother or—well, someone in my family." She had started to say 'other than a fiancé,' but had swallowed her words at the last moment. She certainly did not want him thinking she was hinting at marriage. "It isn't proper."

He laughed. "And when have we done anything that is 'proper'?"

"Well, I should at least appear to make an effort to do so." Thea looked back down at the earrings, her finger unconsciously caressing the garnets. Finally, she closed the box and held it out to Gabriel. "No. I cannot accept them."

"What would I do with them? If you do not want them, then toss them aside."

"No!" Thea's hand clenched around the little box, and she pulled it back to her chest. "They are far too lovely to throw away. Return them to the jeweler."

"And look like a proper muttonhead? I think not. No one but a spurned suitor would return a set of earrings. I have a reputation to uphold, you know."

She gave him an exasperated look and started to speak, but he laid his forefinger against her lips, silencing her. "No. Whatever you were about to say, please do not. Tell everyone they came from someone else—perhaps your grandmother left them to you. If you feel you cannot wear them, then do not. Hide them away in a drawer. But I want you to have them. Even if you never wear them, 'twill be enough to know that you have them, that they please you."

Thea had built up the fortitude to give the gift back to him once. She hadn't the strength to do so again. She wanted the earrings, even if she never once put them on. It was enough to know, as Gabriel said, that he had given them to her. That he had chosen them because they reminded him of the highlights in her hair.

"Very well." Thea slipped the small box into the pocket of her dress beneath her cloak. "I will keep them. Thank you." She could feel tears threatening, but she pushed them back. "I will treasure your gift. Always." She went up on tiptoe and kissed him.

His arms went around her tightly. They kissed again and again, hungry after the separation of the past two days. Thea strained up against him, frustrated by the thick layers of clothing between them. Obviously feeling the same way, Gabriel slid his hands beneath her cloak, moving them over her body.

With an oath, he lifted his mouth from hers. "If only there were a roof." He kissed her cheek, her ear, her neck, interspersing the kisses between his words. "And a door. Just a bit more warmth."

"I feel rather warm right now."

"Sweet heavens, I would kill to get your clothes off right now," he growled, digging his hands into the soft flesh of her buttocks and moving her hips against him. Thea could feel the stiff length of his manhood pressing into her flesh, and an answering heat started deep inside her. "There are the storerooms below here," she suggested. "They were in the cellars, so, at least where the roofs haven't fallen in, they are intact."

"Really?" He raised his head in interest. "Where?"

She let out a little laugh and took his hand, leading him out of the room and down the stone walkway. At the end of the columns, a set of weathered stone steps led downward. Part of the cellar roof had collapsed, letting in enough light to see dimly. The corridor was small and musty. They peeked into the ruins of the first room, then moved down the hallway to the next opening.

"You see? It's a room—and comparatively warm since we are belowground. It's almost livable. Now, if only there were—" Thea stopped abruptly and turned to him as a sudden thought entered her head. She could see the same idea dawning in his eyes. "Do you think—"

"That someone could have taken shelter down here?" he finished.

Thea nodded, and they stared down the corridor. There was light at the other end, where much of the ruins had collapsed into the rooms below, creating an effective end to the cellars and lighting the nearby portions. But in the middle of the corridor between the two cave-ins, where the roof was still intact, it was quite gloomy. They would need more light if they were to see anything.

"There's an old lantern in the back room of the church," Thea offered.

It did not take them long to go to the church and return with a lamp. They walked down the old corridor, holding the lantern high and peering into each doorway they passed. In the third doorway, their light at last revealed something other than an empty earthen room.

Against one wall was a lumpy pile covered by a blanket, and another blanket lay in a heap at one end. A small, flat-topped rock stood beside the crude bed, and on top of the rock was a saucer with the stub of a candle. A jug sat a foot or two away from the bed, and a pail was in one corner of the room. A piece of crust lay on the floor before them. Clearly, someone had been living there.

"Could it have been your sister?" Thea asked.

"It would certainly explain why no one saw her. But I cannot imagine Jocelyn living here—even for a day or two." Gabriel shook his head and backed out of the room. "We might as well check the rest of the place while we are about it."

At the end of the hallway, where the ceiling and walls had collapsed into a jumble, with nothing above them but the sky, they found the remains of a small campfire. Gabriel poked thoughtfully at the ashes with the tip of his boot.

"How could Jocelyn have done all this? Made a fire? Lived so primitively? She never even dressed without the help of a maid."

"It wasn't necessarily your sister who was living here."

"True. But I have little faith in coincidences."

"Do you think she is still living here? Perhaps if we waited . . ."

Gabriel shook his head. "Whoever was here, they've not been around for at least two days. The snow around the cloisters was untouched, remember? No human tracks."

"You are right."

"I shall set a man to keep an eye on it. We could put up a little shelter at a distance and keep watch with a spyglass, just in case someone does return. But I think Jocelyn came to Chesley only to leave Matthew. Perhaps she stayed long enough to make sure he was placed in my hands. But it seems clear that, if my sister was ever here, she has long since departed."

# Sixteen

*Thea spent the next few* days refurbishing her wardrobe. She pulled the light blue dress that had once been her favorite out of the chest to which she had relegated it and set to altering the gown to better suit today's styles. It took a bit of work to lower the waistline and narrow its lines, but with the extra material from those alterations she added a flirty little ruffle at the hem. She attached the new blue ribbon as a sash, which not only added a little brightness but also covered her less-than-expert re-sewing of the waistline. Hopefully no one would recognize the old dress after its modifications, and even if someone did, it didn't matter. Gabriel had never seen it, and it was prettier than anything else she currently owned.

Once that was done, she did what she could for her other clothes, adding a bit of lace or ribbon to one gown or another. She even went up in the attic and searched through the trunks of old clothes, finding a clump of bright red wooden cherries on an old bonnet, which she added for a splash of color to her dark blue winter hat.

She could not help but wish for an elegant dress for Damaris's upcoming Twelfth Night party. She had no desire to wear the same dull evening gown she had worn to the Cliffes' Christmas ball. The haberdashery in Bynford might have a bolt of cloth that would do for an evening gown, and she would have enough time to sew one if she worked diligently. Thea did not consider herself a good seamstress, but she thought she could make up for her lack of skill with determination, which she possessed in abundance. Daniel had given her money as a Christmas present, which she had planned to save for books, but now she thought a ball gown would be infinitely preferable.

It would be a long and chilly journey over to the haberdashery in Bynford in her brother's pony trap, and she was sure that Daniel would find the reason frivolous. But it occurred to her that Damaris might be interested in such a trip. With that in mind, she set out for her friend's house the next morning.

She found Damaris's household in a frenzy of activity. Rugs were being rolled up and carried outside to be beaten, silver was being polished and crystal washed, and every nook and cranny was being scrubbed.

Thea commented on the bustle as Damaris led her into the smaller upstairs sitting room. Damaris chuckled. "Yes. I think my butler and housekeeper are vying to outdo one another. Greeves hired two extra footmen, and Mrs. Clemmons countered that she must have as many new maids. Then, of course, they had to prove that they had ample use for all of them. So they are turning the house inside out cleaning and polishing. I have been driven up here if I hope to have any peace. And they have not yet begun to decorate."

"I am sure that everything will look lovely for the party. Have you received the stationer's cards for the characters?"

"Oh, yes, I must show them to you. I shall allow you to have first choice of who you wish to be." She brought out the box, and the two of them bent their heads over the cards, chuckling over the names and discussing the merits of the characters.

"Dame Veracity would be far too dangerous for me," Thea told her. "I hate to think what might leave my lips, given that temptation."

"I had thought of adopting Lady Vanity," Damaris responded. "I could go about the entire evening with a hand mirror, admiring myself. But I decided that was unfair; 'tis far too fun a character to take for myself. I thought Jack Mischief would suit Sir Myles."

"Yes." Thea laughed. "He would play it to the hilt, I am sure."

"There is nothing called Lord Handsome, unfortunately; that would suit your Lord Morecombe perfectly."

Thea glanced at her, startled, and hoped that her cheeks would not begin to color. "Not *my* Lord Morecombe, surely."

"I hear of him calling at no one else's house."

"Well . . ." Thea was sure she was blushing now. "He comes to visit the baby."

"Of course." Her friend sent her a droll look, but dropped the subject, saying, "I have the perfect one for Prince Arrogant. Lord Rawdon, don't you think?"

"You invited him to your party?" Thea asked in surprise.

"Daniel mentioned it at the Christmas dinner, and it seemed rude not to invite the man." Damaris shrugged. "He did manage not to hit anyone that day—although I must say, it looked like a near thing between him and Morecombe."

"Their relationship is ... complicated."

"So I gathered. Is he really Matthew's father?"

"I think not, despite their looks." Thea shook her head.

"I understand—it is not your tale to tell."

"You're right," Thea responded, grateful for her friend's social acumen. "In any case, I do not think Lord Rawdon will be here for the party. Morecombe told me that he had left town."

"Oh."

Thea was surprised to see that her friend looked a trifle crestfallen. "Are you sorry? I would have thought you would have been relieved."

"Well, he does seem to be a rather ... unsettling guest to have at one's party," Damaris agreed, with a mischievous grin. "But, then, he would add a certain element of excitement. And he is handsome."

"You think he's handsome?" Thea was again surprised.

"Why, yes. Do you not?" Damaris looked back at Thea in equal surprise.

"I hadn't really thought about it." Thea considered the notion. Lord Rawdon could hardly compare to Gabriel's vivid dark looks, of course, but she could see how some women might be attracted to him. "He *is* very unusual. Such pale hair and those light blue eyes."

"Yes, but his eyes are bright, as well—they make me think of the center of a fire, where it is hottest. I imagine he is a hard man to lie to."

"No doubt."

"I wouldn't say he is a comfortable man, mind you," Damaris said with a smile. "But he has a very arresting sort of face."

"Damaris! Do you *like* Lord Rawdon?"

Damaris laughed. "Goodness, no. I don't think he is the sort of man one *likes*, do you? But he is . . . interesting. Still, I suspect the party will do quite well without his presence."

"I am sure it will. I was thinking of making a new gown for it." Thea smiled at her friend. "I have to confess I had an ulterior motive for coming to call on you today. I hoped that you might be interested in a trip to the haberdashery in Bynford one day this week. They had some bolts of material that might do for an evening dress."

"Of course I would be interested. I had been thinking of making a trip to Cheltenham if the weather permitted. It would be marvelous if you would accompany me. But I have a better idea for your gown. I thought of it on Christmas, but I haven't had a chance to tell you. I want to give you one of my ball gowns. All it would take is a bit of alteration, and my Edith can make any changes it needs."

Thea demurred, but Damaris was adamant, taking her by the hand and pulling her down the hall to Damaris's chamber. She rang for her maid, and the woman soon pulled out the dress in question and laid it across the bed. Thea sucked in her breath. The sleek gown of dark red satin was at once luxurious yet gracefully simple.

"Oh, Damaris . . . this is lovely. But, surely you would want to wear it?"

The other woman shook her head. "I have a gown of peacock blue—which perfectly matches my mask, so I must wear that. I have only worn this gown once. Truthfully, 'tis not the best shade for me. It is more on the rust side of red, and I look better in a bluish tone of that color. That is why I thought of you; it is perfect with your hair. Only look."

Damaris gestured toward her maid, who quickly held the gown up to Thea's shoulders and turned her toward the mirror. Thea looked at herself and felt a sudden, almost physical hunger for this gown. Damaris was right. The deep red, with its amber undertone, picked out the reddish highlights of her brown hair and warmed her skin. She could not help but think, too, how perfectly the garnets Gabriel had given her would match the dress. Not, of course, that she would wear the earrings; it would be improper, even if no one knew that Gabriel had given them to her.

"But this is far too valuable." Thea wrapped her arm around the waist of the dress even as she made her demurral, with her other hand holding the neckline up to her chest. Edith, the maid, stepped aside quickly, leaving Thea to gaze at her reflection alone. "And you might want to wear it some other time."

"No, I don't think I will. It truly does not suit me, so it will just languish in the back of my wardrobe."

Thea cast another look at herself and added reluctantly, "But it is red. It wouldn't be appropriate, really."

"To wear red?" Damaris's eyebrows shot upward, and a faint look of hauteur touched her face. "*I* wore it. Do you think that it was improper of me?"

"No, you goose, and you needn't put on that aristocratic look for my benefit," Thea retorted. "I am sure you looked absolutely lovely in it, and I doubt anyone thought anything wrong with it. But you are not the vicar's sister. They will say it is scandalous for me to wear such a dress. And they will say the neckline is too low."

"They, they, they . . ." Damaris said crossly, coming over to stand by her friend. She looped her arm around Thea's shoulders and looked into the mirror, too. "Who cares what they say? It wouldn't be anyone but some old tabby who is green with jealousy, that is all. What matters, my dear, is what Lord Morecombe will say when he sees it."

"Oh, Damaris . . ." Thea met her friend's gaze in the mirror. "I can't . . . I mean, I don't . . . I *won't* think that way."

"Why ever not?" Damaris turned sideways to look at her friend. "Really, Thea, anyone with two eyes can see that his lordship is smitten with you."

"No, truly, I am sure he is not. I—I have helped him, and he is concerned about Matthew and grateful, I'm sure, for my taking care of Matthew."

"What a bag of moonshine. I hope you do not think I would believe such nonsense." Damaris peered more closely into Thea's face. "Do not tell me *you* actually believe that! Thea . . . a man like Morecombe does not dance attendance on a woman because she tends to a baby who may or may not be his sister's illegitimate child. He can hire someone to look after the baby—indeed, he has hired a nursemaid, has he not?"

"Yes."

"Why has he not taken the baby back to his house, as he was going to? Mrs. Clemmons told me he hired the first housekeeper she recommended to him, and the housekeeper has already hired three maids. Lady Wofford is in residence there now, so his household is perfectly respectable, even if she is a bit of a snob. Lolly and young Matthew could move to his house today if he wanted."

"He agrees that Matthew would be happier with me."

"No doubt Matthew is. But I suspect the reason is more that Lord Morecombe does not wish to cause *you* unhappiness. Not to mention the fact that it gives the man a grand excuse to call on you—as he has done each and every day for over a week now."

Thea felt herself blushing at her friend's blunt words. "I will admit that Gabriel has expressed an interest in me."

"I knew it!" Damaris grinned, her eyes twinkling.

"But it isn't in any permanent way. It cannot be. Oh, Damaris, don't you see? I cannot allow myself to hope!"

"But, darling, why not?" Damaris grabbed Thea's hands and squeezed them.

"I am not the sort of woman a man like Lord Morecombe marries!" Thea said in an anguished voice.

"Why not? Thea, dear, your name is quite respectable. Why, you are cousin to an earl—an earl whose son is Morecombe's friend, as well. You've no scandalous past or skeletons in your closet. You haven't a gaggle of impecunious relatives who will cling to him like leeches or mad uncles locked up in your attic. And Morecombe hardly needs you to bring him a large dowry."

"Damaris . . . I am plain! I am fine to . . . to flirt with while Morecombe is in the country for a few weeks. But he will go back to the beautiful ladies of the *ton*. In a few days, I will be forgotten. Gabriel will marry someone sophisticated and lovely, the sort of woman meant to be Lady Morecombe. Not a dowdy spinster from the Cotswolds."

"Thea! Look in this mirror." Damaris turned Thea toward the mirror again, pulling her closer to the looking glass. "Obviously, Lord Morecombe does not find you plain. There are several girls of low station whom he could flirt with—and more—if that was all he wanted. If you will remember, everyone in Chesley was chattering about the fact that he was doing exactly that. He was not lonely for female companionship. He did not need to seek you out merely to keep him occupied until he returned to London. He chose to be with you. He sought you out. And he is, as you pointed out, a man well acquainted with the beauties of the *ton*. He is, I venture to say, a connoisseur of female beauty. Why would you not believe his judgment regarding your looks?"

Thea gazed, wide-eyed, into the mirror. Looking at herself now, she had to admit that she was more attractive than she had thought. Something about her was softer and more pliant, and her face had a glow that she had never before seen. The body that had always been gawky now seemed to have a certain grace. Perhaps she did not have the tempting curves of Damaris beside her, but Thea now realized that her long limbs had their own sort of appeal. After all, Gabriel had told her so—not just with words, but with his desire. Perhaps some of the difference in her was attributable to the changes she had made in hairstyle or clothes, but Thea realized that something more was involved. Happiness, emotion, confidence, had all added an indefinable allure. And maybe, just maybe, she thought, before this she had not looked at herself through impartial eyes. She had never really *seen* herself.

Not as the vicar's daughter, the vicar's sister, the plain contrast to Veronica's beauty. But simply as Thea. A woman completely separate from all those things. And deserving of her own separate life.

She turned to Damaris, an impish grin spreading across her face. "You know . . . I think a red dress might be just what I want after all."

*Once Thea had accepted the* dress, a great deal of measuring and pinning had to be done so that Damaris's maid could alter it to suit Thea, so it was close to an hour before Thea took her leave and started back through the village toward her house. She had not even reached the center of the town when she saw Gabriel striding toward her.

Thea could not refrain from smiling. She had been hurrying, thinking that Gabriel might have come to call on her while she was out and she would have missed him. He had visited every afternoon since Christmas, visits that had been almost as frustrating as they were delightful. Much as she enjoyed seeing Gabriel, being with him, talking to him, her being with him, even for a short time, filled her with desire—a desire that was frustratingly unfulfilled.

When they sat talking, whether side by side on the sofa or across from each other in separate chairs, Thea was overwhelmingly aware of Gabriel's nearness. Only inches separated them. She could reach out a hand to touch his thigh or stroke his cheek; he could caress her skin, kiss her lips. But they could allow none of those things to happen because at any moment someone might pop into the room. Between Lolly and the baby, Thea's brother, Mrs. Brewster, and the day maid, not to mention the usual daily visitors to the vicar's house, the supply of possible interlopers was seemingly never ending. Nor could they meet at the Priory, which would not only test the boundaries of scandal, but also contained even more guests and servants. And the winter weather made any thought of dallying in some glade completely absurd.

Gabriel's hand might brush hers as he handed over Matthew or his gaze might slide boldly down her body, setting up an answering heat, but both of them were well aware that nothing else would follow, no chance to slake the thirst building inside them. As a result, every time Thea saw Gabriel, her desire increased, followed by an equally intense rush of frustration. Even now, just seeing him walking toward her down the street, his long legs eating up the ground between them, Thea's blood began to heat within her veins. Her fingers tightened around her reticule as she reined in her reactions.

"Miss Bainbridge."

"Lord Morecombe." Their eyes met, warm with the feelings that could not be expressed here on the street.

"I was just at the vicarage," Gabriel said, turning to walk beside her back in the direction he had come. "They told me you were visiting Mrs. Howard, so I thought I would offer my escort to your house."

"That is most kind of you." Thea's eyes went to his mouth. She could not help but think how it had felt on her throat . . . her breasts . . . her stomach.

His pupils darkened, and he glanced away. Thea struggled to

think of something to say that did not involve any of the things her mind was dwelling on.

"Um ... I ... I hope your guests will not think you are neglecting them."

"They find it odd, I believe, that I take so many rides in the middle of winter." Gabriel grinned to himself. "Myles is the only one who has guessed the reason."

"That you are coming to see your nephew?"

His grin widened. "That I am using it as an excuse to see you. Ian and Alan, I think, believe I have taken leave of my senses over some stranger's baseborn child."

"They do not think Matthew is your sister's child?"

"I believe they prefer not to think about the baby at all. Lady Wofford endeared herself to me somewhat by insisting that Jocelyn was too good a person to have an illegitimate child, but I fear that is probably more her naïveté speaking than any conviction based on facts."

They had reached the center of the village and were about to turn toward Thea's home when Gabriel glanced up the street in the opposite direction. His footsteps faltered and stopped as he stared at a woman walking past the bakery across the road. The woman glanced at them, then turned and walked rapidly away. Gabriel watched her go, frowning.

"Gabriel?" Thea glanced up at him questioningly. "What is it?"

"I know that woman—but what—? The devil!" He took off at a run.

After a startled instant, Thea hurried after him. He whipped around the corner of the building and disappeared from her sight.

When Thea caught up with him, he was standing in the middle of the street, looking around him in frustration.

Gabriel let out a short, blunt curse under his breath. "I lost her. I was too late. It took me too long to recognize her."

"Who was she? Why did you run after her?"

"It was Jocelyn's maid. Hannah. I'm sure of it."

Thea stared at him. "Then that means . . ."

"Jocelyn is still here. She must be."

They walked farther up the street, looking all around them for any sign of the woman Gabriel had seen in front of the bakery. Thea had not seen the woman's face; all she had seen was a short woman in a dark cloak. However, any woman would have been noticeable on the empty streets. They saw no one.

The shops gave way to houses, and before long they were on the edge of the town. They had crossed a street in their search, with no sign of anyone on it in either direction. They checked in the shops to see if Hannah had entered any of them and even went so far as to knock on the front doors of some of the houses. No one had seen the woman they sought. They received the same answer in the shops near where they had first seen the maid. No stranger had come into their stores that day.

"I am sure everyone in Chesley will now be convinced that I am mad," Gabriel said as they turned away. "I cannot believe I let her slip away! If only I had recognized her immediately." Gabriel jammed his fists into his pockets in frustration.

"Are you certain it was your sister's maid?"

He nodded. "I might have had some doubt about it if she had not disappeared like that. But as soon as she saw me, she turned and ran. Why would a stranger have done that? When I saw her, I was certain I knew her; her features were so familiar. They should be; she lived in my household for years. But it took me a moment to figure out how I knew her. It was just so startling, so out of place to come upon her here."

"It must mean your sister is here, don't you think? And that Matthew is her child? It strains credulity to think they are unrelated."

"I agree. It is also much likelier that Jocelyn camped at the ruins if she had Hannah to help her. Hannah would have been the one cooking over the fire."

"I suppose Hannah could have stolen the baby from her and brought him here herself," Thea mused.

"To what purpose? Why kidnap Jocelyn's baby, steal her brooch, and then abandon them both?"

"It doesn't sound likely," Thea admitted.

"I shouldn't have given up on looking for Jocelyn," Gabriel said as they turned their steps back toward the vicarage.

"But there is no way you could have known. It was clear that no one had been back to the ruins for several days, and we had searched all around."

"I must search again. Could they be staying in any of those houses near where I saw her?"

"I can draw a map when we get home. I don't imagine there are too many places in Chesley that Mrs. Brewster or Lolly or I don't know who lives there."

Her words turned out to be true enough. In the kitchen, Thea took a pencil and piece of paper and began to sketch out the roads and lanes of the village, marking down *X*'s for houses and *O*'s for businesses, paying particular attention to the area where Gabriel had spotted the maid. Lolly listened to them with wide-eyed attention as she fed the baby, every now and then popping in with a name or location.

Thea did her best to keep her attention on her task, but it became more and more difficult with Gabriel sitting so close beside her, his breath sometimes touching her ear or neck or face as he bent closer to see the map. She scolded herself for her obviously wanton nature—how could she be thinking of Gabriel's kiss at a time like this!—but her words had little effect on the heat that twined and twisted through her abdomen.

"I don't think they could be in any of these houses," Thea said at last, setting down the pencil and leaning back in her chair. "One of us would have heard if anyone had two strangers staying with them. Don't you think so, Mrs. Brewster?"

The housekeeper nodded. "Aye. There's not much goes on in Chesley I don't know about. Certainly wouldn't be anybody living on Butcher's Lane."

"I think she turned down that street because it was the quickest way to get out of my line of sight. She could have run down a cross street or alley and circled back. She could have gone anywhere."

Thea picked up the rudimentary map, and she and Gabriel went into the sitting room to continue their discussion. Gabriel poked the coals into life and added another piece of wood to get the fire blazing. He stood for a moment, staring moodily down into the leaping fire.

"You must not blame yourself," Thea told him, going over to him.

He turned and smiled at her sadly. "I think the worst part is that Jocelyn does not want to see me. I thought she brought Matthew here and ran away, and I tried to accept that she felt humiliated or ashamed or afraid to face me. I thought she had intended to come to me, but at the last minute could not work up the courage. I thought later she would regret it or see that I welcomed the baby, and perhaps she would come back. Or at least write me a letter—give me some way of reaching her. But this . . . to know that she has been here for the past weeks, *hiding* from me!"

Gabriel turned and wrapped his arms around Thea, holding on to her tightly and leaning his head against hers. "Thank God you are here with me. I should hate to face this alone."

"Of course I am here." Thea encircled his waist with her arms and returned his embrace. She would not have cared at that moment if half the village had walked in and seen her in Gabriel's arms. All she could think of was his need for comfort. "I will do anything I can to help you."

He kissed the top of her head. "You do more than you could know. Thank you." She could feel his smile against her hair. "I should very much like to kiss you now. Properly, I mean." His lips brushed her hair again, and he sighed and set her aside. "I have to find her. I cannot be at ease until I at least speak to Jocelyn about all this."

"What are you going to do?"

"Obviously, Jocelyn is willing to live in much less comfort than I had assumed. If it's unlikely that she's staying in the village, I think I should search the area surrounding the village. Perhaps there is an abandoned cottage or a barn or other outbuilding where she and Hannah might have sought shelter. I cannot think that she would be staying outdoors in this weather, but there must be some out-of-the-way places or huts or something in which she could live temporarily."

"That will be a long and difficult task."

He nodded. "I know. But I think my friends will help me search. I will divide the area up and search it methodically. I think she must be staying within walking distance of the village if her maid is going back and forth to Chesley, so that will curtail the area a good deal."

Thea nodded. "I wish I could be of some help to you."

"You already have been. Just keep an ear out for any news about strangers in the village. You and your housekeeper are bound to hear if there is any gossip."

"True. That is one of the things that is so peculiar—that all this has happened yet no one seems to have noticed any strangers in the village." Thea paused. "I cannot help but wonder what the man who abducted Matthew has to do with your sister and her maid."

"I know. 'Tis a complete puzzlement to me."

"Do you think—could he be Matthew's father?"

Gabriel looked at her, startled. "I suppose he could be. It would make sense if the man was connected to Matthew."

"Perhaps he did not want your sister bringing the baby to you or seeking your help. Maybe he tried to steal it from her, and that is why she is hiding."

"You are kind to come up with reasons for my sister's avoidance of me that do not include her disliking or fearing me." He smiled at Thea. "But if that is the case, why would Jocelyn hide from me, too? I would think she would come to me for help against the fellow."

"It does not make much sense."

"Nothing about this whole affair makes much sense," Gabriel responded drily.

"There must be a reason; we simply cannot find it."

"I applaud your faith in rationality. I hope you are right. But I should go now. I need to talk to the others so we can start looking tomorrow." He took Thea's hand and lifted it to his lips, kissing it rather more warmly than was customary in departure. "I fear I will be out riding most of the day."

"Of course." Thea was determined not to show her disappointment at the thought of not seeing him the next day.

Still holding her hand, Gabriel moved a step closer. Thea turned her face up as he bent closer. At that moment, they heard Daniel's voice in the hall, speaking to Sally. With a muttered oath, Gabriel stepped back.

"If there is any news . . ." Thea said, primly polite.

"I will come as soon as I can," he promised. With a quick bow and a last glance at her, Gabriel left the room.

Gabriel spent the next two days crisscrossing the land around Chesley with the help of his three friends. He managed, though, to find the time to visit Thea each evening after they had finished searching. Unfortunately, the first evening was spent in a stilted, all-too-brief formal call, for not only was Thea's brother, Daniel, in the sitting room when Gabriel arrived, but also Mrs. Cliffe and her two oldest daughters as well. Thea had to cover a smile when she saw the flash of horror in Gabriel's eyes as they lighted upon the Squire's family, and she was not surprised when Gabriel left after twenty minutes of meaningless social chatter.

The next evening, he hesitated outside the door when she answered, casting a wary glance down the hallway behind her. Thea laughed and reached out to take his hand, pulling him inside.

"There is no one here. My brother has gone to pay a visit on old Mrs. Brenham. And Mrs. Cliffe is safely at home—I sincerely hope." Thea led him back toward the sitting room. "Come in and tell me your news."

"I have none to report, really. Or at least, nothing but failure. We have searched every foot of land around here, I think, and none of us spotted any sign of Jocelyn or Hannah."

"I am so sorry."

Gabriel sighed and sank down into the nearest chair. "Either she is too well hidden for me to find or she is not here."

"What will you do now?"

"I have to keep looking for her. I gave up too easily before. It occurred to me that perhaps Jocelyn is not here. What if she left the baby here, then went to one of the other villages near here? Maybe she only sent Hannah over here the other day to see what she could find out about the baby. For all I know, Jocelyn has been in some other town this whole time, and she just sent Hannah to Chesley with the baby. Maybe Jocelyn was never at the ruins. That would seem more like the girl I knew."

"Do you think she could be waiting to see how you receive Matthew before she comes here herself?"

"I would like to think she will come home, but I cannot count on it. In any case, I must explore farther afield."

"Perhaps I could drive with you to Nyebourne, as we did to Bynford."

He turned to her, his eyes heating. "I thought about it. I even considered borrowing Lady Wofford's closed carriage, so you and I could ride together inside, closed off from all eyes."

"Gabriel!" Thea could not help but smile even as her voice registered shock. Just the thought of what could happen inside a closed vehicle with Gabriel was enough to start a coil of warmth deep in her abdomen.

"What?" He widened his eyes innocently. "Surely you don't think I meant to propose anything shocking or improper? Miss Bainbridge, I do believe it was your mind that immediately went to the possibility of something lewd transpiring in Lady Wofford's carriage."

"Me?" Thea laughed. "It was you! I could see what you intended in your eyes."

"Miss Bainbridge, really . . ." He assumed a pious face. "You are imputing your own wicked thoughts to me. Whatever did you think we might do in a carriage, all alone?"

He reached out and took her hands, pulling her up and over onto his lap.

"Gabriel!" Thea cried out in protest as she wriggled and twisted, shoving halfheartedly at the arm he clamped across her waist to hold her down. "Someone might come in."

"You just said your brother was not here." He interspersed his words with kisses up the side of her neck. "And I'll warrant it's too late for Mrs. Brewster to still be about." He seemed fascinated now by her ear, kissing and nibbling at it while his hand began to roam over her breasts.

"But . . . um . . ." Thea lost the train of her thoughts as his fingers began to circle her nipple in a most interesting way. "Oh, Gabriel."

She could feel his breath on her skin as he chuckled, and it sent more shivers through her. His tongue traced the curves of her ear, and his hand slipped down to bunch up her skirts and slide beneath them, his fingers trailing up the inside of her thigh. He let out a low sound as he found the hot secret center of her, already damp with desire.

"Thea . . ." He breathed her name, burying his face in the juncture of her neck and shoulder. "I would like so much to take you with me. I dare swear we would have no rest the entire trip. And we could partake of a long lunch at the inn."

His fingers stroked her gently, almost lazily, as he talked, sending shudders of unabashed hunger through her. Thea moved instinctively against him, and she felt him harden beneath her. She thought about turning and sitting astride him, imagining his reaction if she did.

From upstairs came the sound of footsteps, and Thea let out a groan of frustration.

"Lolly. Lolly is here with Matthew. And, of course, Peter, the footman you sent over."

"Blast. We could lock the door."

"It doesn't lock," Thea said regretfully. "Not to mention that it would be quite scandalous."

Reluctantly, Gabriel released her. Thea stood up and moved away, making sure her clothes were straight and giving her cheeks time enough to cool.

"We cannot do it. Go together to Nyebourne, I mean." Gabriel's voice was clipped as he stood and went over to the fireplace, poking at the fire rather harder than was necessary. "Much as I would enjoy a trip with you, I cannot take the time for a leisurely journey. I need to cover as much ground as possible."

"Of course," Thea agreed colorlessly.

"I plan to go to all the towns around Chesley one after another. 'Twill be faster not to return home each day."

"Oh." Thea's heart sank lower. "Then you will be gone several days."

"I fear so." The expression of regret and frustration on his face picked up Thea's spirits a bit.

"Are you planning to return?"

"Of course!" Gabriel strode over to her, grasping her by the arms and looking down at her fiercely. "Believe me, there is nothing I look forward to more than coming back to you. And I promise that when I do, we will find some way to be alone and private."

"For longer than a half hour?" Thea tossed back saucily.

Something in the smile he returned was wolfish. "For longer than a few days. It will take at least that much time to do all the things I keep imagining doing with you."

Casting a quick glance past her out into the hallway, Gabriel pulled Thea to him and kissed her thoroughly. Finally his mouth left hers, and he held her tightly against him for a moment before letting her go.

"Hopefully I can live off that for a while." He smiled faintly.

"Will your friends go out to look, too?"

"Myles offered, but I told him I wanted him to stay here and make sure you and Matthew are all right. We cannot trust that the fellow who took Matthew will not try again. So if you need anything or are frightened or suspicious for any reason, send a note to Myles at the Priory."

"Very well." Thea felt warmed by Gabriel's making sure that she and Matthew would be protected. "But I am certain Peter will be more than enough. Nothing else has happened. You must have frightened him off."

"Perhaps. Alan, I think, has decided that the lights of London are calling him," Gabriel went on with a smile.

"Chesley has proved too dull?"

Gabriel's smile widened. "I think it is more that Lady Wofford has civilized life at the Priory."

"Oh. I see."

"But he promised me he will check at the inns in the first few towns on the road to see if Jocelyn is there. Ian will take the northern road for me . . . provided he can withstand his lady's determined pleas to return to Fenstone Park for Twelfth Night."

"Will you be back for Twelfth Night?"

"I am resolved to. I do not intend to miss dancing with you. Or seeing how bewitching you look in a mask."

"What nonsense."

"Not nonsense at all." He kissed her again and released her with a sigh. "Now, I must go."

He made it to the doorway before turning around and coming back for another kiss . . . or three. Finally, he set her aside and strode from the room determinedly. Thea heard him in the kitchen, issuing last-minute instructions to Peter. She climbed the stairs and went to the window to watch Gabriel ride off down the street. With a sigh, she turned away, trying not to think about how lonely the next few days would be without him.

Before long, she knew, Gabriel would leave Chesley for good. His true homes were in London and on his estate. The Priory and Chesley—and she—were only diversions for him, ways for a bored aristocrat to amuse himself. To dare dream anything else would be setting herself up for misery.

Thea opened a dresser drawer and drew out the small box Gabriel had given her. She gazed at the set of garnet earrings inside the box, touching the jewels with a tender finger. What had this present meant to Gabriel? She was afraid to put too much hope in such a thing as a gift. After all, even a vicar's sister from a small village was worldly enough to know that wealthy bachelors often gave jewels to the women they set up as their mistresses. It was entirely possible that the earrings were simply in return for her having given herself to him, a sort of sophisticated thank-you. Or perhaps it was what a man such as Gabriel did to ease the sting of parting.

She slipped the earrings out of the box and into her ears. She was not going to wear them anywhere, but it couldn't hurt to just try them on. Thea turned her head, admiring the way the light caught the deep-red jewel, the glittering gold. They would look splendid with the dress Damaris was lending her.

Thea shook her head impatiently. She could not let herself think this way. She pulled the earrings from her ears and set them back in the box, closing the lid firmly. They must stay hidden away, just like her relationship with Gabriel. Nothing could have spoken more clearly about any future she might have with him than that fact—she and Lord Morecombe were a cause for gossip, for scandal, because everyone knew that there was no chance of marriage between them. If he dangled after her, he would not be looking for a wife.

She had known that from the beginning. Perhaps Damaris was right, and she was not so plain. But Damaris was wrong in suggesting that Gabriel had any long-lasting interest in Thea. He was a sophisticate; she was a church mouse. This was the most wonderful, exciting period of her life, but to Gabriel it was only a brief interlude, easily forgotten.

Thea sighed and turned away from the dresser. The next few days were, she feared, going to be only a foretaste of what her life would soon be like. A life without Gabriel.

# Seventeen

With a great deal of surprise, Thea answered the knock on her front door two days later and found Lady Wofford standing on her doorstep. Belatedly, she realized she was staring, and she stepped back. "Lady Wofford. Please, come in."

"Thank you, Miss Bainbridge." Lady Wofford nodded and swept in, taking her hands out of her fur muff and glancing around expectantly.

Thea realized that the woman was looking for a servant to take her outerwear from her. Thea smothered a smile and reached out for the muff. "Here, allow me."

"Oh. Oh, of course." Emily handed her the muff, followed by her fur-trimmed pelisse, clearly somewhat uncomfortable at her hostess's performing such a menial task. She gave Thea a determined smile. "Things are so much more . . . informal in the country, are they not?"

"Indeed, Lady Wofford, I am afraid I have little to compare it to. I have lived here all my life."

"Yes, of course." Emily's smile wavered a bit, but she went on, "It must be quite . . . reassuring to have known everyone here all your life. I grew up in London, you see. I am a bit of a fish out of water here. I fear that perhaps I have made the wrong impression on you. So I hoped we might start again. We are, after all, cousins, are we not?"

Thea softened. She had, perhaps, judged the woman too harshly. Chesley must be quite a change from London. And the circumstances under which Lady Wofford had met Thea had been decidedly peculiar; she could not blame her, she supposed, for looking at Thea rather askance.

"Of course." Thea offered a more genuine smile to her unexpected guest. "Would you like some tea?"

Thea showed her to the sitting room, then popped into the kitchen to ask Mrs. Brewster to bring the tea tray. She suspected that Lady Wofford found it odd, too, that Thea had not simply rung for a servant. Thea settled down on the chair across from the other woman, and silence descended on them.

Finally Thea said, "I hope you are enjoying your stay in Chesley."

"Indeed, Lord Morecombe is an excellent host. Of course, he and Lord Wofford have known each other since they were children. He comes from an excellent family."

Thea made some murmur of agreement.

"Do you know his family?" Emily asked after another short silence.

"No, I have not had the pleasure."

"His sister is a lovely girl. I was quite surprised when she became engaged to Lord Rawdon. Very long lineage, of course, but, well ... somewhat suspect, nevertheless. I am sure you know what I mean; you are one of the Bainbridges, after all."

"One of the lesser branches, I'm afraid." Thea managed not to add anything sharper.

"Oh, dear, have I offended you? Are you a friend of Lord Rawdon?"

"He has not offered me a reason to dislike him. I cannot say that I know him well."

"Of course." Lady Wofford glanced around, and Thea suspected that she was counting down the minutes until she could politely leave. Thea was rather counting them, as well.

Fortunately, Mrs. Brewster brought in the tea tray, and they were able to expend a few minutes on the ritual of tea before the silence became awkward again.

"How is the . . . um . . . child?" Lady Wofford asked. "The one you found in the church? Such a remarkable thing. I am not sure I have ever heard the like."

"Yes, it was most unusual. He is well. Would you like to see him?"

Alarm touched Lady Wofford's face and was quickly covered. "Oh, my, no, no reason to disturb him. I gather no one in the village saw who left him there."

"No. No one that we have found."

"Well, we must not dwell on such unpleasant topics. Do you plan to attend Mrs. Howard's Twelfth Night party? Sir Myles and Lord Morecombe seem to be quite looking forward to it."

"Yes, my brother and I will be there. Will you and Lord Wofford attend, as well?"

"If we are still here, I suspect we will. No doubt it will be most entertaining. However, I know that Lord Fenstone is most eager

for us to return to the Park. Such a lovely place, even in the winter.
I believe you have been there?"

"Yes, a few times."

"A beautiful estate." Lady Wofford's smile was a more genu-
inely pleased one than Thea had seen on her face before. "Now,
there is an elegant ballroom. And the long gallery— I enjoy strolling
there and looking at all the former earls and countesses."

This seemed an odd pastime to Thea, but she refrained from
saying so. She merely smiled and nodded during the woman's
detailed description of the gown she would wear to the Twelfth
Night ball if they remained in town. Thea found it a great relief
when Emily made her polite good-byes a few minutes later. Thea
arose from her seat, hoping that the movement did not look too
much like a leap for joy. She saw the woman to the door, helping
her on with her pelisse and handing her the muff and hat. When
Lady Wofford at last started down the path toward her carriage,
Thea closed the door and leaned back against it with a sigh of relief.

Lady Wofford had been more pleasant, it was true, but the
result had been, well, boring. Thea could not help but wonder if
Lady Wofford's style of conversation was typical of the ladies
of the *ton*. Was Lady Wofford a true example of her breed? If so,
Thea thought with some dismay, nothing could demonstrate more
clearly the enormous gulf that lay between her world and Gabriel's. He might enjoy Thea while he was here, but his real life, the
one that awaited him back in London, would have no place for her.

*Gabriel strode past the ruins* of the abbey, glad to be off his horse
after three straight days of riding, broken only by going into inns

to question the innkeepers. He had stopped at the Priory only long enough to stable his mount and clean up before he set out for the vicarage. He was a trifle stiff and tired, but none of that weighed against the hunger to see Thea.

If anyone had told him a year ago that he would miss any woman as much as he had missed Thea the past few days, he would have laughed. Much as he enjoyed the company of women, never had one's absence caused him more than a twinge of regret or loneliness. After all, there had always been another woman to take her place, whether she be a lady or a lightskirt. Never before had he sat by himself in front of a fireplace of an evening mooning over a woman, instead of going to the tavern to entertain himself with drink and a hand of cards—and probably a tavern wench for his bed, as well.

Each evening of his journey, he had gone into the public room of the inn to have an ale and ask the patrons if they had seen Jocelyn or Hannah. But invariably he found himself thinking what Thea would say about this tavern guest or that and what he would answer in reply. He wanted to tell her what he had done that day and what he had learned. Any attempts at cards or dice soon palled, and the tavern wenches seemed much too dull-witted for him to enjoy flirting with them. Once he had discovered all the information he could, he soon went up to his bed.

Absurd as it seemed, his time with Thea appeared to have spoiled him for anyone else's company. The loneliness and the boredom were bad enough, but worst of all, he could not keep from lusting after her. The rides from village to village left him with ample time to think, and most of his thoughts consisted of recalling the all-too-brief occasions when he had made love to Thea. These were broken up primarily by visions of coupling with her in the future, along with a smattering of innovative ideas concerning ways to get her alone. As a result, he had spent almost his entire trip in frustrated arousal.

He had done his best to stop thinking about her mane of wild curls and how it had looked floating down around her shoulders and over her breasts, the tendrils parting just enough for the pink-tipped nipples to peek through, tantalizing and beckoning, as she sat astride his hips, riding him to her climax. Or the way her hair had tumbled over the pillow, spread out like a fan from her head, as he sank deep within her, driven by a heated desire so intense it was almost pain. He remembered the glisten of her nipple, damp from his mouth, the slick satin of her nether lips beneath his fingers. He remembered the soft touch of her fingers on his bare skin, the taste of her tongue in his mouth, the soft moan of her passion in his ear.

It had been the very devil getting to sleep every night. He told himself to choose a likely wench from the tavern to slake his thirst. That had always been his way in the past if he lusted after a lady he could not have, and it had worked well enough. But no longer, apparently. None of the women he saw about him appealed—this one was too short, that one too coarse, the other too overripe. The truth was, not one of them caused a single spike to his desire, and he had the distinct suspicion that if he bedded any of them, there would be no lessening of his need for Thea. What he wanted was to feel her long legs wrapped around him, her lips exploring his skin, her sweet mysteries opening to him.

The realization was astounding ... and just a bit frightening.

Was he doomed to spend the rest of his life on this knife edge of desire? Desperate and hungry, panting after a woman whom only two or three weeks ago he had scarcely noticed? It was mad. Nonsensical.

What he ought to do, he told himself, was go back to London until this madness passed. There, among the beauties of the city, he would forget those cool gray eyes and the way they sparkled when she was amused. His fingers would stop itching to sink into her hair and pull it down, sending the pins flying. He would not spend every waking minute dreaming of losing himself in her, vaulting into that dark, blissful abyss.

But it was even more nonsensical to tear himself away from her when all he wanted was to see her again. What he really needed, he knew, was to find some way to be with her all the time, to drink his fill, to expend his lust in long, heated nights of lovemaking. The answer would be a week or two ... or three ... alone with her. What he wanted was something like a ... a honeymoon.

That idea brought him up short. Was he actually thinking of marriage? Surely not. He enjoyed his life as a bachelor. Someday he would marry to carry on the line, but that would not be anytime soon. One did not marry simply because a certain woman drove him mad with lust. There must be much more than that ... companionship and similarity of interest, for example. Love, if one was lucky. Gabriel had come to a stop, deep in thought, and now he glanced around himself. He had reached the graveyard of the church. He looked across the river, where the dark block of the vicarage lay. A warm light burned from behind the windows.

He looked up at the second floor, wondering if the lit window there was Thea's bedroom.

Desire, never far from the surface lately, surged up in him. Whatever was he doing, standing among the gravestones, when the woman he had been thinking of for the past three days was only a few yards away from him?

He strode rapidly past the church and across the bridge. His knock on the front door came quite close to pounding. He waited, every nerve raw, until the door swung open. Thea stood in the doorway, light bathing her from the candelabra on the table beside her. She wore a plain dark dress, and a kerchief covered her head.

She looked utterly beautiful.

"Thea." He stepped inside, sweeping her up into his arms in the same motion, and fastened his mouth to hers.

She threw her arms around his neck, fervently returning his kiss. Frustrated by his heavy coat, he reached between them, undoing the buttons and shoving the sides apart. He could feel the swell of her breasts as she pressed into his chest, the pert, hard thrust of her nipples. Gabriel tore the kerchief from Thea's head and plunged his hands into her hair, holding her head still as his lips found hers again.

Gabriel kissed her as if he would consume her, his mouth leaving hers only to change the angle of their kiss, and all the while he kissed her, his hands roamed her body hungrily, sweeping down her back and curving over her hips. When Thea pulled away, he reached instinctively to draw her back, but she took his hand and tugged, leading him down the hall and into the sitting room.

Thea closed the door behind them, saying, "Daniel is away; he won't be back—"

Her words were cut off by Gabriel, who, having shrugged out of his topcoat and dropped it on the floor, took her in his arms again. "The others?" he asked thickly, raining kisses over her face and neck.

"They're in the kitchen, making supper."

He walked her back until she came up against the door, continuing to kiss her. Bunching her skirts up, he slid his hands beneath her petticoats and in between her legs, caressing her through the cloth of her undergarments. Finding the tie of her pantalets, he jerked it loose and shoved them down and off, his hand seeking out the soft, slick folds of flesh. The sound of Thea's breath catching in her throat sent his hunger surging even higher.

"Sweet heaven, I've missed you," he breathed. "I could think of nothing but you."

Her answer was only a soft moan as his fingers teased and stroked, bringing her to the trembling edge of satisfaction. He reached down and unbuttoned his breeches, and his engorged manhood sprang free. Thea's fingers curled around him, and he stiffened all over, struggling to hold on to his control. Her fingers were maddeningly soft and caressing as they moved slowly over him, and his passion swelled even higher.

He reached beneath her hips, lifting her, and Thea went to him eagerly, opening her legs and wrapping them around him. He slid into her with a motion so achingly pleasurable that he had to sink his teeth into his lower lip to keep from crying out. Gabriel braced her against the door and began to move inside her. He dropped his head to her neck, muffling his hoarse, muttered words against her flesh. The need was so fierce in him he thought he must explode, and yet it continued to build, pushing him ever closer to the edge. There was nothing in the world but this moment, Thea's body surrounding him, her long legs clasping him to her, his driving need buried deep in her softness, the two of them melded together in a white-hot joining.

He heard the soft noise that issued from Thea's throat as he felt her convulse around him, and the world shattered into pleasure. Passion swept through him in a massive wave as he shuddered against her, his seed pouring into her.

Gabriel was not sure how long it was before he returned to reason. They could have stood there, pressed against the heavy door, for a minute or an hour; it was all the same to him. Slowly he released her and moved back, letting her slide down to the floor.

"I would say I am sorry," he said hoarsely, his breath labored, "but I am not."

"Nor am I," she replied, her voice barely above a whisper.

"I am accustomed to having more control. But there is something about you that drives me nearly mad." He smiled and kissed her lightly on each cheek. "I had not meant to greet you quite this ... effusively."

Thea giggled and reached up to touch her hair, where several strands had escaped and fallen down. "I must look a mess. I was cleaning upstairs when I saw you walking up the path."

"You look beautiful." It astonished him that he had once thought her looks only passable. She dazzled him now.

Thea colored prettily at his words. "I should . . ." She made a vague gesture toward her clothes.

He turned away and righted himself, giving her a bit of privacy to adjust her own clothes. When he turned back around, Thea had gone to the mirror against the far wall and was busy trying to pin her hair back in place. Gabriel dropped down into a chair and watched her, enjoying the intimacy of the scene. He felt happier than he had in days.

Thea gave her hair a final pat and pivoted back to face him. She looked put together again, but the flush in her cheeks and the soft curve of her mouth gave her away. Gabriel's smile widened, and her cheeks reddened a little more, but the flashing look she gave him did not seem displeased.

She went to the door and opened it, casting a quick glance out in the hallway. Turning back, she said, "Daniel is in Lower Leckbury today. There is a smaller parish there that he visits once a week."

"Smaller than Chesley?"

"Yes, though you may not believe it. They have a church; it used to be a bit larger. But they have no pastor. So he will not be home until rather late. I was planning on having supper at the table in the kitchen, but perhaps you would like to stay and dine with me? It is quite informal, I'm afraid."

He smiled, amused by her attempt at polite small talk after what had just occurred between them. "I should enjoy that very much, Miss Bainbridge."

Thea grinned and sat down in the chair across from him. "How was your journey? Did you find any information?"

"No." He sighed. "There was one man who was having supper in the tavern in . . . I cannot recall exactly, a village on the road to Oxford, in any case. He thought that he had seen a woman with a baby in the inn a week or two ago. Apparently he frequently eats there. He cannot be sure of the date, though he is fairly certain it was before Christmas. He does not remember two women, however, and he was unsure whether she had brown hair or blond, so I cannot put a great deal of faith in his account."

"I am sorry."

"Thank you. I suppose it was not entirely a waste. I don't believe that Jocelyn and Hannah are currently at an inn in any of the nearby villages. Which leads back, of course, to their being somewhere in Chesley or the countryside around it. I would have thought we had checked everywhere close by, but obviously they must have gone aground somewhere."

"Something will turn up," Thea said consolingly.

"How have things been here? How is young Matthew?"

"I will go fetch him." Thea popped up and left the room, returning a few minutes later with the baby.

Matthew greeted Gabriel with a squeal of delight, and Gabriel spent the next few minutes swinging him up above his head while Matthew erupted with laughter. Afterward, he set the baby down on the rug, and Thea handed Matthew a wooden rattle. He seemed uninterested in it, however, and was soon on all fours, rocking back and forth. Then, surprising them all, including himself, Matthew stuck out one hand, then another, followed by his legs.

"Look! He's crawling!" Thea cried.

Gabriel laughed as the baby stopped, looking shocked, then moved forward again. "Good boy!"

Gabriel stood and pulled Thea into his arms, inexplicably filled with pride. Thea laughed and hugged him back. "That is the first time he's done more than rock there as if he's going to launch himself forward."

"You will doubtless never have a moment's peace from here on." Gabriel watched the baby traveling on, already almost to the edge of the rug.

At that moment a knock sounded on the front door, and Thea and Gabriel glanced at each other in surprise. Thea started toward the front door, and Gabriel followed her, pausing to swoop Matthew up and take him along. As Gabriel stepped into the hall, he heard the front door open and Lord Rawdon's voice saying, "Good evening. I hope I am not disturbing you. I had thought to see young Ma—"

Rawdon's gaze went past Thea to Gabriel, standing in the hallway with the baby. "Oh."

"Rawdon."

The other man inclined his head briefly toward Gabriel. "Morecombe." He turned back to Thea. "Please forgive me, Miss Bainbridge. Perhaps I should come back another time."

"No. Wait." Gabriel went forward quickly. "Stay. I would like to speak to you." He glanced at Thea. "I mean, if that is all right with you, Miss Bainbridge."

"Of course." Thea looked from one man to another. "Please allow me to take your coat, Lord Rawdon. Why don't you gentlemen talk in the sitting room?" Thea hung Rawdon's coat on the rack and went to take the baby from Gabriel. "I'll just, um, see about some tea."

With those words, she whisked the baby down the corridor and through the door into the kitchen. Gabriel regarded Rawdon for a moment, then led him to the sitting room. Rawdon went to the fireplace to warm his hands.

Gabriel stood for a moment, then said stiffly, "I must apologize to you."

Rawdon looked up at him, surprise registering on his face.

"I tried to tell you the other day, after I read Jocelyn's letter. But you had already left Chesley. I was wrong to assume that Jocelyn left because of you. Or that you were the father of her child. I greatly compounded that error by concluding that you must have forced her. I sincerely beg your pardon."

Gabriel waited, watching Rawdon. It had never been easy to read Rawdon's face, but the man was utterly inscrutable now.

"In your place, I probably would have thought the same thing." Rawdon gave a careless shrug. "The world knows that the Staffords are a bad lot."

"I did not judge you on your family."

"No?" Rawdon turned his attention to picking a bit of lint off the sleeve of his jacket. "It must have been on the basis of the wrongs I had committed on you then." He raised his head and focused on his gaze on Gabriel, the firelight glinting in his light eyes.

The implication of Rawdon's words stung. "I am well aware of the quality of your friendship. Your loyalty," Gabriel replied stiffly. "But I did not judge you without good reason."

"Indeed?" The corner of Rawdon's mouth lifted cynically. "Ah, yes, those rumors and innuendos regarding my bad behavior."

"You are not one to accept an apology gracefully, are you?"

"I have little interest in grace. I am more enamored of honesty."

"Honesty? You want honesty?" Gabriel stiffened, stalking toward Rawdon. "Very well then, yes, I had heard a great many rumors regarding your family. I paid no attention to them, for I *knew* you. Even when I heard rumors that you did not treat women as a gentleman should, I ignored them. Because I *knew* you. I trusted you as a man, as a friend; I trusted you so much I was willing to give my sister to you. I believed you would care for her, honor her, protect her. But when a woman runs away only weeks before her wedding, when she flees her home and family and the life she has always known because she cannot bear to marry a man considered by most to be one of the most eligible men in Britain, it becomes harder to ignore stories of that man's mistreatment of women!"

"I have *never* mistreated a woman!" Rawdon roared, his eyes flashing and his hands doubling into fists, and he took a long stride forward.

Gabriel did not back away, but moved to meet him. "I might have believed that then—if you had reacted with the slightest anxiety or pain or even concern for that nineteen-year-old girl whom you professed to love. But when I came to you, when I asked you if you knew where she had gone or why she had left, you sat there, as cold as always, playing cards, without a care in the world. You shrugged—shrugged, as if Jocelyn was as unimportant as one of the fobs on your watch chain—and said you were not going to mourn because some girl decided to cry off. And I realized then that I had been deceived in thinking you a friend. Or the man to whom I should entrust my sister."

"You did not *ask*! You accused! You shouted at me that I had hurt Jocelyn, that I had driven her away. You demanded to know what had happened. What was I supposed to say? That she had ripped my heart from my chest and trampled on it?" Rawdon's eyes were blazing blue, electric in his pale face.

"Your pride was hurt." Gabriel's lips curled. "The woman you said you loved was missing, and you did not bother to look because your pride had taken a fall."

"Of course I searched for her. Are you mad? I sent men out in every direction I could think of—agents and grooms and Bow Street Runners, all looking for her."

"But not you yourself."

"No. Not me." Rawdon's stiff form sagged a little, his fists loosening at his sides. "Not at first. I thought, if she wants to throw me over, then I would bloody well let her go. I refused to beg a woman to marry me. Not even Jocelyn. Later . . ." Rawdon shrugged and turned away. "When I saw that she had run from you as well, when my agents could not find her, I . . . looked for her. I drove down every blasted road out of London. I went to Southampton, to Liverpool; I went to bloody Gretna Green."

"You thought she had run away with someone."

"I thought everything. I even sent inquiries to Paris and Rome. To Brussels."

Gabriel looked at his former friend, half-turned away from

him. Something about Rawdon's powerful frame was forlorn. Gabriel hardened his jaw. "And what of Grace Fortner?"

"Who?" Rawdon glanced at him. A puzzled frown began to form on his brow.

"Grace Fortner. She was the daughter of a gentleman from Sussex, the cousin of Anne Buntwell, and she came out with Anne two years before Jocelyn made her debut. You fancied her for a while."

"Oh." The other man's face cleared. "Yes. I remember her. A pretty girl. Why do you ask?"

"What happened to her?"

"Happened? I don't know." Rawdon paused, thinking. "She—wasn't there some sort of scandal? She left London, didn't she? I believe I heard she married some fellow in Sussex." His gaze narrowed, the frown returning. "What does it matter?"

"A few days after you shrugged off Jocelyn's leaving, I learned that she was not the first girl to flee London because of you. Grace Fortner had, as well. You loved her; you pursued her. You maneuvered her into being alone with you. And when she rejected your advances, you would not let her go. You struggled, and she was hurt. She fled home because of her fear."

The other man simply looked at him for a long moment. "And you believed this?"

"She had no reason to lie. The story compromises her honor. She had every reason to keep it hidden, so the telling of it makes it hard to disbelieve."

"You heard this from Miss Fortner herself?"

"No. But the person who told me had it from her. And I trust that person."

"More than you ever trusted me, obviously." Rawdon came closer. His voice was flat, his gaze direct and cold. "If you were any other man, I would call you out. But for the friendship I once held for you, I will tell you this: I admired Miss Fortner a bit; I danced with her a few times and called on her once or twice. I believe I might even have sent her a nosegay. I did not pursue her. I did not trap her in a compromising position. I did not offer her any harm. I have never in my life laid an angry hand on a woman. I have never hit a female nor have I forced one. Miss Fortner lied or your friend lied. I frankly don't care which. But I will swear to you on my own sister's life that I have never harmed a woman. The only woman I ever loved was Jocelyn, and God help me, the only wrong I did to her was to allow our engagement to go forward even though I knew she did not love me as I loved her."

Gabriel stared into Rawdon's eyes, and in them he saw a cold, hard truth. He knew, with an empty sensation deep in his gut, that he had been wrong, terribly wrong. How could he have taken the word of a stranger, no matter how convincing the circumstances, over that of his trusted friend?

"My God . . . Rawdon. I am sorry." Even as he said them, he knew how terribly inadequate his words were. He took a step forward, his hand reaching out.

Rawdon shifted and half-turned away, his voice cool and remote. "It is all in the past."

"Yes, but . . . I . . ."

The other man shook his head once, briefly. "Please, present my apologies to Miss Bainbridge. I should go now. Tell her I shall return another time to see the boy."

Rawdon strode away, but he paused at the door and turned back. "The reason I left the other day was to meet a man in Oxford—a Bow Street Runner I have used in the past. I hired him to look for Jocelyn. If I hear anything from him, I will let you know."

"Thank you."

With a nod, Rawdon left the room. He must have met Thea in the hallway, for Gabriel heard the murmur of voices, Thea's lighter one mingling with Rawdon's crisp tones. Gabriel stood, unmoving, still stunned, his thoughts spinning, until Thea walked into the room a moment later.

"Gabriel?" She paused just inside the door, then hurried forward. "What is it? What happened? You look like—well, I don't know what."

"Like a man who's been kicked in the midsection?"

"What happened?" Thea repeated as she slipped her hands around his arm and looked up at him in concern. "Lord Rawdon looked a bit . . . overset, as well."

"We talked. I—he told me that everything I'd believed was wrong, and I knew . . . I *knew* when I looked in his eyes that he was telling me the truth."

"You mean, more than what you learned in the letter?"

Gabriel nodded. "Yes. Not just that Jocelyn did not fear or hate him, not just that he isn't Matthew's father. He swore that he had never touched the woman whom I was sure he had hurt and compromised. He swore that he had never hit a woman or forced her, and . . . I believed him. I think . . . I think perhaps he loved Jocelyn more than I ever realized."

"But what about the things he said to you when you confronted him? The callous disregard for where Jocelyn had gone?"

"A pretense." Gabriel shrugged. "That rings true enough. Pride was always Alec's besetting sin. He was never one to let anyone learn the extent of his injuries, whether they were to his body or his heart. I should have known it at the time. I should not have confronted him like that. He would never back down, never let his weakness show if he was attacked. He would lash out instead—and Rawdon always went for the jugular."

"I'm sorry."

"So am I." Gabriel looked down at her, his face etched with regret. "I did a terrible thing, Thea. I think Jocelyn broke Rawdon's heart when she left. And I . . . I turned on him, too. At a time when he needed a friend the most. I didn't believe him, didn't trust him. I assumed he was wicked, not even giving him a chance to explain."

"You were in pain, as well," Thea pointed out. "And he could have acted differently. He could have explained himself, answered your questions."

"Yes. He was proud. I was furious. The result is our friendship was destroyed."

"Perhaps it can be repaired."

"I think not. Rawdon is colder, more bitter. And he was never a man who gave his friendship easily. Things change, and one can rarely return."

Thea slipped her arms around Gabriel's waist and leaned her head against his chest. The pain inside him, he realized with some surprise, felt eased by her touch. He bent and kissed the top of her head. She was warm and soft in his arms, and immeasurably precious. He wondered what he would feel if she suddenly disappeared, leaving only a note behind, and his insides tightened painfully.

He kissed her again, then stepped back, releasing her reluctantly. "There is something I have to do. Will you forgive me if I do not stay?"

"Of course. Where are you going?"

"To the Priory. I have a few questions I need answered."

*Gabriel found Ian in the* smoking room at the rear of the house. He was relieved to see that his friend was alone. Ian looked up as Gabriel entered, his expression wary, but he relaxed when he saw Gabriel.

"It's you. Thank God."

"Who were you expecting?"

"Emily. She has been after me to leave for the Park since Christmas. It was hard to convince her we needed to remain when our host had disappeared."

"My apologies," Gabriel answered drily. He closed the door behind him and walked over to where Ian sat.

His friend watched him approach. Ian set the drink he had been sipping down on the low table beside him. "What is it? You look—" Ian stiffened and rose to his feet. "Did you find Jocelyn?"

"No. I have no idea where she is, any more than I have for the last year. I wanted to ask you about something else. Do you remember what you told me, not long after Jocelyn left, about Miss Fortner and Rawdon?"

"Yes." Ian frowned. "What about it?"

"Are you absolutely certain that it was true?"

Ian's brows rose in surprise. "What? Of course it's true. I would not make something like that up. Gabriel, what are you on about?"

"I talked to Rawdon this afternoon. He denied that anything happened between him and Grace Fortner."

"Well, he would, wouldn't he? He's not going to admit that he tried to seduce her and, failing that, tried to force her."

"I believe him."

Ian stared at Gabriel. "No. He's lying; he has to be. You know the kind of fellow he is. He hurt Miss Fortner. He hurt Jocelyn. That was why Jocelyn fled. It must be. Otherwise . . ." Ian's voice trailed off.

"Otherwise we have been wrong in blaming Rawdon all this time," Gabriel finished. "He showed me a letter from Jocelyn, Ian. She asked *him* for forgiveness."

"What? What did she say?"

"That she wronged him. That she had been deceived. She thought herself in love. I can only assume she meant that she had given herself to this man she was in love with, that he is Matthew's father."

"Good God!" Ian stared at Gabriel, thunderstruck.

"Apparently she has been living on the Continent this whole time. But she decided to return. She said she was coming to me for help."

"Then she *is* here? You said you had not found her."

"I haven't. I don't know where she has gone. But that is what she said to Rawdon in the letter. That is why I have been out searching for her. After he showed me the letter, I was even more certain that Matthew is her child."

"This is—I don't know what to say." Ian passed a hand over his face. "Are you certain the letter was from Jocelyn? Perhaps Rawdon made it up."

"I read it. It was in her hand. I've received hundreds of letters from her; I know her writing well."

"How can this be? I thought—" Ian's voice dropped almost to a whisper. "I thought that he had killed her. He was always a cold, hard bastard when he chose. You know that. I thought he got angry with her and hit her, perhaps not even meaning to kill her, but . . . you know."

Gabriel nodded. "I know. Sometimes I thought so, too, when she was nowhere to be found."

Ian dropped heavily into his chair and picked up his glass again, taking a long drink of it.

"Did Miss Fortner herself tell you the story of what Rawdon did?" Gabriel asked.

Ian glanced at him, startled. "I—what does it matter?"

"It matters, Ian. You told me you knew it to be true. I received the impression that Miss Fortner revealed this to you herself. That it was not merely a rumor."

"It was not a mere rumor!" Ian jumped to his feet, looking agitated. "No, she did not tell me herself, but I was told by someone who would have had no reason to lie." He frowned. "It involved a woman's honor; it was too important to have been mere gossip."

Gabriel sighed. Whatever Ian said, the doubt was clear on his face. Ian had obviously believed what he had told Gabriel, but it had been no more than rumor and gossip. And Gabriel had believed it; he had jumped to believe that Rawdon had wronged his sister. To have believed otherwise, he realized now, would have been to admit that his beloved little sister had simply wanted to leave them. That she was not the innocent victim, but the one who had wronged those who trusted her.

"I can't believe that Jocelyn—" Ian began, then stopped.

"I know. It is hard. We regarded Jocelyn too much as the little girl we had known and not a fully grown woman."

Ian nodded and sat down again, picking up his now empty glass. "I think I'll have another of these."

"I believe I will join you."

*Thea went to Damaris's house* the next afternoon to pick up her gown for the party. The snow from Christmas had all melted away, but a bitter chill was in the wind, and Thea was glad that she had left Matthew at home with his nursemaid. Damaris's house was still a beehive of activity, though it was now aimed more at decorating than at cleaning. As Thea followed Damaris up the stairs to try on the dress the maid had altered, Thea noticed that the servants were all whispering to each other as they worked.

When she asked Damaris about the low buzz of chatter, Damaris glanced at Thea in surprise. "Have you not heard? I thought nothing got past Mrs. Brewster."

"It rarely does, but I was busy at the church today, and I haven't really talked to her. Has something happened?"

"Apparently a number of people have seen a strange man lurking about the village the last day or two. The apothecary's wife

said she saw a stranger in her garden two or three days ago, but ..."
Damaris shrugged.

"Mrs. Foster has an active imagination," Thea supplied.

"Exactly. But Mr. Gilchrist also looked out the window as he
went to bed and saw a stranger walking past. It created a bit of a
stir, though my opinion was that the butcher was right in saying
it was probably only a peddler passing through. But this morning, not one but two different people reported seeing a man last
night. I would discount it as hysteria, frankly, except that my own
housekeeper was one of those who saw him."

"What? You mean here?" Thea felt a leap of alarm. She could
not help but think of the man who had taken Matthew from his
bed, and she had to fight back an urge to run back to the vicarage to make sure Matthew was safe. After all, it was daylight and
several people were watching over the baby, including the sturdy
guard supplied by Gabriel. Matthew would be fine.

"Yes. I did not see him, but Mrs. Clemmons did, and she is
a most phlegmatic woman, not the sort given to fits and starts.
She said he was in the back garden, and he slipped through the
hedge and was gone when she came out of the house, shouting
and wielding her broom."

Thea had to chuckle. "I would have slipped away, too."

As they talked, Thea had pulled off her dress, and Damaris's
maid had dropped the remade gown over Thea's head. Now, the
maid fastened it up the back, and Thea turned to look at herself.

"Oh." She let out a quiet sigh of satisfaction. The ball gown
was even lovelier than she had thought it would be. With the bodice taken in to suit her more modest curves and the hem lowered

slightly to compensate for her extra inches of height, the dress suited her perfectly. She turned this way and that, admiring the way the jewel-like tones of the dress caught the light. "Damaris, it's beautiful. Thank you."

"The dress isn't all that is beautiful," Damaris assured her with a smile. "It looks much better on you than it ever did on me, and I am so happy to see you looking as you deserve."

Thea did not linger long at Damaris's house. She knew that Damaris doubtless had a number of things to do to prepare for the party the next day, and Thea was eager to get home and reassure herself that Matthew was all right. It was all very well to say that ample people were looking after him, but until she could look at him and hold him herself, she could not help but worry about the man who had been seen in the village. After the kidnapping incident, the presence of a stranger here seemed far too coincidental.

One of the maids folded the red ball gown and put it in a box for Thea to carry home, and she set out for her house, thoughts of the stranger occupying her mind. She wondered whether she should send the footman over to the Priory to tell Gabriel of the news from the village. Gabriel usually came to call at some point during the day, but she could not help but feel a sense of urgency.

"Lolly?" She walked into the house, and her sense of alarm heightened when she found the kitchen empty. "Lolly?"

Thea hurried into the hallway and stopped, letting out a sigh of relief as she saw Lolly coming down the stairs, holding Matthew. Peter sat at the foot of the steps, waiting for them. He popped up as soon as he saw Thea, offering her a bow.

"Miss."

"Hello, Peter. Lolly. There's my boy." Thea smiled, setting the box down on the hall table and stretching out her hands to the baby. With a grin, Matthew dove into her arms, and Thea laughed. She glanced at Lolly. "How has he been?"

"A bit fussy. I think he's starting to teethe, miss."

"Really?"

"Aye. Look at his gums." Lolly pulled down his lip, pointing to the lower gum, where a bit of white showed through.

"A tooth!" Thea grinned and lifted the baby's chubby hand to kiss. "Well, aren't you the little man?"

Lolly offered to take up the dress box to Thea's room while Thea played with Matthew. Thea went into the sitting room, where she spent the next half hour sitting on the rug and entertaining Matthew with games of peekaboo, singing, and patty-cake. Later, after Lolly had returned and whisked Matthew off for a snack, Thea went upstairs to put away her dress. Lolly had taken the gown out of the box and spread it out on the bed. Thea smiled at the sight of it. She could not help but wonder what Gabriel would say when he saw her in it. Carefully, she folded it up and put it away in the dresser. Turning, she started toward her secretary, stopping when she almost stepped on a square of white on the floor. She bent down and picked up the piece of paper.

It was folded, with a red wax seal holding it closed. On the other side, in uneven block letters was written LORD MORECOMBE.

Thea stared at the writing, her heart slamming in her chest. Turning, she ran out into the hall. "Peter! Peter!"

The footman came running through the door to the kitchen while Thea was still on the stairs. "Miss! What is it?"

"Have you seen this? Did you see anyone leave this in my room?"

"No, miss." Behind him, Lolly came out of the kitchen door. Her eyes big, she shook her head, as well.

"I'll sit with Lolly and the baby," Thea said, coming the rest of the way down the stairs and going over to lock the front door. "Peter, you run over to the Priory and tell Lord Morecombe that someone came into the house and left a note for him. Tell him I need him."

# Eighteen

*Thea locked the kitchen door,* as well, after Peter left and sat down across from Lolly and the baby, the sealed note on the table before her. It seemed an eternity before she heard the sound of a horse's hooves on the road outside, but she knew it had been little more than thirty minutes. She ran to the door to look out, and seeing Gabriel tying his horse to the fence, she flung open the door and rushed out to meet him.

Gabriel vaulted lightly over the low iron fence and scooped Thea up in a hug, which she later realized would have been scandalous had there been anyone on the road to see it, but at that moment, she did not care for anything except that Gabriel was there.

"What is it? What happened?" He turned and walked with her to the kitchen, his arm still around her shoulders. "Peter said someone had come into the house?"

"Yes. I don't know how or when, but they must have. I went to call on Damaris this afternoon, and when I returned, I found a letter on the floor of my bedroom. It was addressed to you. I am positive it was not there when I left."

"Did you see anyone come in, Lolly?" Gabriel asked.

"No, sir." The nursemaid shook her head. "I don't know how anyone could come in without one of us seeing. I was up and down the stairs a lot with Master Matthew. And Peter was down here in the hall, sir, like he always is, where he can see anyone what comes in the kitchen or the front."

Gabriel nodded. "That is what Peter said, as well."

"I was only gone for an hour or so," Thea said, thinking back. "I went to my room right before I left, and I would swear the note was not in the room then. But it was there when I went upstairs after I came home. Lolly, did you see it when you took the box up there?"

"Box? What box?" Gabriel asked.

Thea could not keep from smiling a little to herself. "Nothing important. Just something I brought back from Damaris's house."

"I didn't see any note, miss. It was on the floor?"

Thea nodded. "It was between my bed and the window; you wouldn't necessarily have noticed it unless you walked around the side of the bed." She frowned and let out a sigh. "Perhaps it could have been there before I left. I cannot remember whether I was in that side of the room. But I *know* it was not there when I awoke this morning. It has to have been left there sometime today. Perhaps it was earlier when I was at the church."

"Well, let's see what it says." Gabriel glanced toward the table. "Is that it?" He started forward.

"Do you think it's that man, miss?" Lolly asked. "The one everybody's talking about?"

"Man? What man?" Gabriel stopped and turned to look at the girl. "Why is everyone talking about him?"

Between them, Lolly and Thea related the various stories of the stranger seen by the residents of Chesley the past few days. Lolly's version was somewhat more dramatic. Gabriel looked toward Thea, his brow raised, and she nodded.

"I know it sounds a bit . . . fanciful, perhaps, but Damaris said that her housekeeper had seen him, too, and that she is a most unfanciful person. Damaris has no doubt that the woman was telling the truth."

"The devil!" Gabriel scowled. "Do you think it's the kidnapper?"

"That is what I thought, as well. I don't know. But it certainly seems suspicious."

Gabriel picked up the square of paper from the table and examined the front. "It looks like a child wrote this. And it is in pencil, not ink."

"Not a lettered person, I'd say," Thea offered.

He broke open the seal and looked down at the signature, letting out a soft oath. "It's from Hannah! Jocelyn's maid."

"That woman is like a ghost! She seems to appear and disappear at will."

Gabriel nodded as he scanned the letter. "She wants me to come to Mrs. Howard's party tomorrow evening."

"What? How does she know about that?"

"I have no idea—no more so than how she manages to be everywhere and yet no one sees her."

"Why would she sneak in here to urge you to come to the party?"

"There's a bit more. She says that she must see me and 'explain all,' whatever that may mean. She says she is frightened and she begs my help. Then she asks me to come to the party, and she says she will meet me there."

"Nothing about your sister? Or the baby?"

Gabriel shook his head and held out the letter to Thea. "See for yourself."

She took the proffered note and read it. It was as disappointingly brief as Gabriel had said. "What will you do?"

Gabriel shrugged. "Go to the party and hope that she contacts me. I know of nothing else. Do you?"

Thea shook her head. "No. I fear not."

"I hate that someone was able to get into your room unnoticed," Gabriel went on. "I am going to send another servant over, in addition to Peter."

"Gabriel, no, that isn't necessary. I will make sure the doors remain locked during the day as well. We had been locking them only at night. I did not dream anyone would be bold enough to come in during the daylight hours, with several people in the house."

"But someone was."

"I know, but I will keep the doors locked now."

"Good. I still want the men here. They can take shifts, so that one is awake at all times." Gabriel stepped forward and placed his hands on Thea's arms. "Please, Thea. Allow me to do this. I cannot take you and Matthew home where I can guard the two of you myself, so let me do what I can."

Thea looked up at him, seeing the warmth and concern in his eyes. "Very well. Although what Daniel will say, I cannot imagine."

"I am sure he will be happy to know his sister is protected."

Gabriel smiled, and she knew that he was thinking about kissing her.

Giving him a warning look, she stepped back, though she could not keep from smiling back at him. She cast a glance over at Lolly, who was watching them as though she were the audience at a play. Thea turned back to Gabriel, assuming a more formal role. "Thank you for your help, my lord."

"You are most welcome." Gabriel winked at her, but swept her an elegant bow. "Miss Bainbridge, may I have the pleasure of escorting you to Mrs. Howard's party tomorrow evening?"

Thea gave him a regal nod. "You may."

"You are as kind as you are lovely." He took her hand and lightly kissed it. "I must leave. I have business to attend to. But I will look forward to tomorrow evening with great anticipation."

Thea walked Gabriel to the door and locked it behind him. She turned back to Lolly, who grinned at her unabashedly. Thea had the feeling that their little charade of formality had not fooled the girl one bit.

The girl heaved a romantic sigh and said, "Your man's a grand gentleman, miss."

Thea started to point out that Gabriel was not her man, but she did not. She could allow herself to dream for a day or two, couldn't she? "Yes. He is a very grand gentleman."

**Gabriel strode into the inn** a few minutes later. The proprietor hastened forward to greet him. "My lord. Good evening, good evening. Would you care for something to eat? A glass of brandy, perhaps?"

"Is Lord Rawdon in?"

The innkeeper stiffened apprehensively. "My lord, my inn is a very quiet establishment..."

"Don't worry. I am not here to start a row. I want only a moment's conversation."

"Of course. Of course." Hornsby did not look entirely certain, but he led Gabriel down the hall to a private sitting area. Opening the door, he spoke to someone inside, then stepped back and bowed to Gabriel, ushering him inside.

As the innkeeper backed out of the room, closing the door behind him, Rawdon rose from a chair by the fire. "Morecombe."

Gabriel nodded. "Good of you to see me." He paused, but could think of no easy way to broach the subject. "I am here to ask a favor of you." Rawdon's brows rose slightly, but Gabriel pressed on. "I realize I have no reason to expect such from you." Gabriel smiled faintly. "I must pin my hopes on your good nature. Or perhaps upon your sense of curiosity."

Rawdon did not smile, but something softened at the corners of his eyes. "Indeed. Well, you have already piqued that. What is the favor?"

"My sister had a maid named Hannah."

"Yes, I recall. She accompanied Jocelyn when she went for a walk."

"Do you remember how she looked?"

"Yes. Short, light brown hair, a bit rabbity." Rawdon frowned slightly. "Why do you ask?"

"Apparently she is in Chesley."

"The maid? Have you seen her? Talked to her?"

"I have seen her." Briefly Gabriel described spotting Hannah on the street and giving chase, only to find she had disappeared. "And today, Miss Bainbridge found this letter in her house, addressed to me." Gabriel pulled the note from his pocket and handed it to the other man.

Rawdon read the letter and looked up at Gabriel. "What is this about? Why is she here?"

"You know as much, or more accurately, as little as I do." Gabriel refolded the note and stuck it in his pocket.

"Do you think Jocelyn is with her?"

"I don't know. I still have not seen nor heard from her. This note is as close as I have come to her. I hope that if I can find Hannah and talk to her, I can at least find out where Jocelyn is."

"What do you want from me?"

"To come to the Twelfth Night party tomorrow night at Mrs. Howard's house. I believe she invited you."

"She did." One corner of Rawdon's mouth curled up in wry amusement. "Not perhaps an entirely enthusiastic invitation, but she did indeed ask."

"It's a masque ball, so everyone's face will be partly concealed. I would like an extra pair of eyes—and, perhaps, an extra pair of fists. She is frightened of someone. There have been rumors of a stranger loitering about the village."

"The man who took the child?"

Gabriel shrugged. "Perhaps. I am walking into this whole affair blind."

"Very well."

If Gabriel was surprised by Rawdon's easy agreement, he did

not show it. He simply nodded. "Thank you. I will see you there tomorrow evening."

"Tell me one thing," Rawdon said as Gabriel turned to go, and Gabriel swung back to face him. "Why did you ask me? Why not one of your friends?"

"Because right now, you are the only man I am certain of."

*"Oh, miss!" Lolly let out* a long sigh as she stepped back from buttoning Thea's gown. "You look beautiful, you do."

Thea smiled as she took a slow turn around, examining herself in the mirror. With Lolly's help, she had done her hair in an artful arrangement of curls, and her dress glowed against her skin in the candlelight.

Matthew, crawling on the floor, headed for the hem of Thea's dress, and Lolly swooped down on him. "Oh, no, you don't, Master Matthew." She swung him up to a burst of giggles.

Thea turned and leaned forward to kiss the baby on the cheek and run her hand over his soft curls. "Promise you will watch him closely tonight, Lolly."

"I won't take my eyes off him, miss. Peter will check my room before bed, and after that, he promised to make his bed in the hall across the doorway. The new man is going to stand watch downstairs in the hall."

"Good." Thea smiled and murmured a good-bye to Matthew, giving him a final light kiss.

Lolly carried the baby out of the room and Thea returned for a last look in the mirror. It was perfect ... well, almost perfect. She could not help but think how well the earrings Gabriel had given her would suit the dress. Opening the top drawer of her dresser, she pulled out the box. The golden earrings glowed against the black velvet background, the garnets twinkling in the candlelight. She pulled one out and held it up to her ear. And her internal argument was over.

She slipped the earrings into her earlobes and turned her head from side to side, studying the effect. They were the finishing touch, the last little bit of perfection. And, really, what did it matter if it was improper to accept them from Gabriel? She had done things with Gabriel that were a great deal more improper. The thought of the look in Gabriel's eyes when he saw her wearing his gift was simply more than she could refuse.

No one need know, anyway, where the earrings had come from. She did not plan to volunteer the information, and hopefully no one would be rude enough to ask outright. If someone did, she would . . . well, she would simply lie. It wasn't as if she hadn't lied hundreds of times to the parishioners. After all, she had assured Mrs. Templeton that her singing voice was beautiful, and Thea had sworn that the Thompson baby was handsome; it would be hard to find two more egregious bouncers than those.

She heard the knock on the front door, and a moment later the deep timbre of Gabriel's voice as he greeted Mrs. Brewster. Thea took a deep breath, picked up her mask, fan, and gloves, and started down the stairs. Gabriel was standing in the entry, chatting with Daniel, as Thea came down the stairs. He turned at the sound of her footsteps and looked up.

The expression on his face was everything she had hoped it would be.

"Thea." The word was little more than a breath as he came to the bottom of the steps, gazing up at her.

Thea beamed, unaware of how her face lit up. Gabriel reached up his hand as she came to the last few steps, and Thea took it. His fingers tightened on hers, telling her, as did his eyes, the things he could not say in front of her brother.

"You are a vision," he told her, bowing over her hand and lightly brushing his lips across it.

Thea caught sight of Daniel, behind Gabriel, goggling at her in amazement, and she let out a giggle of sheer happiness. "Thank you, Lord Morecombe."

"Only one thing could make you even lovelier." Gabriel held out a box. Nestled inside was a delicate corsage of mingled white and red rosebuds.

Thea took it with a gasp of delight. "But how—where—it is the middle of winter!"

"I had it brought from a florist in Cheltenham." He chuckled at her expression. "Surely you did not think I would let you go to a ball without flowers. What sort of an admirer would I be?"

"Is that what you are? An admirer?"

"Of course." He bent closer, murmuring, "Among other things that it is perhaps better not to mention here."

"Well, my dear, you look most lovely," Daniel said, coming up and surprising Thea by kissing her on the cheek. "I am quite looking forward to seeing everyone's expression at the ball tonight." He patted her shoulder. "Now, if you will excuse me, I must run up and change. Save me a dance. I suspect your card may be crowded this evening." With a chuckle, he trotted up the stairs.

"Your brother is right," Gabriel said, taking the corsage from her and reaching down to pin it in place. "I shall have to write in my name on your dance card before we leave, or I shan't have a hope of getting on the floor with you."

"Don't be absurd." Thea's heart fluttered as he bent over her, his fingers lightly brushing the bare skin above her dress as he pinned the flowers. "It is just the absence of my spectacles. You may have to lead me about, I fear." She held up her mask by the strings. "Glasses simply don't work with a mask."

"It is far more than that, I assure you. But it will be my pleasure to 'lead you about.'" He reached up to touch one of her earrings with the tip of his finger, and he smiled. "They look just as I thought they would on you. Beautiful."

Thea felt her throat close up, and she knew she was perilously close to tears.

"Here, let me tie on your mask." Gabriel took it from her hand and reached around her to tie it on. "There, look." He stepped aside, turning her toward the mirror on the wall.

Thea had bought the mask on her shopping expedition to Cheltenham with Damaris last week. It was far dearer than anything she would normally have purchased, but she could not resist the temptation. Sprinkled lightly with tiny glittering rhinestones, the corners arching up into saucy points, the black velvet was a sensual contrast to her milky skin, and it gave her face a hint of exotic mystery. Her gray eyes were luminous and large, outlined by the intense black, and the mask's concealment of her upper face seemed to emphasize her mouth below it.

She met Gabriel's eyes in the mirror, and the sensual softening of his mouth, the heat in his eyes as he gazed at her, confirmed the allure. He moved closer behind her, his arms sliding around her waist.

"I am not sure I can keep my hands off you tonight," he murmured in her ear, his breath on her skin sending flickers of desire down through her.

"Perhaps we should leave, then."

"Mm. But first." He put his hands on her shoulders and turned her around to kiss her. His kiss was long and slow, an establishment of possession as much as it was a promise of delights to come. When at last he released her, Thea took a shaky step backward, her eyes wide and slightly dazed.

"If you keep looking at me like that, I think we *will* have to stay here," he growled, reaching out to take her in his arms again.

But Thea skipped out of his reach laughingly and took her cloak from the rack by the door. "Oh, no, not after promising me a dance. I intend to collect on that."

"You may have every one. Thea . . . I wanted to ask you . . ."

She turned to look at him. A dark look that she could not read was in his eyes. "What?" she asked somewhat apprehensively, unconsciously taking a step backward.

"No, not now." He shook his head. "Later, after this party is over." He smiled and swept her a bow. "After you, Miss Bainbridge."

It would have taken a more saintly person than Thea not to have been pleased by the reaction from the other guests when they entered the party. Damaris, smiling broadly, kissed her on both cheeks and assured her that she would outshine all the other women in attendance. On all sides, Thea saw the amazed stares of the people who had known her all her life. She was gratified to see that even Lady Wofford was gaping at her.

"Cousin, you are looking lovely tonight." Ian recovered more quickly than his wife and stepped forward to claim the right of a cousinly kiss on Thea's cheek. He cast a thoughtful glance over at Gabriel beside her. "Morecombe. Once again you surprise me."

"Miss Bainbridge." Lady Wofford's nod and brief smile were more reserved, but Thea could see the same quick calculation in her eyes as she looked from Thea to Gabriel.

Sir Myles, who had been standing with Ian and Emily, took Thea's hand, his bright golden-brown eyes laughing down into hers. "I have been suspecting for some time that Gabriel was hiding you from us, and now I understand why. You are far too lovely for us mere mortal men."

"You, sir, are a shameless flirt."

"I am," he replied with no apparent regret. "And I intend to flirt with you a great deal tonight. I confess, I enjoy it twice as much when Gabriel is shooting jealous daggers at me with his eyes."

"Now, Myles," Gabriel drawled. "You know I have no objection if you only look …"

"What character did you draw?" Lady Wofford apparently decided that it was time for a change of subject. "I am Mrs. Melody; Ian says I shall have to go about singing all evening."

Thea unfolded the card she had been handed by Damaris as they had entered. "Miss Pinchpenny." She laughed. "That should be an easy one."

On any other night, she would have enjoyed the role, too,

exclaiming over the extravagance of everything and vowing that she could have bought this or that more cheaply, but tonight she could think of nothing but Gabriel's meeting with Hannah. Even as she stood, talking and laughing with the others over their character roles, sipping at her warm cup of mulled wine, her nerves were stretched to their fullest, waiting for what would happen.

A ripple of excitement ran around the room, and Thea turned to see that Lord Rawdon had entered. Even wearing a mask, Rawdon's pale hair and eyes immediately gave away his identity. The tall stranger drew everyone's attention, and a low buzz started, building as whispers passed from guest to guest. Thea sensed Ian and his wife stiffen at the man's entrance, and after Rawdon paid his respects to the hostess and headed in Gabriel's direction, both Lord and Lady Wofford drew back a little. Myles cast a wary glance at Gabriel, but it was soon replaced by surprise as Gabriel stood calmly beside Thea, awaiting Lord Rawdon's approach.

Rawdon stopped and bowed slightly to their group. "Miss Bainbridge. Lord Morecombe."

Myles's eyes widened further when Gabriel returned a polite greeting and bow. "Lord Rawdon."

"Myles." Rawdon's firm mouth lifted slightly as he turned to the other man.

"Alec," Myles replied with unflappable aplomb. "Thought you'd left."

"I returned."

"You would not wish to miss Mrs. Howard's Twelfth Night."

"Naturally."

The greetings between Rawdon and the Woffords were chill-

ier but polite. Ian cast Gabriel a questioning glance, but said nothing to him. For a long, awkward moment, silence reigned, but they
were saved by the musical quartet striking up a dance in the other
room. With relief, Ian turned to his wife and requested a dance,
and the couple left.

"Does anyone want to explain what is happening here?" Myles
asked after a moment, looking from one man to the other.

"Let us just say that Gabriel and I have reached an agreement,"
Rawdon told him.

Like Gabriel and the other men, the Earl wore a plain black
loo mask, which gave him a rather wolfish look, in Thea's opinion.
On the other hand, Gabriel . . . Thea looked up at him and realized, with an underlying dark ripple of desire, that Gabriel resem-
bled nothing so much as a pirate in his mask. A smile curved her
lips as she imagined him in a shirt with billowing, full sleeves, a
rakish scarf tied round his head.

Myles, receiving little satisfaction for his curiosity from his
friends, invited Thea to dance. Though she would have liked to stay
while the men hunted for the maid Hannah, she knew that she was
able to contribute little to the endeavor, since she had no idea what
the woman looked like. So she accepted Myles's invitation with a
smile. Fortunately, the dance was an active country dance rather
than a waltz, so there was little chance for Myles to ply her with
questions about Gabriel and Rawdon. Obviously, Gabriel had
not told Myles about Rawdon or Gabriel's plan to talk to Jocelyn's
maid tonight, and she could not help but wonder why, but she did
not want to let slip anything that Gabriel wished to keep hidden.

After their dance, Thea went out into the wide central hallway of the house, where she found Lord Rawdon, arms crossed, gazing down the hallway toward the front of the house, where Damaris stood talking to two of her guests.

"Having any luck?"

"Not a bit," Rawdon replied. "The fact that everyone is wearing masks makes it rather difficult." He nodded toward Damaris. "Our hostess—Mrs. Howard. Do you know her well?"

"She moved here a few months ago. We are friends."

"She gave me the character Lord Frost." He cocked an eyebrow at Thea, and the ghost of a smile curved his mouth. "Purposeful, do you think?"

Thea chuckled. "Mrs. Howard has a mischievous sense of humor."

"Mm." He was silent for a moment, then said, not looking at her, "I am curious, Miss Bainbridge. Why did you invite me that day to your Christmas feast? We had, ah, less than a harmonious introduction."

Thea glanced up at him, then away, and said quietly, "I understand feeling . . . lonely."

He glanced at her, startled, but before he could speak, Gabriel joined them.

"I have seen no sign of her," Gabriel said. "You?"

"None."

"I am beginning to think that it is a wild-goose chase. I can understand that Hannah felt safer meeting here, with everyone in disguise, but it's bloody inconvenient. How am I supposed to find her?"

"I suspect that she will find you," Thea told him.

"I am wearing a mask, just like everyone else."

Thea gave him a speaking look. "You do not look like the local men. None of you do."

"None of us do what?" Myles asked, coming up beside them.

"Look ordinary," Thea said.

"Is that a polite way of saying we look like popinjays? I think my attire is quite unexceptionable tonight." Myles looked down at his bottle-green jacket, then turned his eye toward Gabriel and Rawdon. "Not somber like some, of course. Gentlemen, has no one ever told you that black breeches and jacket are not required dress for a ball?"

"It's easier," Rawdon replied.

"Particularly if one happens to be color-blind." Myles glanced around, then narrowed his eyes as he glanced toward another group of guests, who were accepting drinks from a black-and-white-clad maid. "I say ... that girl looks familiar."

"Who?" Gabriel straightened and glanced around. "The girl in green? That's one of the Squire's daughters."

"No, not her. The maid behind her. Wait, she'll turn around again. She looks like ..."

"Hannah!" Gabriel and Rawdon said almost in unison.

Thea looked at the maid. "Of course! I saw her here; she's one of the new servants Damaris hired to prepare for the party. But I didn't see her face that day, Gabriel, so I had no idea she was the one you were looking for. What better place to hide than in plain sight, among a bunch of servants?"

"I never thought of looking here for her. Under our noses the entire time."

"And her note—she must have slipped it in with my dress that day, and it fell out when Lolly took the dress out of the box."

"Who are you—you mean Jocelyn's maid?" Myles asked, looking confused. "What the devil is she doing here?"

"That is what I'm about to find out." Gabriel started toward the maid, with the others on his heels.

At that moment Ian came out of the room on the other side of the hall. Without glancing around, he seized Hannah's arm and whisked her away with him around the corner and into the long gallery.

"Ian!" Gabriel halted. His face turned white, then flushed, and he ran after them.

Some of the other guests turned to stare as Thea and the others hurried after Gabriel. Thea cast a pleading look at Damaris as she went, and Damaris moved in quickly behind them to get the other guests' attention, clapping her hands and suggesting that they all move into the other room for refreshments.

Gabriel opened the first door along the long hall and startled the people inside, who were gathered at tables, playing cards. With a bow and a muttered apology, he withdrew and started down the hall to the next room. It, too, was empty, but as they neared the next door, they could hear a man's voice inside, shouting.

"...until you tell me? Where the bloody hell is Jocelyn?"

Gabriel flung the door open and charged inside. Thea, Myles, and Rawdon rushed in behind him. Ian whirled and gaped at them. His eyes widened with a sudden, horrified realization.

"You!" Gabriel spit. "All along it was you who seduced my sister!"

"No! No, I swear!" Ian glanced around frantically. "Gabe! Myles! Please, I saw Hannah, and I was trying to find out where Jocelyn is. For you! I was questioning her for you!"

"Not bleedin' likely!" Hannah screeched, jerking out of his grasp. "It was you what seduced my lady. It was you what told her you loved her and pined for her and cried great crocodile tears because you had to marry Miss Pot o' Gold! I tried to warn her about you, but she wouldn't listen! She was so bleedin' in love with you she couldn't see what you really was. An' you broke her heart, you did, when you sent her packin' like that. Treated her like she was nothin'. Just some trollop."

"Gabriel, no, don't believe her!" Ian cried, but with a roar Gabriel was already charging him.

He slammed into the other man and they crashed to the floor. Gabriel's fist smacked into Ian's face, splitting his lip.

"Gabriel!" Thea turned to Myles, then Rawdon. "Do something!"

"What would you suggest?" Lord Rawdon asked politely.

"Stop him! He'll kill him."

"Oh, I'll stop him before he goes that far," Rawdon said, his eyes glinting. He pushed his mask up onto his forehead.

"Myles!" Thea turned a stern look on him. "Help me!" She ran over and began to tug at Gabriel.

Myles joined her, and with a sigh Rawdon did, too, grabbing both Gabriel's arms and dragging him to his feet. Gabriel stopped struggling, though his hard gaze never left Ian's face. "It's all right. I won't hit him again. Not just yet."

He shot his cuffs and straightened his jacket as Myles stepped over to Ian and shoved his snowy-white handkerchief into the other man's hand. Ian cast a glance toward the doorway, and Rawdon casually stepped in between Ian and the door. Ian slumped and brought the handkerchief up to his face, dabbing at the blood that trickled from his lip and nose.

"You've been lying to me all this time," Gabriel said, his voice low and hard. "You fed me lies about Alec to protect your own cowardly—"

"No! I swear to you! I didn't lie about Rawdon. I heard all those stories. He did attack Miss Fortner." At a low, growling noise from Rawdon, Ian edged closer to Myles. "I'm telling you the truth. Yes, all right, I was jealous of Rawdon—hell, he was going to marry the woman I loved! But I believed everything I told you. The stories were true: I heard them. I—" Ian glanced at Rawdon and swallowed, then looked at Gabriel and Myles.

"Where is Jocelyn?" Gabriel asked. "What did you do to her? Where did you send her?"

"I did nothing! I swear it!" Ian waved his hands wildly. "Please, you must believe me. It's true: I loved Jocelyn. I tried not to, but I could not help myself. She was so beautiful and fresh, so full of vivacity."

"Which you promptly drained from her!" Gabriel glared. "A man who loved her would have come to me and asked for her hand, the way Rawdon did. My God, I trusted you! And all the while, you were dishonoring my sister!"

"I wanted to marry Jocelyn! I did! If I had known she was carrying my child, I would have married her. I swear to you. But she didn't tell me. I didn't know. That must have been why she accepted Rawdon's proposal. I tried to talk to her after that, but she just cried and sent me away. She said she had to do it. I never heard from her after that. I was in despair."

"I ought to break your bloody neck."

"Gabriel, I promise you—I knew nothing about her leaving. I was as lost and confused as you were. I assumed—" Ian stopped and again cast an uneasy glance at Lord Rawdon, looming on one side of him. "I thought that Rawdon must have found out about Jocelyn and me. That he threatened her, sent her away somewhere to avoid the scandal. I thought . . ." Ian's voice dropped. "I thought he had killed her to keep her from shaming him and his name."

"Not everyone thinks like a coward as you do," Rawdon told him.

Ian did not look at him, only at Gabriel. "I don't know where Jocelyn went or why. And I know nothing about her coming back here or about that baby. I don't even know if it's mine."

"I remember now," Myles said suddenly, straightening. "You had blond hair when you were a child, didn't you, Ian? It just got darker as you got older. Blue eyes like Matthew's."

"We don't know that," Ian said in a cajoling tone. "That is why I was talking to Hannah. I was trying to find out where Jocelyn was and—"

"Oh! So this is where everyone is!" said a bright female voice from the doorway.

"Sweet Lord," Myles muttered under his breath as they all turned to find Emily standing at the edge of the room, smiling at them.

"Oh!" Her hand flew to her mouth in consternation. "Ian!

Dearest, what happened?" Lines formed between her brows and she looked from one man to another. "What is going on here?"

"Um . . ." The men glanced at each other.

Thea, turning her gaze from Ian to Gabriel, stiffened, gasping, "Gabriel! She's gone. The maid is gone!"

"The maid?" Emily asked. "What maid?"

"The devil take it!" Gabriel whirled and looked around the empty room. "Now we've lost her." He spared one short, hard glance for Ian. "I want you out of my house tonight. I don't want to see your face again. Ever." He turned. "Excuse me, Lady Wofford."

Gabriel hurried out of the room, with Myles and Rawdon right after him, leaving a stunned Lady Wofford with her husband. Thea followed at a more sedate pace. As she strode back toward the party, Thea heard a sharp cry of "No!" from Emily, followed by a crash of something breakable and the sharp staccato of a woman's heels. Apparently her cousin had gotten little succor from his wife.

Thea turned into the wide central hallway of the house and glanced about, debating where to search for the missing maid. She could see the three men had spread out through the rooms of guests, looking for the maid.

It did not seem to Thea, however, that the girl would try to hide among the guests. Hannah's instinct, surely, would be to flee. She might fear that Ian would come after her again even though she had already revealed his secrets. Thea was unsure why the maid had not simply come to Gabriel from the beginning, but her pattern so far was to run and hide. And that, Thea thought, meant running out into the night.

Hurrying into the small cloakroom, she grabbed up her own cloak and headed toward the back of the house. Her hope was that Hannah would not have simply fled into the cold, but would first have gone upstairs to her room to get her coat—and probably the rest of her things, as well. Instinct, Thea surmised, would send the maid up to and back down from her room by way of the servants' stairs in the rear, and she would exit by one of the rear doors.

Thea slipped down the back hallway behind one of the servants carrying a tray. At the end of the hallway, where the servant turned left into the kitchen, was a short hall leading to the back staircase. At the base of it was a door to the outside. Just as Thea reached the hallway, she saw a woman in a cloak slipping out the back door. Excitement surged in Thea.

Turning, she grabbed a servant who was walking toward her with a full tray. "Quick, fetch Lord Morecombe! Quickly! It's terribly important! Tell him she's gone outside!"

Not waiting to see if the servant obeyed her, Thea darted out the door after Hannah. Fortunately, torches had been planted festively at intervals all around the house, so that the evening was not completely dark. Thea saw the maid slip around the corner of the house ahead of her, and she took off running after her. She did not want to yell and thus spur the girl into running faster.

But Hannah was well in front of her, almost to the front of the house by the time Thea rounded the corner after her. Hannah was hurrying, almost trotting now as she reached the front garden and started up the path to the street. Just as Hannah reached the road, a man stepped out of the shrubbery and grabbed the girl from behind, clamping his hand over her mouth before she could scream.

"No! Let go of her!" Thea shouted, and started toward them. "Gabriel! Help! Help!"

Suddenly, out of the corner of her eye, Thea saw a flicker of movement. Startled, she half-turned just as a heavy stick crashed down on her, knocking her to the ground.

# Nineteen

Because Thea had turned, the stick slammed into her shoulder rather than her head, so even though the blow threw her to the earth, it did not knock her out. Thea hit the ground and rolled, twisting back to grab at her attacker. Thea was shocked to realize that she was reaching for a woman's skirts rather than a man's ankles, but she did not stop to think about it, just latched onto the woman's legs through the skirts and pulled as hard as she could. The woman hit her again and again with the stick, her blows landing with thuds on Thea's back, but Thea held on grimly, crawling forward to wrap her arms more tightly around her attacker's legs.

The woman let out a high shriek and began to kick and pull away from Thea in a panic. It was her undoing, for she fell heavily to the ground. She tried to crawl away, but Thea sprang forward and gripped her by the shoulders, wrestling her around. The woman let out another shriek and whirled, striking out wildly, and for the first time Thea saw her face.

"Lady Wofford!" Thea was so stunned that her grip loosened, and Emily's hand connected with Thea's face, landing a sharp, hard slap.

Thea responded by doubling up her fist and punching the other woman on the jaw. As she pulled back her fist to hit her again, a man's arm went around her and lifted her from the ground.

"There now, my love," Gabriel's amused voice said in her ear. "That was a splendid facer you planted, but no need to continue the mill. Everything is all right. It's over."

"Gabriel! The maid! Hannah! He—" Thea pointed toward the street where the man had grabbed the fleeing maid.

"Don't worry. We have them."

Thea relaxed as she saw that Lord Rawdon had a firm grip on the man who had attacked Hannah, while Damaris and her housekeeper were on either side of the maid, leading her back into the house.

Myles hauled the still-struggling Lady Wofford to her feet. She let loose a string of curses that made Myles's brows rise. "You stupid, insufferable hussy!" she screamed at Thea. "You interfering old tabby! I ought to tear every hair from your head!" She jerked against Myles's restraining arms. "Let me go, you fool!"

"Not just yet, my lady," Gabriel said grimly. "No one is leaving until we get this straightened out."

*Twenty minutes later, they were* all assembled in the library. The party had ended abruptly, with Damaris and her servants politely seeing the guests, agog with curiosity, on their way. One of the card players, the Squire, was also the local magistrate, so he had remained, settling himself at a table and adopting a judicial air. Lord Rawdon was planted in front of the closed door into the gallery, barring the exit.

Emily sulked in one of the chairs facing the Squire, her husband, Ian, beside her. Ian wore a dazed expression on his battered face. The blood on his lip had dried, and the rest had been wiped away, but his nose was swollen and one cheek reddened, his eye above that cheek puffed and red, as well. Emily, with bits of leaves and dried grass clinging to her hair and clothes and her hair straggling down on one side, looked bedraggled but defiant, an appearance only heightened by the noticeable swelling on her jaw where Thea had punched her.

Gabriel loomed beside the Woffords, arms crossed over his chest, his face stony. A few feet away from Emily sat the man who had attacked Hannah, his hands tied together and the other end of the rope tied to the arm of the chair. Myles was planted behind him. At right angles to the Squire and to Emily and Ian, completing the square, sat the maid Hannah. Her face was splotched from tears, and bright red spots were on her face, promising future bruises, where her attacker's fingers had dug into her skin as he clamped his hand over her mouth.

Thea sat between Damaris and Daniel a few feet away, watching. Her cheek still stung from Emily's slap, and she was certain that she would have a number of black-and-blue marks down her back the next day, but she liked to think that Emily's jaw was equally sore.

"Now," Squire Cliffe said heavily, sending a majestic glare all around. "What in the name of heaven has been going on here tonight?"

"Nothing that need concern you," Emily said, dismissing the country squire and turning to Gabriel. "Really, Gabriel, this is nonsense. The local law has nothing to do with any of this. It will only cause us all embarrassment to drag these people into it."

"If you think I am going to ignore the fact that you attacked Miss Bainbridge or that your hired thug over there assaulted Hannah and kidnapped my nephew, you are in for a rude awakening. I can assure you—"

"Kidnapped!" The Squire turned his glare on the man tied to the chair.

"I never," the man said shortly.

"The devil you did not," Gabriel responded. "You struck me with a log! We wrestled in the snow. You are the man who stole Matthew from Miss Bainbridge's house."

"I don't know that man," Emily said firmly, "and I haven't the slightest idea what you're talking about."

"The hell you say!" The kidnapper straightened and glared at Emily. "You ain't pushing this off on me. I been doin' your dirty work for two years now, and you're not gullin' them into thinkin' I done it alone. You hired me, right enough, and you told me to take that brat. You think I'd a come up with that on me own?"

"And why should I hire you to do anything with some by-blow that Miss Bainbridge"—Emily shot a venomous glance at Thea—"found in the church?"

"I presume because that child is your husband's son," Gabriel replied bitingly. "Though I cannot imagine what you hoped to accomplish."

"She was trying to keep you from findin' out, that's what!" Hannah spoke up, her voice hoarse. "She didn't want the world knowin' it was her husband's side-slip. Nor that she was the one what sent my lady out of the country!"

"What!" Ian recoiled from his wife, his dazed face sharpening. "You knew about Jocelyn?"

"Of course I knew, you fool!" Emily rounded on Ian, her eyes blazing. "I am not an idiot! Unlike your friends." Her scornful gaze went to Gabriel and Rawdon before she turned back to her husband. "I offered you everything! I was willing to take you and all your debts. My father even made good your father's obligations. I gave you a carriage and four, a hunter, a hack, fine clothes, anything and everything you wanted. And all I ever wanted in return was your affection! Your respect! Instead you made a fool of me, whoring around with that trollop Jocelyn! Getting her with child." Her lip curled. "I knew. I knew it all!"

"But how could you know? I didn't even know she was carrying my child!" Ian exclaimed.

"You are a simpleton," Emily told him bitterly, the anger draining out of her voice, replaced by contempt. "I intercepted the letter she wrote you. You are not the only one who enjoyed getting his hands on my gold; your valet was happy to take my coins as well."

"You bribed Jossman?"

"I *paid* him, which is more than you were prone to do. My grandfather may have been a cit, as you were so fond of throwing in my face, but he taught me the value of well-paid employees. I knew all about your secret correspondence with your paramour. It was easy enough to send her a note, pretending to be you. Jossman is also quite adept at forging your hand."

"No doubt another task you paid him well for!"

"Indeed."

"Enough of this nonsense!" Gabriel's voice cracked out. "I don't care about your squabbles. I want to know what happened to my sister! Where is Jocelyn?"

"I have no idea where she is," Emily retorted. "Nor do I care. The last time I saw her was when I pointed out to her the impossibility of her marrying Ian."

"What did you say to her to make her leave?"

"The silly goose thought that she would run away with *my* fiancé!" Emily flared. "She wrote telling him that she was carrying his child. She had planned to marry Rawdon to hide her shame, and I was prepared to live with that. I knew that eventually Ian would tire of her or she would lose her heart to Rawdon or some other man. But then she wrote Ian, saying she could not marry without love and begging him to run away with her so that Ian and she and the bastard child could be a family. And I knew that Ian might very well be besotted enough to do it, however idiotic it was. So I had Jossman write her as Ian, saying he would leave with her, but I was the one who met her."

"Dear God!" Ian stared at his wife as if he had never before seen her. "What did you tell her?"

"I told her you would never marry her. You were so thoroughly in debt you would be thrown in debtors' prison in a matter of months if you did not wed me. I told her you had no intention of marrying her or acknowledging her bastard, and I offered, out of the kindness of my heart, to help her. I gave her money to live on. I gave her the services of Pendergraft over there to get her out of the country to Italy and establish her in a pleasant house there. I even paid her a comfortable stipend to support her and her maid and the child."

"Yes!" Hannah cried. "So long as she never contacted any of her loved ones again! You broke her heart, you did. Not just giving up his lordship, which she was too fine a woman to have wasted her love on, anyway. But you wouldn't let her even write her brother or her mother! Always crying her heart out, she was, missing everyone. She wouldn'ta got so sick if it wasn't for that."

"Sick! What are you talking about?" Gabriel strode over and pulled Hannah up from her chair. "What is the matter with Jocelyn?"

"I dunno. She was sick ever since she had the wee one."

"Was sick?" Gabriel paled, his mouth tightening. "What do you mean? Is she . . . dead?"

Hannah nodded, and Thea heard the harsh intake of Lord Rawdon's breath, the only sound that broke the utter stillness of the room. Gabriel turned blindly away, and Thea jumped up, going to him. He wrapped his arms tightly around her.

"She gave me the baby and told me to bring him here to you, my lord," Hannah went on after a moment.

"Why, then, did you try to sell the brat to me?" Emily retorted caustically.

"I didn't try to sell him!" Hannah retorted as Gabriel swung around to fix his sharp gaze on her.

"What exactly *did* you do?" he asked her.

"I was goin' to take him and bring him up meself, that's what. 'Twas I who'd taken care of him, anyways, ever since he was born. My lady couldn't. It was the wet nurse and me. And I needed money, that's all, to keep me and the baby from starvin' to death."

"What a bag of moonshine! It was extortion, pure and simple," Emily told her. "You promised to keep quiet. You said you didn't have to take the baby to Morecombe as Jocelyn told you to—with her dying breath, I might add. You said you could take the baby off and no one would have to know. And if I did not pay you, you were going to take him to Morecombe and tell everyone what I had done! You threatened to ruin me!"

"I deserved something! It was me what took care of her ladyship and the little one. I was the one who did all the work. What was I going to get if I handed him over to her brother? Nothing! A job back maybe if I was lucky, and if I wasn't, being blamed for my lady running away in the first place! I shoulda got something!"

"Yes, well, you would have, if you had brought the baby with you!" Emily retorted, jumping to her feet. "If you hadn't decided to stick him in the church for Miss Propriety over here to find!"

"And if I hadn't hidden him, you'da knocked me over the head and taken him! That's why you had that man there with you. I ain't a fool. I knew better than to bring the babe with me. I know you been searching for me, and it weren't to pay me. You'da killed me tonight if they hadn't stopped you, and you'da done it back then, too. The same reason you had him try to steal the wee one away from her!"

"Enough!" Gabriel roared. "Enough of these recriminations! I don't care which one of you is a more wicked person. Neither of you have enough humanity in you to fill a teacup." He fixed his gaze on Emily. "The truth is out now, and Hannah was right: you are ruined in the *ton*. Whether you will go to jail will, I suppose, depend upon what the magistrate decides and whether Miss Bainbridge wants to press charges. I will count myself fortunate never to see you or your husband again."

Gabriel swung to Hannah. "As for you, you should probably be locked up, as well."

"I took care of her! I did. Miss Jocelyn depended on me."

"So did we all, and you betrayed us. All I want from you now is to know where Jocelyn is. Where did she die?"

The girl shifted and looked down. "She's in Oxford, sir. That was as far as we could get afore she gave out."

"Very well." Gabriel turned to Thea. "I must go. I have to take care of her."

"Of course." Thea looked up at him, her eyes welling with tears for his pain.

Lord Rawdon stepped forward. "I will go with you."

Gabriel turned to him. "Thank you."

Gabriel took Thea's hands in his and squeezed them, lifting them to his lips. "I shall return."

Thea nodded, the tears spilling onto her cheeks. Gabriel bent and kissed her forehead, and she threw her arms around him, clinging to him for one long moment, not caring what anyone thought or said. She stepped back, and Gabriel strode out of the room, Lord Rawdon beside him.

*Thea arose from the prayer* bench in front of St. Dwynwen's statue, where she had given up the same prayer of thanks she had uttered for the past two weeks, and walked out of the church. Turning toward the ruins, she wound her way through the gravestones.

She stopped at the edge of the graveyard and looked at the pile of stones that were the ruins of the old abbey. Her eyes paused on the arches of the cloisters, and she thought of the afternoon she and Gabriel had spent there and the kisses they had shared inside the sheltering walls. A longing as sweet as it was painful pierced her, and she looked past the ruins to the trees, imagining beyond them the sturdy bulk of the Priory.

The Priory was empty now except for a cadre of servants. Gabriel's guests had left the day after Gabriel rode off with Lord Rawdon. Sir Myles had come by to bid good-bye to Thea. He was returning to London, where he would rejoin Gabriel and Rawdon. Thea had no idea where Ian and Emily had gone. Squire Cliffe had tossed Lady Wofford's man in jail, though he had not had the will to bring charges against a peer's wife. In any case, much as she disliked Emily, Thea had not cared to press charges, either. Matthew was healthy and unharmed, and Emily could no longer do anything to him now that her secrets had been revealed. And whatever pain Lord and Lady Wofford had caused Gabriel and his sister, Thea doubted that any of it was punishable by law. It would only cause scandal for Gabriel and his family if Lady Wofford were hauled into court. Thea suspected that Ian and Emily's life together, exiled from the life of the London *ton*, would be punishment enough, anyway.

It had been a fortnight since Thea had last seen Gabriel. At first, in her sympathy for him, she had not thought about what his leaving meant for her, but gradually, as the days stretched emptily into one another with no word, she had realized that her time with Gabriel was over. Oh, she knew that he would briefly return.

Matthew was his nephew, and Gabriel would want to raise him, so he would come back to Chesley to take Matthew off to live at the Morecombe estate.

That would only increase her pain, for she would lose Matthew as well as Gabriel. Sometimes when she thought about it, Thea feared that she would be unable to bear losing them both. She loved Matthew; in the short time he had been here, he had stolen into her heart. Just as Gabriel had. It seemed absurd to think that she had at one time wondered if she was falling in love with Gabriel. It was so clear, so obvious to her now.

Both man and child had opened her up to love. To life. They had given her something precious, a joy and fulfillment that would always live in her even after they were gone from her. She knew that she would never willingly return to the dry, narrow path she had lived before. She was grateful for the added richness in her life, and she could never regret meeting Matthew or Gabriel.

But, oh, it was hard sometimes to remember that when she was alone.

Thea turned away from the view of the ruins, firmly blinking away the tears that threatened, and started back through the graveyard. Deep in her thoughts, she lifted her head as she rounded the corner of the church. And there, walking across the bridge toward her, was Gabriel.

Thea stopped, her breath catching in her throat, and for a moment she was unable to speak or even to think. Gabriel's face was intent, and he strode forward purposefully. When he saw her, his face shifted, suddenly alight, and he hurried forward. Thea started toward him, her feet moving faster and faster. He was doing the same, picking up speed until he was running, and so was she.

They met in the churchyard, his arms reaching out to her, and Thea went into them without hesitation. He wrapped his arms around her, holding her to him tightly. The world spun around her dizzily; the only solid, secure thing in it was Gabriel, his arms like iron around her, his body warm against hers, his voice muffled in her hair.

"God, I've missed you!" He squeezed her more tightly for emphasis. "You don't know how much. I've gone out of my mind the past few days, wishing you were with me. I should not have rushed off like that. I hardly knew what I was doing. It wasn't until afterward that I realized that it would be even worse without you there."

"I'm sorry." Thea clung to him, scarcely able to believe that he was here, that her life was not being snatched away from her just yet. She had no idea how long it would last, but at least for the moment, Gabriel still wanted to hold her, be with her. "I know it must have been awful for you, having to deal with your sister's death."

He released her, moving back a little, but he did not break contact with her, still holding her hand as he gazed down at her. "It was hard. Worst was having to tell her mother. Rawdon stayed with me through it all. That helped." Gabriel shook his head. "I wouldn't say that we are exactly friends again . . . but just knowing that he had loved her, too, that we shared the same loss and confusion, that we'd both been in limbo the past year, waiting and wondering, somehow made it easier to bear. Myles joined us for the memorial service at the estate. And Alan. It was strange . . ." He sighed and started walking toward the church, still holding her hand.

"Strange not to have Ian?" Thea asked, matching her steps to his.

He nodded. "We were friends for so long. I knew him before any of the others. His mother was a friend of my mother's. I knew he wasn't perfect, but I would never have thought he could have done that." Gabriel shrugged. "Well, he was always weak, I suppose. He didn't have the toughness that Rawdon does—stupid, really, that it was that hardness that made me believe that Rawdon had hurt Jocelyn, and all the time it was Ian's weakness, instead."

They reached a bench outside the church and sat down. Gabriel took Thea's hand between both of his.

"I stopped by the vicarage." He smiled faintly. "I believe Matthew has grown in just the time I've been gone."

"Did you see his new tooth?"

"Indeed I did." Gabriel smiled, but it faded rapidly. "I'm sorry that his mother won't get to see him grow up."

"It's very sad."

"I wish . . . oh, I wish a hundred things had been different." Gabriel sighed. "I had become accustomed to thinking of Jocelyn as dead, it had been so long since we'd heard from her. But now . . . it's as if the wound has been reopened."

"But at least you know that she meant to bring Matthew to you, that she still trusted you, loved you."

He nodded. "She was trying to return home, and that brings me some peace. I know now what happened, why Jocelyn left and where she went; we no longer have to wonder. And I understand why she hid it from me."

"Not because she feared you but because she wanted to shield her lover."

"Yes. She gave her heart to the wrong man." Gabriel glanced at her and then away. He shifted on the bench. He was acting, Thea thought with some surprise, *nervous*. Abruptly, he stood up. "Thea, there is something I must ask you."

Thea's heart clenched within her chest. It was coming now, she thought—he was about to tell her that he planned to return home and take Matthew with him. Her brief period of happiness was over. She wanted to turn away, to run from him rather than have to hear the words, but Thea made herself stay. She had always believed in facing whatever came straight on. So, clasping her hands together in her lap, she looked up at him, waiting.

"I planned to do this the night of the Twelfth Night party," he started, not looking at her. "I began right before we went to the masque ball that night, you may remember?"

"I do recall you said we would talk about it afterward," Thea said stiffly. Had he already been planning to leave then?

"Yes. Then everything happened. And, well . . ." Startling her, he dropped down on one knee before Thea and took her hand. "Miss Althea Bainbridge, will you do me the honor, the very great honor, of giving me your hand in marriage?"

Thea stared at him, unable to speak.

Gabriel raised an eyebrow. "Thea? Don't leave me hanging. I am making you an offer."

"Gabriel!" She giggled, even as tears started in her eyes, and her hands flew to her mouth. "Oh, Gabriel! You can't be serious!"

"Dash it, Thea!" He stood up. "Of course I am serious. I am asking you to marry me."

"But I—but you—"

"I do believe I have rendered you speechless." He chuckled, pulling her up and linking his hands behind her waist. "Come, my dear, I will help you. Just say, 'Yes, Gabriel.'"

"But you are a lord, and I am a nobody. I am sure everyone would be shocked to see you marry a vicar's daughter. And a spinster, as well."

"I have no plans to choose my wife based on what others think."

"But you are so handsome that all the girls doubtless drool all over you, and I am plain."

"What a very off-putting picture you draw." He bent to kiss her forehead lightly, following it with kisses brushed on the tip of her nose and the curve of her chin. "And you are not plain. You have beautiful, wild, silky hair that I want to bury myself in, and you have the most speaking gray eyes. And the longest, most devastatingly gorgeous legs."

"Gabriel!" Thea laughed. "Stop. You are talking nonsense."

"Not I. Look at me." He assumed a stern face and pointed with his forefinger to his vivid dark eyes. "I have the vision of an eagle. You, on the other hand"—he reached up and plucked her spectacles from her nose—"have to wear these to see. Which of us do you think sees more clearly?" He leaned down and kissed her again, his mouth lingering. "Now say, 'Yes, Gabriel.'"

"Are you really certain?"

"I have never been so certain in my life. You are the woman I want to spend the rest of my life with. The woman I want to raise Matthew with me. To bear my children. I cannot picture growing old without you. You are all I want. I love you, Thea."

"And I love you. I love you so much!"

"Then why are we shilly-shallying about here? Just say—"

"Yes, Gabriel." Thea smiled. "Oh, yes—"

Her words were cut off as his mouth covered hers.

Mark your calendars!

*New York Times* bestselling author

# CANDACE CAMP's

sizzling new series continues in

———∞∞∞———

# A
# Summer
# Seduction

———∞∞∞———

Look for it in mass market and eBook
Summer 2012!

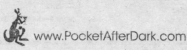